Shirin Azad is an ex-headhunter, investor and philanthropist from London, where she resides with her family.

In the middle of her career, she relocated to Hamburg, Germany to be with her newly-wedded husband. Shirin immersed herself in German life, experimenting with many different passion projects, from property design to an unfinished career in counselling. However, following the traumatic premature birth of her son, Shirin and her family decided to move back to the city she grew up in, London.

Shirin's lifelong pursuit has been to become an author. She penned many romance dramas throughout university as a hobby, but felt the early nineties to be ill-prepared for an ethnic minority female author. She laid her writing dream dormant and decided to enter the corporate world. Shirin loosely revisited writing again in her mid-twenties, during a spontaneous move to Rome to work in fashion. However, again, she put it on the back burner to focus on her career.

Over the last few years, Shirin has rediscovered her love for literature, particularly in romance, tragedy and drama. She has finally picked up her pen once more and embarked on her true passion: writing.

the *light* *of* *darkness*

SHIRIN AZAD

First published in Great Britain in 2021
by Book Brilliance Publishing
265A Fir Tree Road, Epsom, Surrey, KT17 3LF
+44 (0)20 8641 5090
www.bookbrilliancepublishing.com
admin@bookbrilliancepublishing.com

A CIP catalogue record for this book is available
at the British Library.

ISBN 978-1-913770-32-7

Typeset in Adobe Caslon Pro.
Printed by 4edge Ltd.

Front cover artwork by Tammy Clark of Art by T Clark

I dedicate my first novel, *The Light of Darkness*, to all those who are struggling with mental insecurities, loneliness and confusion.

The Light of Darkness was written to raise awareness, provide light and hope for all those with Alzheimer's and their carers.

1

The wind swept his floppy blond hair to the side of his face, smacking it violently against his cheek. The ferocity of the storm would easily push him off the cliff if he didn't jump himself, which he thought would solve his misery. Trembling with fear, Harry looked down, his heart pounding. It would be certain death if he jumped. No recovery. Chilled to the bone in just his blue pyjamas, he froze on the edge of the clifftop. The waves beneath him hollered as they crashed against the rocks. Pitch dark, with nothing but the moon as his light, and the white of the breaking waves like tiny crystals of snow, Laura's face, full of concern, flashed before him.

In the far distance, the boys' voices faintly echoed in and out of his ears.

'Daddy!' screamed Charlie. 'Don't do it! Don't do it, Daddy! I love you!' Tears streamed down Harry's cold, purple face. He took a deep breath, closed his eyes and leapt off the cliff.

In a frenzied scream, he forced himself to wake up. Dripping in sweat and panting for breath, Harry broke away from his brutal nightmare. Relieved Laura was away, he lay in bed, still and silent. Three o'clock in the morning. How could he continue like this? The last few months had become a real challenge. Sharing a bed with his darling wife, the most natural thing in the world, had begun to be a constant, dreaded anxiety. How had Laura not noticed?

How had it managed to escape her attention for so long? His insomnia, the disturbing dreams, the sudden frequency of his bizarre sleep travels around the house. How had Laura just accepted his vague, 'I am very stressed at work' explanation? Laura, being a deep sleeper, and Harry's recent and relentless excuse of snoring, meant he was able to sleep in the guest room without too much suspicion. What other choice did he have? With his tossing and turning, and his often-violent nocturnal movements, Laura was grateful to have the bed to herself, but she would soon cotton on that all was not well. He could, of course, start his medication as he had been advised, or, better still, open up and confess to his wife and share his unpleasant secret. Or he could continue to hide behind her long hours and increased workload, which fortunately seemed to be working to Harry's advantage. However, living with a colossal burden and hiding it from his wife was nothing short of impossible. How long could he maintain this exhausting pretence that all was well?

ooooo

Harry picked up his phone and read his messages again.

Okay, darling, yes the kids are fine. Have a great time. Don't worry about anything. I love you. See you when you get back.

Laura was away in Athens with her girlfriends for a girls' weekend. Harry had all the freedom in the world to stress and worry, without having to explain anything to anyone.

Diverting his thoughts away from his extraordinary dreams, he thought about the red dress he had bought for his wife; it was beautiful. He smiled dryly, and felt a tiny bit pleased: he was going to surprise her with it for their tenth wedding anniversary dinner.

Harry sat up on the bed looking around the room. It was dark and silent. He temporarily forgot about the enormity of his nightmare; after all, it was nothing new. If anything, it was fast becoming the new norm. He remembered he had to do something. What was it? He played with the phone as he began to reconstruct his previous movements before he fell asleep. *So where was I in my thoughts?* he pondered. *The phone call. The red dress. The anniversary dinner. Aha!* He suddenly remembered, tapping his calendar app on his iPhone, and reading out loud. 'Twentieth July – Anniversary dinner for two booked at Boy on the Moon at eight o'clock. Give Laura the dress!' Harry checked the dates on his busy calendar, full to the brim with notes and reminders. *It seems to be getting worse*, he thought; he could hardly remember anything. *I'm only forty-seven years old. It's far too early for all of this.* He stared at his phone. A curious feeling ran through his body, almost paralysing him with fear. The lack of sleep rendered him tired and grumpy.

He went to check on the boys again; they were his only source of comfort at the moment. Bursting with love, Harry stared at them, fast asleep on their bunk beds. Their faces shone bright in the dim sidelight that was always left on in their room. Gently, he kissed their blond heads and slowly crept out of their room. It was the middle of the night; he couldn't sleep, so he might as well work. He strolled downstairs and fired up his laptop: sixty-eight new emails. *Nothing important that can't wait till Monday morning*, he assured himself, scanning the messages quickly. He cross-checked his calendar again, this time on the laptop to make sure it was synced with his phone.

He could hardly afford to make any more mistakes; imagine how ridiculous that would look. He was still reeling from last week. How could he have allowed such a thing to happen? He shook his head in regret. How could he have forgotten? After arranging a board meeting for the senior partners, then forgetting all about it and failing to show up. What a disaster! All the senior partners gathered around the large table, patiently waiting for the host to chair the meeting, and he doesn't show! He had to make sure this didn't happen again; do whatever he could not to arouse any suspicion; he must not slip up; no one should get even the slightest hint that something was wrong.

Harry printed off his calendar for the entire month. Every day was busy. He took his printout and his phone back to the bedroom. He opened his bedside drawer, took out a green highlighter and a thick notepad, and began to read through his appointments for Monday morning. He re-read them a second time. Nothing too overwhelming, thank God. A normal day's work, all good. Slowly, he returned the highlighter and the notepad back to its original place, hidden away underneath a large book, and thoughtfully closed the drawer again.

He lay back in bed, trying to rest his mind. Faint, rhythmic beats steadily rose in the air from a distance, disappearing into clouds of nothingness. He imagined little puffs of smoke rising and disappearing as his mind played tricks on him. He closed his eyes, hoping to shut down his brain. His eyes opened automatically. Again, he closed his eyes and tried to sleep. It was no good. Helplessly, Harry looked up at the ceiling and took a deep breath, unable to find any peace in his troubled mind.

Have I forgotten something? Did I check on the boys? Did I switch off the cooker? Did I lock the back door? Did I close the front door? Did I close the fridge? Yes. Yes, I did. The answer to all of his questions was a resounding, *Yes. It's okay! I did everything I was supposed to do.*

Mum is coming tomorrow to take the kids to her place. Dad will take them the weekend after. Laura's parents will take them the weekend after that. Laura, mmm... I wonder what Laura is doing? I hope she is having fun; she really deserves some time out.

Harry and Laura, the envy of their friends, were still as much in love today as they were back when they first married which was very unusual for their social circle. Harry turned his head wistfully, gazing at the empty space where Laura would usually be lying. He could occasionally smell traces of her perfume that lingered on the duvet. How unnatural it felt to sleep alone in this giant-sized bed.

He tried not to need her. How easy life was before this numbness struck his life. Confined to his vague state of consciousness that evoked a profound sensation of vulnerability, where static screams tore through his mind, suddenly her absence rendered him lifeless, making matters even worse. Preoccupied in his thoughts, he sank down deep in his bed, as though it was swallowing him up whole. With a yank, he pulled the duvet over his head, trying to force himself to sleep. He must not think any more. He was exhausted. He thought about the sleeping pills. Should he take them? He could just slip one in his mouth without any effort, and all would be well. No, he wouldn't risk it. He closed his eyes, begging for nature to do its magic and let him sleep.

ooooo

6.30 - *Beep beep…* the blaring alarm pierced through his ears, practically deafening him. Had he become unusually sensitive to loud noises, he wondered? With a heavy yawn, Harry dragged himself out of bed. Despite the disturbance, he felt reasonably calm and rested. He had somehow managed a few hours of sleep. A positive curiosity piqued his mind, eclipsing the negative thoughts of the night before. After all, it was a new day. With the push of a button, the dusky cream velvet curtains opened, revealing a glorious clear blue sky outside. A smile illuminated Harry's face as he imagined a world of possibilities awaiting him on this bright sunny day. Even the birds shared his positive sentiments as they sang melodiously. It felt as though the heavens had opened up, sending these tiny winged creatures to support his laid-back mood. *It's going to be a good day*, he assured himself. *The boys will be so happy.* No rain predicted. It was a perfect day for them to enjoy a barbecue at Grandma's.

Downing a shot of espresso, Harry sprinted to the attic where he had built himself a fully functioning gym; a decent-sized room, boasting a state-of-the-art treadmill, cross-trainer, weights, and a brand new power plate machine. *Let's aim for seven kilometres and see how I get on*, he challenged himself. As he began to run on the treadmill, Harry's thoughts once again started to take shape in the form of his daily to-do-list. *What do I have to do today? Where do I have to be? Laura is away, I have the boys; what have I planned to do with them? What was plan B, in case plan A failed? What's the alternative plan if it pours with rain? What are they having for breakfast?* The faster he ran, the more his grey T-shirt began to get soaked. Certain he had diligently planned his day, he felt confident all was well, and that he had answers to his questions. What were those plans again?

Unable to precisely identify an answer, he continued to run faster. *It's fine*, he assured himself, *it's still early. The day has just begun. I'll check my phone and figure it out.* He continued to run and tried not to think. Staring aimlessly out of the window, he hoped the penny would drop and everything would miraculously fall into place, making sense of the last few torturous months.

Following an exhausting four-kilometre run, Harry finally stopped. Dripping with sweat, he barged into the boys' room.

'Good morning, boys! Rise and shine.'

Charlie leapt out of bed. 'Daddy, what are we doing today? Is it raining?'

'We're going to Grandma's,' grunted Ollie, annoyed, with his eyes still shut.

Ah, those are the plans, thought Harry. What a relief. He wiped his face and his head, still very much out of breath.

'Grandma's coming to get us, and Aunt Jane will be there with Luca and Mia. You're too stupid to remember.'

'I'm not stupid! Daddy, Ollie called me stupid. You're stupid and an idiot!'

'Now now, boys. Stop that. No one is stupid. What shall we have for breakfast?' Harry looked at his face in a small mirror hidden from the boys' reach. His face was red and still glowing from the sweaty workout. There was no hint of stress.

'Pancakes or fried eggs?'

'I want eggs,' replied Charlie.

'I want pancakes. I don't want to eat what you eat!'

Ollie jumped out of his bed, and Charlie grabbed his father's arms.

'Ollie, be nice to your brother; we can have eggs *and* pancakes.'

Harry liked making breakfast for his boys. It was the only time he went to the kitchen or anywhere near the cooker. Though a great cook, he no longer found the same pleasure in preparing meals as he had done previously. Work was a good excuse to avoid visiting the kitchen. After breakfast, Harry helped the boys choose their clothes, and at ten o'clock sharp, Elizabeth rang the doorbell.

'How are my babies?' Harry's mum squeezed his face, and planted a big kiss on his cheek, ignoring the fact he was a grown man.

'Come in, Mum.'

'Something smells good.'

'Grandma, I'm really excited about the bouncy castle. I can't wait!' The boys ran towards Elizabeth, almost knocking her over in a frenzy of excitement.

'Bouncing castle's going to be so much fun,' Charlie repeated. Charlie copied everything his older brother did. Ollie was his idol. Ollie, in turn, was mean to Charlie and tried to bully him whenever he got the chance.

'Yes, my darlings, we have an amazing bouncing castle today, and your aunt and cousins and their friends will all be there. We'll have a barbecue and eat lots of delicious things and play lots of games. We're going to have a lovely day.'

'Have you checked the weather?' interrupted Harry.

'Of course I have. It's going to be nice all day. Are you going to join us at some point before everyone leaves? Jane and the kids haven't seen you in ages. Why don't you come for a late lunch?'

'I'll try, but as you know, Gemma, my PA, is moving house today. She broke up with her boyfriend and needed some help to move into her new house. I felt obliged and offered.'

'Well you can bring her with you if you want; there'll be plenty of food. Just call me in advance so I know if you're coming.'

'I'll see how we go. I don't want her taking time off during the week and using the move as an excuse. I really need her in the office; it's a very busy period at the moment.'

'Harry, that's what you always say! I wish you wouldn't think about work on a Sunday. It's God's day. It's a day to relax with your friends and family.'

'I'll come to pick the kids up at around seven, if I don't make it sooner.'

'Have you packed a small bag for Charlie with his creams and anti-allergy meds in case he flares up?'

Harry stared at his mum blankly. *Damn! How did he forget?* The thought hadn't even crossed his mind.

'Mum keeps an emergency bag packed for Charlie in his cupboard,' Ollie said to no one in particular.

Harry ran upstairs to fetch the little bag. How stupid and dangerous to send Charlie anywhere without his anti-allergy pills and creams. How could he have forgotten?

ooooo

Harry flung himself on the sofa as his mum's estate car disappeared from his driveway. *Stupid to have forgotten, but*

I must not give myself a hard time; it could have happened to anyone. Was he overtired? Yes, but no more than usual. What happened last night? He lay in thought, recollecting his disturbed night as though mentally flicking the pages of a novel. Gradually, flashbacks of the suicidal dream appeared in front of him. He leapt up from the sofa, immediately seeking distraction, looking for his phone. He wandered around the room, wondering where he could have put it. 'Where is it?' he asked himself out loud, resisting the urge to get hot under the collar. 'Where did I put it?' He found it under a kitchen towel.

Twenty-two messages awaited him. Laura's high-resolution photos from the Acropolis and other famous Greek sites dazzled him. It was impossible not to admire the photos. He gazed at them in amazement. He hadn't been to Athens for such a long time; what a fun city it was. Laura had caught a tan; she looked lovely. Her face beamed with happiness. Zooming in and zooming out of one particular photo, he couldn't help but notice she was also wearing a new dress. He hadn't seen the dress before; she had never worn it out with him. Her boobs looked bigger and she was pouting; how unlike Laura this was.

He stared at the picture intensely, as though he didn't recognise the person in the photo; it really didn't look much like his wife. Her normally wavy, auburn hair was now dead straight and far lighter than usual; her make-up was bold and remarkably noticeable. Studying the photo from different angles failed to make her any more recognisable. The photos provided Harry with great satisfaction: Laura was definitely prettier than her friends. Harry comforted himself with a sense of pride.

The colour red suited her and the décolletage of the dress was quite stunning. Her skin glowed under the hot Greek sun. Her hazel eyes dazzled. She was the picture of health; the extra pounds she seemed to have gained escaped Harry's attention. Looking closely at the photos, he could have sworn she looked almost a decade younger. 'I will be sure to ask her why she doesn't dress like that for me when she returns,' he muttered to himself.

Hello Harry, beeped his phone, instantly distracting him away from his wife's photos. *Hope you're okay. Thanks so much for offering to help me. I really appreciate it. The delivery guys are almost done; we envisage being at the new house in about an hour. Do you still have the address? See you there soon, and thanks again.*

ooooo

'I think that's it. I'll just give it a last check and meet you guys at the house.'

Gemma, Harry's fiercely loyal personal assistant, closed the door as the removal guys set off for the new house. Regretfully, she looked around one final time. Thick stains had turned the grey carpet a smutty green, looking almost sinful. A thick layer of black dust veiled the house in its entirety. Guilt-ridden brown marks blemished the once perfect white walls. Traces of furniture marks were conspicuously visible around the empty room. All that remained were the floor and the walls. Each room was engulfed with an eerie nothingness. The house was empty. Everything was gone.

Gemma's eyes welled up with tears. What a magical house this was! So many incredible things had happened here. Hundreds of enlightening experiences, cleansing of souls, healing of minds, the heavy chanting amidst the deep beating of the drums. What a shame it had all come to an end. Though she was tough as nails, it was still hard for Gemma to realise it was all over and that it was time to move on.

It had been just a matter of time before the relationship had run its course, and Gemma still felt raw inside. How she wished it could have lasted a little longer. Although unplanned, she'd fallen in love with him, even though he'd made it crystal clear it was all going to be temporary. She knew he never stayed in one place for too long, and she'd made the grave mistake of falling for him. Alas, she couldn't blame anyone but herself. Wiping away her tears, she picked up the phone. Thank God it was Harry.

'All done?'

'Almost,' she sniffed.

'Are you okay?'

'Yes. Just a bit sad.'

'Where are you? Old house or new?'

'I'm still in the old house. I'm just saying my last goodbyes. Such a powerful house. So many good vibes; so many experiences. So much has happened here; it feels a bit surreal.'

Harry could afford little sympathy. Wrapped up in his own bizarre emotions, he lacked empathy for others. In his eyes, Gemma was smart; she would figure it out. In fact, she was one of the most exceptional women he had ever met. Adamant she never wanted to have kids, happiest on her own, no need for anything; she was as brilliant as she was versatile.

'Do you want me to come there, or shall I meet you at the new place?'

'Maybe come to the new place. My boss probably shouldn't see this house or feel the aura surrounding it. It might be a bit too much for you.'

'Sure. Say in about an hour or so?'

'Great. Thanks. Do you have the address?'

'Uhh... can you send it to me again, please? Thanks.'

Hmm... What have I done with that goddamn address? Harry tore into himself, frustrated. *Where is it? Where did I put it?* He wanted to punch something. *I'm sure she's given it to me many times already. Why didn't I write it down? She knows me so well; she knows I would have forgotten it, so she kindly offered to send it to me again. Gemma is a good girl; I really should help her. But she is so competent and so able. Why does she need my help? That man she was involved with, how mysterious he sounds.* Harry continued to check his messages, and slowly started to drive to Gemma's new flat the minute he saw her text.

○○○○○

Do they have a plan, and are they aware of which box goes into which room?

Yes, of course. All the boxes are carefully labelled.

Okay, let them unload and we can start unpacking once they're gone. Do you want to jump into the car? You can't see me; I'm parked behind the truck.

Okay. I'm coming.

Harry watched Gemma approaching his car. He couldn't help noticing how attractive she looked. Never before had he seen her wear tight jeans and a tight T-shirt. Her office attire was always strict and formal. Though not a conformist, she kept her personal life strictly separate from her professional life. Always impeccable at work, it had recently come to Harry's attention that there was far more to his personal assistant than one could possibly imagine. *It might be worth investigating*, he observed to himself. This was as good a time as any. Even her hair seemed unrecognisable, the usual grandmother bun now replaced by bouncy blonde hair messily cascading down around her face; it looked great.

This all-American Barbie doll look, a far cry from the mysterious spiritual healer she seemed to be in her private life. For the first time since she had been working for him, Harry caught himself staring at her, actually seeing her. He noticed that she was a woman, a real woman, not just a machine that carried out his instructions, managed his diary and organised his life. Hiding behind his Aviator glasses, he realised he knew practically nothing about her.

He opened the passenger window of the car.

She bent down. 'Thanks for coming.'

'No problem. Get in.'

Gemma smiled gratefully as she opened the car door. *What was so different about her boss today?* The gold-rimmed sunglasses matched his dark blond hair; he looked like a movie star. The expensive but casual black jumper and the relaxed blue jeans fitted perfectly around his waist. Had he lost a bit of weight? He looked great.

'Let's give the boys time to unload the van. Coffee meanwhile?'

Composed and back to reality, Gemma responded instantly, automatically reverting to the professional assistant she was.

'Let's go to the high street. We can park, and there are lots of nice little coffee shops tucked away.'

'Actually, I just had a coffee, but of course I'm happy to accompany you. I can't help with the heavy lifting. I cannot risk slipping a disk, or doing my back in. Sorry. Lame, I know.'

'I know.' Gemma smiled as if she knew everything about him. 'We can wait till all the hard work is done and the men have all gone. We can go then and start the unpacking. Again, thanks for helping me, and for being here. All my friends are busy, and as you know...

'Yes, I know you've lost your licence,' Harry interrupted.

'It's ridiculous.'

'Actually, I've been meaning to ask you about that. How *did* you lose your licence?'

Gemma smiled, embarrassed. Blushing, she said nothing.

'Please don't tell me it was drink driving. Actually, if it was, definitely do not tell me; it's best I don't know.'

'No, it wasn't drink driving, I promise. I lost control of the steering wheel.'

'How?' he quizzed.

'It's a long story.'

'I'm curious.'

Her tight pink T-shirt was very distracting. She had great breasts. Harry wondered why he had never noticed them before.

'I don't drink. However, I was very slightly under the influence, but it wasn't alcohol, and it wasn't my fault. One of the girls I was driving home started to freak out and I lost control. I'm normally an excellent driver.'

'Under the influence of what, may I ask?'

'Do you really want to know?'

'Now, yes. I do.

'I'm not sure if I should really be telling you, I don't want you to get the wrong idea. But what you should know is that it's nothing too dangerous; in fact, alcohol is by far more harmful to your body and health than this is. It's all-natural, no chemicals. My boyfriend, or should I say ex-boyfriend, is a healer. Amongst other things.'

'A what? I thought he worked for a tech company.'

'Yes, he does, but this is his other profession.'

Harry parked his car on the main road and they made their way to the coffee shop.

Harry looked at Gemma as he held the café door open for her, wholly confused. *Actually, she could have a great career as a pin-up in a lads' magazine*, he thought. She had the right make-up and clothes, the perfect buxom blonde.

'Oh, Harry, you look so freaked out!'

'I am,' he agreed. 'How many professions does a person have?'

She smiled. 'Don't be freaked out. It's all innocent! You remember he is half Brazilian and half Irish? In his teens, he trekked the Amazon rainforest and came into contact with a local tribe there. Since then, he has learned their ways and how to work with their medicines.'

Harry was now very confused.

'For many years, he has been working with plants and trees. He knows and understands them very well. He has permission from the medicine keepers, also known as shamans, to give the medicines to people.'

'*Shamans?*' Harry raised his eyebrows. *What was she talking about?*

'Healers. Let's call them healers.' Gemma laughed, wondering what he could be thinking.

'This is crazy. And this chap was your boyfriend?'

'Yes.'

'How long were you two together?'

'Two and a half years.'

'Was he genuine?'

'Yes.'

'Did he have powers?'

She smiled. 'Yes, you could say that.'

'Are you into all of this stuff as well?'

'Well, yes, but I am not a healer. I just helped Paulo. He built up a community of people in Europe years ago. He often brings tribes here for ceremonies, and sometimes travels with them. He used to invite people to our old house and help them. We had many workshops there.'

'I'm very surprised. I never imagined you to be into this kind of thing.'

'Never judge a book by its cover,' Gemma smirked.

'No, never. So what else did you guys do?'

'It was just basically helping people to cure them of their illnesses. Alternative therapy, if you like. Depression, addiction, paranoia, insecurities, all sorts of things.'

'How interesting. I had no idea.'

'I don't discuss my personal life with anyone in the office, least of all you. You're my boss!' She laughed, very comfortable with herself. She had nice teeth. Harry compared her to Pamela Anderson. *Maybe not as pretty but certainly that type*, he agreed with himself.

'It's good that you don't. People wouldn't really understand. This kind of thing is frowned upon in our conservative, uniform, corporate way of life.'

'I know. I don't confide in anyone, just a handful of people. But this is who I am. What you see in the office, yes, of course, it's me. I love my job and I need the money, but I am really not a corporate being.'

'Well, you are very convincing. You do what you do very well, but it's great you're involved with other things, have other hobbies. So do you guys have seances?'

'No, of course not! We're not witches.' Gemma laughed. 'It's more meditation – we have workshops, courses, programmes; people come for different needs. Different people require different medicines.'

'What kind of medicine?'

'It comes in different forms, usually tea, or chocolate, or cakes.'

'Like psychedelics?'

'Yes.'

'Wow. I haven't thought of psychedelics since I left college.'

'Psilocybin to be precise. Magic mushrooms, a hallucinogenic substance. Some people need them. They cure depression! Psilocybin has mind-altering effects, similar to LSD. You have to know what you are doing. You have to do it responsibly, do it under guidance, supervision'

'Do they help people?'

'Oh my God, hundreds, perhaps even thousands, of people. Psychedelics are proper medical alternatives, though not for everyone, of course, but very effective and with a very high success rate. It was great to be able to help people. I wonder if I will ever get the chance to do so again, now that Paulo and I have broken up.'

'I'm so sorry about that. Why did you break up?'

'He wants to move back to Brazil, and I suspect he has found someone else, someone who probably has the same powers as he does.'

'Why do you say that?'

'It's just a feeling. I have spent so much time in this environment, I can see and feel things. Besides, he flatly refused when I asked if I could come with him.'

'I'm so sorry. It can't be easy. What things do you feel and see?'

'Are you worried?' Gemma grinned mischievously.

'No, I'm just curious. I don't have a spiritual side at all. I know it's so en vogue to be in touch with one's inner conscience and things, but I'm just... I don't get it.'

'You don't need to, I guess. You're married, you have children, an amazing career. It's probably not appealing for someone with your profile.'

'But you say it cures depression?'

'Yes. Very often.'

'I'm very open. Or at least I'm trying to be. Who knows... one day I may want to try it myself.'

'Well, I'm right here if you ever want to.' She gave him a big open smile. 'In fact, I have the perfect thing for you!'

'Really? What?' Now he was really interested.

'It's called Ayahuasca.'

'Aya *what*? It sounds super scary.'

'Trust me. It's not. When you're ready, if you're ever ready, you can try it.' She winked at him.

Harry stared at her blankly. Should he tell her? Should he tell her how desperate he was to try it? To try anything to rid him of this constant state of forgetfulness?

'Thanks, Harry.' Gemma broke the awkward silence. 'I really appreciate that you have given up your Sunday to help me.'

'You don't have to thank me.' He shook his head slowly. What she had just told him had been a most enlightening experience for him. 'It's the least I can do. Laura is away, Mum has the kids, I would have been bored sitting at home all by myself.'

Gemma looked sad. Harry, rather uncomfortable, wasn't sure what to do. Should he comfort her by putting his arms around her? He sipped his green juice and offered another apology. *What was the name of that psychedelic she mentioned? And what was Ayahuasca*, he wondered. He wanted to be alone so he could research what she'd told him.

'Shall we start making our way back to the house soon?' Gemma sensed his discomfort.

'Yes. Let's. I'll just pay and we can go. I promised my mother I would have a late lunch with her and my sister and her kids. Also, Laura will be back tonight so I thought I'd whip her up some supper.'

Gemma smiled. 'Okay, let's see how much we can get done before you have to go.'

The removal guys were finishing up when they arrived. Fortunately, most of the hard work had been done. Harry and Gemma took a room each and got to work, unpacking the large boxes. Harry, still in shock from what Gemma had told him, nevertheless felt elated. Not comfortable enough or ready to confide in her as yet, but if anyone could help him, he thought she could. Alternative therapy is not something he had thought much about or previously given any consideration to, but now knowing it was so readily available offered him a great sense of comfort.

A close confidante as well as his trusted PA, Gemma was very fond of Harry. She loved working for him. A senior partner in a successful hedge fund, he could, and probably should, have been egocentric, but he wasn't. Always polite and balanced, he treated his colleagues with respect and dignity. Sometimes she felt she knew everything about him, but other times wondered if she knew him at all.

Gemma admired and consistently supported Harry; he in turn felt extremely comfortable around her, even though their relationship seldom left the office building. Perhaps that was why it worked: it was purely professional. Maybe he should keep it that way and keep away from this alternative therapy. As it was, Gemma had access to his diary and his bank accounts; she did his expenses, she knew how often he had medical appointments; in fact, his whole life lay openly exposed to her. Only today had he begun to understand her true value, how much she did for him, how much he needed her. Perhaps she was more than an assistant? Perhaps she could be a friend? Suddenly it became clear to him that, going forward, he might need her one day. He might even need her more than he needed his wife.

ooooo

'Daddy, I hurt my head. Can you come pick me up? I wanna go home.' Charlie had tried to call Harry three times, but Harry had missed the call every time. For some bizarre reason, Charlie's messages diverted straight to his voicemail. The minute Harry read Charlie's text message, he bid Gemma a quick farewell at the door and rushed off to his mother's house, hoping and praying it wasn't serious. Fortunately, it wasn't. He made a note to himself; *check phone, maybe time for an upgrade.*

'I would have called you had it been serious. It's just a little scratch. Actually, he is missing his mum, and is also a bit tired. Have you eaten?' Elizabeth was not concerned. She was busy hosting and in control as usual.

'I'm going to say a quick hi to Jane and the kids, and then I'd better go. The kids have school tomorrow. I'll get them to do their homework and then give them a bath.' After a few minutes with his sister, Harry grabbed the boys and headed home.

ooooo

Keen to create a seductive, romantic atmosphere for Laura's return, he observed the flames flicker as he lit the candles. The boys fell asleep almost immediately once they were in bed, leaving him free to entertain his wife without disturbance. Harry took great pleasure in thinking about Laura. It pleased him greatly knowing he still loved and desired her, almost as much as when they first met. Proud and somewhat arrogant, rarely did he feel compelled to give in to moments of weakness that many other men were guilty of subjecting themselves to. He felt he had married the right woman, and he was happy to remain faithful to her. Jumping from tune to tune on his iPod, he felt consumed with desire as he thought about Laura, longing to make love to her, for it had been a while. They had both been so consumed with work lately, and what with him changing beds so often, they had neglected sex.

Laura had been exceptionally busy, and she hadn't been in the mood. Very often she would bring home big folders from the office and sit in front of her laptop, working till late at night. This generally proved advantageous for him, given his recent night disturbances and his willingness to sleep in the spare bed. However, as Laura had been away, he hoped she would be relaxed and would have missed him a little.

Leaning back on his chair, he realised how much he had missed her. He wasn't great at being alone. He wondered how she would take the news when he finally told her. *She will help me*, he assured himself. *She loves me.* Thrilled she was on her way home after what seemed like weeks of being away, he sent her a text message in anticipation.

Hey, where are you?

I've just got into an Uber. Should be home in about twenty or thirty minutes. I'm very tired and a bit hungover. Can't wait to get to bed.

Really? I thought we could have some "us" time together. I've missed you.'

Oh darling, I've missed you too. I brought you some delicious Greek snacks, and some cured meat and cheese.

Thanks, but I want you more than the meat and the cheese

Are the kids okay? Are they asleep?

They're fine and in bed. Charlie had a little scratch on the trampoline, but they're both fine and fast asleep.

Oh, my baby, how did that happen? Wasn't Elizabeth keeping an eye on him? How did he hurt himself!?

It's nothing. It's just a little scratch. The kids had a great time. Jane was there with her children, and they all played together and had a whale of a time. I promise.

Hmm… I'll believe that when I see it.

Laura's not in the mood. Harry became deflated. *Let's watch Netflix instead,* he thought bitterly.

Harry observed Laura as she bit into the lamb cutlet he had bought back from his mum's barbecue. The perfect lady, her table manners were always impeccable, even when tired and at home. His secret fetish was watching her eat. A passionate foodie, but now a reluctant cook, one of Harry's favourite pleasures was to dine out with Laura. Watching her devour her food left him ecstatic. Elegant and graceful, Laura possessed the ability to make everything look and taste delicious. Temptingly she would suck on a cherry, her lips a wild shade of red, as though she were filming a TV advert. Laura frequently ended up in fits of laughter during such boozy nights, while Harry would become crazy with desire. Sex, however, didn't seem to be on the cards right now.

Reluctantly, Laura spoke about her weekend away, about her love for her friends, and of course how much she loved travelling.

'I love you very much.' Laura kissed Harry on his lips. 'Thank you for the food, it was delicious. I'm very tired. I'll go to bed. Come when you're ready.' She went to bed and fell asleep straight away. Harry lay next to her feeling gutted. He had missed his wife, had done his best with the kids, helped Gemma move, and now his wife was fast asleep and he was lying in bed unable to sleep and feeling horny. What a disastrous evening. Reluctantly, he went downstairs to watch a film, but tired after the past few nights, fell asleep almost immediately.

2

While driving to work the next day, Harry thought about Gemma. He looked forward to seeing her and wondered how she had spent the night. He thought again: should he confide in her and tell her his concerns and problems? It was a tough call to make. He knew she was loyal to him and that she was fond of him, but was confiding such a big thing to her, or, indeed, to anyone, ever a good idea? Maybe he should talk to his sister Jane instead. It'd be fine to tell her; at least he knew he could trust her implicitly.

At the office, things ticked along as usual. Another day, another set of challenges. Cancelled meetings, internal conflicts, clashing egos, budgets waiting to be implemented, hiring and firing discussions – there was no end. Fortunately, being a senior partner in a reputable hedge fund afforded Harry the maximum freedom to be involved as much as he pleased. His only real job was to make money, a lot of it. A natural-born leader and an expert in his field, Harry's superior skills and infallible ability distanced him from others in the same industry. Simultaneously embracing risk and responsibilities, Harry prevailed as 'the magician' to his peers. Highly regarded and professionally unrivalled, he thrilled in his reputation, exceeding his own expectations. Early intensive years of exposure, an excellent network, the right family connections, not to mention numerous self-improving, self-empowering tailor-made courses, catapulted him to a highly accomplished position.

Long gone were the days of overselling, vicious competition, savage backstabbing. The industry had cleaned itself up. Nevertheless, the ruthless manipulation and abhorrent thoughts of destroying every threatening obstacle were still present, although strategically concealed. The Harry Hoffmans of today were a far cry from the smug, cut-throat young bankers of yesteryear. Charming and intelligent, he'd successfully carved a niche for himself and had excelled in his profession, undoubtedly one of the finest in the unpredictable world of finance.

There was a knock at the door. 'Come in.'

'It's only me.'

She looked different again. Serious, boring, hair up, thick glasses, unflattering clothes. How could this 'plain Jane' be the same sexy, smiley, bouncy girl from yesterday? He'd compared her to someone yesterday... Who was it?

'Here it is!' She held up a manuscript in her hand, smiling excitedly.

'Oh, yes. I forgot about that. Great. It's done.'

'*The Unconventional Future of Finance* by Harry Hoffman,' Gemma added.

'Finally! I'm so happy.'

'This is how it will look. I just want you to be a 100 per cent sure before it goes off to the printers.'

'I can't look at it any more. Please get one of the tech team to go through it one last time. Actually, you probably don't need to; I think it's all done.'

'Positive?'

'Yes. I think so.'

'Okaaay. Off I go.'

The book! The damn book was another reason for his sleepless nights. He felt as though it had fried his brain. It had certainly kept him away from his wife. Writing a book was meant to be a no-brainer for Harry, a financial expert and a literary enthusiast. However, it had ended up taking months to complete, and seemed to have cost him a loss of brain cells, resulting in strange mood swings and a bizarre form of memory loss. *Could writing a book be the reason?* he wondered to himself. *Could this be the cause of all my problems?*

'I hope it was all worth it. I won't be writing another book any time soon,' he muttered to himself, relieved it was over. 'Will I ever be able to write another book with my sudden lack of focus and concentration?' he wondered out loud.

Just then, his work phone rang.

'Your sister is on the line.'

'Jane, hi, what's up?'

'It's Dad. He's in hospital! He slipped and hurt his hip. You need to come over. Mum's playing golf and not reachable, and Maria is not answering either. I need to go and pick up the kids. We are in A&E. Please come. And why aren't you picking up your bloody mobile?'

'Oh God! I'm coming. Stay there till I arrive.'

Where's my mobile? he thought to himself as he searched his office.

'Gemma, my dad has had an accident. Please cancel all my meetings today. And where is my mobile?'

He continued to search for his phone. Oh dear God, where was it? Ringing it was pointless; it was most probably on silent.

'Here it is!' Hiding under a pile of papers, he could hardly believe he missed it. It was so obvious.

Harry hailed a black taxi, almost tripping over as he dashed to get in it. 'I hope the old fool is okay. Where is his wife? Why isn't she with him? Why isn't she picking up?' He spoke to himself inaudibly in frustration.

Harry and Jane despised Maria. Things had still been reasonably okay between Eric and Elizabeth, until one day when their father announced that Maria, Jane's highly paid au pair, was having a baby, and that he, Eric, was the father! Previously, the main concern had been that Jane's dysfunctional husband was likely to have been the one to 'tap the nanny', not Jane's father; no one could have predicted that.

'Oh thank God you're here. I didn't know what to do.' Jane was very distressed. She flung her arms around Harry and kissed him on the cheek. 'I hate him so much, but I also feel sorry for him. He's in a really bad way. I can't believe he left Mum for Maria… and now, where is she?'

Jane, a compassionate, free-spirited young woman, was a fraction of her old self since her father Eric's affair with her children's au pair had come out in the open. Fiercely independent and with a joie de vivre, she was a keen feminist, high in morale and passionate about her beliefs. Harry was very close to his sister, though recently he'd not seen much of her.

'I really don't know. I'll try to call her. Have you been able to get hold of Mum?' Though not as resentful as Jane about his father, Harry was irritated with what had just happened and would have preferred not to be dealing with it right now.

'We are thinking of releasing him tomorrow morning,' the doctor announced, unconcerned. 'He needs the medication I've given him, lots of rest, and shouldn't be alone, if at all possible. Is there someone to take care of him?'

'Yes, there is. Thanks, Doctor.'

Harry kissed his dad on the forehead, wondering who on earth was free tomorrow. He tried to leave the hospital as soon as he possibly could. He hated hospitals. Ever since he could remember, he'd borne a strong loathing for them; the fear and anxiety never seemed to ease.

'Mum, thank God you called. Have you heard?' Luckily Elizabeth had picked up Jane's messages. 'Someone will have to stay with him from tomorrow when they discharge him at midday; he cannot be left alone.'

'Where is his wife? She needs to be told. It's her problem. She has to be there for the bad and ugly times, not just when it bloody well pleases her.' Elizabeth's tone was disgruntled and bitter with sarcasm. She was not impressed. The mere mention of her ex-husband peeved her. Eric's recent antics rendered the once revered and admired family to nothing but ridicule and embarrassment.

'We need to keep trying to get hold of her. I can't take Dad to my place. I'm not sure what's going on with Laura; she's been a bit distant since she returned.' Harry nervously fidgeted with his wedding ring while trying to ignore the heavy stench of cheap air freshener circulating in his Uber. At least the driver appeared to know where he was going and he hoped the traffic would ease up back to the office, Harry consoled himself.

'Your wife certainly has her moments. What's wrong with her now? Too much of an easy life?' Harry's mother and his wife made no secret of their disdain for one another.

'Let's save that for another day, please, Mother. Tell me what you want to do. I can pick him up tomorrow, but I'll have to drop him somewhere and dash back to the office. I have a lot on at the moment.'

'I'll try to get hold of this dragon woman. If not, you can drop him at my place, though it is absolutely not my first choice.'

Relieved, Harry hung up. The incessant stream of sudden bad news had all but drowned him. How did things suddenly get so arduous and exhausting?

'Spare some change, mate.' Unfortunately, beggars continued to flock into the glamorous streets of London, and clearly had no intention of stopping this habit. Mayfair remained an attractive destination for these poor destitute guys. Heavy rain bounced aggressively off the pavement, causing large puddles everywhere. London streets were prone to flooding. Covering his head with a newspaper, Harry cautiously ran into the office from the cab, careful not to slip. One member of the family already lay wounded from a fall; it didn't need another.

Would it be inappropriate to gulp down a shot of whisky? he thought, carefully studying his calendar. He squinted, looked around, and peered out of his office window to ensure no prying eyes in the opposite building were in a position to catch a glimpse of him swigging alcohol in the office. *I've had a terrible day; I deserve it.* At the speed of light, Harry gulped down a large shot of alcohol, pretending nothing had happened.

'Oh shit!' he suddenly hollered. 'I forgot the dentist!'

'It's Harry Hoffman; I had an appointment at five today which…'

'No problem, Mr Hoffman. It's already been cancelled. Would you like to re-schedule for another day?'

'Absolutely not!' he muttered under his breath. 'No, sorry, not yet. I'll call you back soon with a date. Thank you.' He let his phone fall on his lap. He didn't feel well. Leaning back on his chair, he threw his head back while attempting to rest his feet on the table. A loud bang followed.

'Oh no!' His phone had plunged to the floor. *Don't be broken*, he frowned in dread. Luckily not. 'Oh, thank God,' he sighed, relieved.

The phone flashed a new message.

Hi, what time are you home? Kate has invited me to a concert last-minute. The babysitter will pick up the kids and feed them. Think there's food in the fridge, if not just get a take-out. Will text after the concert. Love you xx

Again? She's disappearing *again?* Harry felt no doubt in his mind something was really off with Laura. He felt compelled to question her perplexing behaviour. What's going on with her? She was purposely avoiding him. None of it made any sense. Without further thought, Harry made his way home.

ooooo

Christine, the babysitter, had made an effort with a chicken and mushroom pie, which was rather commendable; it smelt and looked delicious. Harry was starving and therefore delighted to have a warm, home-cooked meal. He tossed some leaves in a bowl and poured himself a large glass of wine.

'Do you want one?' He held up the glass, half smiling. Christine smiled politely, shaking her head.

'How was your day, Christine?'

'Splendid, thank you. Yourself?'

Christine had worked for the family for five years. Twenty-five years old, she understood both his and Laura's sarcasm and mood swings. It was very likely they'd had a small fight, or he'd had a bad day at work. Harry was unable to hide his feelings; the way he moved and his tone of voice clearly indicated his mood. She knew he couldn't care less about what she thought. He found her nosy and judgemental, but dared not to say anything for fear she would walk out.

'Yes. Great, thanks.'

Harry looked at the kids, munching away happily at their pie.

'Are they both okay? Anything I need to know or do?' He took a big slurp of his wine and a bite of the creamy pie.

'No, everything is fine. I'll bathe them; they've done their homework and are both quite tired. I'll go home as soon as they're down. Is that okay or did you need me for longer?'

'No. Please do what you have to do. I'll be okay. Anything nice planned?'

She smiled. He took another large sip, eyes fixed on her.

'I have a date.' She had a twinkle in her eye. Christine was no looker. Harry thought she was overweight and didn't like her tight, dark curls. However, she intrigued him in many ways, even though sexually she did nothing for him, much to his relief. His father Eric was not his role model when it came to nannies. He wondered who her date was, and if he was also overweight.

'Good for you. I hope you have a lovely evening, and make sure he is nice to you.' Harry walked to his study, concentrating carefully on the tray holding his meal and drink. He took out his phone and checked all his appointments for the following day, writing down his to-do list. It had become a ritual. He switched on his laptop, checked his Outlook calendar, double confirming everything was correct. Chomping at his supper and downing his wine, he found himself thinking about his wife. Where was she? It was a struggle not to get suspicious. Was she up to something? He looked back through their WhatsApp messages: no clues. All her messages were normal and positive. It was impossible to guess; he didn't want to become paranoid about this as well. *Perhaps she needs space. Best to leave her to it.*

Harry scrolled through his emails that he'd missed during the day and caught up with his outstanding work. No emergencies, no great problems, just day-to-day concerns. No drama. All okay. He poured himself a second glass of wine, knowing full well that drinking with his condition was not wise.

Christine knocked on the door and popped her head in. 'I'm off now. The boys are in bed; would you like to say goodnight to them?'

'Daddy,' called Charlie at the sight of his father. 'Daddy, Oliver hit me. I hate him!'

'Shut up. I hate you more!' Oliver barked. Harry was shocked at Ollie's aggression. Why was he so unkind to his little brother?

'Ollie, stop being so horrible to your brother. What's got into you? This kind of behaviour is not on. Please say sorry to Charlie.'

'No, I won't, I hate him. He's stupid and can't even spell his name properly.'

Where was this coming from? Harry was unable to understand Ollie recently. What prompted this aggression towards his little brother? Something was going on with him, but what was it? It completely slipped his mind that he had already visited Oliver's school on account of complaints about Oliver's behaviour. Harry made a mental note: *Must discuss with Laura.* He wondered what Laura would make of this behaviour. Did she already know? If so, why hadn't she told him about it? Or had she told him and he had forgotten? It felt as if he hadn't had a proper conversation with Laura in ages. Unexpected melancholic thoughts began to creep into his mind. He felt a sharp cramp pierce his gut. Calmly he pressed his hand against his stomach, aware that Ollie was watching him. The future looked bleak; Harry wasn't sure what was going on around him. Once again, he felt things were getting on top of him and he was losing his strength and control. Harry hated losing control. In his whole life so far, he had always been in full control of his actions and emotions.

'I hate you too!' Charlie screamed at Ollie. 'You are disgusting and even more stupid!' He began to scream at the top of his voice.

Ollie threw his teddy at Charlie. 'Just shut up! Shut up, you retard!'

'Alright, alright, that's enough, both of you. I'm telling Mummy. I don't want to listen to this anymore.'

Off went the light and bang went the door. Even the kids were acting weird.

Laura could deal with this. *I can't right now*, he thought.

Harry shot to his desk in a panic and frantically opened the top drawer. Hands shaking, cheeks flushed, he yanked out the leaflet deeply hidden away – that he'd been desperate to avoid forever.

'Alzheimer's at an early age'

The big, bold words were right there in front of him, staring at him. Holding the leaflet in his hand, Harry stared blankly. Unable to find any emotion, his face turned to stone. His head pounded. His instincts told him to open the leaflet and find out once and for all what was written inside, and this time, read it properly. Was there anything different to what he had researched on the internet? Surely it was the same information he already knew? Browsing the web or discussing the situation with a doctor seemed much easier, more casual. The leaflet posed a different scenario. It seemed to suggest it was there for him, and him alone. It was *his* disease.

For almost four months, he had been feeling lost within himself, forgetting things, with inexplicable headaches, depression, and uneasiness; he knew he had to open this leaflet filled with toxic words that promised to ruin his life. He owed it to himself to read and understand what was happening to him; the words were, after all, designed for situations specific to what he was experiencing. If not directly for himself, then at least for the sake of his loved ones.

Where was Laura? It would be nice if he could share this burden with her. Harry could not find the courage to navigate through this leaflet on his own. In a frenzy, he opened the drawer and threw the leaflet back inside, poured himself a Cognac, and ran into the garden, lighting up a Cuban cigar.

Perhaps I'm overthinking everything. Laura is busy, the boys are playing up, my memory is bad. I have slight headaches; it's hardly the end of the world. Harry sat back on a chair, resting his feet on the table outside and puffing calmly on his cigar. The Cognac tasted good. He wished torrential rain would flood the streets outside his house, outside his office. He wished it would hail, and that thunder and darkness would dominate the skies and the streets would be desolate, void of all humans, reminiscent of a zombie movie. Harry felt anger and resentment towards the world; he wanted everyone to suffer. Why should he be the only one? The Cognac seemed to be finishing quicker than he was drinking it. Should he drink more slowly or should he pour himself another? What should he do?

Just at that moment, Harry's phone began to ring. He ignored it. 'You can wait,' he snarled spitefully at his mobile as if it were a person.

He took another small sip of his precious Cognac. *Well if I am going to die, I may as well enjoy myself.*

The phone rang again. Harry didn't flinch. 'Leave a message!' he ordered.

Beep beep. Whoever it was took his instructions and left a message.

He held his phone close to his face, squinting his eyes as if he were going blind. A big smile spread across his face.

He heard the voicemail. His best friend, delighted to hear from him, was sorry he hadn't called sooner. Harry couldn't help noticing how content and excited his friend's voice sounded. Subconsciously, he felt a pang of envy. He wanted to light another cigar, but was that wise? It would have been nice to smoke inside. Ever since they'd installed smoke alarms, they'd ended up smoking far less. Going all the way to the garden was a tremendous effort, especially when the weather cooled. This infuriated their privileged, hedonistic guests, who often liked to chain-smoke.

Laura and Harry, the perfect hosts, had entertained incessantly back in the day. However, since his best friend and his wife had moved to Hong Kong, their rich, snobby work-shy friends had all but faded into oblivion. Their social life was now half of what it had been in its heyday. Harry's house had served as the perfect venue – they frequently hosted many lavish, decadent, self-gratifying parties. Harry could no longer imagine that time ever returning. His best friend had left the country. Laura was moody, and he was at great risk of developing full-blown Alzheimer's disease. He wondered if any of these gilded people would still come to his house or be his friend if they had the slightest inkling that he was sick. Sick with such a perplexing disease that was probably unheard of at his age. It was inconceivable to Harry that other young people could remotely be at risk with similar symptoms. As far as he was concerned, he was the only unfortunate being in this position and therefore felt terribly sorry for himself.

ooooo

The next morning, Laura hurried off to work before Harry found an opportunity to speak with her. Thankfully his day was also busy. Back-to-back meetings meant there was little time to solve the mystery that had become his wife. A detailed partners' meeting discussing the year's pipeline greatly pleased Harry. His overseas travel, minimal for the next six months, meant only a handful of trips had been pencilled in. The older you get, the less fun these trips become. He scowled to himself, grateful there was nothing immediate.

Reaching for his phone, he noticed his wife had written to him.

Free for dinner tonight?

Yes, he replied instantly. He was amazed she had found time for him in her busy schedule.

Great. Seven-thirty at the Old Bistro. Christine will be with the kids. xx

Dreading bad news, he tried to bury himself in complex spreadsheets, which undoubtedly required his full attention. Harry stared at what lay before him. There were a lot of numbers. He looked at the rows and the columns. All he could see were numbers. Numbers that made little sense. Was this his spreadsheet? Had he done it? He couldn't remember. He closed the window. He didn't want to see it any more. Staring at his screensaver was a far more pleasant experience. Laura and the kids posing on the sandy Koh Samui beaches, smiling at him, was as unreal a sight as the spreadsheets were incomprehensible. He thought about Laura again.

That's right; she wants to meet for dinner. What does she want to say? He couldn't imagine what she wanted to say, what unsavoury announcement she wanted to make. Why didn't she just come home? *How strange she wants to meet at the Bistro.* Crazy thoughts spun in his head; he dared not acknowledge them. His mind boggled. So much suspense.

Is everything okay? he typed back, hands almost trembling. *Should I be worried?*

I'll tell you when I see you, please don't be late.

What kind of a bullshit answer is that? He clenched his teeth. What a challenge not to overwhelm himself with worry. If only she knew what he was going through.

Harry, a man of vast talents, had yet to master the art of manipulation. Perhaps it was ignorance or naïvety, but his brain was rather one-dimensional. A straightforward, logical man, who saw only black and white, he found it almost impossible to understand Machiavellian, cunning thoughts. Astrophysics, quantum physics, algorithms, mathematical formulae, complicated themes and structures were his world. Women, their moods and their thoughts, he found alien, outright outlandish and inexplicable.

He adored his wife; not only was she a wonderful wife and mother, she was also intelligent and grounded. However, like most men, he didn't understand women and neither did he try to. He lived in his safe, warm little bubble, not questioning or overthinking. He'd been happy and content in his nirvana. However, recently things had changed. Suddenly he'd been forced to take responsibility for himself. He was faced with things he didn't have the capability to understand. Ignorance was bliss. A creature of his environment, he couldn't cope with change.

ooooo

Dreading every step, he made his way to the restaurant. Part of him wanted to get there first and consume something strong in preparation for the worst. The other part of him was drowning in concern. His fears exaggerated his negativity. A desperate urge to turn back and run away, though not an option, did cross his mind. He could faintly see Laura through the window fidgeting, both hands wrapped tightly around a warm mug. Trying to hide from view, he ducked as he drew closer. Slowly he raised himself up. A waiter blocked his view. 'Move,' he motioned with his hand. Nope, the waiter was talking to Laura. Harry paused. Should he go inside? He had no choice. He lived with the woman; how could he possibly avoid her? Bravely and boldly, he walked into the restaurant.

A nervous-looking Laura clocked him right away.

Should I kiss her? he wondered, realising how ridiculous this sounded as he approached her. She stood up and leant over. He pecked her gently.

'Here, this is for you.' A cold pint of beer awaited him. He felt like drinking the whole glass in one gulp.

'Thanks.' He sipped gently, careful to remain in control.

'Are you okay? Busy day?'

Harry was silent. He hated small talk.

'Laura, why am I here?' He looked at her questioningly. 'You've been so distant. Whatever is the matter? What is going on?' He reached for her hand. His eyes, icy blue. She was freezing. Laura frowned apologetically as if she were about to break down in tears. She took a small sip of green tea from her mug.

'Harry. I... I need to tell you something.'

'What is it? Please tell me.' Harry's eyes narrowed; he felt a nervous twitch at the tip of his nose. The restaurant was buzzing as usual. Groups of friends, among them young couples, sat happily eating, drinking, chatting, giggling with laughter. Warm and cosy, the lighting was dim and inviting. *The Best of Frank Sinatra* played faintly in the background. Harry ignored everything and everyone. Right now, he had no interest in anything. Normally he loved to people-watch when life was a little less complicated. A blissfully happy marriage, beautiful children, a fantastic career, Harry had everything one could possibly want. He was incredibly happy. He had been fortunate enough to live a life fully in control of his actions, lacking in nothing. Most things fell into place just as they were meant to. But suddenly everything had taken a turn for the worse; for the last few months or so, he felt he had not been in control of any aspect of his life.

'I don't know how to say this...' Laura was in the same boat. She was a strong, confident, successful woman. Able and competent, she hardly ever struggled with anything. Harry didn't recognise this nervous, desperate woman sitting in front of him.

He looked at her expressionless. 'Just say it, Laura. What on earth is going on?' It was serious.

She looked down at her mug. 'I'm pregnant.'

3

That night, Harry and Laura lay in bed. 'How? How did this happen? When?' Harry could hardly get the words out.

'I'm not sure.' Laura shook her head. 'I've not been to the doctor, but I suspect it could have been when we went to Geneva for Paul and Kevin's wedding. Remember we drank so much that night? We were both so drunk, we could hardly even find our room. I believe it was that night. I had recently just come off the pill and we were both just trying to be careful. The whole day, we were drinking; in fact, we had been drinking since the day before. We obviously took it a bit too far.'

'We don't make mistakes like that.' Harry was still in shock. He didn't know what to think. How could he bring another baby into this world knowing his fate, his future? Staring at the ceiling he felt himself paralysed, unable to speak or think. A big crack on the ceiling made him feel as if the ceiling was about to collapse on top of him. This might be a good time to confess to Laura and tell her what was going on in his life. She was being honest with him; shouldn't he take this chance and do the same? But again, he felt himself consumed by fear.

'A baby at this age? It can't be.'

'It can be and it is. I did the test three times.'

Laura stared at the ceiling, hoping she could see what he saw. She seemed as much in shock as he was.

'How long have you known?'

'I had a feeling something was wrong for a while. I missed my period, but just thought I was more menopausal than anything else, and besides my periods have recently been very irregular. I didn't think anything of it. I did another pregnancy test in Athens.'

'Does…'

'Yes, Kate knows. She's my best friend; of course I told her, but no. No one else knows.'

'Okay, let's not tell anyone anything right now.'

'No, of course not.'

'Do you want to go to the doctor for a check?'

They both continued to talk to the ceiling, avoiding looking at one another.

'I've made an appointment for Friday. You don't need to come. In fact, I'd prefer it if you don't.' She turned to look at him.

I prefer I don't, he thought to himself.

He continued to look at the ceiling, remaining silent. Words failed him. Harry had never been the silent type. He loved the sound of his own voice and wanted everyone else to love the sound of his voice. Laura was well aware of the shock he was feeling.

She drew close to him and laid her head on his chest.

'Are you very, very shocked?'

Harry was still silent.

'Darling, Harry, please say something.'

'I don't know what to say.'

'What are you feeling?'

'I'm shocked.'

'Besides that.'

'That's it. I'm too shocked to feel anything else.'

The room was silent.

'We discussed this for many years. I didn't want a third child; I'm not able to help look after it.' Laura remained silent, listening to him intently, still as a stone. 'You want to work. Your career is the most important thing to you. I still need to focus on work. I can't take time off, we have no space in the house, and, above everything else, we are both old. Having a third baby at your age is a huge risk. A risk I do not want to take.'

Laura continued to stare at the ceiling, breathing heavily as though she were out of breath. Neither of them moved.

Suddenly, Laura stood up. 'I'm hungry.' She left the room. Harry remained glued to the same position, deep in thought. His head was heavy, his eyes fatigued. His nose started to run. Was he getting sick? He wondered how much of his new ailments were real and how much was in his mind. *I don't want to become a hypochondriac*, he thought, *I must learn to differentiate what's real and what's in my head. If there is something seriously wrong with me, it needs to be properly dealt with. It must not get trapped with that which is not real.*

Harry made his way to his study quietly, trying to avoid Laura. He emailed his PA. Since breaking up with her boyfriend, Gemma was far more available on email at unconventional hours. He hoped she was on her phone now and sporadically checking her messages.

Gemma, could you please book me a flight to Chicago? Sunday to Thursday. I'll stay at the Hyatt as usual.

Gemma messaged him back immediately. It was good she was online and so responsive. If she had noticed some irregularity in his behaviour recently, she'd kept it to herself.

ooooo

Dear team, old and new,

Hope all well.

I will be in Chicago next week. I have a few meetings and would like to meet you all, especially the new members. I'll email my full agenda when all meetings are confirmed. I need to discuss a few urgent matters. Happy to take all meetings. Staying at the Hyatt.

Look forward to catching up and meeting the new faces.

Best regards,

Harry

Harry read through the email a couple of times and hit send, feeling a blitz of adrenaline rush through him. In desperate need of a break and a quick escape, he wished he could leave this very moment. The baby news had tipped him over the edge. Too much information. Too much news. Too much happening. Nothing in his control. He hoped a change of environment would help him put his life into perspective.

Communication that night between the normally happy couple remained minimal. Behaving like strangers, they ignored each other. Praying for the night to be over as quickly as possible, each stayed in their respective positions, careful not to touch the other. Harry couldn't think of anything to say to his wife, and Laura felt tremendously let down by Harry. They both wished desperately to be elsewhere; morning couldn't arrive soon enough.

ooooo

Dr Arnold sat stiff and upright on one side of a desk, hands tightly clasped together, listening intently to Laura. As usual, his poker face, hidden behind thick-rimmed glasses, gave nothing away. A full head of white, curly hair, his face blank and expressionless, this man was paid to show no emotion.

'Mrs Hoffman, I'm sure you are aware of the dangers of having a baby at your age. I'm obliged to tell you this.'

'I understand that, Doctor, but I am pregnant; it's been confirmed. I just need to know the baby is healthy.'

'Very well. I have to warn you of the problems you may face. Please take a look at this leaflet.'

Your risk of pregnancy complications, such as high blood pressure and gestational diabetes, increases after the age of 35 and continues to rise in your 40s. The odds of genetic problems also jump as you get older. At 40, your chance of conceiving a child with Down's syndrome is one in 100; at 45 it's one in 30.

This was the last thing she wanted to read. A large stack of leaflets lay waiting for her attention. Dr Arnold had been their family doctor for many years. The last two times she'd told him she was pregnant, he'd insisted she read through all the risks. This time, she detected visible concern on his stern face.

'First, let's do all the tests that are needed, and we can take it from there.' Laura tried to put on a brave face. She was petrified. She knew the drill from her last two pregnancies, but then she'd been years younger; it was much easier then. Forty-eight was not a safe age to have a baby. She was fully aware of this, but what other options did she have? This baby had not been planned; it was a mistake.

She left the surgery, dreading the results that were due in a few days. Calming herself down, she tried not to worry too much so she could deal with whatever was awaiting her.

She made her way to Ollie's school. What on earth could his teachers want to discuss with her so urgently? Why did she need to see the headmistress? Surely his form teacher could deal with it? What could be so important? What a terrible inconvenience.

'Thank you for coming at such short notice, Mrs Hoffman. We appreciate it.'

Laura nodded casually, hoping the woman would get to the point quickly. She tried to force a smile, but found it very difficult.

'Is everything okay?' she queried, confusion visibly spreading across her tired face.

The teacher sat up straight. Stern and indestructible. She looked rather youthful to be the headmistress. Though sharply dressed in a pale pink, pussy-bow shirt, her hair was a messy mass of limp dark hair, cut in a short bob.

'Unfortunately, we've had a few more incidents with Oliver.' Mrs Douglas held her pen firmly, leaning forward from her desk. 'He's hit three kids and bitten two of them.' Her eyes narrowed behind her glasses. She looked gravely serious.

Laura couldn't believe her ears. *Not again!* she thought to herself. She raised her eyebrows, almost scowling in nervous disbelief. Harry had so diligently dealt with this the last time it had happened a year ago; she had hoped it was a one-off.

Mrs Douglas continued. 'It first occurred a month ago; we dismissed the incident as kids play-fighting. Then it happened again, but as both boys were telling fibs we couldn't determine who was at fault. Unfortunately it happened yet again, and at that point we had no choice but to take action. It was lunchtime, and Oliver punched and kicked a boy a couple of years below him. He threw the boy's lunch box on the floor... and,' she hesitated, '... and called him the F-word.' Mrs Douglas frowned. Her expression was harsh and unforgiving. It was not a conversation she liked to have with a parent, but it was certainly one she was used to.

Laura sat listening gobsmacked. What was she hearing?

The headmistress went on. 'Yesterday, Oliver hit one of the younger kids. The little boy has a bruise on his arm. He was screaming in pain. Oliver's response was to laugh loudly at the boy and repeatedly shouted "Cry. Cry. Go on, cry!" It was a nasty sight; the poor little thing was screaming and crying out in pain. We have informed the parents of the boy; they will not be sending their child back to the school until Oliver is suspended.' She paused.

Laura was spinning her wedding ring with her thumb, aghast.

'We're trying to deal with what's been happening professionally, but as you can appreciate, it's a very delicate matter.'

The teacher looked attentively at Laura, as though awaiting some form of reaction from her.

'I'm very sorry. I've no idea what has brought this on. I know there was that one time previously, but he is so different now. Oliver is usually a very well-behaved boy, at least at home. He is a very bright child and is usually obedient. I'm very saddened and shocked by what you are telling me. I cannot imagine this behaviour from him.' Words could hardly explain Laura's consternation and embarrassment. She wished Harry could be here with her now.

'We have an educational therapist we can call to examine and assess certain children. With your permission, we can investigate this matter further.'

'Should I take him to a child psychiatrist?' Laura wanted to close this matter and leave. She felt out of breath and flustered.

'We think that's the best way to deal with this. Oliver may need some external help and may need to be observed. Unfortunately, we cannot keep him in the school as he is deemed to be a risk to the other children. The therapist the school uses will be available to do home visits, together with your own psychiatrist. If, after a short time, they assess that Oliver is ready to return to school, I would be happy to discuss this with you.'

'Where is Oliver now?'

'In a separate room with a supply teacher.'

'Do I need to take him home with me now?'

'Yes. I'm sorry we cannot allow him to be with other children without supervision, and unfortunately we don't have the resources to hire special needs teachers.'

'Fine. I'll take him home with me.'

'Very well. Follow me.'

Quietly bent over a desk, arms wrapped around his head, Oliver sat in the middle of the classroom. A round, middle-aged teacher with white hair and a harsh, wrinkled face sat at the front of the class, ignoring Oliver, whose head seemed to be buried in a book.

'Oliver!' called his mother angrily. 'Lift up your head,' she demanded.

Ollie peeped through his arms. With a red, flustered face, he looked at his mother, angry and tired.

'Let's go. Get up! We're going home.'

She grabbed her son and dragged him out of the school.

Silently, mother and son got in the car and drove home. Laura was in no mood for conversation, preferring that Harry deal with the situation when he returned home later.

'Elizabeth, hi, it's Laura.' She took a deep breath. 'Oliver has been suspended from school. Please give me a call when you get this message. Thanks.' Laura struggled to understand or explain her dislike of her mother-in-law. There seemed to be no reason for this; Elizabeth was a kind, intelligent woman, still very attractive and quite glamorous, given her age. A retired university lecturer, she was an academic and an intellectual, with an army of letters after her name. Back in the seventies, she had even modelled part-time, to pay for her frequent round-the-world trips. Despite her glamorous lifestyle and enviable career, she had embraced motherhood with grace and ease, teaching her kids everything she knew, always pushing them both to excel. Careful not to neglect her duties as a wife, her marriage to Eric had been a happy, solid union. To the outside world, it was nothing but perfect, and would have continued to be so had not an ominous character, Maria, entered the scene.

By now, Elizabeth had forgiven Eric and often felt sorry for him. She had been diagnosed with breast cancer, her chemotherapy had been long and hard, and her mood swings often almost unbearable. Needless to say, with Elizabeth's condition so bad, and given their age, their sex life was wholly non-existent. It had probably been unrealistic to have expected Eric to have stayed by her side and continue to be a loving husband and carer. Elizabeth had always felt their marriage wasn't eternal. Eric was a wonderful husband and father; however, his manly needs had prevailed in his twilight years.

Laura admired Elizabeth in her own strange way. She was also, however, very suspicious of her kindness, as her own mother was a harsh, critical woman who had hated her children and rejected them for most of their lives.

'Laura, it's Elizabeth. What in heaven's name is going on? Where are you?'

'Thanks for calling back so soon. Can you come to the house? I'm driving now, so can't really speak.'

Laura found Elizabeth patiently waiting in the car outside her house. She was confused; she had just spent the weekend with the boys, and she'd seen no signs of anything strange. Ollie was just a normal ten-year-old boy. Surely there must be some mistake?

'Thanks for coming.' Laura felt stupid for disliking Elizabeth all these years; what a waste of time, but still she couldn't bring herself to like her either. Elizabeth nodded when Laura got out of the car, giving her half a worried smile.

Automatically, they both focused on Ollie. Elizabeth made sure to watch Ollie's movements carefully, and be particularly interested in how he reacted when he saw her, but that was pointless. Ollie hardly acknowledged her. Head down, he ran to the door ignoring his grandmother as though he hadn't seen her.

'Hello, Ollie.' Elizabeth greeted him as she usually would, not sure if she should hug him, especially as he was purposely ignoring her. Ollie pretended he didn't hear or see her. *This is going to be difficult*, she thought as she sighed. Ollie ran straight to his room as the two women sat at the kitchen table.

Laura poured herself a glass of wine, Elizabeth waited for the kettle to boil. Laura re-played the scene to a worried-looking Elizabeth. The violence in Ollie made no sense to either of them. They both tried to play it down as a one-off, though Laura was well aware it wasn't. Kids go through this phase, they agreed, but deep down they both worried, especially Laura. What if there was something terribly wrong?

'Shall I go and talk to him, or do you want to do so first?' said Elizabeth.

Ollie was Laura's favourite child and Charlie, Harry's. Was Ollie a bit spoilt? Was what happened somehow her fault? The thought often crossed Laura's mind, especially today.

'No. I'll go. I'll finish my drink and then go.'

Just at that moment, Harry showed up. 'Mum!' He bent down to greet his mother with a kiss. 'What are you doing here?' Before his mum could answer, he glared at Laura. She barely glanced at him.

'Are you crazy, drinking in your condition? What are you doing?!' Silence ensued. Laura looked at him in shock, unable to utter a word.

Elizabeth didn't know what to think. Puzzled, she looked at both of them, questioningly. Nobody spoke.

'You may as well tell me now.' She first looked at Harry, then at Laura, seeking an answer.

'I'm sorry.' Harry took a deep breath. Laura shook her head, looked down at her glass and paused. She wanted to kill him. She lifted her face and pursed her lips together furiously, her eyes glowing in anger.

'I'm pregnant!' she hissed angrily. Startled, Elizabeth tried to muster a half-smile. Tall and slim, she stood straight and firm. Her grey, shoulder-length hair perfectly coiffed, her blue eyes glimmering in both shock and wonder. She remained silent.

'I'm guessing it wasn't planned.' Elizabeth broke the silence, her voice a loud whisper. Laura once again felt a bitter distaste for Elizabeth. Her sentiments knew no consistency regarding Elizabeth. Love turned to hate, hate turned to love, all in a matter of seconds, and in this precise moment she was bursting to the brim with contempt for her Pilates-honed mother-in-law. How bitterly she now regretted having invited this over-domineering woman to judge her personal mess.

'What do you think?' she snarled aggressively.

'This is probably a private matter between the two of you. I will go and talk to Ollie.'

'Leave Ollie alone! I'll deal with him.'

'Then I will go home. There's nothing for me to do here.' Elizabeth stood up impatiently, not wanting to prolong her stay for a second longer.

'Is Ollie home? Why?' Harry asked.

Without another word, Elizabeth walked out of the kitchen door. They could hear her car speed off.

Laura sat still looking at her drink, running her forefinger round the rim gently, biting her lip.

'I can't believe you just did that.' She looked up at him angrily. 'For fuck's sake, Harry!'

'I'm sorry. I saw you drinking and just freaked out.' Harry wished he could turn back the clock. How careless. Why couldn't he have just kept his mouth shut? 'Besides it's only my mother; she's not going to say anything. Now, can you tell me what's going on with Ollie?'

'Okay. You want to know?' her voice was patronising and unkind. 'He got suspended!' She smiled wickedly.

Harry pulled up a chair and sat down where his mother had sat before.

Laura continued to speak with animosity. 'I should record the number of times I have to repeat myself.'

Still processing the pregnancy, and now this with Ollie, Harry thought back to the weekend and remembered how Ollie had spoken to Charlie, and how obnoxious he himself had found his first-born child. He had forgotten the time he had been called in to Oliver's school for the very same reason.

'He needs to be professionally analysed, but what do we do in the interim?' Laura took a deep breath shaking her head. 'I just can't figure it out. We'll somehow have to manage between us. I'm so confused.'

Harry hoped Laura had figured something out. 'I have to go to Chicago,' he announced, worried she would throw the glass at him.

'*What?* Oh, bloody great!' Laura screamed. 'Just bloody great. Anything else? Any other announcements to make? Come on, anything else?' Laura broke down, battling with herself not to cry.

'I'm sorry. I know it's bad timing.' Harry put his arms around her. He wanted to cry too.

'Just leave me alone, please.' Laura buried her head on the table. 'Please just… just go away. Just leave me alone.'

'I'll go and talk to Ollie.' Harry tried to be helpful in any way possible. There was no point trying to reason with a pregnant hormonal woman, especially one whose son had just been suspended from school. Laura began to sob quietly.

Harry made his way to the boys' bedroom, dreading each step. He hated confrontation unless it was work-related. Even then he was beginning to lose his mojo, given the new unsavoury developments in his life. Gently, he knocked on Ollie's door. No response. He knocked again, still no answer. Slowly, he pushed open the door, surprised how silent the room was. Still as a rock, with arms and legs draped across the bed, lay an exhausted child with flushed cheeks and a sweaty forehead. He was fast asleep, dribbling from fatigue. How could this small child hit and bite to such an extent that he managed to get himself thrown out of school at the grand old age of ten? Relieved he didn't need to confront the issue right then, Harry heaved a huge sigh of relief, and slowly crept out of the room.

He sat in his study and sent an email to his mother.

Hi Mum,

Sorry about what happened before. So much is going on, and as you can imagine it's a very bad time. Laura is obviously not herself and I have a lot going on at work. I've been called to Chicago and cannot avoid having to go. Please try to support Laura; she really needs help, though will probably not ask for it. I know you already have Dad at your place and are managing that situation. I promise I will help when I get back.

Thanks, Harry

Like every other dedicated father, Harry adored his kids, but struggled with small children. Now his boys were finally at an age where he could begin to enjoy them. He revelled in overseeing the Lego projects, helping them with their homework and all things nerdy. However, the mere thought of babies frightened the life out of him. If he never laid eyes on another nappy, or a cot, or a buggy, or indeed anything baby-related, it would still be too soon. He absolutely could not go through that again, and couldn't imagine anything worse. A corporate beast, both inside and out, fatherhood was no natural feat for him. He lacked the basic instinct needed to be around children, openly admitting he found it an arduous endeavour. But he assured all those concerned his relationship with both of his children would most certainly improve in their teens. In fact, he looked forward to them both growing up. Life was meant to get easier.

ooooo

For a senior executive, business trips, though not as luxurious as in previous years, still offered a reasonable level of comfort and enjoyment. A self-perpetuated, busy few days awaiting him, Harry used his noise-cancelling headphones to silence away the unavoidable racket of the plane while educating himself on a SEC case.

One of the companies in which Harry's firm had a large share, was unfortunately being investigated by the United States Securities and Exchange Commission, more commonly known as the SEC. This had thrown everything into jeopardy and had resulted in the stock price tumbling. Important decisions awaited, justifying his trip, though the American arm of the company could have just as easily dealt with this without Harry needing to fly over. Dump the position or keep it? Though there was nothing serious to stress about, the challenge for Harry was remembering things: names, places, people, and in particular, sequence of events, which was the trickiest part.

What excited Harry most about this trip was the promise of a peaceful night's sleep. How he looked forward to an undisturbed night. The freedom to be carefree. He would lock the door to avoid the danger of sleepwalking.

He hoped his violent outbursts wouldn't occur but if they did, then at least no one would know. Exploring his inner thoughts, whilst hidden away in the comfort of his hotel room, made him feel very comforted.

Pleased to see his mother had responded to his email, he read what she'd written immediately, hoping all was well. Harry adored his mum. She was truly one of a kind, a spectacular woman. It was great that she had planned to take Ollie and Dad away to the country for a short respite; it was the perfect solution for both of them. Somehow Elizabeth always knew what to say and how to manage every situation.

Laura reminded Harry of his mother; it was one of the main reasons he'd married her. He'd identified the strength and compassion of his mother in his young wife. However, recently he'd begun to question himself on this issue. Was all this an illusion? Did Laura really possess similar attributes as Elizabeth? Could they really be compared? The more he dwelled on the issue, the more uncertain he became about his wife and her recent actions. How well did he know his wife? Did they still want the same things? Were they on the same path? Was it possible they had slowly been growing apart and that he'd been so consumed with his illness that he hadn't noticed? He knew he had to dismiss these negative thoughts and focus on something else, but something bizarre was definitely going on. Laura was not her normal self.

The flight, thank God, had been smooth and reasonably empty. Harry stared at his screen, trying to read, but his interests lay with his wife. He had to support Laura, no matter what. After all, it was his mistake too. Grateful to have some time out, he had to try to relax his mind and go with the flow. He would certainly support her when he returned, he assured himself.

The hotel room was bright and spacious, just as he'd hoped it would be. No matter where in the world he was, the Hyatt usually lived up to Harry's expectations. For business trips, he preferred to take no risks. The standard, the quality, was all it promised to be, and, most importantly, no hidden surprises awaited him. Delicious, dark chocolate surrounded a complimentary bottle of Champagne.

As always, Gemma had printed out a copy of Harry's itinerary, which he soon learnt to keep on his person at all times. His agenda, reasonably transparent, held no big surprises, except for one peculiar meeting which had managed to slip his mind, or he hadn't previously been informed about. A meeting room had been especially reserved for it. Scheduled attendees pencilled in were simply Miles Matthews, Head of Chicago, and a certain Miss Serena Markhieva. Who was this woman and why hadn't he been aware of this meeting? Why had Gemma not told him? A web link under her name resulted in error. The more he clicked, the more errors. Google listed endless Serena Markhievas, rendering it impossible to decipher which one was his target. This lady, whoever she was, clearly did not want to be found. He made a note to quiz Miles on the meeting the moment he got the chance.

ooooo

The drive up to the country was always a scenic, pleasant affair. The route was full of happy memories. The Hoffman family frequently holidayed in the region, be they warm summers or icy winters. Innocent childish laughter echoed in Elizabeth's ears. She could still hear her small children running across the fields, rolling down the hills, eating fruit off the trees, happy and carefree. These very hills, these trees that had never known any sorrow; how different things were now, she thought: there was so much ambiguity and uneasiness. Lost in her thoughts, Elizabeth sped through the windy country roads, ignoring all the speed limits.

Eric and Ollie sat in dark silence. Not even the picturesque charm of the idyllic countryside helped soothe Eric's broken heart. Large cups of yellow sunrays burst through the car window, temporarily blinding his vision. Despair and betrayal were his only companions now; he couldn't help but feel humiliated, followed by a tremendous amount of self-reproach. What a bittersweet pill to swallow: the very woman to rescue him was the same woman he'd abandoned when she needed him most.

Crippled with grief, he sought solace in the thought of disappearing, tucking himself in a corner beyond the hills where no one could find him. What had he done? What was his crime? All he did was to fall in love. While it was a fact that Maria was much younger than he was, and it probably wasn't ideal that she was hired by his daughter to look after her small children.

His marriage to Elizabeth had been pretty much over. Everyone knew that. He deserved to be happy; it just happened to be with a much younger woman, who wasn't his wife. Embarrassing or not, he was certainly paying the price now. Dumped, alone, an injured hip and his ex-wife for company for God knows how long, who seemed to take it in her stride. What he wouldn't do now to see Maria just one more time? After all, what was her reason for leaving without so much as an explanation?

Eric observed Elizabeth from the corner of his eye as she drove in silence, forehead full of frowns. Classical music played in the background, agitating the hell out of Ollie, as he stared blankly out of the window, oblivious to the picture-perfect surroundings.

Eric hadn't looked at Elizabeth properly for many years: she looked fabulous. 'You haven't aged a day since we broke up,' he said to her in regret.

'You think so?' Elizabeth grinned, concentrating on the road.

'What's the secret?'

'I don't know. I try to stay positive and not let others get to me,' she chuckled, her sarcasm no longer a surprise to him.

He smiled humbly. 'I deserve that, I guess, but it wasn't entirely my fault.' He shrugged his shoulders.

'Please, not now. I'm not in the mood. Ollie, are you okay back there?'

Silence.

'Ollie, your grandma is talking to you.'

Silence.

'Ollie. *Ollie.*'

'*What?*' hissed Ollie, his voice full of aggression.

'Are you okay?' Elizabeth raised her voice.

'Yes!' he screamed back.

Elizabeth shook her head in frustration. This was not the time to get wound up.

ooooo

'Is he asleep?' Elizabeth asked, staring into the open fields at nothing in particular. Beautifully assembled clay pots adorned the pretty terrace. The night air was calm and pleasant. Slowly, she rocked back and forth on an old rocking chair and smoked her own hand-rolled spliff. An expert at rolling joints since the beginning of her breast cancer, she smoked openly when she needed, ignoring social barriers and the need to explain. 'Who's going to interrogate an old lady?' she would reply when questioned.

'Finally. It took ages.' Eric sat down next to Elizabeth, politely asking for a puff of her joint. She passed it to him without speaking or turning her head. Her royal blue silk dress was perfectly complemented by the darkness of the night.

'What is going on with this poor boy? I can't believe he's been kicked out of school. The first person ever in the family. If I'd been suspended from school, my father would have expelled me from home. Kids have no idea how lucky they are these days.' Eric coughed as he spoke, no longer in the habit of smoking. He handed the joint back to his ex-wife, who still had not made eye contact with him since his release from the hospital.

Eric lightly tapped his walking stick on the concrete floor, waiting patiently for Elizabeth to say something to him. The atmosphere between the two of them tense.

'I am just as shocked as you are,' Elizabeth said, looking ahead as though speaking to herself aloud. 'Something isn't right with him. He's suffering; we need to help him.'

Eric sat in silence. He realised how indifferent to him his ex-wife had become; she didn't even look at him. His presence, or equally his absence, seemed to have little effect on her. The ticking sound of the rocking chair soothed his mind as it rocked back and forth. Without any malicious intention, Elizabeth continued to ignore him, miles away in her own thoughts. The estranged couple remained sitting, enveloped by the still darkness.

Eric suddenly felt insecure around his ex-wife. He looked twice her age; how did this happen? A bald head, a face rich in wrinkles, false teeth: he looked horrendous. She, on the other hand, looked regal and serene, unaffected by any of life's harshness. Eric tried to see what it was that fascinated Elizabeth so much, but all that was visible was nothing but blackness and silence.

'Well, if you're going to continue to ignore me, I'll go to bed. There's no point me sitting here waiting for you to speak to me.' In haste, he tried to stand up, exerting immense pressure on his walking stick.

'Sit back down!' ordered Elizabeth. She turned around to face him, angry and unforgiving. 'Just sit back down, and stop feeling sorry for yourself.'

Eric did as he was told, looking sheepish. Still reeling from the pain from his fall, a sharp pain lingered, travelling up and down his limbs. 'I'm not feeling sorry for myself. How long do you want to punish me?'

Elizabeth scowled. 'Who's punishing you?' she swiped at him, looking him straight in the eye.

'Who's punishing me? Well... you. You're punishing me. Harry is punishing me. Jane is punishing me. The kids are punishing me, my son's wife is punishing me, my daughter's husband is punishing me, everyone is punishing me, and I'm sick of it. I know what I did, and I know everyone is livid, but I had my reasons. I'm still the father of my kids, and they shouldn't treat me that way. I had my reasons for what I did. No one ever wanted to know what

I was going through; they all sided with you, and that was that. I was treated very unfairly.'

Elizabeth was silent. 'Do you want a glass of wine?' She poured him a large glass of Burgundy before he could respond. 'No one is upset or treating you badly; no one cares. Believe it or not, we all have our own problems. Taking on someone else's problems right now is a luxury no one can afford.'

'Well, I would be happy if I wasn't treated with sarcasm and contempt. All I feel is constant sniggering from everyone. Isn't it enough for everyone that my wife has left me and... ,' he wanted to say, *emptied my bank account*, but held back on this, '... and disappeared off the face of the planet?'

'Yes, I meant to ask you about that. Where on earth has this crazy woman disappeared to? I've tried to get hold of her so many times, but no luck. Where is she?'

Distraught, Eric turned to face Elizabeth as she spoke. He felt his heart implode, his arms and legs numb from his overwhelming grief. So immense was his sorrow, only screaming at the top of his lungs would afford him some relief. Sipping his wine, he looked up at the dark sky adorned with the most magnificent stars.

'I don't know. I can only guess she has returned home to Portugal.' He reclined in his chair, sighing loudly.

'What did you do to drive her away so mercilessly, without any explanation? People don't just run off like that without a word; something must have triggered it. Were you having problems?' Elizabeth looked at him inquisitively.

'I've already said I don't know, and, no, we were not having problems. I don't have any answers. One minute she was my soulmate, or so she told me; the next minute she has disappeared into thin air. I loved and trusted her; I can't believe she could do this to me.' Tears rolled down Eric's puffy, battered face. There was no point in him trying to wipe them, or pretend he was not crying. Let Elizabeth think what she wanted; he was now past caring what she thought.

'If you don't mind, I'm going to bed.' Eric cut a sad, forlorn figure. Elizabeth couldn't help sympathising. It was impossible not to feel his torment. Even though he had caused her ample suffering and heartache, only the coldest of hearts could have lacked sympathy. She must forgive him. There was simply no point of holding a grudge at their age. If truth be told, it was hardly his fault, for he probably could no longer think straight, or resist a young woman for that matter.

'Okay. Goodnight. Tomorrow is another day. It does get easier, I promise you.' She flashed him half a grin.

'Thanks.' He got up and walked inside, slowly fading inside the house in deep gloom. Elizabeth rocked back and forth, calm and serene, thoroughly enjoying her cannabis joint.

What an expensive mistake the old fool has made, she thought. She often missed him. She missed lying next to him, discussing nothing in particular, or sharing her thoughts about Harry and Jane, or their grandkids. She missed his presence. In the beginning, their relationship had been so uncomplicated. So full of love. So transparent, natural and, most of all, predictable. *Would they still have been together had cancer not taken over these recent few years of her life?* she wondered, lost in an almost hypnotic state. 'Probably not,' she said out loud. 'I would never have been able to cope with his sexual needs at my age.' She shook her head. Her mind wandered off to Harry and Laura. Problems in that marriage were clearly visible, though Harry, consumed by love, oblivious to his wife's deeply concealed insecurities, hardly saw them. She shook her head, tutting loudly, eyes heavy, deep in thought. *How irresponsible of them both*, she thought. *How could they make a mistake like this at their age?* As far as she knew, neither of them had wanted a third child; they could hardly cope with the two they had.

Laura had always somewhat baffled Elizabeth, but Harry remained the light of her eyes. Always exceptionally close, she was almost able to read his mind. Now, however, she found no explanation for the present situation. Also, his sudden abrupt departure for Chicago made no sense. Was he avoiding something? If so, what?

'Enough.' In anticipation of her action-packed planned day ahead, she thrust herself up from her rocking chair. Unsteady on her feet, she giggled, striding into the house. Two miserable children to deal with, she needed full energy and a clear head.

4

Harry sat in a diner close to his hotel, staring at his diary. So accustomed had he become to writing things down and referring to what he'd written over and over again, it almost seemed to come naturally to him. It was the only way he felt confident enough to face the world. He couldn't deny the comfort it gave him, and it was his secret. Laura, thank God, hadn't yet caught sight of him studying his calendar. To a stranger it would appear as though he were revising for an important exam. Inside the diary, neatly folded in half, lay a flyer he had successfully avoided looking at for months.

Harry gazed outside. Large, spacious American streets, and a pace of life worlds away from the hustle and bustle of the daily Mayfair grind would normally bring a sense of calm to Harry's hectic life. The last days of spring would soon fade away without so much as a murmur, welcoming in the summer season where the days would last forever. People walked around in T-shirts, in anticipation of embracing the warm climate. The unpretentious folk of Chicago, content with the warm, humid weather, strolled along casually, happy and carefree.

A sour note of bitterness flooded Harry's thoughts. How was it possible only he had problems? Why was his world crumbling? How did Laura fall pregnant? He could easily drive himself crazy thinking about it. No logical explanation presented itself. When did it happen? They were always careful; she was careful; he was careful. How had this happened? He buried his head in his hands, desperate to trace back the steps. Wracking his brain was not enough; he couldn't remember. He looked at the leaflet fearfully and took a deep breath. It was time. He had to read it.

> *This leaflet aims to give an introduction to **early-onset Alzheimer's disease**, a form of young-onset **dementia** ... **Dementia** is used to describe a group of symptoms – including memory loss, confusion, mood changes and difficulty with day-to-day tasks.*

Harry folded the leaflet shut. How could he possibly be suffering from early-onset dementia? Who does this happen to? He wasn't even fifty years old; how could this be happening to him? How could he possibly remember when he impregnated his wife if he had dementia, memory loss, confusion and mood swings all at once? He gulped his coffee down, almost spilling it on himself, desperate to get back to the hotel.

He walked out of the coffee shop, finding himself at a loss. He didn't know where the hotel was. Where should he go? In which direction should he walk? What should he do now? He took out his phone, frantically searching for the address. He looked in Notes on his phone: there was no address. He checked his calendar, 'Staying at the Hyatt Regency Chicago' but there was no address. He felt in a state of panic. What should he do? How did he get so lost? Slowly he typed the name of his hotel into Google Maps, feeling relieved, but the internet connection was slow, not to mention temperamental. *Oh God! Why did I come?* he thought to himself in a panic.

I really need to see someone, to speak to someone. I can't go through this. How do I get to the hotel? He swallowed his pride, and asked a passer-by for directions. Once again it painfully dawned on Harry that ignorance was not the way forward, he needed to take some responsibility; the next time he might not be so lucky in reaching his destination.

ooooo

Flustered, he lay in bed, resting the laptop on his legs, grateful he was able to get back to the hotel. The warm bright light lifted his spirits. Once again, he typed the words 'Dementia' and 'Alzheimer's' on his laptop, this time without looking over his shoulder. *Was there any new research?* he wondered.

Mayo Clinic's description hadn't changed much. No life-altering updates, no new discoveries had been recorded. It was the same as the last time he checked.

But others with early-onset Alzheimer's have a type of the disease called 'familial Alzheimer's disease'. They're likely to have a parent or grandparent who also developed Alzheimer's at a younger age.

Harry re-read this sentence continuously, thinking, wondering, torturing his brain, desperately trying to remember if his parents or grandparents, great uncles, great aunts, great grandparents or anyone he was related to had suffered from dementia or anything similar. Something must be hidden away deep inside; he just had to locate it. Harry and Jane had had a great relationship with their grandparents. He would have known if they had dementia; he remembered them well. His maternal grandmother had died of ovarian cancer, his maternal grandfather simply of old age, having lived a long and healthy life.

On his father's side, again nothing special. His grandpa had died of a heart attack, and his grandma, general illness, but none of them had anything remotely linked to Alzheimer's or other types of dementia. It could well be possible that one of his great grandparents or great uncles or aunts, someone in the family way back, may have had it – that would at least make some sense.

Harry continued to read, and as usual doubted he'd understood what he read. Was he processing the information in the way it was meant to be processed? Another challenge he could possibly do without. To remember information, he would first need to process it. He couldn't very well remember something he hadn't even understood in the first place. Consumed with his daily struggles, he once again found himself questioning whether what he was experiencing was simply paranoia. Maybe there was nothing wrong with him. Maybe it was all in his head. Had he invented all of this in his mind? Perhaps he was delusional.

'Focus!' he told himself. Harry continued to read. The more he read, the more frightened he became: what mental torture. How ironic, Harry lamented to himself, both his parents still reasonably healthy, except for his mum's cancer which was quite common in women of her age, and his dad's recent hip injury, again nothing too grave, yet here he was with this strange disease at his young age, a disease for which no cure was available.

Should I speak to Mum? Maybe she has signs of it. Maybe Dad does too. What about Jane? With only two years difference between him and her, she could just as well have it. Maybe she has it and is keeping quiet; maybe all three of them have it and they're all hiding it. How can he be the only one that has it? *Maybe I should send them all a message and just ask them outright; maybe they all have it and need to talk about it. Perhaps I should break the ice and tell them I have it too, and that way it's not so difficult for them to discuss it. Perhaps I'll be doing them a favour by forcing them to talk about it. Or perhaps they don't have it and that's why they haven't said anything.*

Harry picked up his phone. He really should tell his wife and discuss all this with her first. But is Laura able to deal with it right now? She's pregnant. She has Ollie and Charlie. How can I burden her with what I've got on top of what she has to deal with? It felt as though the weight of the world rested solely on his shoulders, and he didn't like it one bit.

ooooo

The blaring sound of the alarm tore him away from the same horrifying, jumping-off-the-cliff nightmare. Despite the frequency of the dream, it seemed not to get any easier, but curiously, on account of its predictability, meant he was somehow getting used to it. Or was he? He lay in bed, still as a mouse, allowing himself sufficient time to wake up calmly and collect his thoughts, carefully reconstructing his previous steps. Though this was not his first time in the Chicago office, Harry wondered if he would feel comfortable, if things had remained the same since his last visit. Keen to always make a good impression, it was essential to remain calm and focused.

It's a mindset, he thought. People had high expectations; he must not disappoint.

A charismatic leader and an excellent poker player, Harry could act the dazzling politician and position himself perfectly if need be. From the outside looking in, it all appeared gloriously perfect. Far less arrogant than his counterparts, sincere and ethical, he often wondered if he was in the right industry. Always known to play fair, Harry was a pleasure to work with. He invested time in his junior colleagues, building up their careers, teaching and mentoring, frequently paying the best bonuses in the business. Always a perfectionist, Harry liked to be liked. His aim had always been to maintain both his personal and professional standards for as long as he could. His elegant reflection in the full-length mirror still pleased him.

Perfecting his hair, he splashed on some aftershave on his face and checked his image from all angles. 'Screw you, Alzheimer's,' he muttered.

He left the hotel room on a high. Using the taxi ride to go through his to-do list and emails, it transpired that the mysterious meeting with Miss Markhieva had been scheduled for today. He couldn't help a certain amount of excited anticipation throbbing inside him. Again, he tried to Google her, but once again there was no available information on this mysterious woman.

ooooo

Laura sat behind her desk feeling flat and static. Dehydrated and nauseous, she could hardly keep her head up. Increasingly, she felt as though she was losing the will to live. Well aware that urgent decisions begged her attention, she questioned whether she could find the strength to make them. Her heart grieved and she wished, just this once, the 'situation' could solve itself. Placing a loving hand on her tummy, her imagination began to run wild, with the rapid beating of her heart. Her crazy thoughts gave way to the same vivid images in her head. The picture played over and over again. The haunting vision of a little girl playing in the sand with Charlie and Ollie dominated her every thought. A white cotton sun hat sitting on her soft, bald head. Oh, how beautiful the little darling was. She wanted to scoop her up in her arms and shower her with kisses. But could she really bring another child into this flawed world? What was she going to offer her? How would she look after her?

Youth no longer on her side, her job as a mother to small babies was already complete. She simply couldn't go back there. Breast pumping, bottle feeding, the sleepless nights; the thought horrified her. Her career had already taken a beating, not once but twice, and each time it had become harder and harder to readjust, rebuild, fight, compete with younger, more dynamic, colleagues. The male-dominated legal world hadn't changed much; equal opportunities were a lovely idea but, in all honesty, it was a myth.

She had finally found a great work-life balance, found equilibrium in all aspects of her life; having another baby would throw her off balance once again. Was she able to deal with that for the third time? That is, of course, assuming the baby was healthy. She clammed up with fear at the possibility of this poor child being born with problems. Could she live with herself, knowing she was subjecting this innocent creature to a very probable likelihood of a lifetime of unfathomable issues? Did she have the right to do this? How would the boys cope if this child was sick or disabled?

The baby would need her full time; she couldn't leave it with a nanny. What if the nanny was incapable of looking after such a needy child? What if the nanny was evil? What a terrible fate that would be. Laura pressed hard on her tummy, heartbroken. How could she have been so stupid? Why had she allowed this to happen? She felt like a dumb teenager. Covering her face with her hands, she wanted to scream. There was certainly another option, almost inconceivable though it was. Maybe she should give it some consideration. Did she have it in her heart to do the unthinkable? The mere thought of it sent shivers up her spine, leaving her miserable and despondent. She felt her blood pressure rising sky high. What a terrible mess.

Laura, just like Harry, hated not being in control. Highly ambitious, ruthless and determined, she had lived her whole life with the sole intention of winning. Losing simply was not an option. Competitive and focused, once she set her sights on something, she pursued it relentlessly, crushing whatever obstacle faced her. Marriage and motherhood had had a calming effect on her, but failure had no space in her life.

Harry and Laura complemented each other perfectly; their mutual love of winning and being the best was the first thing that had attracted them to one another; it somehow remained the glue that kept them together. Their respect and admiration for each other's strengths and passions kept their relationship alive and healthy, though Harry, somewhat less competitive than Laura, enjoyed playing second fiddle to his wife. He revelled in his wife's victories, finding her triumphs not only sexy but highly desirable. Her ego marginally bigger than his, worked to his lazy advantage, for he happily sat back watching her make the decisions. Managing the household, making arrangements for the kids, the holidays, her wish was his command. All he asked for in return was peace, and she was happy to grant him that providing she remained in control at all times.

ooooo

Hi, darling, what was the name of that psychiatrist that posh mother at the school went to see recently? After thinking for a while, Laura WhatsApped a friend from the kids' school.

Dr Stephan Raza, came the instant WhatsApp reply. *Very expensive, and very good.*

Thanks, she replied, ready to contact him immediately.

And did I mention gorgeous? Five smiley faces followed.

Laura smiled. *How do you know?*

Everybody knows. I've met him. And, of course, Google. Lots of info and pictures. Quite a superstar. More smiley faces.

Okay, wait, let me check…'

Will wait. Quick. Tell me what you think.

Wow.

Told you.

I'm shocked. He really is very handsome. I must admit.

Told you. Very charming, and quite good.

Thanks, darling, really appreciate it.

Sure. What's up anyway? Is it for you? Surely you are the last person in the world that would need a therapist. All okay?

Fine. Tell you later. Thanks a lot.

Big kiss.

Laura called the practice without a minute's hesitation. Fabulous! A last-minute cancellation meant she could be squeezed in for an appointment that afternoon at four o'clock.

'Georgia, please cancel my four p.m. today; I have to go to Charlie's school. He isn't feeling well.'

'Of course, will do so immediately,' replied Laura's PA, obediently.

ooooo

Dr Raza's biography was as impressive as his face. Laura, half expecting the description to be nonsense, could hardly believe what she saw and read. He was quite a sensation. Wasn't it more of a bored housewife's fantasy, or Mills and Boon and trashy romantic novels, the only places where handsome doctors existed? She read the bio repeatedly, referring back to his face as she read. Something definitely stood out. How engaging he looked. Perhaps his picture was a result of intense Photoshopping; everyone seems to be doing that these days. Laura's own corporate photo had been re-edited to perfection, resembling someone half her age. Those arresting blue eyes, so bright and intense, could hardly be real. If one was to believe everything they read in his bio, it could safely be assumed this was the right man; he seemed to be as good as it gets regarding matters of the mind. Stephan Raza, a man of extensive knowledge and expertise, promised to cure all sorts of emotional issues. Positive reviews and beautifully crafted testimonials certainly seemed to justify his steep price.

Laura once more examined his flawless face, which seemed to reveal a humble, kind smile. She profoundly hoped he was the real deal and could help bring some relief. The handsome photo and the enchanting smile certainly

77

made it easier for her to see him, but was it therapy she needed? Had she sunk so low? For the first time in her adult life, the magic wand had jumped out of her hands, without the possibility of her instantly scooping it back up. She was suddenly incapable of solving her own problems, compelled to rely on outside intervention. She looked at her reflection in the mirror and thought that her usually Botoxed 'business' face was reduced to nothing but a pale, haggard old bat. She decided she looked horrible. Turning to an angle, she examined her stomach; nothing visible, still flat. Pushing her tummy out as far as she could, in front of a full-length mirror discreetly hidden inside a large filing cupboard, she breathed in and out, inspecting it from every angle, not sure of what she expected to see. She rubbed her tummy lovingly with both hands as she thrust it out further in the hope of once again capturing how she would look full term, now that she was considerably older. Feeling her tummy made her emotional which only confused her further.

'This is so depressing,' she mumbled to herself, shaking her head in self-pity while banging the door closed with a loud thud. She sat back at her desk, carefully hiding any visible facial blemishes with a thin layer of foundation. She pulled her limp auburn hair into a loose ponytail. Her dry, chapped lips benefited from a light healthy coat of lipstick. A few lashings of mascara later, she headed off to see Dr Raza an hour early.

ooooo

With all of Harry's attempts to discuss the curious meeting with the unknown lady with Miles in vain, he was left none the wiser. It remained shrouded in mystery, as did this intriguing Russian-sounding person herself. He made his way to the meeting room a few minutes ahead of schedule, having successfully cast his emotional issues to one side. Ready, and in anticipation of something exciting to divert his attention from his problems, the urge to meet this woman was nevertheless incomprehensible.

The empty, spacious meeting room was minimally furnished, with a large, expensive glass office table in the centre. Fourteen state-of-the-art, comfortable, dark wooden chairs were neatly arranged around it. In addition to a telephone and remote control for an old-fashioned projector, three glasses, three bottles of water, and a few napkins had been neatly laid out. Downtown Chicago, clearly visible from the large windows, transfixed Harry. Curiously, he looked down. He had a newly developed relationship with heights since his horrific nightmares; Harry claimed that he now had vertigo. Laura's face rushed into his mind: she looked as she did in his dream. 'Please, God, let her be okay!' he prayed under his breath.

Lost in his thoughts, he was slightly taken aback when the door flung open and a panting Miles tore inside, quite out of breath.

'So good to see you, buddy! How are you?'

Harry shook Miles's hand eagerly.

'I'm sorry I've not been around.' Miles caught his breath. 'I've been inundated.' He shook his head, flapping his arms around like a waddling duck. 'Serious problems with Shanghai again. I've been stuck in conference calls almost the entire week. The Chinese are so bureaucratic, and oh, so very impatient.'

'No worries. I just wanted to ask you about today's meeting. I don't have any info.' Harry smiled. 'Who is she?'

'Actually, I don't know any more than you do. She's the daughter of a prominent Azeri businessman who recently passed away. She inherited some insane amounts of money and wants to park it somewhere. She asked for you specifically.' Miles raised his eyebrows up and down, smiling mischievously.

Harry also raised his eyebrows, somewhat bewildered.

'Me? Asked for *me*? How strange.' Harry frowned, pulling a glassy-eyed, confused look. 'Really? I've never heard of her. I wonder why she would ask for me…'

'We'll find out very soon, Harry, my friend.' Miles grinned smugly, as excited as Harry was curious. A dashing, athletically-built Harvard-educated ex-lawyer, Miles hailed from a distinguished wealthy American family, consisting largely of Republican politicians. A ruthless, persuasive businessman, born into extreme privileges, he lived in his rich little bubble that consisted of like-minded people. Having never known real hard work or struggle, he was usually relaxed and composed, with an unrivalled habit of making others feel comfortable and at ease.

Harry respected Miles tremendously. The two men shared a common gentleman's agreement to keep each other's secrets, or turn a blind eye when necessary, resulting in a mutual understanding between them. Not quite equal in their social standing, Miles was a man of considerable power, often referred to as the guy never to oppose, a fact Harry was also privy to.

'I'm also quite intrigued. I wonder what she looks like.' Miles had a twinkle in his eye. Harry recognised the look, but preferred not to acknowledge it. Before he could find a moment to comment or reflect on what his colleague had just said, they were interrupted by an insistent knock on the door.

'Come in!' Miles shouted excitedly.

The door opened slowly. Serena Markhieva was shown into the room by a sharply dressed receptionist. Harry and Miles remained still, with their eyes fixed on what they saw at the door. Speechless, they both looked in silence as she breezed into the room. Casually hanging off her shoulders, a large, pale grey pashmina shawl covered a luxurious white satin shirt. Her long legs were encased in a pair of tight jeans, accompanied by a pair of high-heeled shoes. Tall and dazzling, she approached the two men, offering her hand.

'Serena Markhieva,' she smiled warmly.

'Miles Matthews. A pleasure, Miss Markhieva. This is my colleague from the London office, Harry Hoffman.'

'Nice to meet you both.' Harry blushed as he shook her cold, dainty hand. His cheeks were hot and flushed and his heart was throbbing as though he had been hit by a thunderbolt. *What is this I see before me?* He had never set eyes on a woman like this before. Her lips were ruby red, her light brown hair was pulled back loosely in a low bun. With her translucent, soft pale skin, he was spellbound. Simple and classy, he could hardly resist gazing at her pearly white teeth as she smiled and spoke gently. For a few moments, nothing else existed. He forgot about all his problems. His heart fluttered, his knees felt weak and feeble. Like an angel from heaven, she was simply mesmerising. The pearls adorned around her neck paled in comparison to the sparkling diamonds drooping from her ears. Indeed, she was a picture of grace and elegance. Struck by her beauty, it was inconceivable to Harry that this gorgeous woman had asked to see him specifically. Why?

'You too. How do you do?' Her hand remained in his, followed by a gentle squeeze, as though she were meeting an old friend.

'Please do take a seat,' interrupted Miles, pulling out a chair at the head of the table. Serena crossed her legs as she made herself comfortable. Fascinated, the two men watched her closely, instantaneously realising how unsubtle they may have appeared to her. Miles discreetly nudged Harry with his elbow. Harry fast understood and swiftly resumed his composure. He broadened his shoulders, closed his mouth firmly, gently raising himself even taller. A strapping six foot two inches tall, he had nothing to fear. He could only hope she hadn't noticed his lack of composure. She must know what effect she had on people. He decided to forgive himself. He stared at a beautiful woman. So what?

Captivated, Harry and Miles sat close to one another, doting on her every word. They could have been mistaken for two obedient schoolboys.

'I have to be honest; we've had little briefing or knowledge of how we can be of help to you. Please advise us.' Miles smiled his most charming smile, 'What can we do for you?' Harry sat back as Miles laid on the charm. 'It's a pleasure to have you here, and both Harry and I would be delighted to accommodate you however we can. We are a fifty-year-old business, and even though I say so myself, we are very good at what we do.' He smiled innocently. She smiled back. 'We are very performant and pro-active in terms of our risk management; we will be transparent every step of the way. Please be assured you can trust our strategies and our asset-management, and always feel comfortable and relaxed. You are in good hands. Whatever the markets throw at us, we will handle it.'

Miles talked as though cream were being poured into a bowl of strawberries. The tone of his voice, his body language, his delicate mannerisms; what a mighty salesman, and what wonderful, sugar-coated words. Harry was in awe of him. Rarely was there so much generosity in a boardroom. *Watch and learn*, Harry thought to himself. He loved pitching with Miles, the absolute epitome of class and sophistication.

'Thank you.' Serena smiled in appreciation.

'Can I offer you a drink before we begin, perhaps?' He poured water for the three of them.

'I'm fine, thank you. I had a coffee before I came. I need your help. I have come into a large sum of money, which I don't know what to do with. It is possible I may receive more, though I cannot say for certain. I will need to do something with it, whether I invest it, move it around. I don't know how to do any of it. I have no financial brain. I will need some help and advice.'

'Of course. That's our job. We do that for our clients every day. This is our expertise. We would be more than happy to help you in every which way we can. We will take all the work off you and do everything to protect and grow your money. You have come to the right place.'

'We do, of course, have to ask the source of funds, and quickly go through the very boring "know your client" checks, as a first step. My apologies, I know it's not very glamorous.' Harry interrupted, trying not to sound too abrupt or administrative.

'I will provide you with all the details you require, Mr Hoffman. It's all clean, I assure you.' She smiled. 'My father died last year. I'm an only child, so of course the natural beneficiary. Everything was left to me. Of course, I always knew I would inherit everything, but wasn't sure it would be these amounts.'

Harry and Miles listened fascinated. It was by far the best part of their job. Never a dull moment.

'I'm afraid it was a case of bad politics. Large amounts of my father's money were taken away and our assets unlawfully frozen. Now, with a new government in Azerbaijan, they have taken a more lenient approach and are willing to return the money to its rightful owner. Sadly these things are not such a rarity in that part of the world.'

'Where is the money now?' asked Miles.

'It's all over the world. Part of it is here with me, some of it is in Cyprus, some in Switzerland and Lichtenstein. My father had bank accounts in many different places. Trust funds were set up for me overseas. I'm not exactly sure myself; all I know is that I would like to have the whole lot here in the US, or at least have whatever I can. As you may imagine, I wasn't really aware of any of this previously, but now that I am, I want it all under my control.'

Serena spoke with a gentle American accent with a slight French twang. One might be forgiven for assuming that she, given her attire and mannerisms, had been educated in Paris. Her appearance seemed more French than American.

'As I mentioned, I am an only child and have no other living relatives. I have to take sole control of everything. Unfortunately I don't have a financial background, and have no clue how to manage such a large sum of money.' She paused thoughtfully. 'I wish my father had managed it better before he died, or at least had told me about it, but his death was very sudden and unexpected.' She clasped her hands together. 'Can you help me?'

'Yes. We will do everything we can to help you, I promise. We are sorry to hear about your father. It sounds very sad and unfortunate.'

'Yes, it was a tragedy.'

'Are you an American citizen?'

'Yes. I have both French and American passports. I have been US-based for a while. However, I remain open to relocating someday. I considered maybe moving to London, hence asking to meet Harry Hoffman. Also, I am told British banks are often a safe bet and less bureaucratic than other countries. But I don't know anything about banks or the finance industry. Since I came into this money, I was forced to make decisions about what to do with it; I can't possibly spend it all.' She gave a little nervous laugh. 'It was all very unexpected. I started doing some research and stumbled upon you guys, so I thought I'd give you a call.' She spoke openly with a serene air of integrity and calmness.

'I called your London office, wanting to speak to you,' she said, looking at Harry. 'They said you were in Chicago, which happened to be perfect for me.'

Harry, quite unsure of what to make of all this, focused on her every word. Though she sounded perfectly genuine, something niggled him. It all appeared somewhat peculiar, almost like a cliché, some elaborate espionage movie scene from a bad Bond movie. *Beautiful, mysterious Russian-ish lady walks into a skyscraper wanting to hide an obscene amount of money. Her red lips and high heels captivate all the men, leaving them madly in love with this beautiful spy.* All a bit surreal, there must be something dodgy in all of this. Can this woman really be who she says she is? It was all very cryptic.

'Do you live in Chicago?'

'Yes, I do.'

'May I ask your profession?' The more he focused on her face, the more real she began to appear. Microscopic little blemishes on her face started to surface, as though they had suddenly appeared from nowhere. Faintly detectable wrinkles formed around her eyes when she smiled; these smallest imperfections further endeared her to both men. Harry found himself the more enamoured the more he looked at her.

A no-nonsense, down-to-business type of guy, Harry remained focused on his little world, primarily his job, family, and now his health. As beautiful and intriguing as this lady was, ultimately, she was a client. He had to treat her like any other client or person of interest. There was, however, more to this lady. She was a far cry from your average wealthy client; her mere presence commanded attention. He greatly looked forward to presenting her with the 'know your client' questions, and would wait with bated breath for her to pass the due diligence process. *How compelling and spicy would it be if she were really a corrupt femme fatale sent by Russian intelligence to fleece them for information and park dodgy KGB money?* He chuckled to himself at the absurd thought.

'I am an artist and sometime student. I study journalism part-time. I was learning to become an opera singer, but didn't make it. I wasn't able to hit the high notes.' She laughed out loud. 'My career didn't go as I planned, I'm afraid.'

The men laughed along with her.

'I don't think anyone's does. I wanted to be a baseball player when I was young, like every American kid, but was forced to study law and economics and work in a bank.'

'What about you, Harry? What did you want to be when you were younger?'

They both looked at him. It was his turn to be on the spot.

'Oh, I used to change my mind all the time. I wanted to be a football player; you guys call it soccer here. Then I wanted to be an actor, a photographer, an architect; you name it, I wanted to be it. Luckily, I liked studying, and studying economics and finance didn't seem so bad.' Serena made no secret that she was watching him as he spoke, almost as though she were scrutinising him. Harry was far more interesting to her than Miles, but why?

Unable to define her strategy, again Harry questioned her motives. Was he overthinking and dramatising everything out of insecurity and his current fragile state of mind, or was it all above board and normal? No, he shouldn't doubt himself; there was definitely something questionable about this; something was strange. This woman certainly seemed to have him in her sights, but the question was why.

ooooo

Laura nervously filled out the new patients' form, trying her best to be as honest and precise as she could. She skimmed through the questions until presented with the 'Are you pregnant?' question. Chewing on her pen anxiously, she paused and sighed. What should she answer? Nothing. She left it blank.

A state-of-the-art waiting room, it seemed as though the dermatologists next door had had some influence on the décor. It was all very shiny and pleasant. The clean-cut receptionists wore white, blending in perfectly with the bright, gleaming walls. Laura longed for a glimpse of the patient list, having heard the practice was a firm favourite of A-list celebrities.

'Dr Raza will see you now. Please follow me.' Laura stood up obediently, walking behind the woman in the white outfit, wondering if confiding in a perfect stranger was the right thing to do.

'Please take a seat. He will be here shortly.' It was a warm, inviting room and Laura sat down staring into nothingness, hardly noticing her surroundings. She inspected her phone: no new messages. She flicked through her photos, looking at nothing in particular. She flicked through her text messages, glimpsed her emails. Nothing required immediate attention.

'Mrs Hoffman, sorry to have kept you waiting. I'm Dr Stephan Raza.'

Somewhat baffled by his arrival, Laura stood up awkwardly. The doctor smiled graciously and shook her hand firmly.

'Please do sit down.' He sat opposite her, looking nothing like his profile picture from the website. Much older in appearance, his hair was grey and unkempt. His aged face was white and leathery, and he smiled at her sympathetically. His sharp steely blue eyes gave nothing away. Laura sat silently, daring not to flinch. Though she looked at him intensely, her mind full of indefinable thoughts, she didn't really see him.

'How are you, Mrs Hoffman?' Dr Raza questioned softly. His expression was gentle; his eyes suddenly warm and encouraging.

'I'm… fine. Thank you. I'm okay.' Her voice was croaky, and unclear. She cleared her throat. 'I'm okay, thank you,' she repeated, louder this time.

She forced a smile and repeated once more: 'I'm okay, thanks, Doctor,' she said again, assuring him all was well.

'Good.' He smiled at her. She gazed at his face. What was all the fuss about? She failed to understand why people thought him such a stunner; he was just an average looking chap, and an old one at that. There was nothing special about him.

'How are you?'

'I'm very well, thank you.' He paused for a while. 'Would you like to talk?'

'Yes.' She nodded. 'Yes, I would like to talk. I'm here because I need to talk. I need to talk to someone. I'm… I really need to talk.' She smiled sadly.

'You can talk to me.' He nodded at her reassuringly.

She looked down at her hands gently, rubbing her thumb along her palm, moving on to her engagement ring and nervously playing with it, swirling it round and round profusely.

'How are you feeling?' the doctor asked.

'Pregnant. I'm feeling very pregnant, Doctor.' She chuckled hysterically.

'I see.' He clasped his lips together. 'Was this pregnancy planned?' He lowered his head to level hers.

Laura's eyes swelled up with tears. She shook her head, sniffing her tears away. The doctor gave her a few minutes to gather her thoughts.

'Would you like to talk about the pregnancy?' His voice was deep but kind.

Laura burst into tears. She wiped her nose and her tears with a crumpled-up tissue. 'I'm sorry.' She continued to cry, blowing her nose as she hid her face in her tissue.

'Take your time. It's okay. You don't need to speak if you don't want to.'

Laura blew her nose again, slowly wiping her tears away with her tissue. Dr Raza allowed her as much time as she needed.

'I'm pregnant. I'm forty-eight years old and I am pregnant.' She looked towards the doctor, then averted her gaze away from him deliberately, as though she didn't want him to see her or know her real age. She focused on the crystals dangling off the lampshade behind the doctor's chair, staring at them blankly. Her eyes welled up again with tears. Fiercely, she wiped them away before they rolled down her cheeks. She felt mascara running down her cheeks, which she continued to wipe away with her wet tissue.

'Does the father of the child know that you are pregnant?' asked Doctor Raza calmly.

'Yes. Yes, he does. He knows.'

'How does he feel?'

'He is shocked and disgusted.' She shrugged her shoulders matter-of-factly. 'He cannot believe I could get pregnant at my age.' The doctor let her catch her thoughts. She shook her head in disbelief.

Dr Raza focused his gaze on Laura. 'Are you married? he asked, almost in a whisper.

'Yes.'

Do you live together?'

'Yes.'

'Do you have children?'

'Yes. Two boys. Oliver and Charlie.'

'How old are they?'

'Ten and eight.'

'Have you told anyone about the pregnancy?'

'My best friend and my husband. His mother also knows; my husband slipped up and told her.' Her voice suddenly turned sarcastic and aggressive. 'He accidentally told his mother; can you believe that?' She shook her head.

'You didn't want her to know?'

'No. I really didn't want her to know.'

'Do you have a good relationship with your mother-in-law, Mrs Hoffman?'

'Laura. Please call me Laura.'

'How's your relationship with your mother-in-law, Laura?'

She shrugged her shoulders. 'Good and bad. Mostly bad. I don't care for her much. Actually, I don't really like her.'

'Okay. Do you have someone you can talk to about this with?'

'I can talk to my best friend.' She looked at him sternly. 'But I don't really want to talk to her or anyone about it.'

'Okay.' The doctor smiled. He looked nice when he smiled. 'Would you like to talk to me?'

'There is nothing to talk about. I need to decide what I am going to do. It's very simple. I need to make a decision and… and then execute it.'

'I understand.' Dr Raza edged forward from his seat. 'What would you like me to do? How can I be of help to you?'

'I need to make a decision and I need you to help me.'

'Yes. I will help you.'

Laura laughed hesitantly. 'I want you to help me live with myself.'

Once again, she began to sob. Dr Raza got up from his seat and offered her a box of tissues. He sat back down and faced her.

'Why do you need to make a decision?'

Laura stopped crying and looked at him in amazement. 'Sorry?' She blew her nose. 'Why do I need to make a decision? Did you ask me why I need to make a decision?'

'Yes. Why do you need to make a decision?'

She continued to look straight at him, confused.

'I need to make a decision because… because… I need to make a decision. I need to make a decision, because… well, of course I need to make a decision, Doctor.' *What a stupid question*, Laura thought. *How can I not make a decision? I have to make a decision.*

'Why do you need to make a decision?'

'I need to make a decision because I need to know whether or not I should keep this child.'

'How are you going to make this decision?' Dr Raza asked calmly as if he were talking to a five-year-old child.

Laura, almost on the verge of hysteria, felt as though she'd lost her voice. Words refused to come out of her mouth. How should she answer this question? All the years training as a lawyer, staying confident, composed, analytical, yet now she found herself sitting in front of a psychiatrist unable to explain herself rationally. She really hated herself right now. Why was it so difficult to explain what she needed to do; why could this man not understand? Wasn't it clear? Surely it was.

'I am going to make this decision once I have thought it all through.'

'Okay. What do you need to think through?'

'What I need to do.'

'What do you need to do?'

'Make a decision.'

'Make a decision about *what*?'

'Whether I keep the baby.'

'Do you know how you will make the decision?'

'I will weigh out the pros and cons.'

'… and then?'

'And then I will make the decision.'

'Okay. Can I offer you some help?'

'Yes. Yes, please.'

'How do you think I can help?'

'By supporting me.'

'Of course I will. I will help and support you in any way I can.'

'Thank you, Doctor.'

'It's a pleasure.'

'Please don't judge me.' Laura looked down in remorse.

'No. I will not judge you. It's not my place to judge you.'

'Everybody judges, Doctor. No matter what we all say, everyone judges. It's the way it is.'

'I really will not judge you. I couldn't do this job if I was going to judge you or be judgemental. You must ultimately do what's best for you and, of course, your family. If you make a decision or choose not to make a decision, I will support you either way, and be available when you need to talk.'

She nodded, rubbing her palms together anxiously.

'What does your GP or gynaecologist say, I mean from a health perspective?'

'My gynaecologist is gay; he is not fond of kids. He thinks the world is already overpopulated and that we needn't pollute it with more people. He hasn't outright given me a concrete opinion, but he is 100 per cent sure it's a risk and would probably advise me to... to not go ahead. He is a nice guy, but he is very risk-averse. He knows me, and my whole family, and he knows my giving birth again would be disruptive for us. He also thinks two kids are more than enough and that the planet simply doesn't need more children.'

Dr Raza smiled. 'I'm sure he has his reasons for his opinions.'

'He is worried I am simply too old, and that my eggs aren't what they used to be, that my body is unable, etc. etc. He is just being cautious and is probably dreading my endless visits to his surgery.'

They both smiled.

Finally, she could see the attraction in him. He was actually very handsome. His wrinkles had hardly destroyed his looks, *au contraire* they defined him. Laura sat still. She liked his aura. She took a chance to gaze at him sneakily, head to toe.

'It was good you came in to see me today. Would you like to make another appointment to see me again, perhaps next week?'

'Yes please, I would like that. Are you going on holiday, or quitting or leaving the country? Will you still be available when I need you again?'

Dr Raza smiled amiably. 'Yes. I will be here whenever you need me. Make an appointment whenever it is convenient with my secretary; she will put it in my diary.'

'Thank you, Doctor. It was really helpful.' She squeezed his hand, a nervous wreck. He held on, trying to give her strength.

'You will be okay,' he reassured her. She hesitated, looking directly at his face, before nervously looking away. She found herself standing extremely close to him, the faint whiff of aftershave mixed with a sterile, minty smell hovered around him.

Dr Raza stood six foot four inches tall. A monster of a man, he towered over Laura. Strong and broad, he looked remarkably fit for someone his age. Laura felt weak and jittery, her hand still locked in his hand, her five-foot-six-inch frame practically dwarfed by his presence. She raised her eyes and lifted her head to look at his face. He smiled kindly, bending his head down towards her, slowly letting go of her hand. With teary eyes, crimson cheeks and strange sentiments fluttering in her stomach, she whispered goodbye and hurried out of his practice.

ooooo

Staring out of the window from the top deck of a bus, she watched the cars standing still. Traffic-heavy, the slow bus was exactly what she wished for that moment. Somewhat in a heavy daydream, Laura's thoughts drifted away, leaving her reality far behind. Purposely shoving the baby issues to one side in her thoughts, she easily forgot the stresses and her problems.

The conversation with Dr Raza played on her mind; she reiterated his every word to herself: the way he spoke, the sound of his voice, which echoed in and out of her mind. His masculine, comforting baritone voice, the way he said her name… She replayed in her mind his intense, analytical stare, his calm reassuring presence. She took comfort from the visit, feeling as though she had found a friend, or at least someone neutral to talk to.

Thanks for the recommendation, well worth the visit, and you are right, very handsome indeed. She signed the message to her friend with a big smile visible on her face.

5

The sun tore through the dark curtains in Elizabeth's room, spectacularly brightening up every corner. The central England weather promised its inhabitants a splendid afternoon. Determined to cheer up both grandpa and grandson, Elizabeth planned an elaborate, fun-filled day, although she faced a major challenge, given there was almost seventy or so years age difference between the two of them.

Oliver woke up in his usual cantankerous mood, with a grumpiness that was fast becoming his identity. Though only ten years of age, his behaviour was more teenage than child, the regularity in which he expressed his tantrums were a cause of concern for most of the family except his mother, who, until recently, had thought him perfect, often encouraging his aggressive exploits.

Eric, on the other hand, was upbeat and agile.

'I've decided to enjoy this delightful weather and cheer up... as much as I can. I think Oliver should do the same.' Eric and Elizabeth both glanced at Ollie chomping away at his cereal. Ollie decided to ignore his grandparents.

'I want to speak to my mummy,' he grunted.

'After breakfast, darling.' Elizabeth sipped her coffee. 'First of all, I want us all to take a moment and acknowledge where we are.' She peered at Oliver. 'Especially you, my darling Ollie.' Ollie ignored her again. 'Oliver, did you know the Cotswolds has been declared an Area of Outstanding Natural Beauty, abbreviated to AONB? It's a vast area of almost eight hundred square miles, covering the counties of Gloucestershire and Oxfordshire, and extending into parts of Wiltshire, Worcestershire, Warwickshire and Somerset.'

'I don't care,' hissed Oliver, still not looking up.

Elizabeth shot a frustrated look of disapproval at Eric who sympathised with her helplessly. Not one to be deflated, she continued to speak loudly.

'I thought we could go and visit Highgrove Estate which belongs to the Prince of Wales, and Corsham Court, another former royal manor, which boasts an incredibly beautiful garden. It's the perfect day for a little excursion.' Ollie didn't flinch. The boy was simply not interested. He was indeed in a very funny mood; he wasn't going to appreciate anything today. 'Okay, change of plan,' she whispered to Eric, miffed.

With both Eric and Ollie on board, Elizabeth set off in her car to visit her dear friend Lucinda. Though only a forty-five-minute drive away, and the roads reasonably quiet, it seemed like a very long distance. Lucinda lived in a very large beautiful old house, rich in years of history. Enclosed by steeply rising hills and surrounded by beech woods, the entrance of the house, a naturalist's dream, was framed with deep lawns overlooking a vast lake. The house, though unique and resplendent to people who lived outside the region, was in fact nothing but another stunningly unaffordable dwelling for the locals. As they drew closer to the house, Oliver's interest finally piqued.

'Wow, look at those apple trees. Amazing!' Rows and rows of pristine, immaculately groomed apple trees formed endless neat lines. In full blossom, they filled the air with the sweetest smell. Oliver was stunned; he had never seen so many apple trees before.

'Wait till you get inside,' winked Elizabeth at her eldest grandson.

'Why? What's inside? What is it, Grandma? Tell me. I can't wait.'

'Interested now, are we?' Eric and Elizabeth chuckled at the animated boy who was now over-excited and finally alive, full of energy, almost as if he had been swapped with another child, a well-behaved one.

'You'll see.'

Ollie stared at the window, intrigued.

'Such a gorgeous house, but how does Lucinda live here alone? Doesn't she get lonely?' asked Eric.

'She doesn't; she is used to it. She has her dogs, a few friends, she has her organ, the church choir. She is very content. You haven't seen her for ages, have you?'

Lucinda, a widow for many years, a long-time friend of Elizabeth's and godmother to Jane, was also a very harsh critic of Eric's since his shenanigans with the Portuguese au pair. Eric had not seen her since their divorce.

A kids' paradise, the grounds not only boasted a well-stocked lake and swimming pool, but there was also an indoor pool and a spa. Elizabeth's favourite was the tennis court.

'How many wonderful memories, how many competitive games we've played here! I'm looking forward to beating you at tennis again.' She smiled at Eric.

He glared at her stunned. 'Tennis? With my injured hip? Are you crazy?'

Elizabeth bit her lip.

'Sorry! I totally forgot. You look fine from here.' She grinned at him sheepishly. 'You know, Lucinda confided in me that she is running out of money and cannot afford the maintenance of this house anymore.'

'Really? That's sad. It would be a tragedy to lose a place like this.'

'I know. I wish Harry had the means to buy it. It would be so lovely to own something like this. Perhaps I'll mention it to him when I next see him.'

As anticipated, Ollie thoroughly enjoyed himself. Both he and Eric successfully distracted themselves from their recent problems and made the most of the sumptuous house, entertaining themselves to their full ability.

For Elizabeth, it was mission accomplished. How shallow men of all ages seemed to be; at the click of a finger they forget all their problems and then a few minutes later find themselves moping around once again. They ended a perfect day with a delicious meal in a quaint picturesque country pub, buzzing with friendly locals, happy to engage in long, relaxed conversations.

ooooo

'I know what you're both thinking,' Serena spoke lightly. 'You are wondering what's going on. There must be more to this woman than meets the eye. She is probably some dodgy KGB agent, sent on a secret mission to obtain classified information.' She gave a little playful laugh and continued calmly. 'Or perhaps she is here to somehow launder her war criminal father's blood money,' she smirked, reading both their minds and simultaneously trivialising the sensitivity of the subject.

Harry and Miles remained silent, unable to muster up a witty, polite comeback.

'What a cliché that would be.' She laughed, and shifted her gaze back and forth between the two men. Unable to avert their gaze from this electrifying, charismatic woman, the two normally assertive men watched open-mouthed as this dazzling creature casually got up and wandered towards the window, staring outside as though she were seeking something. She turned around and faced them both, confident and seemingly wise beyond her years. Serena's poise and self-assurance betrayed her very youthful appearance.

A young lady of Eastern European origin, she was accustomed to dealing with frequently ignorant, unkind advances and comments. She had learned to develop a thick skin and cope with the negativity and criticism she had endured daily in her youth. The confidence and inner strength she had learned to display often gave the wrong impression, compelling most people to assume her to be something she wasn't.

'I am willing to pay whatever fees necessary for an attractive return. I want my funds in competent hands and accessible to me, without any questions or any bureaucracy. We can set up a meeting with my father's team of accountants who will go through the books with you, and will be able to answer all your questions far better than I can. I cannot do the admin process with you.'

'I do apologise if we are giving the wrong impression, Miss Markhieva. There is absolutely no judgement on our part, but there are things that cannot be avoided. We have to have compliance checks, audits, anti-money laundering checks, due diligence, etc. We also have certain questions we need to ask you, certain boxes we need to tick before we can take on any new clients. Everything has to be accounted for and legitimate. I do apologise if somehow we are giving you the wrong impression; it is certainly not intentional.' Harry was grateful for Miles's monologue. He wanted him to put her at ease.

'Thank you, I appreciate that. I am used to people viewing me in a certain way, which was before I came into the money. I can't begin to imagine what they might think now. Sometimes I tend to be paranoid and over-think. My money is clean. All of it! There is, unfortunately, nothing more to me than what I am saying.' Miles and Harry empathised with an all-knowing nod of their heads. 'I can only imagine that if I were a spy or an unorthodox government official, how much fun that would be. Unfortunately, I don't have that skill set!'

'I'm sorry if we appear to have overactive imaginations. I can assure you it's not our intention to malign you. It would be an absolute pleasure to help you in any way we can. We would be delighted to meet your father's team, whenever convenient. I'm here for another two days; it would be great if we could do this before I leave.'

'Perfect. I will be in touch. Thank you, gentlemen.'

'It's a pleasure.' They both stood up and handed her their business cards, making sure that both their mobile numbers had been included, and watched her leave the room.

Miles slumped himself down on a chair as though suffocating. He hit both hands on the table with a large thud.

'Harry, Harry, oh Harry! I think I am in love! What an incredible woman. She is out of this world. Wow! I mean, I couldn't take my eyes off her! She is gorgeous. We don't come across women like that in Chicago. What a dream. She can park any amount of money with us, providing she has a hot, dirty, illicit affair with me...' Miles then impersonated a Dr Evil laugh.

Harry pulled up a chair next to him, nodding his head in dazed ecstatic disbelief. 'Who is she, where did she come from? She waltzes into our office so confident, so gorgeous, and has us both eating out of her hands. I could have stared at her the whole day.' Harry stroked his chin pensively, 'She was so different from the average rich heiress that we usually meet. Down to earth, fun, pleasant. So beautiful, surprisingly not arrogant, and oh so sexy!'

'If I didn't have a few hundred years of family fortunes to lose, I would be pursuing Miss Markhieva in a way that would blow her mind.'

'I hear you,' Harry considered encouragingly. 'I so hear you. What an extraordinary woman. You don't see her walking down the street every day. And I wonder just how much money she is talking about.'

'Obsceeeeene amounts,' retorted Miles, imitating Richard Gere in *Pretty Woman*. They both laughed loudly.

'I agree. Obsceeeene amounts. Obscene amounts of dirty, filthy money.' Harry laughed.

'I wonder what she is like in bed.' Miles's eyes narrowed, lips pursed together, his face excited and serious. His gelled-back hair shone from the wax holding it in place.

'I wonder where she got all that money from, or where her dad got it from? It sounds dodgy to me.'

'Who cares about the money? I wonder if she would consider running away with me.'

Harry squinted. 'This conversation is getting too dangerous for me; I'm a married man. I cannot talk or even think like this!'

'Really? So, you're trying to tell me the thought never crossed your mind!? The whole time you were sitting there in front of her and, as you English say, "gawking" at her, you thought absolutely nothing?' Miles's tone rapidly changed from playful humour to serious and assertive. 'What hypocrites you English are. You say one thing, yet mean something completely different.'

Harry was taken aback. What had just happened? Miles had switched. His face had turned pale, his lips curled and his expression was harsh and arrogant, all in a matter of seconds. Suddenly, he was a different person.

Harry took a deep breath, trying to appease the awkwardness. 'Miles, I'm a happily married man.' He cleared his throat gently. 'Of course, I can appreciate a beautiful woman, an extremely beautiful woman, but other than that, what else?' Miles stared at him blankly. 'Besides, I have a lot going on in my life, I can't think about much else at the moment.' Harry wondered why Miles had become so contentious. He couldn't understand.

'So, you're this sweet, innocent, perfect dude, so madly in love with his wife that he doesn't even look at another woman, huh?'

Harry was stunned. *What was up with this guy?*

Miles's phone blared.

Saved by the bell, Harry sighed.

Miles averted his gaze away from Harry with a strange, almost pitiful look and quickly picked up his phone. 'Mr Kim. Hello, sir. How are you?' Miles gestured to Harry to leave the room. Relieved, Harry sprinted out of the boardroom.

He jumped into a taxi, immensely grateful to be out of that stuffy room. *What extraordinary behaviour*, he thought. Reasonably well acquainted with Miles, Harry knew him to be nothing but charming and professional. He was fully aware that Miles could easily change into someone threatening and vicious, but why had he taken such offence, and why especially towards him? It was all very strange. He frowned to himself and gazed out of the window. He thought of Serena, her porcelain face, her kind smile, the gentle, unassuming way she looked at him with those bright, bewitching eyes. Miles was right: he would have absolutely loved to have whisked her away in his arms and run off into the sunset. What a goddess she was, so gorgeous and exquisite. She was an extraordinary creature, yet what was her angle? What did she really want? Who was she? It was inconceivable to Harry that this woman was as genuine as she claimed to be. He was perplexed. Something didn't add up. Something wasn't right.

Struggling to understand the last few hours, Harry glanced at his mobile phone, skimming through the messages, interested only in what Laura had to say. Oddly enough, however, there was nothing from his wife. 'Why hasn't she written? How odd.' Immersed in anguish and concern, he typed her a brief message.

Hi. All okay?

Fine. She responded immediately.

Okay, great. Will be home day after tomorrow. Want anything from duty-free?

No thanks. See you when you get back.

Cold, frosty and abrupt. He sighed to himself, rolling his eyes. Yearning to be back in his hotel room, to indulge in a bit of porn or Netflix, he rushed through his emails. The thought of lying in bed with his laptop made him smile.

ooooo

'Mr Hoffman. Good evening, sir. I hope you had a lovely day. Your guest is waiting for you at the bar.' The concierge smiled politely, motioning with his head.

'My guest?' Harry gaped, somewhat taken aback.

'Yes, sir. A Miss... I'm sorry, sir, I'll just check the name again.' The friendly young chap walked towards his desk.

Harry interrupted. 'No, it's okay, don't worry. I'll go see for myself. Thank you.'

'You're welcome, Mr Hoffman, sir.'

The hotel was unusually busy and seemed to be hosting large conferences of Chinese business men. Faint Chinese music played in the lobby to honour their visit. *Surely not*, thought Harry. Elated, his heart raced as he noticed a tall waif-like figure rise from a distant chair upon spotting him. She waved at him gently. It was her! Astounded and awed, he approached her calmly, dumbfounded as to why on earth she was here.

'Hello Harry,' she purred. Her lip had a subtle upward quirk.

'Miss Markhieva! What a pleasant surprise! How lovely to see you,' Harry beamed, eyes gleaming. 'I don't know what to say. I wasn't expecting you.'

'Serena. Please call me Serena.'

Harry smiled, unsure how to proceed, dazzled by her presence.

'Can we sit for a moment?'

'Of course. Please, sit down. Can I get you something, a drink?'

'Just still water, please.'

'Okay. I'll have something stronger; are you sure you won't join me?'

His earlier suspicion of her turned into something else, something he could hardly define himself. As he sat facing her, he considered she couldn't possibly be anything but innocent and transparent. His heart pounding, he could only pray she didn't hear its loud beating, for its noise deafened him. How he wished the clock would stop ticking; he could then remain sitting in front of her for hours, just admiring her angelic features.

'How did you know I was staying here?' Contrary to his fluttering heart, his voice was firm and strong.

'It's the Hyatt. Everyone stays here!'

'That's not a satisfactory answer.' He grinned.

'I have decided to move to London.'

'Really?'

'Yes. I will be living in central London. I believe you are south of the river, not too far.'

'How do you know where I live?'

She smiled.

'Why do you know where I live? What else do you know about me?' His eyes glinted.

'I know you are happily married with two kids, Oliver and Charlie.'

'What else?' *Hmm… I wonder if I need to be concerned,* he thought.

'I know you are good at your job. I know you are honest and loyal, unlike your friend – or shall I say "the main man of the company", Miles?' She waited for a change of expression from Harry. He offered none.

Cool as a cucumber, he replied, 'Why, what has he done?'

'A lot.'

'Gin and tonic for sir, and a bottle of still water for madam.' They continued to look at each other. Harry averted his gaze and thanked the waiter.

Serena sipped her water calmly.

'It seems as if you've done your research well.' He looked at his drink. 'Is it spiked?'

She burst out laughing, as did he. Did he just say that? How silly of him.

'Yes,' she joked, 'all this time and effort just to kill you.'

They both giggled. She grabbed his gin and tonic and took a large sip. 'There you go. See, I'm alive.'

'For now,' he smirked.

She smiled broadly.

'Is there something specific you would like to tell me? Is everything okay?'

'Yes, everything is okay.' She took a deep breath. 'Harry, I am not hiding anything from you guys. Everything I told you is true. My father died recently. He died very suddenly, leaving me all alone. He was my last, only living relative left in this big crazy world. And, yes, he died having left me a lot of money. That's it. I promise you it's all true.'

'Okay, but I don't understand,' he smiled dryly. 'Why have you come here to see me? You could have made an appointment and seen me formally in the office, the conventional way. Seeing me in my hotel in the evening, won't people talk?'

'I don't want Miles.'

'Excuse me?'

I don't want Miles handling my finances.'

'Why not?'

She shook her head in silence.

'Then why did you involve him? You could have come straight to me.'

'I was worried you wouldn't take on any new clients, or at least take on me. I probably wouldn't have passed your due diligence. I couldn't risk it.'

'How did you know Miles would agree?'

'Miles is predictable. He would never say no to money, or to a beautiful woman for that matter.' She gave him a sarcastic look.

Harry sipped his drink slowly. 'I see.'

'What do you see?'

'You think I am different from Miles?'

'Day and night, Mr Hoffman.'

'Harry, please.'

'Miles and his family are very well known in Chicago. He comes from a very old moneyed family. A very powerful family. Miles and his uncle George are particularly famous. For all the wrong reasons, I might add. They have very effective ways of making people say "yes"; there are constant rumours that they have most of the important judges in their pocket; they all belong to the same old boys' clubs. Miles knows all the important people here. He is very well connected and not to be messed with.'

Harry listened intently, overwhelmed.

'A lot of Miles's own family are retired lawyers and judges. They write their own rules. They can't be challenged. Everyone here knows not to get in their way. I have nothing against him personally; I just don't know if I want to be involved with him, and I'm also not sure I want him managing my money, or knowing anything about me. He is very arrogant. I... I... don't know what he will do.'

'I'm speechless. I didn't know any of this. I don't know Miles very well. Also, I am actually not sure I want to know any more. I mean I work for him... His father and uncles are the founders of the company.'

'Well, I hope it won't affect you. We will both be in London soon. Away from here.'

What a bold statement. How exactly did she want him to respond to that? He twirled his straw around his drink, her eyes burning through him.

'Why are you moving to London?'

'It's easier for me to manage my money from London. My father always preferred I was London-based rather than being in the US, and Europe is generally easier than the US.'

'Is that the only reason?'

'What do you mean?'

Harry blushed, playing with his glass.

'Do you think I am moving to be closer to you?' She giggled.

'No, I don't think that. Is it just for financial and tax reasons you want to move, or are there other reasons?'

'You want to know what more I know about you and how I know it? Am I right?' Harry looked up at her without uttering a word.

'Gemma told me.'

'You spoke to *Gemma*? My PA, Gemma?'

'Yes. Gemma. Your PA, Gemma.'

'What did she say?'

'Everything.' Serena grinned, cheekily.

'Like what?' Harry's voice quivered.

'Relax, I'm just joking. She was very friendly, she briefly described what you do, how many awards your company has won, how excellent at your job you all are. She directed me to your website and said I should request information on the company and maybe join the mailing list if I want to know more. I told her I was based in Chicago, at which point she happened to mention that coincidentally you were going to be in Chicago for work too. I pretended to be a finance student doing some research for my thesis. I kept her on the phone for ages; she must have been in a particularly good mood that day to talk to me for so long.'

'She believed you?'

'I'm very convincing.'

'Did she say anything about my personal life?'

'Of course not.' Serena brushed him off dismissively. It's all written on your profile. She didn't even tell me where you were staying in Chicago. Everything else I already knew via testimonials and basic research.'

Ah well, nothing sinister then. He was getting worked up about nothing, as usual. It all made sense. She could still be hiding something though.

'I want *you* to manage my money. I don't want Miles involved. My money, my choice. It's as simple as that.'

'I'm happy to manage your affairs, Serena. I'm just extremely cautious before I accept new clients. I have to be; things have changed – we need to be a 100 per cent sure. Compliance is a bastard these days. I have to be extra risk-averse, extra cautious. Our world is now so different. I am sorry; it feels as if I am ranting, I don't mean to put you off. I would love you to be my client.'

'But you have to be extra careful with me?'

'No, that's not what I mean. I'm not expressing myself well. I'm just a bit tired. Jet lagged, and I have a few things going on…'

'Marriage troubles?' she sneered unsympathetically, as though she expected to hear this.

'No, no, nothing like that, thank God, It's my son, my parents, their health. My father had a fall recently and worried us all...' He paused. 'I need to keep my finger on the pulse... always.'

'You won't have any problems with me.' Serena raised her glass for a toast. 'You have to look into my eyes while we toast, even though its only water.' Now he was in trouble. He had been trying to avoid direct eye contact. Those dangerous turquoise-blue eyes would surely put a spell on him; he didn't trust himself.

They clinked their glasses together. He had no choice but to look at her properly. She drew him in like a moth to a flame. He had been reasonably relaxed up until this point.

'To a successful partnership!' She smiled confidently. Perhaps Miles was right and it was better to admit that she was the one in power; he was helpless in her company.

'How do you suggest I manage the situation with Miles? You are more his client than mine; he will expect full authority. I don't want to repeat this conversation to him, and Miles... he was... quite taken by you. I would assume he would expect to take over your account solely and fully.'

'You can leave that part to me. I can manage him myself. I don't want to provoke him, but I don't fear him. I can personally relay my message to him.'

Harry leant forward. 'You do know that he was very impressed by you at that meeting, don't you...?'

'Was he?' Serena leant forward alluringly. 'What about you, Mr Hoffman? Were you also very impressed with me?' Serena fluttered her eyelids at him playfully. Could she get a reaction out of him? He was even more impressive in person than from his many flattering internet references.

'You're a client, Miss Markhieva. I don't mix business with pleasure, as charming as you may be.' He pouted teasingly. 'I'm not going to fall for it!' He smiled as his eyes twinkled. The damage was done; she saw right through him. They gazed at each other for a split second.

She was happy. Once again, she felt the rush of chemicals and hormones that flooded through her brain and body at their morning meeting, leaving her in a semi-state of euphoria. Despite the happy photos of Harry and his glamorously-dressed wife attending industry galas, despite pictures of his two children with their faces blurred, splattered in images when Googling him, despite her good judgement, she had fallen for him. Did he feel something too, she wondered? Neither of them spoke. She took a deep breath and smiled back.

'I hope we can be friends, Harry. My father was the only person I had, and now he has gone. I'm alone. Totally alone.' She broke the silence, back in the moment.

'I take it you are not married…?'

'Sadly, no.'

Harry wished to explore this subject further and fire a storm of questions at her. How could it be possible she could be single, given that she was so beautiful, yet hadn't been snapped up by some eligible bachelor? However, she seemed not to want to elaborate.

Every word, every expression he exchanged with her, became a struggle; sitting opposite her stirred many confusing emotions. With Laura so far way, acting so bizarrely and rejecting him, and now sitting in front of this stunning woman who seemed to take great pleasure in his company, unreservedly throwing enigmatic innuendos at him, he felt something that simply didn't suit him. He desired her. She was the first woman ever to get under his skin since his wife. Never one to doubt his feelings about his wife, or the state of his marriage, he had previously reigned superior to these situations. Extramarital affairs, office romances, mistresses and the like, simply had no space in Harry's world. Yet now, within one day, Harry felt himself a victim of turmoil and uncertainty. Serena managed to provoke a craving he didn't know he had. His comfort zone shattered, he had entered a world he didn't understand.

'I'm not married,' she said after a small pause. 'I was in quite a serious relationship, and even thought I was in love, but sadly I wasn't, and we are no longer together.' She shrugged her shoulders, casually implying she had moved on, yet her eyes told a different story.

'I'm sorry. It's none of my business.'

'It's fine. It's a normal question. These things are going to come up. Unfortunately, it's complicated, and though I try not to be complicated... I am.' Harry absorbed her every word and analysed her every whim. 'Unfortunately, my ill-fated destiny follows me everywhere I go. I try to be happy and positive, but somehow end up lonely and miserable.'

'Oh come on, it's not that bad. At least you're rich!'

'Yes, that I am. At least for now.' They both grinned and toasted their glasses again.

6

'Honey, I'm home! Oh, I forgot. No one is home.' Laura curled her lip sarcastically, unaccustomed to her current state of mind, translating to a lack of sympathy towards her husband and children. Usually a loving, doting wife, recent events had driven her to question the concept of both marriage and family, unfortunately leading her to view it all with cynical derision. Outraged, she inspected the living room, clutching her shopping bag tightly.

'Good heavens, what's this?' The living room appeared to have been hit by a bomb. How unbearable! Charlie's school uniform, his homework, his reading books, empty crisps packets, all lay scattered on the floor in possibly the biggest mess ever made in her house.

'Dear God!' she cried out loudly. 'What on earth is this?'

On the table lay an A4 piece of paper with a message from Christine, the babysitter.

Have taken Charlie to football. Sorry for the mess, we were in a rush. C xx

Laura tutted, as she microwaved a ready-made quiche, thirstily gulping down a large glass of water. She scanned through her messages on her phone. Harry, Harry, Harry. Almost all of the messages were from Harry. She ignored them. She read all the other messages in her inbox, but brutally swiped Harry's away. Acrimonious thoughts prevailed in her mind, contempt and anger now being the only feelings she held for her husband. Laura's sentiments towards most people had largely taken on an exaggerated turn, and not in a positive manner. For now, Ollie was on her mind. Could it be possible that he could sense something was not quite right and was acting up because of it? Or maybe the poor child had always been out of control and she, his mother, had been oblivious to his bad behaviour.

Her eyes focused on the beautiful display of family photos neatly paraded around the kitchen. She was the author of this family tale. This diligent display of a perfect family was her idea, her creation. How lovely the pictures looked, and, more to the point, how happy everyone appeared in them. Nothing contrived, nothing fake, a genuinely happy family stared back at her from the photos.

The picture of Charlie and Ollie laughing with Jane's kids caught her attention: all four kids grinned at the camera, blissfully happy. The boys adored their cousins, especially Mia; she was their favourite, a kind, lovely girl. If Laura ever had a daughter, she would want her daughter to be just like Mia. Laura placed her hand on her stomach. A few years ago, she was willing to turn the world upside down for a daughter. A beautiful little girl with curly, blonde locks that she would love more than anything else in the world, but Harry didn't want another child. Harry didn't let her have another child, and now she had a child growing inside of her, now that it had become almost impossible for her to mother a child, she was pregnant. How terribly unfair.

She stared at the photo, wondering how Oliver and Charlie would feel about having a sister. Eyes full of tears, she reached for a tissue, noticing that Elizabeth was writing to her. Ignoring it, she tapped the internet icon on her phone, and Dr Raza's face flashed in front of her. The sour expression on her face fast replaced itself with joy and a sprightly, thrilled smile. This man was pleasure itself. Just the mere sight of him immediately distanced her from her problems.

Christine and Charlie burst in through the back door, screeching with laughter. Christine ran after Charlie, playfully shouting at him. Instantly, Laura navigated away from her internet page and ran to the door.

'Hi, darling!' She whisked Charlie into her arms and kissed him. 'I've missed you. How are you? Hey, Christine. Come in.'

'Hi, Laura.' Christine caught her breath.

Charlie was overjoyed at seeing his mummy. 'I hurt my knee, Mummy.'

'Oh, sweetheart, where? Oh, my poor darling, let Mummy kiss it better for you.' She rubbed his knee and proceeded to kiss it, while she held him tightly.

Suddenly from nowhere, she felt discomfort in her stomach and an urge to vomit, forcing her to almost shove Charlie to the floor. Hot flushes ran through her body like little bolts of electricity. Hurriedly she excused herself, and ran to the bathroom, lips dry, throat parched, hormones racing around wildly. She looked at herself in the bathroom mirror, feeling nauseous, her head bent over the loo, desperate to throw up. *Good grief, I did not miss this feeling*, she lamented, staring into the toilet bowl feeling like death.

She tried again and again to vomit but was unsuccessful every time. What a dreadful feeling! Huddled up on the floor and holding on to the loo, she sat still, feeling incredibly sorry for herself, feeble and weak.

Desolate and contrite, uncontrollable tears poured down her hot, flushed cheeks. In the distance, Charlie and Christine's voices echoed as they played games. Relieved Charlie was happy and Ollie away with his grandparents, she could silently be sick without burying herself in too much guilt. The kids were okay for the time being; she would deal with Ollie when she had solved her own problems. All she needed to do now was to focus on herself.

Later, Laura lay in Charlie's bed holding him tightly in her arms, gently stroking his soft cheek, his angelic face content and free of concern. It had been a good idea to separate the boys and give them their own rooms. Charlie was far more relaxed now. It was late, but she couldn't sleep. *I wonder what my husband is doing in Chicago?* she thought. She looked at her watch: seven in the evening in Chicago. *I wonder if he is seeing another woman?* Charlie's greasy hair forced her to admit her priorities were not at home with her family, and his Spider-Man lamp had gathered a significant amount of dust. She glanced around the room, unable to remember the last time it had been properly cleaned. What an incredible accumulation of rubbish in this poor child's room, he had only moved in! She had been neglecting her maternal duties.

Laura thought about her psychiatrist... *Was he gay? Was he married? What did his wife look like? He must have grown-up kids; what did they look like? What did Dr Raza think of her? What did he think of all of his patients? Did he ever flirt with them? Was he a good husband?* She grabbed her phone to read his bio again, this time in peace. Harry's name persisted on her screen. *Why is he ringing me so late?* The ringing continued. She let it ring. Should she pick it up? She really should, she hadn't spoken to him in what seemed like many, many days.

'Hi,' she said distantly. 'How are you?' her voice, faint and unenergetic. In no mood to speak to him, she hoped he would understand and leave her be, but Harry couldn't hide his concern.

'Sorry to call so late. I've called and left so many messages. Why haven't you responded?'

Leave me alone, she begrudged under her breath. 'Is it important? I'm tired; I want to go to bed.'

'How are you?'

'Fine.' Her casual, abrupt answers infuriated Harry. *Three thousand, nine hundred and forty-five miles between us, and all she can say is 'fine'. Why do I bother?* he wondered. Uncomfortable silences followed between them. This sudden irrational behaviour his wife was displaying was as frustrating as it was hurtful. Was he losing his wife? What was the reason for this bitterness, especially towards him? Harry felt he was wrestling with a stranger on the phone. Her frosty, snappy answers baffled him, leaving him unsure what to feel and what to think. If she intended to hurt him, she was certainly succeeding. He couldn't begin to imagine what was going through her mind.

'I'm fine,' she repeated, clearing her throat.

'How are the kids?'

'Ollie is with your parents and Charlie is here with me. I am lying next to him.'

'Have you spoken to Ollie?'

'No.'

'Any updates on his school situation?'

'No. I'm stalling it. I'll deal with it when I'm in the mood.'

Silence.

Laura was dreading hearing his next question. Harry was dreading asking his next question. 'How's your health?'

'I'm fine.'

'Are you going to say anything else besides "I'm fine"?'

'I'm tired. I want to go to sleep.'

'Really? You have nothing else to say?'

Silence.

This is futile. It's like talking to a brick wall. I don't understand what's wrong.

Silence.

'Okay. Goodnight. I'll be home the day after tomorrow.'

'Goodnight.'

Disheartened, they both hung up simultaneously.

Laura tiptoed to her room. Feeling flat and sombre, it was time to try and sleep and say goodbye to the day. Tomorrow was a new day. New sets of challenges would undoubtedly require new answers. She would wait patiently for dawn. An early riser, she hoped to find some energy and inspiration. God knows, she needed it.

ooooo

Harry calmly made his way back to the table. If the conversation weighed heavily on his mind, this was not the time to show it, and did he really expect the conversation with his wife to be easy?

'Could have been worse,' he told himself. 'It can't be easy for her. I can't believe I've left her alone to deal with this.'

It appeared as though all of the Chicago office had come to dinner, well at least the people that mattered – and everyone had one thing on their mind: to 'team build' (probably to secure a promotion). To Harry's relief, the atmosphere remained relaxed and comfortable, the team, friendly and informal, contrary to his doom and gloom-laden thoughts. The idea of socialising and making small talk was nothing Harry was much in the mood for. However, as he was the supposed guest of honour, the least he could do was cheer up.

The impressive turnout, the excited chit-chat surrounding the long, homely wooden table, was largely in his honour. Harry fascinated the Americans: his mannerisms, naturally, his accent and his quintessential British way of being, were as alien to them as they and their American way of working were to him. Admired and respected, Harry was as courteous as he was polite, always greeting everyone with a smile, taking an interest in people. Generally he liked to be liked, though with the recent changes in his life, his priorities had dramatically changed. He no longer cared to make polite conversation; people, and particularly their opinion of him, remained the least of his worries.

As chuffed as he was with the turnout, it would have been naïve of him to assume the crowd had gathered just to enjoy a drink with Harry Hoffman from the London office who shares a name with a prince. This was in fact Miles's city; Miles called the shots. The night was still very young; it was impossible to predict how it would turn out. Discreetly, Harry watched Miles who sat smugly at the head of the table, laughing out loud as he passionately entertained his team while knocking back margaritas, ordering large rounds, making sure everyone had a drink and generally being the best boss one could hope for. Not a care in the world, rich, successful and powerful, Miles was simply a delight to watch.

He seemed to fascinate everyone lucky enough to be in his presence. A modern-day Gordon Gekko, there seemed to be no boundaries to what he could do. Confidently and happily, he laughed off rules. 'I don't follow rules, I make them!' was his motto. A very seductive schmoozer, few people impressed Harry as much as Miles did, even though he himself had hailed from aristocratic roots and had grown up surrounded by the elite upper echelons of society, which itself had produced notable superstars. Miles, however, was in a league of his own. Everything American was always bigger and better in Harry's opinion, or at least Miles was. Masculine yet empathetic, arrogant yet considerate, professional yet fun, he had it all figured out.

Whether it was all a staged pretence or innate and natural, it was a show worth watching. Miles was the perfect example of corporate finance; people genuinely seemed to feel comfortable in his company. Arresting and electrifying, he drew people to him like a magnet. In a male-driven industry, it amused Harry to witness the scores of perfect blondes surrounding him; surely that wasn't a coincidence? Miles was known for even involving himself in hiring the interns. His excuse was simply, 'Everybody should get a fair chance to have a prestigious name on their résumé'. Women, gays, ethnic minorities, but most importantly, he wanted to be known in the finance industry for hiring as many women as possible.

Harry observed Miles as he flirted shamelessly with the younger women scattered strategically around the table, doting on his every word, fluttering their eyelashes, giggling with laughter, all the while being plied with copious amounts of vodka.

'So who's gonna take her to bed first, you or me?' Miles chewed on an unlit cigar, taking a seat close to Harry while downing a shot of tequila as though it was water. Harry shot his eyes once round the place, but Miles had already ensured no prying ears.

'I doubt she would want to sleep with me.'

'I disagree, Harry, my boy,' said Miles in a phoney English accent. 'I think she would very much like to sleep with you, my dear chap.' Not quite slurring his words, it was apparent he'd already had lots to drink. 'FYI, if you're too precious to do it,' he swayed his head, 'I most certainly will.'

Harry glared at him. 'What do you mean?'

'You think I'm going to let *that* go so easily? She's the real deal, my boy. Where are you going to meet a woman like that? She's having dinner with me tomorrow night.' Miles smiled schemingly, his words piercing a stake through Harry's heart.

Did he hear that right? His ears began to ring. A high pitched shrill almost deafened both his ears. 'You're having dinner?'

'Yup!' Miles took another puff of his unlit cigar looking up at the ceiling, just so that he could then look down at Harry and laugh patronisingly. 'Does this concern you, Harry, my dear?'

'No,' Harry smiled, 'of course not. Why would it? It's great.'

'I don't know. She did ask for you to come along, though.' He lifted his eyebrows up and down repeatedly. 'Why did she do that, Harry?'

The music began to blare, the dance tracks hit the speakers, a group of women excitedly hit the dance floor. A fair amount of alcohol had been consumed by now; the party was on its way to getting started. The less important the staff, the more likely they were to end up on the dance floor. The senior partners, still relatively sober, remained glued to their seats, chatting sensibly. Miles made sure the drinks flowed steadily, keen to witness senior partners misbehave, only to crucify them the next day. He thrilled in moments like these. As the air conditioning seemed to be lowered, the atmosphere began to heat up.

'I don't know,' Harry responded casually, sipping his watered-down whiskey.

'You know I will take her to bed, don't you?' Harry would have loved to punch Miles in the face at that moment. That smug little face of his, how would it have looked with a deformed nose?

Just five minutes ago, he'd held this man in such high esteem, and now he was nothing but vermin. Harry's mood soured; he felt his ears ringing again – or was he imagining it? He probably wasn't. It was on the verge of becoming painful. Were they all conspiring behind his back?

Just a few hours ago, Serena was sitting with him in his hotel expressing her disdain and disgust for Miles with a story about how she mistrusted him, yet the whole time she was planning a romantic dinner with him. Why would she do that? Full of contempt for both Serena and Miles, Harry wanted desperately to excuse himself. He didn't want to hear another word about their date.

'Hi, darling, are you drunk yet?' A woman flung her arms around Miles's neck, kissing him on the lips.

Miles laughed loudly. 'Not yet, darling. I've been waiting for you.' He kissed her passionately on her dark red lips.

'Meet Harry, a senior partner from London and a good friend.'

'Hi, Harry, so nice to meet you. I'm Claudia, his wife.' She greeted Harry with a warm hug.

'Lovely to meet you too, Claudia.' Conservatively dressed, she appeared much older than Miles; a woman very much in charge.

'I've heard so much about you; it's nice to meet you finally. How long are you staying?' Assertive and composed, just like her husband, she reminded Harry of a madam in a brothel, but a kind one. Harry warmed to her. She seemed fun in her own domineering way. Oozing confidence, she looked him directly in the eye, as if she were seeking something. A slim woman of average height, every part surgically enhanced, albeit subtly, she was very striking. Did she remind Harry of somebody specific, or was she just a bit Hollywood?

'Yes. You too. I'm actually leaving...' he thought for a second, '... the day after tomorrow.' He forced a smile. 'Can I get you a drink?'

'Oh no, please don't worry. I'll call the waiter over in a minute. It's a shame you're not around for a little while longer; you could have come to dinner.'

Harry nodded politely. Under normal circumstances he would have loved to have gone to dinner at their place; it would have been a pleasure to have nosed around their house and their lives. How riveting and salacious it would have been to observe them, and see just how genuine their marriage was. Did Mrs Miles know what her darling husband got up to behind her back?

'I would have loved that. I hope to be back soon.' Harry had never given much thought to Miles, let alone Miles's wife, yet now this nice plastic lady aroused his curiosity. What was the story between them? Not really the type of woman he would have envisaged Miles to be with, he would have loved to learn more.

'Oh, Harry is a very busy man,' interrupted Miles bluntly, handing Claudia a glass of Champagne. 'Harry has queues of women lining up to spend time with him. Look, everyone is here for Harry.' He pointed at his staff and smiled. 'He won't have time to come to dinner.'

Miles's provocative statement somewhat embarrassed Claudia. Ignoring him, she continued. 'When you are next in Chicago, I insist you come to dinner, and you must bring your wife. What's her name again?'

'Laura.'

'When *are* you returning to Chicago, Harry?' Miles quizzed him surreptitiously.

'I don't know. I don't have any immediate plans. Are you guys visiting London any time soon?' He addressed Claudia specifically.

'Oh, I would love to! I just love London. We Americans have so many false notions about London. I love going to London and discovering that it's actually nothing like how we imagined it.' She laughed out loud. Harry smiled. Miles remained stern and silent.

'Yes, Americans get a shock when they visit London for the first time. You must let me know when you next visit; we can all get together.'

Miles's intent stare left Harry quite uncomfortable.

'Right. Please allow me to excuse myself, I'm still very jet lagged, and I'm getting a slight headache. Claudia,' he put out his hand, 'so lovely to...' she leant forward and kissed him on both cheeks. 'Lovely to meet you. I hope to see you very soon, with the whole family next time.'

As politely as he could muster, Harry bid farewell and made his exit.

ooooo

The very moment he sat in the taxi, in a frenzy he dialled Serena's number. What on earth was she up to? Her phone rang; she didn't pick up. He rang again; she didn't pick up. He tried to WhatsApp her; she wasn't on WhatsApp. He sent her an SMS, asking her to call him back asap. Why wasn't she picking up? Was this all a set-up? Were she and Miles part of an elaborate plan? Why was she meeting Miles for dinner, and why wasn't she taking his call?

'Screw this!' he complained under his breath, navigating the British Airways website on his phone, desperate to change his flight. He wanted to leave as soon as possible. 'First thing tomorrow, I'm out of here.'

The next morning, he dashed for the airport, having managed to get a seat on a BA flight to London. He wrote an apologetic message to Miles and then firmly switched off his phone. *Miles cannot bother me anymore*, he told himself and firmly closed his eyes. A second later, as though he forgot something, he opened his eyes in a flash, to check his phone one last time before completely shutting off. Alas, Serena still had not responded. He frowned. It was very strange behaviour.

Right! Time to put this miserable trip behind me. I hope I won't have the pleasure of hearing from these people any time soon, he thought. Headphones on, phone off, eyeshades on, he pushed his seat back. Over and out.

7

Alone in the clinic, Laura sat trembling, desperate for this moment to be over as soon as possible. Mentally drained, eyes wide open, she felt dizzy and faint. She was quite sure she had made the right decision; approaching this without emotion and sentiment was the only way to manage it. A few minutes, and this colossal grief, this inexplicable burden, would be over.

A woman in a white nurse's outfit with a stern face approached her. 'Mrs Laura Hoffman?'

'Yes.'

'Follow me, please.'

ooooo

When she opened her eyes, she was lying on a strange bed, cold and tired. Her eyes wandered around the room as she sought her bearings. Two other women lay on beds next to her, a disoriented look on their faces. Without a moment's hesitation, Laura rushed to her feet, found the bag with her clothes, got dressed, and discharged herself immediately. Frantically, she directed the black cab straight home. Her heart sank to the ground as she struggled to open her front door, leaving her empty and helpless. She felt destroyed. Out of breath and heavy-headed, she pulled the curtains shut in Ollie's room with all her strength and lay down in his bed, sobbing. If she was lucky, she would never wake up.

Slowly the sleep started to wear off, leaving her lethargic, as though very heavy weights pulled her down. Her eyelids felt like heavy bricks. After a short struggle, she opened her eyes. Through a dim, blurry vision, she could just about make out a figure on the chair next to her. Harry gently lifted his hand off her head, staring at her with a guilt-ridden face. His concerned frown changed to a sweet smile. Slowly she tried to sit up. Cautiously, he helped to raise her up.

'How are you?' he asked, lovingly.

'How long have you been sitting here?' she mumbled almost inaudibly. Her face battered and hair dishevelled, she looked like she had seen a ghost.

'Not long. An hour or so.'

Laura was miles away. She had lost all feelings of reality; her face was still and expressionless. Her last memory was of the clinic; she was just about to be sedated.

'When did you get back?'

'About an hour and a half ago,' Harry said, looking at his watch.

Laura tried to gather her bearings. 'What day is it? Weren't you supposed to get back tomorrow?'

'Yes. I finished my work early.' He sighed. 'I wanted to check on you; you weren't responsive on the phone.'

Laura looked away from him.

'Are you okay?'

'Yes. Why?'

'You don't really like sleeping during the day. You were in a very deep sleep when I arrived. You were also talking in your sleep.'

Laura looked horrified. 'Oh God.' She covered her face in dread. 'What did I say?' *Why did he come home early?* She cursed herself.

'You were mumbling. You said something about your baby. I couldn't understand what you were saying.'

Laura glared at her husband. 'I'm thirsty. I need a drink.' The bottle next to the bed was empty.

'Why are you sleeping here?'

'I'm thirsty,' Laura repeated. Aiming for the kitchen, she thrust the blanket away from her. Tiny stains of blood were half-visible beneath her. She looked at him horrified and burst into a fit of tears. Harry, not seeing the stains, threw his arms around her. 'I'm sorry. I'm so sorry,' she wailed.

Harry held her tight. 'No, no, I'm sorry, I love you. I shouldn't have left like that, so abruptly.'

'I feel a bit dizzy.'

'You need to rest. Let me take you to our bed.' Gently he helped her up, she tried to move his arms away, but didn't find the strength. Harry took her to their bed.

'I'm fine, honestly, you don't need to walk with me. I just need to lie down.'

Harry dimmed the lights, leaving her to sleep in peace. He realised he had to tread carefully and give her time and space to breath. There was so much on her plate; she must be mentally and physically exhausted; he would talk to her when she was rested.

ooooo

Harry brewed his favourite herbal tea and sat in front of his laptop on his desk. Following his normal ritual, he compiled a list of people he needed to contact and immediately started typing. Gemma, as usual, was first on his list.

Next on his list, was his mother:

Hi Mum, hope you're all well. I arrived back a day early, Laura is very unhappy and a bit down, I found her lying in bed very distressed. I would like to take her away for a week or so. We need some time alone. How is Ollie? Would you be able to help with both the boys this week? I will ask Christine to work overtime.

Please let me know if that is okay so I can book. How is Dad? Any luck finding Maria?

Harry x

Consumed with his systematic emailing and planning, Harry tried to ignore his phone, but the same croaky frog sound he had chosen as his ringtone all those years ago seemed to get louder and louder. He ignored it. It continued; it wasn't going to go away. Did he really want to pick up an anonymous call right now? He put it on silent, and watched it ring profusely. Someone, somewhere was desperately trying to get hold of him.

Where are you? Five messages, asking the same question. His WhatsApp was buzzing, full of messages demanding to know where he was. Serena was looking for him. He felt her desperation; she seemed to get angrier and angrier in every message. Should he ignore her or should he write back? He couldn't decide. It was probably more important that he prioritise his wife and his marriage rather than this luxury pain in the backside that could surely wait.

Sorry, had a crisis - had to rush; will explain soon. Enjoy your meeting.

Where are you?

London.

What? I cannot believe that. Why did you go without telling me?

Harry laid the phone next to his laptop face down.

Continuing with his email orgy, the last on his list was the travel agency that took care of his travel needs; there was no other choice, they needed some time out. He had to support his wife. He had to prioritise his marriage. Nothing was more important to him than his wife; he needed to be there for her. He needed to save his marriage.

ooooo

The painful realisation came too late. Harry was meant to stay in Chicago one more day. Serena was sure he would be at the dinner she had so cunningly planned. En route to the restaurant, it was just too late to turn back now. He'd abruptly returned to London, leaving her none the wiser. Reluctantly, Serena took her place opposite Miles. She looked at him, her contempt deeply hidden behind a fake smile. He, on the contrary, stared at her with obvious delight. Subtle yet ravishing, Serena's look, sharp and edgy, ready for her rendezvous with the man she had so looked forward to seeing, was a waste of time and effort. Lucky enough to be able to carry off any look elegantly, she enjoyed dressing up; clothes hung off her body as though they had been tailor-made just for her. Her face radiant from the natural glows of youth, she wore little make-up, opting for a light blush and a lash of mascara.

'What a disaster!' she hissed under her breath. *How could Harry do this? Not a single word; how could he just leave like this?* she kept asking herself.

'I'm a bit surprised Harry left so abruptly. I expected him to be here. Do you know what happened?'

'No, I don't, and, yes, it was very strange the way he left. I'm also quite surprised. I saw him only last night.'

Serena looked at him stunned. 'Oh, you saw him last night? Where did you go?'

If Miles had had any doubt about Serena's attraction to Harry, he did so no longer. He could almost taste the disappointment she so carefully tried to conceal. All dressed up, inordinately excited to spend the evening with him… (and Miles, of course), it was palpably obvious she was infatuated with Harry. No longer in the mood to provoke, the more she desired Harry, the more Miles found himself longing for her.

'We had a team-building evening. The team wanted to meet Harry, especially the women it seems.' He smiled.

Serena contrived a disappointing smile. 'I see.'

'We went out for drinks, and it quickly became all about the Englishman. American women can never resist the charm of a classy English gentleman. Hugh Grant has a lot to answer for!' He grinned in that smug, sleazy fashion which Serena was rapidly finding repulsive.

'Yes,' he continued, 'it was all about our darling, Dirty Harry, as I like to call him.'

Utterly disappointed at how the evening had turned out, *what could be a polite reason to excuse myself?* was her only thought.

The waiter approached the table with a bottle of vintage Louis Roederer Cristal Champagne, two Champagne flutes and a large tray of beautifully assembled Beluga caviar, with blini and other Russian delights on the side. The perfect start to the perfect evening, Miles calculated, and meticulously planned a glorious few hours, taking full advantage of Harry's absence. Careful not to over do it, but impressive enough to intrigue her, he was a man with a plan.

Regrettably, however, the lady was not in the mood. Serena was in no way endeared to Miles, a fact Miles could not understand. Impeccably polite and ever charming, she would normally have forced herself to tolerate his company, but today, no. Explicitly planned around Harry, Miles was timed to leave after a brief conversation, and the evening was to be for her and Harry. *Quel dommage*. What a failure. The tiny bit of flirtation with Miles she was going to tease Harry with, the little experiment she was going to carry out to see if there was a morsel of affection he felt for her, was all in vain. This whole chapter was futile, borderline disaster. How ridiculous she had been! Harry was married. What had she imagined? What had she hoped to achieve? Why had she wanted him so badly? He was taken. He lived in another country. What had she expected to happen between them?

'Nothing,' she muttered to herself, as though she were having a conversation with someone else. 'I just wanted to see him one last time; I know he is married and happy.' The actual plan had been to avoid bad blood and make it clear that she had chosen Harry to be her investment manager and orchestrate everything from London, and Miles was to butt out and perhaps also to have an innocent little flirt with the Englishman.

'I hope you don't mind, I took the liberty of ordering something I thought you might particularly enjoy, and I must say I too am very partial to a bit of caviar every now and then.' As distracted as she was, she had to admit Miles knew his game. There was nothing average about him, whatever his intention might have been; he had made a tremendous effort.

'Thank you; it looks delicious.' She looked at her watch. 'You probably won't believe me, but I hadn't intended on staying very long tonight.' Fully transparent, nevertheless she continued. 'I just wanted the three of us to have a quick drink. Both of you seemed a little unsure when we met in the office. I thought we could get to know each other informally so you could see that I am real and that my money is real. I hadn't planned on much else.'

'I have no doubt you are real, Serena. I'm delighted you invited us for a drink, it's very good to meet outside of the office; it's great to see each other over a casual drink.'

Thrilled with the way things had turned out, enthusiastically Miles toasted his glass against hers. She had no choice; she was obliged to stick it out – leaving now was not an option. What a mess she had got herself into! In future, perhaps she should leave the game playing to the big girls. What should she talk to him about?

Once she'd accepted the outcome, she began to realise that perhaps it was not all doom and gloom. The evening might still provide some mysteries and surprises. Serena had somewhat misjudged Miles. Not nearly as obnoxious and sleazy as she had first thought him to be, well at least not with her, he was really good company, thoroughly entertaining and fun. No stranger to rubbing shoulders with the crème de la crème of society, Miles was the master of seduction, very comfortable among high-profile women who found him a pleasure to be around. Far better adept at laying on the charm offensive than most other men, he was in a league of his own, far superior to Harry, who had been happily and faithfully married to the same woman for almost ten years.

Miles almost made a career out of setting the ideal seduction scene; it was nothing more than fun and games for him, with little regard for anyone who got hurt or destroyed. The difference this time, however, was that he cared passionately about the person he was attempting to seduce.

After what seemed a long night, the evening finally came to a successful end. Miles, a far better friend than foe, was more besotted than ever. Admitting defeat, Serena stopped fighting with herself and accepted his kind gestures, including the chauffeur-driven Maybach to drop her home, not even contesting Miles's kind offer to walk her to her building.

'I'm sorry it didn't go exactly as planned; I hope I didn't bore you too much.'

'Not at all. Thank you. Thanks for a delicious meal, it was all wonderful. As I think I mentioned before, I will ask our family accountants to prepare all the information for you. I'm hoping it will be ready soon.'

'We will wait for it patiently.' Miles watched her enter her building after a polite and formal farewell. Serena discreetly peered out of her bedroom window, making sure Miles had gone. *Oh my God*, she thought in agitation, *his car was still in sight in the very same spot as when she had left.* Instantly jumping back out of view, she waited. *What on earth is he doing? Why doesn't he leave?* She waited a little, then took another glimpse, and sure enough, he was still there. What a strange, unpredictable evening. It had not been how she'd planned it; it was very cruel of Harry to leave without a word; and Miles, hmm... Miles. *I hope I haven't led him to believe something that is not true*, she thought. Once again, she crept back to check if he had gone, and this time thankfully his car had finally vanished. One last check on her phone before calling it a night; unfortunately, nothing from Harry. 'I give up!' she cried out loud.

ooooo

The doorbell rang loud and long. Who could that be at the door at eight-thirty in the morning? Serena's friend, Amory, the porter, stood still, hiding his face behind an ethereal cascading bouquet, nothing short of a floral fantasy.

'Someone loves you, ma'am,' he said in a deep southern drawl, handing her an antique Chinese lantern vase, adorned with elegant white dahlias, peach spray roses, all assembled perfectly next to large pink peonies.

'Enjoy, ma'am, you surely deserve them, they're beautiful.' She hoped Harry was apologising; the thought stirred her heart with excitement, but when she found the bouquet was from Miles, she dumped the sweet-smelling flowers which stood silently on her large dining table. Distracted and bored, she strolled into the shower. She shrugged. Maybe the lobby would appreciate Miles's expensive gesture.

ooooo

First thing in the morning, Gemma read Harry's detailed emails. *He must have had another fight with his wife*, she thought, sharing Harry's meticulous planning with the company florist. Laura's day would start perfectly with breakfast in bed, flowers and a well-deserved lie-in.

Just as Harry predicted, Laura slept late; not even his piping hot colourful fry-up and a fragrant cinnamon latte, her usual favourite, could cheer her up. Thanking him coldly, she wolfed down the food as though she hadn't eaten for days. Harry could only observe silently; very rarely did she eat with such gusto. As planned, the doorbell rang. Laura received the flowers showing little interest, laying them on the kitchen table, ignoring them completely. She continued to eat her breakfast, nonchalant and emotionless, staring up into space as though nothing and no one existed.

'Aren't you going to open your flowers?'

Slamming her cutlery on the plate, as though greatly inconvenienced, Laura walked over to the flowers, and with a quick glance at the note, faced Harry. 'Thank you, they're lovely.'

She continued to eat her breakfast. Crushed, Harry resorted to arranging the flowers himself. *What was the point of all this?* he lamented, sitting opposite her so she couldn't escape. Laura took no notice of him; her eyes were gaunt, her body weak.

'Laura, we need to talk.' No reaction. 'Laura, darling, are you listening to me? We need to talk.' Harry tried to speak without sarcasm, careful not to upset her, not knowing how she would react.

'What do you want to talk about?' Laura answered without looking at him, playing with her food.

'Don't you think we need to talk?' he asked, shaking his head.

'I don't know what you want to talk about.'

Harry didn't want to hurt her feelings, but he was fast running out of options. She seemed to have no interest in anything he had to say. He might as well have been invisible. 'We need to talk about these last few days.' He paused. She turned to face him, her face blank and confused. 'Is there anything you want to tell me?'

'No.' She looked away from him and stared at the garden. 'The lawn needs mowing.' Harry looked at the garden, speechless.

They both sat in silence.

'I was thinking we could go away for a few days.' He waited for a reaction; there was none. 'Somewhere warm and nice. Not too far. Somewhere where we could be alone, just the two of us.'

She shook her head. 'No, thanks. I don't want to go away right now.'

'Have a think about it...'

'There's nothing to think about. I have work. I won't get any time off right now.'

'Why not?'

'I don't want to go away,' she snapped. She got up and locked herself in the bathroom.

Harry ran after her and banged on the bathroom door. 'Laura! Laura!' He banged harder.

'Leave me alone!' Laura shouted. 'I don't want to talk. Please just go away.'

'Fine!'

Harry sprinted out of the house, calling his sister from his car.

'Have you got a minute, Jane?'

'Sure. What's up?'

'Have you got time for a quick coffee?'

'No, but you can come over to mine. I'm working from home today. Are you okay?'

Moments later, Jane opened the door to a very stressed-looking Harry.

'What's up, big brother?' She grinned, though she could see Harry was not in the mood for humour.

Distraught, he began to pour his heart out to his sister. Laura's trip to Athens, her cold, distant responses, her indifferent behaviour. Ollie getting suspended, the baby. Serena, Miles... and then he paused.

'I can't believe this, poor you.' Jane flung her arms around Harry. 'Why didn't you tell me any of this before? I could have helped, at least with the kids.'

'I thought it was all under control; it all happened so suddenly. Laura changed almost overnight. I don't understand her behaviour.'

'Laura was always a bitch.'

Harry glared at his sister, horrified.

'What do you mean? Why do you call her a bitch? Jane! Why did you call her a bitch? Please explain.' Harry was both shocked and upset.

'She *is* a bitch. I'm sorry if I am hurting your feelings; your darling wife is not the sweet little angel you think she is. Nobody likes her.'

Harry could hardly believe his ears. He could do nothing but stare at his sister in utter shock.

'Okay, maybe I'm exaggerating. Or maybe I'm not. Harry, Mum and I have both given up.'

Harry shook his head in disbelief. 'Given up with what?'

'Given up with her. Look, for years and years now we've both tried to be her friend, but she's made it impossible. She doesn't like any of us. It was always touch and go with her; she made it very clear from day one she didn't really want us around, except, of course, to babysit. She pretty much hates us all.'

Harry shook his head; his sister's words were as cruel as they were unbelievable to him. 'Why haven't you ever told me you felt this way about her?'

'Why? What would it have achieved?'

'I would have known.'

'And? What good would that have done? It doesn't matter what anyone thinks; we thought you guys were happy. It's got nothing to do with anyone else. Besides, my personal opinion hardly matters.'

'No, but I thought you all liked one another. I had no clue you felt like this about Laura, I thought she was very likeable. I'm very, very shocked.'

'Do you like my husband?'

'Nobody likes your husband.'

Jane burst out laughing; Harry laughed too.

'No, but seriously, you don't like my husband and it doesn't matter. I mean *I* don't like my husband either, but it's okay. We're unconventional; we make no secret of it, but you and Laura, you're the perfect couple, or so everyone thought you were.'

'We sort of were. I don't know what's happened, and what's even worse is that she doesn't seem to care. She won't even talk to me.'

'She's very selfish. Mum always said she was extremely manipulative, and has you wrapped around her little finger.'

Harry had always thought very highly of his wife; in his eyes she was an exceptional human being. He'd believed everyone was as fond of her as he was, but this was evidently not the case.

Jane continued. 'If you must know the truth, I wasn't so keen on you marrying her and neither was Mum, but you were so in love, we decided to leave you to it.'

Harry listened in amazement as his sister continued to speak.

'We found her very arrogant and very ambitious, no empathy or kindness. To be honest, I'm surprised you are still together. We expected problems a long time ago.'

'Everything is "we" – so that means both you and Mum?'

'—and Dad,' Jane interrupted. 'Dad didn't like her either. He says he has never warmed to her.'

'Him as well? Great. Just great. So did you all sit together, gossiping about poor Harry who married a witch?'

'Yes, something like that. Sorry. Do you want some strawberries?'

'Do you guys really dislike her so much?'

'No. We just don't like her very much. But we respect the fact that she is your wife, and we like you, so there really is no problem.'

'Well she hates me at the moment; she doesn't want to talk to me. I've booked a holiday, but she doesn't want to go.'

'Leave her. She needs to be alone. The more you press her to do things with you, the more she'll reject you.'

'I can't live with her like this. Christine is looking after Charlie almost full-time, Oliver is in Oxfordshire with Mum. It can't continue like this. She has to tell me what she wants. I was hoping you could perhaps talk to her, but after hearing all of this I can't believe I thought that could even be a possibility.'

'I can talk to her, of course. I will if you want me to. But you know what she will say?'

Harry glared at her. Jane was silent.

'What will she say, Jane?'

'Oh, Harry, I'm so sorry about all of this.'

'What will she say, Jane?'

'Oh, come on, Harry, you *know* she is jealous.'

'Jealous of *what?*'

'Jealous of your relationship with your family, Harry.'

'*What?* Laura? Jealous? Jealous of you guys? That doesn't make any sense. Why should she be jealous of you and Mum? That's nonsense, surely?'

'Think what you want. It doesn't matter anyway; who cares? These strawberries are really good, you should really try them. I have some cream too if you want.'

Surely his sister was exaggerating? Laura was the most self-assured, confident woman he knew. Why shouldn't she be? She had everything going for her. Jane is biased; she just doesn't like her.

'Did she ever say that?'

Jane smiled sarcastically, 'Damn right she did!'

'When?'

'Her entire life.'

'What exactly did she say?'

'Many things.'

'Like what?' Harry shouted. 'Sorry.' He took a deep breath. 'I didn't mean to shout. Please, Jane, it's really important. I'm having a crisis. I'm really confused. I... I just don't know what to do. Laura has been acting so strange these last few days; I don't recognise her any more. And now what with everything you're saying... I didn't know any of this.'

'What I am saying isn't important. It doesn't matter how she feels about us. The important thing is that you sort things out with her. You can't live like this; it's terrible for you and the kids. You need to talk to her. Right now you are freaked out, quite rightly, but forget everything I have said, it really doesn't matter.'

'I will, or at least I'll try. But look, please don't say anything to her or to anyone. I'll deal with it myself. She'll go mad if she knows I'm involving my family in our affairs, especially given how she feels about you guys.' He shook his head again in disbelief.

'You need to be able to communicate with your wife, Harry; that's the least that's required in a marriage. I understand she's going through a hard time, but you deserve a little more from her. Take her out to dinner and try to have a chat.'

'I did. I tried to book a bloody holiday to have a bloody chat, but she locked herself in the bathroom and is avoiding me.'

'I don't know what to advise. Try to speak to her; I'm happy to help if I can.'

Harry kissed his sister and left. So, all these years, all these years he had been in the dark. His wife hated his family, and his family hated his wife, and no one had told him. Was he just a naïve fool? Was he so much in love with his wife that he couldn't see anything else? Had he been wrong about her? Was she not what he had thought her to be all these years? Or was it his family who had provoked Laura? Were they somehow responsible for everything? Even if Laura felt a bit threatened by them, she didn't deserve such strong feelings of dislike from his family. His Laura, his beautiful Laura, his beautiful wife, how could anyone hate her?

Harry drove straight home, more determined than ever. He was going to force his wife to talk to him, bring Ollie back, and make sure they were a proper family again.

Harry flung open the front door, charging into the house like a bull in a china shop. Bursting with empathy for his wife, he was going to do all in his power to make things okay. He would help her. Support her. Whatever he needed to do, he was going to do it. *Who cares what the family thinks; she is my wife and I love her.* They were going to get through this. Excited, he ran up the stairs into the bedroom shouting Laura's name. He was going to tell her he loved her and apologise for everything. Laura was the love of his life, the mother of his children.

'What are you doing?' He panicked.

'Packing.'

'Why?'

'I'm going to go and stay with my parents for a while.'

'*What?* Why?'

She continued to pack while a desperate Harry looked on helplessly. 'I spoke to Christine. She will continue to look after Charlie. You just need to drop him to school in the morning. Christine will do the rest. Your mum can drop Oliver off to me. I will decide what to do with him.'

Harry sat on the bed devastated. 'Why are you doing this?'

'Doing what?'

'Why are you leaving? At least talk to me. Why are you breaking up our family?'

'I'm not doing anything. I need some time out. I need to sort myself out.'

'But *why?*'

'I'm just going to take one bag, for now. I will decide what to do later.'

'What about the baby?'

'The baby?' Laura stopped packing.

'Our baby, the one inside you.' He pointed to her stomach.

Laura paused. Now she was confused. 'Are you serious?' She sat on the bed next to him, turning to face him, bewildered. 'You're asking me about the baby? Seriously, you're asking me about the baby?'

Harry was even more confused. 'Yes. I am asking you about the baby. Why are you so shocked? I am asking you about our baby.' He looked deep into her eyes, wondering if he was going mad. Why was she so shocked?

Then Laura realised he didn't know. *He hadn't figured it out. What an idiot!*

'There is no baby. I… I… made sure there is no baby…' she replied slowly. Unable to face him, she looked away, eyes welling up with tears.

Harry felt stiff, as though he were paralysed. He was frozen. Was it possible his spine was slowly twisting itself around his neck like a tight rope?

'You did *what?*'

'You heard me.'

'You made sure there is no baby… what does that mean? What did you do?' He glared at her icily, dumbstruck.

She continued to pack calmly. 'I got rid of it.'

'What? When? You made this decision by yourself?'

Eerie dark silence ensued. A gust of wind burst in through the open window. Harry felt shivery from the sudden chill. Laura did not want to speak to him, but Harry was relentless, he needed some answers.

'You didn't think to discuss this matter with me? Are you seriously saying this to me? You decided to get rid of our baby and you didn't even tell me?' Blindsided, he erupted into a screaming match with his wife. 'How could you do that?'

'Oh, don't sit here and pretend.' Laura stood up angrily. 'Don't pretend you wanted it. Who the hell are you kidding? You didn't want this baby. It's because of you I got rid of it. If it wasn't for you, I would have kept it. I would have kept it; do you hear me?' Laura yelled at the top of her lungs. 'You! You forced me to get rid of it. This is *your* fault. It was obvious you didn't want it. It's because of *you* that I got rid of it.' Laura's irate screams turned into a frenzy of uncontrollable tears.

Just then the door flung open with a loud bang. Charlie ran inside, crying hysterically and throwing his arms around his father. Thrown back by his presence, Harry swept his son off the floor, holding on to him for dear life, squeezing him tightly. 'Charlie! It's okay, sweetheart,' he said as he kissed him on the cheek. 'It's okay, darling.'

'Why are you and Mummy screaming? Please stop!'

Harry pressed him even closer, consumed with sympathy and regret.

'I'm sorry, darling. Mummy and Daddy are just speaking. Come on, I will take you to bed.' Overwhelmed with compassion and regret, it hadn't crossed his mind in the slightest that Charlie had been dropped home by the nanny. Holding Charlie around his shoulders, Harry took the distressed little boy to his room and lay next to Charlie as though in a trance. Charlie's voice buzzed in and out of his ears, like a big blur.

'Daddy... Daddy...' Charlie called. Harry stroked Charlie's hair, unsure what to do or say, hardly hearing him. *Poor kid*, he thought. How devastating for him to have to witness something so awful. Separated from his brother, his parents hardly around, and when they are, they fight each other with screaming matches.

Amid his scrambled thoughts, he heard the front door closing with a gentle but discernible thud and then the sound of a car's engine. The stillness of the night heightened even the quietest of sounds; there was no mistaking that Laura had left the house. Harry lay in silence, powerless. He knew following her would be senseless. Numb from the stifling day, he had no choice but to let things be. The universe was turning its back on him; he felt deflated.

I just have to give in to what's happened, he thought. Jet lagged and drowned in sorrow, a faint ringing sound protruded through his ears, finding its way slowly to his brain. It seemed to be getting louder and louder… blocking his ears with his hands, he hoped to shut it out, but it persisted.

He lay on the sofa calmly and waited for the ringing to disappear. It couldn't last forever; at some point, it would have to stop. With Laura gone, all responsibilities undoubtedly fell on his shoulders. His priority was his kids; he would need to take care of them and manage himself accordingly.

Without further ado he leapt off the sofa, swallowed a few drops of melatonin, and ensured he had set as many alarms as possible for tomorrow morning. Getting Charlie to school tomorrow was now his first responsibility.

ooooo

'Daddy, Daddy, wake up, we are going to be late for school. Daddy, you are so lazy, come on, wake up. Dad, Daddy…'

Charlie tugged at his father's arm with all his might. 'Daddy, you need to make me breakfast and get my bag ready, Daddy…' the child was relentless.

Dragging himself away from a state of oblivion, Harry slowly began to come to life. Reluctantly he forced open his eyes. Charlie continued pulling his arm, gently, a bright smile beaming across his tired little face. Charlie was the grown-up, now forcing his dad to wake up.

Harry pulled him to his chest and gave him a huge kiss on his cheek. 'I love you, Charlie.'

Charlie smiled at his father. 'I love you too, Daddy, but you should hurry. You will probably take ages in the shower; we are going to be late for school.' Harry raised his head to check the time: ten past seven. Thank God. At least he didn't need to rush.

After dropping Charlie off to school, Harry sat in a coffee shop, slowly sipping herbal tea and consumed in reflective torment. Unfamiliar with any kind of burden or trauma, he battled with this new way of being. So far removed had he been from the daily stresses and concerns suffered by other people, he didn't know where to begin. How does one cope with problems? Where had it all gone wrong? How was this his life now? Always on top of his game, Harry had previously had his past, present and future perfectly mapped out. So airtight was his forecast of how his life was going to be, there had been no space for any hurdles or surprises. Shocked and overwhelmed by the unpredictability of the last two weeks, his life seemed to have spiralled out of his control. Such misfortunes had no place in his life. This was not meant to be happening, either to him or his family. Harry stared at his cup: what a bizarre, zigzag pattern. *Why would anyone design a mug like this?* he wondered. What was he even looking at? Was this meant to be clever artwork? It was ugly. There was no rhythm, no story to it. What was he was supposed to see? He avoided taking out his mobile phone; he couldn't bear to look at it right now; he needed a few minutes of nothingness before the madness of the day. Ignorance is bliss. This should be his new mantra; he needed to deploy these words; he needed to adopt a new route and shield himself from the anxiety of the last few weeks.

And then, just like that, Harry decided it was best for him to ignore what had happened and to continue living his life, devoid of pain and grief. Without any emotion, any drama, he settled on a plan of action going forward. Peace. He would make peace, and he would proceed. The dreaded conversation with his wife hadn't happened, nothing she said had happened, none of it had happened, everything was fine. His priority was his kids and himself. Not known as a man of much emotion, or rather, a man able to shove his emotions to one side, Harry rarely allowed obstacles into his life. Why should he start now? Harry and Jane hailed from both a financially and socially affluent background; their childhood had been blissfully happy. Strong and confident by nature, blessed with intelligence, drive and ambition, their future had been carved out towards success from the start. Harry had lived his bachelor days wildly and irresponsibly, like most men of his ilk. Decadent parties, jet set crowds and a vast range of exotic women, his single life had been bound primarily around his personal satisfaction and his own, thrill-seeking pleasure. Having previously indulged in extensive hedonistic debauchery and womanising, once he was married, he had decided that would be it. He was going to be the greatest husband and father ever.

A healthy, athletic young man, Harry had successfully reached middle life, seldom experiencing a sick day. How ironic now to be cursed with such a complex, baffling disease, so rapidly devastating his existence. The two things he had most keenly protected, invested most of his time in, seemed to be crumbling in front of his eyes, and most tragically he had lost control over both of them.

Since his wild college and partying days, he had never spent a day sleeping longer than nine in the morning, and he had regularly exercised, challenged his brain, and had succeeded in reading a book every week or fortnight. How did he fall victim to this disgraceful illness?

He remembered a time when women practically threw themselves at his feet; he could have had the pick of the best of the best, the daughter of an earl, the sister of a prince, the cousin of a millionaire, yet he chose Laura. Not an aristocrat, neither a society beauty, nor the beneficiary of a large trust fund, but a 'normal', feet-firmly-on- the-ground, wholesome young woman whom he was sure would never let him down in any way. Having witnessed regular marital breakdowns, he had carefully observed and identified the shortcomings of many couples, and vowed not to repeat their mistakes.

Old fashioned and a true gentleman, Harry made every effort to nourish their married life with happiness and adventure. He firmly believed he had done his level best not to ever purposely cause Laura pain. But now, unprepared to share the blame in any way and devastated at her despair, he was unable to discern an immediate remedy. Staring at the ceiling, he felt as though he was somehow shrouded in darkness. He had no answers. He hoped sincerely all was not lost; he would move mountains to right his wrongs, should there be any.

Mindful and mature for a normal man, he would take it on the chin. Who knows, perhaps it was to his advantage to learn to function and continue without her for a month or two; he would quietly resign from emotion, cease his search for answers by focusing on what needed to be done. First things first: he would round up a team to help him with the household and the kids, bereft of resentment or bitterness.

Systematically, he constructed lists of 'to-dos', planning pick-ups and drop-offs, writing down everything he could think of. Number one on his list was to appoint additional help and hire a part-time babysitter on top of the regular nanny. He knew to anticipate problems and obstacles, and most importantly he must learn to forgive himself. There was little doubt he was going to make mistakes, in fact miscalculating, poor judgement and forgetting crucial things was rapidly becoming his norm. Regardless, he would try his best to manage.

ooooo

A full week went by without drama, so far mostly working according to plan. The extra support had worked well. Harry's tactical planning turned out to be a success. Though pleased with himself, Harry knew he was using his temporary circumstances to avoid the more pressing matters needing attention. Deeply immersed in day-to-day trivia, it was almost a relief not having to attend to the small niggling matter of his illness. Able to deal with most things, the Alzheimer's trumped his other concerns. He sincerely wished this devil away with every fibre of his being. Almost instantly, another week passed by and chuffed with himself, Harry, still on top of things, felt a desire to celebrate his achievements.

Gemma organised a lavish partner lunch, and this time Harry went along leaving his woes behind, thoroughly enjoying business talk with his colleagues.

Energetically, and with a spring in his step, Harry walked back to the office. Lighter in mood, he was calm and relaxed. Lawrence, their company lawyer and a good friend of his, revered and feared within the industry, walked alongside, and they made silly jokes, happy to catch up after many months of not seeing one another.

'Nice lunch, gentlemen?' Gemma batted her eyelids playfully as the two men entered the building,

'Very nice, thank you.' The two men answered at the same time. The men in the company were always delighted at the sight of Gemma.

'Great. I'm just going out to lunch myself; I'll be back soon. Oh, and there's some mail on your desk, Harry. See you shortly.'

Harry and Lawrence parted ways, agreeing to make lunch a regular affair whenever possible. Genuinely happy after what seemed like a lifetime of stress, Harry strolled into his office, cheerful and carefree. The wine had worked its lunchtime magic, leaving him a tad light-headed and giddy. A hint of mischief played on his mind, making him grin as though he was about to do something wicked and sinister. Just as Gemma had said, two small piles of mail sat neatly on his desk. One stack marked 'urgent', one not. Naturally gravitating to the urgent pile, Harry casually tore open the envelope, still on a high from his lunch.

Horror spread across his face as he felt himself hitting the floor with a loud thud.

Laura wanted a divorce.

8

Across the Atlantic in windy Chicago, Serena's maid carefully started packing Serena's bags. She worked through the huge wardrobes, sifting through the old, new, valuable and less valuable possessions Serena had accumulated over the years.

Serena, busy in her studio, immersed herself, fretting to complete the last touches to her artwork in the uncharacteristically messy room. Not only was painting Serena's most cherished hobby, it also served as her solace and her comfort. Happiest with a paintbrush in one hand and a palette in another, her most sincere form of expression came to life in her art, which often depicted her conflicted life and background. Serena's work largely depended on her mood. Happy memories inspired lively, bright and vivid paintings. Dark thoughts and tragic childhood memories resulted in more sinister paintings, which inevitably worried her, hours later, upon careful inspection. A talented artist, she focused mostly on matters close to her heart, namely her family and her previous life before the US.

Her most passionate works consisted of her beloved mother, usually in some tragic form. She drew endless portraits of her, as though she were somehow trying to bring her back from the dead through her drawings. Frequently she painted her siblings, and most recently she had started to paint her father. Agonisingly for Serena, all of her family were dead. Her younger twin brothers, who had died when she was only nine years old, were nothing but a blur to her; no matter how often she drew them, their faces never became any clearer.

Painting members of her family temporarily transported her back home, poignantly contributing to her heartbreak. Expressing herself through her painting was the only link to everything she held dear to in her lonely life. Stunningly beautiful creations of a time so real only heightened her grief, existing solely as a constant reminder, time and time again, that she was alone. Unable to share, discuss or enjoy her wonderful art with anyone she trusted, she would often, in fits of rage, destroy her work, only to break down in tears days later, lamenting the wreckage.

The paintings in her studio told a similar story: a trained eye could quite easily grasp the artist's state of mind. Serena frequently drew her old house, her grandparents' house, her nursery, her school – everything she could remember from her childhood and the dim recesses of her memory. Her reason, she explained, was simply to keep her experiences alive while she was still young and fit enough to be able to capture her memories on paper. Often while brushing the different hues of watercolour onto the canvas, she would find herself in floods of tears; the subjects of the paintings routinely consumed her logical thoughts, frequently illuminating the very fragile emotions she sought to escape from. In moments like these, she would abandon her art and force herself to forget all about it until she was once again strong enough to hold a paintbrush, often leaving the painting untouched for weeks, and almost invariably leaving the project unfinished or fit for the bin.

Serena fantasised of one day having a family that she could paint: her own family, a husband, a few children, a few dogs, and a beautiful house in the countryside. She associated her past life with her passion, instinctively focusing mostly on her childhood in Azerbaijan, visible in her paintings and haunting her art.

She craved new, positive inspiration to capture in her compositions, but that next chapter of her life seemed nowhere in sight. Having been alone for so long, she was beginning to give up on the idea of a family, soon to accept her fate as a lonely spinster. Nevertheless, various incidents compelled her to look on the bright side: at least she wasn't faced with financial concerns. Just for that, she should be immensely grateful.

Unable to decide which angle of the canvas she was currently painting required more time, so she wandered to the back of the studio, uninspired. The fierce portrait of her mother stared down at her, mocking her. Blazing green eyes and razor-sharp cheekbones; was it an honest depiction of this wonderful woman? Serena felt a sudden shiver run through her spine; it was as though she were looking at an older, serious version of herself. She stepped back a little, studying the painting, unsure of whether or not she was satisfied with it. Her mother looked dangerously stern and harsh; had that been her intention or had she once again been slapped with those loathsome, depressive vibes when she'd crafted it? Her memories of a hard-working, kind woman were ill-portrayed. Had she intended to depict a cruel-looking woman, she undoubtedly would have succeeded. Serena took long strides further back to inspect the painting in more detail. It was a rather impressive piece of work; a strange, proud sensation filled her heart with joy.

Her mother would probably have liked it. Serena smiled at her mum, vowing to continue painting until she had captured her perfectly.

ooooo

Serena's trip to Lucerne, Switzerland, had been arranged months ago. Her plans to visit her old friend Maxim thrilled her with excitement. Max was Serena's oldest and closest friend, as well as her first love; they had been high school sweethearts back in Azerbaijan and deeply in love at the time. Over the years they had maintained their friendship, incessantly visiting one another when in need of love and affection.

The eternal bachelor, the mere thought of commitment terrified Max. He took great pleasure in relationships, but much to the chagrin of his counterparts, never felt the need to commit to marriage or anything remotely binding. Eternally fond of each other, first and foremost Serena and Max were great friends, their feelings for each other mutually reciprocated, with the question of romance carefully ruled out many moons ago. Max, the sole person with any meaning left in Serena's life, was the one she turned to after the death of her father. Max was the one she turned to when she broke her leg during a skiing accident. Max was the one she turned to when her previous relationship had broken down. By far her strongest pillar, he was the only person she had left. Having failed in her relationships, Serena generally found friendship a challenge, both with men and women.

The responsibility of friendship consistently landed on Max's shoulders, often pushing him to provide solutions when and as they occurred. Fortunately Max himself, free from commitment and responsibility, expertly dealt with Serena's expectations. Sceptical of relationships in general, Serena's mammoth expectations of Max were nothing new for him. From early on in their childhood, he was aware and understood that he had reluctantly been appointed Serena's unofficial guardian angel.

Joyfully, he responded to most of her needs, prioritising her safety and happiness. He remembered how much he'd loved her when they were young. It was an unspoken love that he hardly realised had slowly began to fade away. Without much fuss, he had given up hope of a fairy-tale ending between the two of them. They lived far away from each other and had grown up very differently from one another; so much had happened in their own lives that it was no longer possible to feel the same way about her. The burning desire he felt for her as a young man had been replaced with something altogether different.

Against her own good judgement, subconsciously Serena waited to hear from Harry, hoping there might still be some remote possibility of them meeting again. Bored and mostly alone, she craved company, often clinging on to her daydreams and the few good memories from her past. There was no question in her mind that she found Harry attractive, but she didn't expect the feelings to linger. Was he so desirable because he was totally unavailable? Was it because he was different? She had met him so briefly; she wished she could have spent some time with him and got to know him. He had something very special about him.

Every day she checked her phone, hoping for something she gave little credence to. Had there been any doubt in her fickle mind, one long email from Miles, bluntly informing her that Harry would be unavailable for a week or so as he was enjoying a romantic holiday with his wife, put paid to her yearning. Serena's decision to move to London had been determined before her encounter with Harry. However, Miles's email, though not such a surprise, made a move to London now seem as senseless as it was foolish.

The change of financial circumstances paved the way for a change of surroundings. Serena longed for a fresh new start. Uninspired by Chicago and her lonely social status, she dreamt of moving to a fun and exciting European city. England had been a great option. Fortunately for Serena, she could pick and choose where she lived. No commitments, cash-rich, fluent in many languages, the world was her oyster. Footloose and fancy-free, her first stop was Switzerland. If things worked out, she could stay longer. If not, she could leave. There were some advantages of being single. She looked forward to her visit.

ooooo

The last few months had shattered and drained Serena. Her father's unexpected death had not only left her paralysed with pain but had forced her to grow up, face matters, and make decisions she could hardly have imagined ever doing previously. She was lost. She often found herself drowning in a bottomless ocean with no one to speak to, and, most painfully, no one to love. Boarding the United Airlines 'red-eye' flight to Zürich to spend time with the only person she had left, Serena felt content and excited, looking forward to a few days of freeing her mind from everything. She flicked through a couple of magazines and ate without concern on the flight; after all, her ticket was flexible, with no return date set. Reclining in her seat, she smiled to herself. She had two choices; she could wallow in self-pity at being alone, or she could try to see the positives in her life. No care, no compassion, no regard for anyone but herself had its own rewards. Never wanting for money, her current financial state thrust her into a limitless world of freedom, opening up doors that hadn't been so readily available before. Suddenly, everything was possible and ready to be taken and enjoyed. She could do whatever she pleased. On this notion, she slept joyously, right through until she landed in Zürich.

ooooo

On a dazzling, sunny day, Serena awoke, her lungs taking in the fresh, clean air of the spectacular mountainous region. Eagerly admiring the stunning sites around Lake Zürich, she felt comfortable and at ease. Many a happy month had she enjoyed in Zürich with her family as a child; the memories rushed back like a waterfall. She felt she could easily belong there. Her planned two-day stop was sufficient to take in the sights before making her way to Lucerne, where the sumptuous award-winning Swiss Spa Hotel was the ideal retreat to relax and unwind. Feeling much older than her years because of the recent influx of bad news, Serena wondered if it was time to succumb to Botox and indulge in some minor plastic surgery; there was no better place than Switzerland for such endeavours. Resisting the temptation was quite a challenge, given every corner of the spa lay adorned with impeccable advertising for the perfect face.

Rested and rejuvenated, she felt a sense of calm soothing her body. Her mind was at peace and her limbs reposed as though in hibernation, completely at ease and tranquil. Meanwhile, her heart raced at the mere thought of seeing Max; she yearned for him. She wondered how things would be between them. Although she'd stopped noticing his rugged good looks, it was impossible to forget or dismiss him. A confident, passionate man, Max lectured on German literature and philosophy; he dreamt of living in a world consisting solely of intellectuals, who read books and lived for art and culture. An unconventional, rare breed, Max's unique character isolated him from mainstream commercialism. Not one to share an affinity with today's capitalist society, he buried himself in his passion. His one weakness, however, was beautiful women and the occasional female lecturer in his faculty, and every so often a student would grab his attention, sending him into a state of madness.

Though German was his forte, Max lectured comfortably in French and his native Russian. The woman Serena had become today was largely down to Max. It was Max who had taught Serena how to paint; he'd spent hours showing her how to mix the colours, how to hold the paintbrush, what the meaning of a blank canvas was. It was Max who'd taught her how to sing, how to dance the Austrian waltz, how to play the cello. She owed him a tremendous part of her life; he'd taught her how to become a woman, how to be, and it was for him, her dear Max, that she had crossed the ocean to spend time with today.

Serena felt her heart leap into her mouth, the butterflies in her stomach raging in a frenzy. Delighted to spot him in the corner of a dimly-lit restaurant, she found it was almost impossible not to scream at the top of her lungs as she ran towards him, thrusting herself forward, longing to embrace him. What a great distraction he was!

'Oh, my goodness, you look great! Where's the beard?' Serena jumped into his arms, as he swept her off her feet. Words couldn't describe how pleased she was to see him, her closest friend. His new, clean fresh look suited him far more than the heavy, scruffy beard he'd worn when they had last met.

'It's gone. It was too messy.' Max stroked his chin reminiscing. 'I miss it sometimes, I must say.' He pulled out a chair for his favourite woman. 'You look gorgeous. How are you?'

'I'm great. I'm happy, and I'm just delighted to see you. I feel wonderful.' Serena threw her arms in the air thrilled to be with him, heavily overstating her state of mind.

'Wow! Great! I haven't seen you like this in a long time. We must celebrate.'

'Yes, let's feast. This dinner is my treat, let's enjoy.'

Max watched his darling friend in amazement, unable to determine why she was so excited. He was curious: was she really genuinely happy, was she really morbidly depressed, or was she simply unsure of what she felt?'

'You do seem happy. I'm so glad.'

'I've had my moments, and to be honest, I'm tired of negativity and bad news. I want to live for myself now. I have no one to worry about any more, I have decided to be selfish and focus on myself.' Max watched Serena as she spoke. She certainly seemed chirpy.

'That's music to my ears,' Max gushed, pretending to look to the heavens. 'Finally! You've always been a wonderful worrier. I found that very endearing, but I do truly believe it's high time that you focus on yourself. It's your time now.'

'I know, I know. What can I say? It's certainly not been easy.' She took a deep breath. 'I lost my father, my relationship fell apart, and it all seemed to happen at the same time. I felt out of control.'

'You should call me more often if you feel like that.' Max was already on his second drink. He was drinking faster than usual, Serena thought.

The food arrived promptly. Serena had ordered roast poussin with asparagus, whilst Max had ordered steak and chips.

'What small portions you have here in Europe! Very delicious though,' Serena smiled.

'Thank you.' Max bowed his head. '… and, yes, tiny in comparison to the monstrous portions you have in the US.'

'Anyway, I don't really want to talk about my problems. Let's talk about you for a change,' said Serena, chomping hungrily on her food. She liked to eat. 'So, what's new in your life? Who is the lady?'

'No lady.'

'Really, no one at all?'

'No. No one at all.'

'That's surprising. How come?'

'I am done with women. You are all the same.'

'Are we?' Serena sipped her Champagne; Max took a large gulp as though he had been parched for months.

'Yes. All woman are the same.'

'How?'

'You want everything… and then, when you finally get everything, surprise, surprise, you don't want it anymore.' He shrugged his shoulders in frustration.

'Really? Is that the case?'

'Yes. You start to complain, and you don't stop. The grass is always greener everywhere else, except where you are.'

'Careful, darling, you are beginning to reek of bitterness.'

'I am always bitter. I like being bitter. I am bitter, but not unhappy.'

'Do you ever stop to think that you too could be a reason for your relationships not working out?'

'No. I don't!' Max was smug, but humorous. Serena smiled with him. She loved his harmless arrogance. There was not a malicious bone in his body, but a creature frequently misunderstood, his bark much worse than his bite. Max's carefree attitude disgruntled many.

'I am an artist! Women need to understand me. Of course, I like to wine and dine them like any other man; however, there is more to me, and to life, than just that.'

Max seldom explained his motives, but he seemed to be on a roll. Serena loved listening to his rather outré opinions.

'Do you date your students?'

Max smiled. 'I try not to.' He ordered another bottle of Champagne. 'I do hope this really is your treat, I cannot afford dinners like this, though I do thoroughly enjoy them, I must say.'

Serena smiled. 'Yes. It certainly is my treat. Order whatever you want; I am more than happy to pay.'

'I am only joking; my family would disown me if they knew I let a woman pay,' he frowned, 'but it is very expensive.'

'So, is it these young and broke students you date that expect to be wined and dined? I have some news for you, my darling friend. In case you hadn't noticed, women are independent nowadays. We don't need men to buy us expensive dinners and designer clothes; we can buy them ourselves.'

'Well, *you* certainly can, that's for sure.'

They both laughed and toasted to good fortune. After dinner, Max invited Serena back to his flat; she accepted on the condition that he cuddle her all night.

He opened a bottle of wine, which Serena made him promise to drink slowly. Although not usually a drinker, Serena was in the mood to drink with him and live recklessly. The effect of alcohol, still somewhat alien to her, superbly lightened her mood and loosened her conservative inhibitions, freeing her from any previous concern. Giddy and light-headed, she wondered why she hadn't indulged in this magic potion more frequently; it was so subtle, yet so powerful.

The soft piano notes rolled off Max's fingertips, gradually sinking, then roaring angrily with passion. Thousands of emotions stirred through Serena's heart. She caught herself drifting away, transcending different worlds, as the haunting melody he was playing came to life, bringing with it both joy and grief. With the dreamy musical notes Max played, and with the fading whistles of the evening rain pounding on the cobbled streets outside, Serena sank further into the sofa, relaxed and inebriated from the alcohol and the loud rhythm of the piano. She scrutinised Max's fingers caressing the ivory keys; his shadow on the wall swayed from side to side as he played zealously. She held on tightly to the photo albums on her lap as the music penetrated her body and mind.

'I have at least ten photo albums of you, of us, in my basement.' Max stopped playing and pulled her away from her trance. 'Photos of school, of college, our homes, our town, our friends. I have kept everything.'

'I long to see them, but now just keep playing. I love these profound melancholic melodies that I associate just with you. Are they your own?' He nodded humbly. 'It's beautiful the way you play. I stopped playing; I must start again.'

'Do you want to play?'

'No, I just want to lie here, drown myself in drink, and listen to you playing. I want to pretend that we are young again and that I am back at home in my little town. Being with you reminds me of so many things I don't usually think about. I want to let my imagination run free… Please play some more.'

Max continued to play. Serena noticed the dim hue of a broken lamp standing tall against the wall, his fingers floating around the keys effortlessly, notes rolling like the waves of a cold stream. He played with passion, as if he were performing in front of an audience. So much time had passed between them; she knew so little about him, the man he had become in his adult life. Watching him play so magically mesmerised her; she had forgotten how enjoyable it was. The effects of the alcohol, coupled with the excitement and the jet lag, gradually began to take its toll, exhausting her until she felt confined to the small space she lay in. Surrendering to her fatigue, she gently motioned for her friend to take her to a comfortable place, her limbs weak from the thrill of her unusual day.

Max swept his childhood friend in his arms and led her to his room. Moderately drunk and a little debilitated, it appeared as though she had already half dozed off. Mindful not to disturb her, Max gently undressed her; she purred with a burst of subtle laughter as he tugged at her clothes. She hadn't changed; she was still the same delicate, vulnerable girl he'd known all those years ago. Gently he flung a T-shirt over her head, careful not to cross any boundaries, or hurt her in any way. She continued to giggle helplessly.

'My beautiful angel,' he observed as she lay on his bed, curled into a ball, passed out in oblivion. With a light stroke of his finger, he swept away a loose strand of hair from her face. Her unblemished skin, her fragile porcelain face, was still as beautiful as the early morning frost, untouched by the harshness of time. *Her beauty is timeless, almost immortal*, he thought. Max gazed closely as she lay on the bed, her coral lips frozen in half a smile. This gorgeous creature whom he'd spent hours just looking at while he was growing up, now lay helpless on his bed. This innocent, mesmerising woman he had spent his young adult life in love with, her head tilted to the side, her lips pursed into a delicate pout, how ravishing she was, even in her sleep. How could he help but remember how profound his love had been for her, how much he yearned for her touch, her smell. Could it be possible the crazy, intense passion, the sexual desire, the woman he would have given his right arm and leg for, now lying in his bed in nothing but a white T-shirt, could it be possible his feelings for her were now replaced by sisterly love? Max had no sisters, so he was unsure how one loved one's sister, he assumed it to be without passion – perhaps how one loves one's mother? No, he didn't love Serena like he loved his mother; maybe he loved her the way he loved his dog, or his books, or his music; could that be possible?

Certain he loved Serena as deeply as he had done all those years ago, he now struggled to understand *how* he loved her. He lay next to her gazing adoringly at her, her breath warming his cheeks. He drew closer, gently kissing her soft moist lips. She giggled in her sleep whispering incomprehensibly. Relieved at his lack of sexual desire, Max wrapped his arms around her waist and tried to sleep, just as he'd promised he would.

ooooo

The glimmer of the sun barely visible through the opaque windows, Serena's head tinged faintly in pain as she slowly scrambled out of her deep sleep. A few moments of wide-eyed searching across the room, she recognised nothing, but luckily remembered where she was. The Roman numerals on the bedside clock glowed in the room, shrouded by the unnatural darkness. Eleven-thirty in the morning! She raised her eyebrows in shock. Flicking on the lamp she raised herself up, feeling a tad heavy-headed. A red rose lay bashfully on a piece of paper next to the bedside lamp.

I leave him in charge of you, for I know he will love you as much as I do. Sleep well, my sweet angel, till you rid your life of fatigue.

Care only for yourself and worry for nothing, your guardian angel shines his light over you from the skies above.

PS: the fridge is full. Call me if you need anything. See you tonight. Your darling friend M.

Kisses

Serena clung on to the paper, pressing it firmly against her heart. The rose seemed to blush a deeper shade of crimson as she held it close against her cheek. Could it be possible? Was her Max still the same darling man she had loved so many years ago? Could he be the answer to all her problems? She read the message again and again, stroking the soft petals of the rose and smiling fondly to herself.

Once back at her hotel after a hearty meal, she pulled the blanket over her head, attempting to sleep away the demon inside her head. Maybe alcohol wasn't such a good idea after all.

9

Laura sat outside Dr Raza's office, stiff as a statue, wondering if she should stay or go. Her mind raced in doubt, her legs fidgeting with reluctance to do anything. The faint scent of lavender lingering in the air reminded her of the camping trips she'd so enjoyed as a kid. She would much rather have been there than here. Not yet ready to open up or engage in deep discussion, she wondered if she was making a mistake. Was it too soon? Did she need more time? Her feelings raw, her stomach whirling round and round as though she was on a spinning wheel, Laura tried to get herself up, but felt powerless to move. She would be called in any minute; she had better make a decision. Was she staying or going? She wanted to see Dr Raza, she had missed him, but what if he was disgusted with her and her recent actions? She would have to tell him. The whole point of seeing him was to tell him things, to open up, to discuss her emotional state. But what if he judged her and thought her disgusting? She stood up, ready to run out of the practice.

'Dr Raza will see you now, Mrs Hoffman.' The nurse stared at her, breaking into a gentle smile of encouragement. 'Would you like to follow me?' Laura obeyed. She took her seat, the same seat as her last visit almost three weeks ago.

Everything was as she had left it: the sterile white walls, the female-focused magazines, the old coffee machine. She curled her lip and began to bite her nails, something she usually never did. Nervously dreading the next hour, it still wasn't too late; she could still leave. How could she honestly confess to Dr Raza what she had done… at her age?

'Mrs Hoffman, it's lovely to see you. Please remain seated.' The doctor sat opposite Laura at a comfortable distance, close enough to read her face and her concerns. 'How are you?'

Laura tried to speak. Defenceless and unable to find her voice, her failed attempt to discuss her feelings remained hidden by a dry smile, leading to a stream of painful tears. Graciously the doctor reached over, offering her some tissues and a reassuring smile.

'I'm sorry,' she whispered looking down.

'Please don't be. It's okay. Would you like a few minutes to yourself?'

Laura nodded, unable to utter a word.

'Okay. I will be in the other room; just knock when you are ready. Please take your time.'

Wishing she had walked away when she'd had the chance, Laura hid her face in her hands and sobbed uncontrollably. Eyes shut tight, ridden with guilt, she felt as though someone had ripped out her insides from within. What had she done, dear God, what had she done? Resisting the temptation of screaming at the top of her lungs, she felt herself stripped down to the core, flawed and vulnerable; a mere shadow of her former self.

'Pull yourself together, Laura!' she told herself. 'What are you doing? Pull yourself together! This is not the place or the time.' With a fierce wipe of the back of her hand, she dried her tears off her moist red cheeks, drowning in embarrassment and shame. Broken and deflated, she took a few steps towards the window, the sky still a beautiful bright blue without a single cloud. She looked at her shaking hand, clenched it into a fist and bit her lip till it almost bled. Pressing her temples with her fingers, she took a deep breath and looked in the mirror at her face. Mechanically she applied a thin layer of translucent powder on her face, followed by a generous lashing of nude lip balm. Laura sat down, took a deep breath, blew her nose, and allowed the doctor back in the room again.

'How are you feeling?' The doctor was calm, as though nothing had happened.

'Better, thank you. I'm sorry.' She smiled, timid and apprehensive.

'It's perfectly okay. Please don't feel embarrassed in here. This is your time. It's okay to cry, and very often necessary. Please don't worry.'

'Thank you.' Laura nodded, wishing things could have been different.

'We can start whenever you are ready.' Dr Raza prompted her to take the lead. She didn't speak.

'How are you feeling, Laura? Would you like to talk?'

She looked up at Dr Raza and took a deep breath. 'Do you really want to know?'

'Yes. I do.'

'You're going to hate me.' She shook her head. 'You're not going to want to talk to me once I tell you what I've done.' She half smiled, not sure what to do with herself, trying to resist her tears.

The doctor smiled back. 'Why do you think that?'

'Because I did something terrible. Nice ladies don't do what I did.'

'What did you do?'

Silence ensued, wrapping them both in its stillness. The white walls were impeccable in the quiet of the day. Fighting her tears, Laura cleared her throat forcefully. Looking directly at Dr Raza, she admitted the truth.

'I got rid of the baby, Doctor.'

Dr Raza was silent. Although he expected nothing other than this very answer, it still felt a little awkward. He let it go and waited for her to continue. She didn't.

He spoke. 'How do you feel?'

'Disgusted. Sickened with myself. I feel terrible.'

'Does your husband know?'

'Yes.'

'How did he take it?'

'He was disgusted and upset. Understandably.'

'Did he not try to stop you?'

'He didn't know; he was in Chicago.'

'Did he know you were planning this?'

'No.' Her eyes became teary again.

'Do you feel you made the right decision?'

'Yes. It was the best thing to do. There was no other choice.'

'Does your husband agree with your decision?'

Laura looked down. 'It was nothing to do with him. He left me alone to deal with everything myself. I didn't want to talk to him.'

The doctor listened. His face was still free of reaction and emotion.

'How are things between the two of you now?'

'I've moved out.'

A concerned smile crept up on the doctor's face. 'You have made some big decisions.'

'I've served him divorce papers as well.' Laura smiled apologetically, yet smugly.

Dr Raza, quite taken aback, remained his normal, placid self, yet was undeniably shocked. Usually a patient came in to discuss such things, to seek advice before diving in head first. *Clearly this is not your average woman*, he thought to himself.

'Perhaps we should consider this step by step, Mrs Hoffman. A lot has happened. We need to break it all down and discuss this: one thing at a time before we move on to anything else.'

'I am okay, Doctor. I'm a tough cookie; I will be okay in time. I don't regret any of my decisions, and neither do I question them. I am not full of hate or resentment for anything, not even my husband.' Laura paused and blew her nose. 'I just feel it's time to move on. Our marriage has run its course. It's over, and everything associated with it.

I need some time… I will be okay. Time, and a little help from you, and I will be okay.'

'Yes. Of course you will be okay, and it's great that you are thinking like this, so rationally and so positive. I am here to help in every way I can.'

What kind eyes the doctor has, thought Laura as she observed him, curious about what he might be thinking.

'Where would you like to start? What would you like to discuss today? Perhaps we can make a plan of action going forward, according to what you might wish to achieve.'

'I don't wish to discuss my actions or what I have done; I want to discuss how to live with my actions and the repercussions on a day-to-day basis, and without feeling guilty. I did the right thing for both my husband and myself, but that's not the discussion I want to have. Right now, he is angry with me; in time he will realise and understand I have made the best decision. We can't continue as a couple after this.'

'How does your husband feel about everything?'

Laura closed her eyes and blew her nose again. The more she spoke, the more her guilt weighed her down. Her shoulders drooped, giving the impression she was far older than her years. Weak and fatigued, her body felt as though all life had been sucked out of it.

'He is very angry, hurt and upset, as you can imagine.' She sighed. 'He didn't see it coming.' Laura whispered quietly; the doctor could barely hear her.

'My husband is a good man. He tries very hard to do the right thing. We both made a mistake, but the truth is that even if we hadn't made this mistake, it would still have been time to move on.' Laura shrugged her shoulders, facing the doctor. She spoke as though she hardly saw him.

'Harry doesn't know this, but my heart hasn't been in this marriage, in this relationship, for a long time. I love Harry very much but... but... but not as a husband.' Her eyes welled up again. 'In my heart, the marriage has been over for a long time. I just didn't know how to break it to him, I knew it would hurt him; I didn't want to hurt him.' Laura looked at the doctor. 'I've been avoiding him and he has started to notice. We frequently sleep in different beds, he has things going on, I have things going on. In fact, he has been acting quite strangely recently, but I haven't cared enough to question it. I'm not interested in him any more. The pregnancy was the catalyst; it forced me to make a decision.'

Dr Raza listened intently. Before he met his patients, he took time to read their files and understand who they were, or at least who they were before they came to him. Laura, a successful lawyer, worked for a big city law firm. A junior partner, her CV was immaculate, her achievements beyond impressive. Dr Raza, no stranger to treating city professionals, sympathised with these young corporates who seemed to excel in their careers, but managed to destroy their personal lives.

He wished he could find a remedy that could offer these lost souls the same success at home as at the office. Here was a perfect example of a successful woman who probably shouldn't have found herself in this situation. Dr Raza always wondered what his patients were like when not in need of therapy. He imagined Laura to be a formidable opponent, dressed in a power suit, sitting in her glossy office and probably winning every case she was involved in.

Laura didn't seem to be a wounded victim carrying heaps of emotional baggage. Like most people, she'd suffered a mid-life misfortune and ended up in a place she hadn't anticipated. He saw a determination in her; she probably wouldn't need a long course of treatment. He certainly hoped this to be the case. He always felt a great sense of achievement when his patients stopped needing him. Laura would probably be fine in less time than usual, before waltzing back to her normality.

'When we suffer sudden tragedies or losses, we deal with them in different ways, often ignoring or avoiding the most simple solutions that we fail to identify because of the overwhelming grief we are feeling. If you feel up to it, my advice would be to try and have a talk with your husband. Don't feel rushed if you are not ready. I don't want to push you, but it might be worth considering. What do you think? Do you think it might be an option to talk to him soon?'

Laura nodded her head. 'Yes, I know. I know I need to talk to him, but he hates me right now. Nothing I say will have much impact on him. He is angry. Perhaps I should let him calm down. He is not going to like what I have to say.'

'Don't feel pressured. Take your time. This is about you. If you don't feel ready to discuss anything, don't.'

Laura despaired, imagining herself entangled in a face-to-face chat with Harry. Ten years of their lives together – over. Just like that! Harry had been blindsided by all of this; at the very least he was entitled to an explanation. As far as he was concerned, everything was fine and dandy, he hadn't seen any of this coming. Cold chills darted down her spine. She pictured her children running around in open fields, both of their parents by their side, laughing and smiling. She was about to inflict a tremendous amount of pain on them, destroying their innocent lives, forever. Thinking about her children left her practically incapacitated. She imagined herself on a fast roundabout, the room turned dark. The darkness spread panic like a virus through her heart. She took a large sip of water to try and clear her thoughts. Perhaps the doctor was right; she should talk to Harry as soon as possible, rid herself of this burden, find some peace in her actions and try to move on.

ooooo

Harry sat at his desk, glaring at the disturbingly ugly word 'divorce'. Suddenly, he felt out of breath. His chest started to hurt. He forced his eyes shut, took a deep breath, and ran to his desk; the jug of water was empty. His face broke out in a sweat. He felt a desperate need to vomit. He ran to the bin, forcing himself to throw up. He sat on the floor panting, his stomach strangely whirling. He felt shivery. He sat still, waiting for this strange feeling to pass. His eyes began to twitch, his head began to spin. He lay against the wall breathing heavily. A sudden urge to go to the lavatory, slowly he walked out of the office as though in a trance. Aiming for the lavatory, which was down the corridor on the right-hand side, Harry turned left, unaware where he was going. His heavy breathing now calmer, he pushed the door, casually walking in.

'Harry?' smiled the head of HR, who was presenting to a team of ten people.

'Harry?' she called again. 'Are you looking for me?'

Without a word, Harry walked out of the office, and barged in to the office next door. He was searching for the bathroom, but couldn't seem to find it.

'Hello, Harry,' smiled a man, head buried in his laptop. Everyone glanced at him. He looked around and walked out again. Banging the door behind him, he stared ahead.

'Hi, Harry,' Gemma smiled at him. 'Are you okay?'

'Laura wants a divorce.'

'*What?*' Gemma couldn't believe her ears. 'I'm so sorry. Are you okay? Can I help you with anything?'

'I have a very bad headache. Can you please call me a taxi? I would like to go home. I need the lavatory first, though. I don't feel well.'

'Of course. Let me help you, then I'll put you in a cab. I'm so sorry, Harry.'

ooooo

'This woman is unbelievable! What is she playing at? Stupid bitch! She's selfish and conniving; has she given any thought to her children? I am so sorry to hear this, darling.'

Beyond grateful to have his mother, Harry couldn't help wondering if his kids would ever feel such love, such emotion for their mother, as he did for his. He would fight Laura tooth and nail for custody of their children; she was unfit to look after the kids by herself. Unable to think much further, he waited for the painkillers to kick in. The headache gradually started to disappear, but his head felt heavy and his eyes were blurry. He was knocked out, and shortly he fell in a deep, blacked-out sleep.

ooooo

Like a bird with broken wings struggling to fly, Harry pulled himself away from his silent sleep. He looked around the deserted room. He felt cold but rested, and his head felt much lighter. Seemingly, he had nothing but his own shadow for company. Plagued by his own demons, in what now seemed a life of forgotten dreams, he couldn't quite make out what was going on. He lay in bed, trying to gather his thoughts. He joined dots with his fingers in the air. Slowly, some things started to come back. He walked downstairs in a state of oblivion.

Elizabeth, a statue-like vision, sat bold and firm at the kitchen table, hands wrapped around a cold cup of tea, still shaking in anger. She swept her arms around Harry. Harry fought back his tears while holding his mother tightly. Cringing with embarrassment, he fought with himself not to break down; it was useless, he was not in control. His mother held on to him. What a disappointment, how humiliating, what must his mum be thinking? Desperate not to trouble her too much, Harry broke away from her. Consumed with guilt and misery, and knowing he had recently burdened her virtually every day with his problems, he apologised profusely for his weakness. He hated feeling like this.

Livid, Elizabeth wanted him to tell her everything from the beginning.

'That's it, Mum. I have absolutely no clue. I simply cannot figure it out. It doesn't make any sense to me at all. I just thought she was a bit frustrated and needed a bit of time, blah-blah. I couldn't begin to imagine she was going to hit me with this.'

'I have noticed a change in her since she returned from Greece,' his mother agreed.

Harry shot his mother a perturbed look of helplessness, dreading what was about to follow.

Elizabeth recognised the anguish in her son's eyes, but nevertheless pursued her thoughts out loud. 'Are you sure she didn't meet someone in Greece?'

A bittersweet image tugged at his ice-cold heart. Black clouds hung over his head, tangled memories and whispers of the past chilled his brain.

'The thought hadn't crossed my mind. But no, I'm not sure.' Trying to uncover the unseen, staring into a universe of lost memories, troubled and forlorn, Harry witnessed his life dangling in front of him. 'It's very possible she met someone there as she has been a bit strange, a bit vacant since she returned.' Without emotion, he continued. 'I didn't even think it possible. I trust her implicitly, or maybe I should say I *trusted* her implicitly.'

'Do you want a cup of tea?'

'No. I'll drink water. I'm feeling very dehydrated.'

'How is your head?'

'Much better, thanks.' Harry gulped down two large glasses of water, one after the other without stopping to take a breath. Elizabeth observed her son's frustration; she felt very sorry for him.

Harry pulled up a chair to face his mother. 'Mum, I need to tell you something.'

Lines of concern protruded through Elizabeth's face. 'What is it?'

Harry paused.

'Harry, what is it?' she said as she frowned anxiously.

'Nothing.' He smiled dryly. 'It's nothing, I'm just concerned about what Laura's plans for the kids are. I will fight her for custody. I will, of course, need your help. Christine is already working full-time, and I have hired a part-time babysitter too. I don't want Laura to have my kids.'

His mother squeezed his hand, 'Of course! Of course I will help you, darling. Don't worry about a thing, I'm right here. I'm so shocked! I've been so careful never to interfere in your marriage. I always tried to maintain a friendly relationship with Laura, and help her in any way I could, but her recent behaviour has been very strange. I never imagined she would do this. What has happened?'

'I don't know.'

'I can't believe she would put the poor kids through this. Has she thought about what she is doing? Divorce is the worst thing for such small kids. I'm speechless.'

'I know.' Harry hung his head low, distressed and embarrassed that his life had come to this, forcing him to run back to his mother for help. Words failed him. Gasping for air, he felt the walls closing in, trapping him in sorrow.

Outside in the garden, the flowers were blooming. The white peonies stood out distinctly amongst the various roses, neither troubled nor apologetic for their existence. Blossoming in their beauty and purity, the very flowers Harry and Laura had planted together, now felt like sharp thorns pricking him through his spine. Harry thought about his dreams. He imagined himself on the edge of a steep cliff once again. How easy it would be to just jump off. Once again, his children's faces flashed back and forth in front of him. Bewildered, he wondered how to break the news to them. Oliver had just returned back to school after the intervention of a therapist; this news would negate all the positive progress he had made in the last few weeks. The weekly therapy would probably now need to continue indefinitely.

'Why don't we take a week out and go on a family holiday?'

'What will that achieve? The kids have school. I can't just take them out. I think it's illegal or something.'

'Not if there is a good reason.'

'I was going to take my dear wife on a week's break so we could "reconnect", but instead she wants a divorce.'

Elizabeth shook her head in distress. 'Chin up, darling. I know it's devastating, but what doesn't kill you makes you stronger. I promise you, it does get easier.' She pointed to herself. 'Here, look at me, I am living proof!' She smiled ironically.

Harry kissed his mother on the cheek. 'I know, Mum. It probably will get better at some point, but right now it seems as if it's the end of the world. I am such a fool; I really didn't see this coming. How stupid I've been.'

'I'm sorry you've had to go through this.' In shock herself, Elizabeth didn't know what to say. Harry's marriage had been the most solid in the family.

'I'm very tired, Harry, I'm going to go home; will you be okay? Think about my suggestion about the holiday; we can take that other fool along with us.' Harry looked at his mum, puzzled. 'Eric, my ex-husband, your father!' She smiled.

The demons in Harry's head set themselves loose, roaming around freely, riding the waves of his life.

Immersed in his deadly anguish, the song of emptiness played loud in his ears; how can hurt reach so deep? He remained glued to his seat: nothing to do, nothing to hold or to cling on to. Echoes of his children's laughter haunted him. The devouring pain, the empty void, the unspeakable numbness. How could Laura do this? Deliver such a bold stab in the back. Each promise she'd made now felt like a punch; every thought she'd shared seemed like a bullet. How was he going to cope? How was he, with Alzheimer's disease, going to bring up two kids?

While Harry had slept, Elizabeth had assembled half a dozen brightly coloured tulips on the table, in a failed attempt to brighten up the kitchen. Having not noticed the tulips all this time, suddenly they fascinated Harry as he sat around the kitchen table, his eyes fixated on them. The flowers seemed to stare back at him almost as intently as he stared at them, as though they had a mind of their own. Drawing his eyes close together, Harry gawped intensely at them, puzzled. Concentrating fiercely, long and hard, suddenly void of emotion as though the last few hours hadn't happened, Harry gazed at the flowers as though he questioned their presence and their intentions; how vulnerable his brain had become. His question was, what colour were they? Looking intensely at them failed to provide an answer. Were they as strangely shaped as they seemed? Why were these flowers blurry? How odd. Was it his mind playing tricks, or was it his vision? *Red?* he asked himself, or *orange?* Hmm… actually the more he squinted, the more a bright shade of pink appeared to be the answer, or were they all different colours? Focusing on different angles, bringing the vase closer, might make things clearer. He gave it another shot. Harry turned the vase around and begun to play a little game, bringing the vase close, then sliding it away, then pulling it close again, then sliding it away again. No matter how much he focused, he couldn't quite figure out what colour the flowers were.

He continued to play this back-and-forth game until he miscalculated the distance by pulling the vase too close. The vase fell on the heavy kitchen tiles, shattering into what seemed like a million pieces. The water spilt everywhere and the tulips lay on the slippery grey kitchen floor. Harry had been dreading moments like this. Grateful it hadn't happened in front of his mother, he felt he now had no choice but to make an appointment and see a doctor as soon as possible.

He had kissed the kids goodnight, and was now lying fully clothed on his bed, trying to absorb his insane day. His life had been easy as a breeze for a long time, but suddenly it seemed to have come crashing down like a pack of cards. His head buzzed with fear, his pulse raced, his heart pounded, as he prayed this was the last bombshell he had to face. He couldn't take any more. Harry's thoughts sailed to Serena. Beautiful Serena, lovely Serena. How easy life might have been with Serena if he hadn't had his ghastly problems and his tragic illness.

Serena's face beamed before his eyes; he longed to have her close. He wondered what she was doing and where she was. Was she still mad at him? Perhaps he should call her; yes, that might be a good idea. But what should he say to her? How should he say it? A mind possessed, thoughts flying through times past,

Harry's mind rushed towards different paths, imprisoning him in nostalgia. Long remembered joys turned to screams of despair. Thinking about his children crippled him with horror; how would he break the news to them? *Mummy doesn't live here anymore.* They would be devastated. He reflected on his sickness; was it all a false alarm? Surely it was just a daunting scare? Surely, he was far too young to be at risk of such a horrific, ugly disease? His rational thinking mind gave him some solace. It was easier to think of his illness than his wife. What a pleasure to be in control of one's own thoughts. He must steer clear of bitterness and negativity. It was far better to focus on the future and seek pragmatic solutions.

Harry's sudden enlightened psyche questioned how he should contemplate caring for his kids, especially with this monster illness. What if it didn't get better? What if it got worse and he deteriorated as most people did? He had hoped to grow old with Laura. He had hoped his darling wife of ten years would look after him in his twilight years, nurse him through his sickness, help with his ailments, and above all love and be with him. Now, however, all he was faced with was getting very sick, very quickly. Deteriorating, and tragically, all alone. 'Perhaps it's for the best,' he heard himself say out loud. 'It's hardly fair for me to expect her to stay and nurse me with my illness. Maybe she would have left me anyway once she found out I was sick.'

Harry found it easy to speak out loud when no one was around. Unable to share his thoughts with anyone else, it was probably best he confided only in himself. His mother and Jane would simply not be able to digest this heartbreaking news; how could he burden them with it? It was best he kept his problem away from them for as long as he could.

ooooo

Within the confinement of his room, another depressing day lay ahead of him. As usual, the struggle to surface out of bed was the first challenge, followed by an avid perusal of the list of chores. Every day Harry prioritised his to-do list, trying to absorb as much information as he could and memorise his meetings. Discreetly he referred to the list continuously throughout the day in case he should forget something. While checking his messages, his heart missed a beat as he realised Laura had sent him a message. Glaring at the screen, he pondered. Should he read the message? His hands trembled as he touched the screen. Could he face it? Did he have the strength, the endurance for more bad news? Could he stomach anymore?

I'm sorry for everything. Can we meet? It would be good to talk face to face. I never meant to hurt you. One day I hope you can find it in your heart to forgive me.

Without further procrastinating, Harry responded immediately.

When?

Tomorrow night. Usual place, eight in the evening?

Fine.

Usual place, thought Harry. She wants to meet in the usual place. She has destroyed my life and she wants to meet in the usual place, as if it was just a casual date. Harry checked his to-do list again, determined to continue his day without further torturing himself or inviting additional grief. He endeavoured to block his mind from negative thoughts and prioritise the unavoidable.

ooooo

With a heavy heart, Harry slowly made his way to Olivio, their usual Greek taverna formerly known as their 'happy place'. Throughout the years the restaurant had shaped itself to symbolise their marital life, catering to all their needs, be it christenings, birthday parties, dinner parties, Sunday brunch, and more. Would this one evening now wipe out all the joy and festivities, replacing all the great memories with misery and tragedy?

Overwhelmed with scathing thoughts of hurt and grief, Harry peeped discreetly through a side window. He saw Laura fussing hysterically with her wine glass, her face a deep shade of scarlet, not so different to her wine. It saddened Harry to see Laura on a different table to their usual spot. Slowly everything was changing. Change, as they say, is life, and change, as they say, is death. For Harry, change now symbolised nothing but death. Wearily, he tasked his inner strength to muster up the courage to charge inside and deal with whatever awaited him.

Laura stood up robotically as she caught sight of her husband approaching her. Try as she might, she couldn't deny that Harry, though paralysed with doubt and regret, looked as gorgeous as he always did, standing tall and firm. In full view, Laura wiped away her tears.

'Thanks for coming.' She fiddled with a tissue. 'I wasn't sure if you would.' They both sat down at the same time.

'Oh, I wouldn't miss this for the world!' retorted Harry acerbically.

'For God's sake, Harry.' Laura shook her head bitterly.

'"For God's sake, Harry" *what?*' he fired back at her. 'Seriously. You send me divorce papers to my office after everything we have just recently been through, and you want me to be kind and polite?'

'If you are going to act like this, I will get up and leave, and we can communicate via lawyers. Let it all get acrimonious, if that's what you would rather.'

'I don't understand what you want from me. I just said I wouldn't miss coming here. That's all.' Harry poured himself a glass of wine. 'So, go ahead. I'm listening.'

Trying to stay calm, he looked Laura straight in the eye, his face frozen, his eyes cold.

Laura, intimidated by Harry's candid directness, averted her gaze. In twelve years of knowing him, she had never experienced his wrath. A blissfully happy marriage, not once had Harry ever raised his voice to his wife; never once had he shouted in anger. Laura remained his princess, his desire, his life. Now it all lay wrecked, wrecked by her.

'I know you are upset and hurt right now.'

'Upset and hurt? Well, that's an understatement if ever I've heard one.'

'Can you please let me finish?' Laura shook her head in frustration.

'Okay. Continue.'

'Right. I am sorry. I really am. I don't know what I can say or do. Everything I'm going to say is going to upset you. I never meant to hurt you. I… I simply… I just don't… I don't think this marriage is working. I…. I… I'm not happy.'

Harry's unforgiving stare proved challenging for Laura to continue speaking. His rage burnt through her skin;

perhaps it was a bad idea to sit here in front of him. Seldom had she witnessed such intense emotion in Harry's face. Deeply wounded and embarrassed, she thought to call the whole thing off, hold him in her arms and go home.

'Why couldn't we discuss this? Huh? Why couldn't we talk about this? You are my wife. Why didn't you talk to me about this, like a grown-up? Why did you make this monumental decision alone, without telling me? How dare you? Do you realise what you have done? I nearly had a heart attack when I read your letter. I'm serious. Why didn't you talk to me about it?'

Laura, by now sobbing uncontrollably, looked at the floor, shaking her head. Harry continued. 'You should have at least given me a chance. Whatever you were going through, you could have told me. Whatever you needed, whatever you wanted from me to do, to become, I would have done it for you. It was incredibly heartless of you to first tell me you got rid of our baby, a decision you made all by yourself. Then you decide to move out, and now, just when I was expecting you back home and my kids were going to have their mother back, you slap me with a divorce. Who are you? I don't recognise you anymore.'

Laura stopped crying, dried her tears, composed herself, and put her lawyer's hat on.

'I'm sorry I didn't discuss this with you. I thought it counter-productive. I had made up my mind. My decision was final. Discussing matters of the heart in this manner achieves no results. We've had a wonderful marriage, two fantastic kids, a great time, beautiful, happy memories. I will take those memories with me. I hope when you calm down, you too will be able to do the same.' Laura spoke with little or no emotion. She had had her bad moment and a little cry. It was time to face the music now. Unaffected by such tragedies, she pragmatically and professionally handled cases similar to this daily. But this very cool, confident behaviour Harry had so adored and admired in his wife, now began to disgust and infuriate him.

'I suppose you will now want to discuss the financial economic side of the divorce, having done with the emotional side.'

Dismissing him as a mere distraction, Laura spoke over him. Her patronising tone was deplorable to him. 'We can keep it clean and simple. We sell the house, split the money, you see the kids every other weekend, you pay for the kids' schooling and holidays. I am not greedy or unfair; you pay a third of your monthly salary. Everything else we can discuss once the basics are cleared.'

'The kids stay with me,' Harry fired calmly. Losing his temper, shouting, screaming, sarcasm was not the best way to proceed, clearly evident by his wife's behaviour.

'That's out of the question. Don't be unreasonable and start an unnecessary fight. You can have the kids every other weekend, one night a week in addition if you really must, but they need to live with me, their mother.'

'Fine.' Placidly Harry stood up, calmly placing a twenty-pound note on the table. 'You will be hearing from my lawyers. See you in court.' In full view of the kind restaurant owners, the regular staff, who all knew Harry and Laura as the golden couple, Harry quietly strolled out of the restaurant, his head held up high, but with his heart blazing fiercely.

ooooo

A long, undisturbed relaxing sleep later, Serena lay in the bath, deliriously happy. What a brilliant decision it had been to make this fulfilling trip to Switzerland to visit her friend. How easy it would be to fall in love with Max all over again, to marry him and have his kids. This would solve all her problems. She knew him, she trusted him, and above all she loved him. But was loving someone as a friend a good enough reason to marry them?

Serena swirled the bubbles around in the bath, creating wild patterns. The zesty scent of the bath crystals and the warmth of the water gave the large suite a pleasurable, calming effect. The steamy windows enclosed her in the room, blocking any contact to the outside world, which could often be unpredictable and hostile. Complacent within her boundaries, Serena felt herself ready to fall in love. So desperate was she to meet someone, nothing was too big an ordeal. Determined to turn her life around, she longed for a companion to love and take care of her.

The past year had been instrumental in shaping her character, as she'd blossomed from girl to woman, aware of the pains of the earth, and she was now ready to embrace responsibility and enter the grown-up phase of her life. Growing up so dramatically brought challenges. Her choices had to be wise, if not outright calculated. Disappointed at the mere thought of Harry, Serena swore to herself that married men were to be avoided at all costs. Hoping it would happen naturally, sometime soon, she told herself repeatedly she must not obsess about finding that special person. It would happen when it was meant to, and it was probably better not to try and force things.

Lucerne, a tourist's dream, offered a substantial amount to its loyal visitors, and it seemed Serena's hotel, the hub of information, delightfully advertised the best cruises right from her doorstep. Practically dressed for the ever-changing Swiss climate, strategically she placed herself on the front row of the river cruise. The anonymity of being a tourist was something she was nevertheless akin to. Having still not found her 'real' home, Serena adapted well to different places; in fact, she made a pact with herself to travel. For as long as she was commitment-free, she would enrich her life with different experiences and adventures. Combining travel with work, wherever she could, painting landscapes, people, towns, villages, whatever might be captured in paints and colours would be her new job. Perhaps she could sell her paintings to the rich and famous, or to some of the acclaimed art galleries dotted around Europe.

Serena's previous life was still very much part of her daily memories; she was regularly disturbed by both her conscious and subconscious world. The trepid conditions of the central Asian mental asylums frequently haunted her. For as long as she could remember, she had promised her mother and herself she would donate whatever she could; the profits from the sales of her paintings had proved her only route to honour that promise until now.

As the catamaran set off, Serena dreamed of island-hopping around southern European islands. Lying on sun-soaked beaches, eating oysters, drinking local wines, sailing, swimming naked in the Mediterranean, waking up to blue skies and sunshine every day. She would round all this off perfectly by capturing her experiences directly on canvas.

The clean Swiss air was fresh and fragrant, the river pleasantly calm; what a splendid day for a river cruise. The cold wind brushed past her cheeks, while the warm sunrays highlighted her long, dark hair. She looked up at the sky; would the sun continue to shine with all its smouldering glory, or would it be concealed and buried by dark clouds? An inquisitive mind, constantly seeking her final destination without realising it, Serena spent most of her time in anticipation of what awaited her. Upbeat and passionate about life, she was open and guileless, despite life's harshness, smiling even through the toughest challenges. Creative by nature, always on the search for her next project, curiously she observed her fellow passengers perched near her. There was an intense concentration of nationalities: everyone on the boat was from somewhere different. Switzerland offered everything to everyone, an international melting point for people of all nationalities basking in charm and elegance. Amidst the sound of the engine, she deciphered many different languages being spoken, from German to French, Italian, Arabic, Mandarin, Russian, Hindi, but very little English. It was pointless to eavesdrop. Not a single conversation interested her. Most people's conversations consisted of general mundane talk, almost everything she understood was a compliment to the Swiss and their beautiful country. Relocating to this magical part of the world might seriously be a consideration. Life in Chicago suddenly seemed very far away. She closed her eyes, inhaling the clear, crisp air, preferring to see and hear nothing. Her mind stopped. Her focus was purely on enjoying the moment.

Strolling aimlessly after the excursion, her heart full of adventure, Serena stumbled upon a charming little coffee shop. Here she had the perfect opportunity to order the authentic Swiss *Birnenkuchen*. Both content and tranquil, she finally succumbed. What a challenge it had been to resist looking at her phone; she had successfully managed half of the day. Every time her eyes drifted to her screensaver, her heart missed a beat. Her father's bright smile and his kind, loving eyes glared at her. Overcome with emotion after his death, she'd taught herself to ignore whatever challenged her. Gazing lovingly at her father, she hoped one day to replace his picture with the bright smiles of her own children. Seeing her dad constantly left her torn inside.

She read Max's message with delight, and a big smile spread across her face. Always so gallant, not only had he taken care of dinner plans, he had also set up a small studio in his flat allowing Serena some space. She could use this space to draw, to paint, however she pleased. What an adorable friend he was. He read her mind as though she were transparent. After careful deliberation, her mind firmly made up, Serena would dig deep within her heart. Though evident her love for her friend was nothing but platonic, things were about to change. Even if she had to force sexual desire, she would try her level best to finally turn this friendship into a romance – after all, what could be more perfect than falling in love with your best friend?

ooooo

Serena squealed in delight. It felt as though she hadn't laughed so heartily in decades as she did in Max's company. Without the slightest effort, he managed to press all the right buttons. Successfully he predicted what she liked to eat, to drink, what would make her laugh, what made her cry. Given the many years since their separation, he had not lost his magic or his ability to read her thoughts and tap into her sentiments. Giggling in girly laughter, wiping away tears of amusement, Serena interrupted their joyous moment. Her serious chat could wait no longer.

'Oh, come on, serious is boring; let's have some tequila!'

Max clapped his hands together, searching for a waiter. This traditional conservative restaurant was probably not the best place for drunk and disorderly conduct. *'Monsieur! Entschuldigen Sie bitte!'* Luckily, with his voice still quiet and calm, they didn't attract much attention. Dramatic panoramic views of the lake surrounded by tall mountains fascinated the guests. Mesmerised, Serena too could not help but admire the beautiful scenery.

'No, listen to me, please, I want to discuss something with you that's been playing on my mind and refusing to go away,' insisted Serena.

'What is it?' A curious Max offered her his full attention. 'What's on your mind?'

Serena gave out a nervous laugh. The waiter approached. Max turned him away, committing himself fully to listening to her.

'It's a bit embarrassing.' She blushed. 'Erm a bit... er... a bit hard to articulate.'

'What's the matter?' He grinned, puzzled. 'I can't imagine what could be embarrassing and complicated between us.'

'I... I... I think we should spend the night together.' She shot him a quick stare, desperate not to miss his reaction.

Max's concentrated face suddenly creased into a frown. A wise, good man, the wrinkles on his face gave nothing away, only making him more interesting. 'Why?' he stroked his chin, careful not to avert his gaze away from her for a split second.

Horrified by his nonchalant response, Serena drew her own conclusions from his response. 'Don't you want to?'

'We spent the night together last night.'

'No, I mean spend the night together, as in properly, together... you know what I mean.' She stared at him, wounded like a bird flapping its wing, quite unable to fly.

After a quick pause, Max spoke. 'It's not that I don't want to, but I am not sure it's such a good idea. I don't know what we have to gain from it.'

'Shouldn't we try to find out?' Serena smiled apprehensively.

'I don't need to find out.'

'Okay... you're not making this easy for me.' Her face was red and jittery.

'I'm sorry, it's not my intention to hurt you. I just think it might not be a great idea for us to make a conscious decision of going down that route. If it were to happen naturally or even accidentally, that's another thing – it might even be nice – but to plan it might lead to disappointment.'

'But at least we would know!' Serena almost jumped down his throat.

'Know what?'

Serena hesitated. 'If we have a future together.'

Flabbergasted, Max had no answer.

He reached deep in his jacket pocket taking out his wallet.

'What are you doing?' Serena, unable to decipher his motives, felt knocked hard in confusion and disappointment. Mysteriously, he presented what appeared to be a photo, laying it gently on the table. He followed it with another photo, identical to the first one, and again laid it on the table. Slowly he turned over both the photos and left them face up for her to see. Dark shades of fear flashed across his face. Serena stared at the pictures. Her face, red and hardened, she croaked, 'Who are they?'

'My sons.'

While Serena had lived a gilded, mostly comfortable life across the pond in the US, Max had been busy. A professor of literature, his long days comprised lecturing young, beautiful women, amongst others, desperate to better their language skills, eager for his attention and to make his acquaintance. A respected senior lecturer, Max's career reigned supreme, without doubt, the most important thing in his life. Careful not to devastate it in any way, he had successfully managed to avoid any form of scandal, until Heidi, his ski instructor, decided she was bored with the slopes, preferring to go back to school to study literature.

'A gentleman doesn't kiss and tell, but she pursued me relentlessly. Beautiful as she was, I was not interested in any kind of relationship. Unfortunately, the more I rejected her, the more it became a game for her. Desperate to have me under any circumstance, she made it happen. Not once but twice.'

Serena, livid, demanded to know why he hadn't told her. 'I could hardly tell you while you were burying your father; that's the last time I saw you. I was actually going to tell you tonight, believe it or not.'

'You had plenty of chances to tell me; I cannot believe this.' Without a further word exchanged, Serena stormed out of the restaurant. Max had no choice but to let her go.

Zürich Central Station, one of the busiest train stations in the world, was an extraordinary place. Trains were departing to Spain, France, Italy, Austria, to name but a few. Unprepared, luggage packed in a frenzy before checking out of the hotel by her side, Serena nervously looked up at the large train timetable.

She had no idea where to go.

<u>10</u>

Gemma, surprised to find a WhatsApp from Harry's mother, called back immediately. A big fan of Harry's mother, Gemma consistently named Elizabeth as the woman she would most like to be in her later years.

'It's nothing serious. I just wanted to be certain Harry wasn't overworking. I'm really quite worried about him.'

Gemma sympathised with Elizabeth, and wondered if she should disclose the concerns senior partners in the office had been sharing amongst themselves. Malicious gossip had started circulating: Harry hadn't been himself recently. Gemma agreed with Elizabeth: a holiday would do Harry the world of good. Harry, however, unfortunately could not be persuaded. He opposed the idea outright, even though he had previously decided to take the time out and go with Laura. He felt helpless and insecure with the recent happenings in his life. Taking a week off would now be counterproductive. When Harry had received his early-onset Alzheimer's diagnosis, his world had turned upside down; he knew then his happy, relaxed life would never be the same again. Adding the divorce to that, time off from work was as effective as a hole in the head.

'I'm sorry, Mum, I think it's a very bad idea; I simply won't manage.'

'Rubbish!' snapped Elizabeth. 'I spoke to Gemma; she checked your diary thoroughly and assured me nothing was outstanding or immediate that couldn't wait. In fact, she even encouraged me to take you away; she herself thinks it will do you good.'

'I won't be able to relax, and it will be a waste of money.'

'It's my treat. You don't have to worry about the money. I will pay. I've spoken to your dad, and he, too, feels he needs a break after everything he's been through. By the way, does the school know about your wife's decision?'

'No, I haven't told them. I haven't told the kids either; I am sure Laura has, but they haven't said anything to me, and I don't know what to say to them. In a way I'm relieved they haven't mentioned it. I've no idea how to handle any of this.'

'Well, that's why the holiday is a great idea: we sit them down and tell them together. And if Eric and I are both there, they will at least understand they are not being abandoned; everything is the same, just that Mummy and Daddy will no longer live together.'

'I've decided to fight for custody.'

Elizabeth paused. She expected her son to fight for custody of his children, but how was he going to cope? Did she have the strength and patience to step up every time he needed her because essentially it would probably be her that would be spending the most time with them?

Elizabeth's silence troubled Harry. 'Why are you silent?'

'I'm thinking…'

Harry wished he had FaceTimed her instead of an audio call. 'You think it's a bad idea and I shouldn't fight for custody?'

'I think you should *think* before you say or do anything.'

'I don't need this. I'll speak to you later.' Harry slammed the phone down, holding his head in his hands in despair. Even his mother wasn't on his side any more.

Deeply concerned for her son, and perturbed by Laura's actions, Elizabeth wasted no time in writing a message to Laura requesting a meeting. The sudden want of a divorce just out of the blue; it made no sense. What was Laura up to?

Can we please meet? she typed on her iPhone.

I'm sorry I'm extremely busy with work. Happy to discuss on the phone, came the answer. Elizabeth barely took her finger away from the keyboard. She sniggered at Laura's response, not bothering to dignify it with a reply of her own, knowing it would inevitably lead to a fight.

Elizabeth proceeded to book the holiday regardless, with Harry's flights purposely left flexible. To her relief, the school reacted with support, even encouraging a short break for the children on compassionate grounds, and it came as no surprise that Laura had already informed the school that she and Harry were on the path to a divorce and that the children undoubtedly would be remaining with her. Wreaking mild vengeance, Elizabeth wrote another message to her soon-to-be ex-daughter-in-law.

Harry, as you can imagine, is going out of his mind. It breaks my heart to see my son in so much pain. I have organised a family holiday for a week to help him deal with things. Eric and I will take the children. I have spoken to the school; they told me they already know about your plans, and therefore were supportive of the holiday. Harry's ticket is also booked, awaiting confirmation from him. Both children will have school work plus their homework with them; they will not miss anything. Elizabeth.

I'm sorry – you did what? Laura shot back, fast as a bullet.

Here we go, thought Elizabeth.

Yes, that's right. The school is very supportive.

Laura responded: *You are taking my kids on holiday during school term without discussing it with me first, and you are discussing my private life with the school teachers? Have you lost your mind? Absolutely not.*

If you care in the slightest about Harry, or at least your kids, you will not obstruct me. Harry needs this time to explain the situation to them calmly; he is worried out of his mind thanks to you.

Laura read Elizabeth's latest message with fury. Every word stabbed her like a knife. The cheek of this battleaxe. How dare she!

PS, I am not going behind your back, I was going to tell you. If you have a shred of decency, you will step back and allow Harry this time before the storm starts.

Why didn't Harry have the guts to tell me this himself? Laura typed back.

Harry has refused to go.

Despite her age, Elizabeth, an expert with technology, prided herself on just how fast she could type on an iPhone. What fun it was to write messages.

This was my idea. Gemma told me he was booking a holiday with you, but as you are not going, I thought we would go instead. Very likely Harry may refuse.

Lie! Of course, he knows, came the response from Laura.

If you prefer to go with him and sort things out, we can all stay behind and look after the kids.

I've made up my mind, Laura responded.

Fine. So have we. Let us go in peace, and don't deprive the kids of time with their father before their entire world gets torn apart.

Fine, go ahead. Please inform your son not to fight me for custody. My children need their mother. We can be amicable and grown-up about all this. He can have as much time as he wants with them. If he fights me, he will lose. It is not worth it.

Elizabeth typed back. *I will relay your message. You should be aware that Harry has his own mind; he doesn't listen to me. And also please try to understand his predicament. These last couple of weeks have not been easy for him, and this bombshell of yours is the last thing he expected.*

Do you think he should have custody? Laura typed.

This is not my fight. My job is to support my son and make sure my grandchildren are safe and protected.

And who do you think can best provide them that safety and protection?

I will relay your message – you have my word, replied Elizabeth.

ooooo

Allowing instinct to govern her actions, Serena found herself sitting comfortably in the first-class cabin of an express train to Milan. What other choice did she have right now but to try and relax and obliterate the last few days from her over-exhaustive imagination? Looking forward, with no travel arrangements in place, and not knowing a soul in Italy, some decisions had to be made. *They can wait*, she told herself, *I will decide once I arrive. Let me enjoy these three peaceful hours.*

Buzzing to the point of explosion, endless messages from Max battered Serena's phone. Determined to be heard, he continued to write relentlessly, much to her annoyance. What had she honestly expected? Why was she so shocked? Wasn't it the most normal thing in the world that he would have children, lovers, friends? Storming out in that childish, aggressive fashion was very unfair, and rather cruel.

No longer able to bear or hear the constant vibrations of the phone, she succumbed. Partly upset, partly curious, what was his explanation? A blatant kick in the teeth, how did he plan to make amends for this? Reluctantly, she read his messages. Ignore them as she might, she knew it wasn't in him her disappointment lay, but within herself. Max had only done what everyone else would do, the most natural thing in the world at his age. He had two beautiful children. *The irony of it*, thought Serena. *Here I am, desperate to give birth and have my own children, and here is a man who absolutely doesn't want children, yet he is blessed with not just one, but two beautiful kids.* The simple tragedy of the matter was nothing if not laughable. Unable to even hold down a relationship, Serena could hardly dream of having children right now.

'He could have told me earlier,' she muttered under her breath. 'What a coward. Perhaps I would have even liked to meet them. Did he purposely hide this from me? Perhaps he's a bit embarrassed; surely it must be complicated. He's not married to her, they are not in a relationship, and the kids looked relatively similar in age.' Was there even more to the story?

Max continued to message her profusely, his tone harshening more and more with each message. She responded.

Not upset, have some things that need attention. All good, please give me some space. Will write soon. Sorry.

There, that should quieten him down. Just like that she put paid to it, simply and casually. There was no need to convey to him the depths of her despair; what was the point? It couldn't possibly get any more embarrassing or awkward.

Where are you? responded Max immediately.

On a train, tired. Need to sleep. No more messages, please :-)

And just like that, nothing. At her request, he stopped writing. Serena closed her eyes, hoping to sleep, fresh for her endeavours. Though a light sleeper, she was able to fall asleep almost everywhere, despite the noise.

Wrapped in a pale cashmere scarf, safe and secure, far away from bad news, Serena, just about to fall asleep, made herself thoroughly comfortable in her seat. Time would certainly fly by now. A high-speed train, reasonably quiet, no disturbances. Perfection, she grinned to herself, content.

Suddenly, she awoke in a frenzy.

'I saw you stare at her. The minute I closed my eyes, you were gawping at her, don't lie to me! You men; you are all the same. I feel like ripping the bitch's eyes out!'

If there was one thing capable of disrupting Serena's sleep, it was the sound of shrieking jealousy.

'You are crazy! I wasn't looking at her. Calm down.'

I must be in Italy. Serena curled her lip, still fatigued, staring out of the window. She had missed her opportunity to sleep. She hoped not to have been the cause of this drama. As innocent as she was, she possessed the uncanny ability to create fights between couples, no matter how desperately in love they were. Keen to maintain distance from even the mere possibility of dilemmas or misunderstandings, she stared blankly out of the window, poems by Pierre de Ronsard in her hand.

The possibility of sleep no longer an option, the events of the night before continued to unfold in front of her, as though stripping her of her clothes. Fighting hard to keep her spirits up, she felt drained and empty. Resisting the forever impending question of 'what next?' she felt her eyes swell up; had she been in the confines of her own home, she would have cried. Deep down inside herself, she felt frustration and a tremendous amount of self-pity. Her vacation had not gone to plan, and now she was on a train heading to nowhere, unsure where she would end up and what her plans were. Burying her father had left her empty with a massive hole in her heart; she had lost her innocence, and her carefree lifestyle had turned to paranoia and uncertainty. She wanted nothing more than to beat this insecurity, to find someone to come and fix the wounds. She missed her girlish naïvety: it had been taken away from her very prematurely. Not quite yet ready to become a responsible, grown-up woman, she desperately wanted to smile again.

As the train drew closer to its final destination, Serena booked herself a night's stay in Milan; the rest could wait, even though Tuscany seemed like a good place to settle for a while. Countless friendly passengers offered to help with her bags while disembarking from the train. Not accustomed to such friendly surroundings, she welcomed the kind gestures, partially suspicious, partially humoured by the relaxed attitude and attention. It was a stark contrast from Switzerland. Encouraged, she felt a sense of comfort: not all was lost. There was still hope. She strode along the platform happily, welcoming the attention; there was nothing wrong with a confidence boost every now and then.

Settling into her luxurious, spacious suite, the time for her next challenge had presented itself. No longer able to put it off, she sought deep inside herself; she did have the courage. She was brave enough. She, too, was able to stand in solidarity with her sisters, the hundreds of wonderful single women. She, too, could join a dating site. The next challenge was navigating through them. It was a world as alien to her as a desert to a sea creature; she wasn't sure what to expect.

Ten minutes of confused surfing, puzzled facial expressions, and a few laughs later, the mysterious world of online dating continued to be deeply enigmatic. 'Fabrizzio the Flying Casanova' or 'Donatello's David' were probably not going to be suitable. Unfortunately the dating apps were destined to be deleted with the same speed as they were downloaded, causing her to give up. Italy, she deemed, was the very last place on earth to seek romance.

The next challenge came in the shape of dinner. Should she order room service and hide from the world, or brave it and dine in the open restaurant alone? Already daunted by endless challenges, she felt defeated: surely there was an easier option? Pasta and a soppy romcom in the room surely made things far more effortless, not to mention painless.

'Such a cowardly route!' she shouted out loud, lying on the bed challenging herself. In a foreign country and in a city so spectacular, yet she was about to resort to dining in the confines of her room all alone, and experience none of the greatness the city had to offer. She had only one night here; surely she should make the most of it? 'Anthropophobia is defined as a fear of people,' according to Google.

'Hmm...' she sighed to herself. 'Is that what I have? Do I? No, I don't.' The room service menu clearly visible, clad in its dark leather cover, lay on the coffee table. She could already predict what it had to offer.

The hotel restaurants, on the other hand, seemed far more inviting and beautifully decadent. Classy mahogany furniture mounted in rich, opulent colours, soft, dim lighting, mesmerising romantic background music; what a shame it would be to miss out on such pleasures. Shouldn't she throw on a nice dress and brave it? She could always request a table at the back, away from prying eyes, and simply hide. If the worst came to the worst, her laptop could act as her fall back: whenever it got too uncomfortable, she could bury herself behind her screen. Serena lay on the bed in her bathrobe, humming and daydreaming, her skin still glowing from a hot shower. Finally, she began to feel relaxed and jovial. Even the hotel magazines offered something for everyone. The list of art galleries, museums and theatres fascinated her; she could sit and read these the whole day long.

Suddenly disturbed by the doorbell, she swung open the door timidly, still in her bathrobe.

'Good heavens' she whispered in amazement at the sight of a smiling bellboy holding up an ice bucket and a bottle distinctly visible as Champagne.

'For you, Signorina.' The bellboy proceeded to enter the room. 'Posso... May I?' he asked barging in.

'Is... er... that for me?'

'*Si, Signorina.*' He took the bottle of Dom Pérignon out of the bucket and began to pour her a glass.

'I don't remember ordering that.'

'A gentleman in the hotel asked me to bring it for you, Madame.'

'May I ask who?' Giddy with excitement, Serena was secretly overjoyed. At least someone was thinking of her. She didn't care whom it was from; she would make it her mission to thoroughly enjoy every sip. The timing was perfect.

'There is a note. Please.' The bellboy handed her a small envelope, bowed his head slightly, and left her in peace.

May I be so bold as to beg your company for dinner tonight?

'Yes, you may.' Serena muttered, and smiled humorously. Convinced she would be dining with a freak or a degenerate, she at least felt relieved not to have to dine alone in her room. Some company is better than no company. Besides, at least there would now be an excuse to get dressed and have someone to talk to. She could always leave after the first course if it was terrible; all she had to do was to get into the lift. Of course, there was also the slight possibility that he wasn't a freak or a degenerate. Perhaps he was a charming, dashing gentleman. Who knows, he might be someone fun and exciting. She marvelled at this thought, looking for clues in the note.

Lo and behold, at the bottom right-hand corner a phone number, clearly visible, caught her attention. Serena pondered a little, impatient to know more, but how? If she wrote from her mobile, he would have her number; if she called from the hotel phone, she would be obliged to speak with him: dilemma, what to do?

Ah, the concierge, of course! She smiled, excited.

Dinner was set at eight o'clock downstairs in the main restaurant. Though she tried to act responsibly, somewhat restraining her feelings, it was hard to deny that she suddenly felt alive with excitement. Just to be noticed was the greatest pleasure. Reprimanding herself amidst the furore, she resorted to drinking slowly. After all, he could be a serial killer or equally something sinister.

Unsure how she felt about her date, she scrambled through her suitcase, undecided how to dress. Should she go the elegant route, should she be sexy, should she look formal, should she look casual? Unfamiliar with the dating game, a clueless Serena examined her semi-naked body in the mirror. Fortunately, she could dress however she pleased; nothing could go wrong. She stared at her reflection in amazement: her long, tanned legs were further elongated by the very flattering mirror. Given that she knew nothing about this man's identity, she decided it was best to remain conservative.

Just at that point, a curious thought crossed her mind: *what if it wasn't a man?* What if it was a woman who'd requested the pleasure of her company? Though not bi-curious, the thought was endearing; how much fun would it be to spend a wonderful evening with a beautiful, intelligent woman? Serena craved female company; her mother, long gone and in such desperate circumstances. Never again had she encountered another female she could truly befriend.

Neatly folded in the corner of the carefully packed suitcase, a gorgeous piece of silk caught her eye. Not recognising it immediately, she carefully pulled it out: bright white and soft to the touch, it opened into the perfect halter neck dress. Never worn before, it seemed like the perfect choice for this mysterious occasion. She poured her slender body effortlessly into the dress. There was no doubt it was tailor-made with her in mind.

She grabbed her shawl, dabbed on her favourite scent, and courageously walked out of the door, momentarily pausing her thoughts. The Champagne had taken effect, the knot in her stomach was rather palpable. She assumed her most composed posture, feeling relatively at ease. Determined to navigate her way around the restaurant confidently, she wished he would just pop up. How embarrassing it was walking around aimlessly; how much she wished to turn around and march straight back to her room.

'*Buona serra, Signorina,*' the maître d' bowed his head, his voice loud and deep

'*Buona serra*,' she squeaked. '*Io sono…*'– stuck at 'I am,' she had a temporary memory block, hardly able to find the words to complete her Italian sentence. Smiling uncomfortably, she immediately noticed a distinctive, almost familiar, figure rising from his seat, obviously looking in her direction. Thanking the maître d', as he continued to speak, she confidently strode towards the man with the salt and pepper George Clooney hair. His expressive eyes were noticeable from the entrance. The maître d' followed her closely, almost running and trying to keep up with her, and then promptly pulling a chair out for her. Her date hadn't stopped smiling since he'd caught sight of her. The entire restaurant watched spellbound as she glided towards this very handsome man. What were the dynamics between these two gorgeous people?

'I'm so happy you could make it.' He sat down once she was comfortable.

'Thank you for the Champagne.'

'You're welcome.' He smiled and bowed his head. 'I hope you enjoyed it?'

'I did, yes. I don't really drink, but it was so good I drank almost half of it.'

'Perfect.'

'It's the only reason I had the courage to accept your invitation.' She smiled nervously.

'I should have sent two bottles.' He smiled. She blushed. 'I took a risk and ordered us some drinks. I took a wild guess what you might like; I hope that's okay?'

'Yes, it's fine. Thank you.' Two peach Bellinis were waiting on the table.

'Shall we?' he offered her a glass.

'Shall we introduce ourselves first?' she asked, aware they were in full view of the whole restaurant, still watching, fascinated.

'Of course. Apologies. I'm Mathias. It's nice to meet you.' He offered her his hand, noticing her hands were cold and trembling.

'Serena,' she whispered. Her voice was barely audible. She cleared her throat, raising her voice slightly. 'I'm Serena,' she repeated anxiously, her knees weak and helpless.

'Serena, shall we have a little drink? Cheers.'

Hands still trembling, she barely sipped her drink, following it immediately with a large sip of water as though she were about to choke.

Mathias, immediately recognising how uncomfortable Serena was, spoke softly. 'You know, I nearly didn't get on that plane today; I was going to send a colleague here instead. I am so glad I changed my mind.'

'Where do you live?'

'Paris. And you?'

'Chicago.'

'Ah, so you are American.'

'Sort of.' She smiled, timidly. He watched her attentively.

'What are you doing in Milan?'

'I'm... well, I'm... actually, I don't know. I wasn't really meant to be here. I was visiting a friend in Zurich, then decided to head to Tuscany, and stopped here for the night to break up the journey,' Serena jittered anxiously.

How she wished she had remained in her room, far away from this confrontation. She grabbed her drink, this time taking a large sip. Mathias smiled sweetly at her; she felt a bit more at ease. *He must know I am uncomfortable.* He gazed at her unreservedly; she took the chance to return his gaze; it was incredible how handsome he was. How could that be possible? What were the chances her blind date could be such a hunk? Was luck finally on her side, or were her eyes playing a trick on her? This must be an illusion … Or maybe she was drunk.

'Are you travelling alone?'

'Yes.' She nodded. 'I do everything alone.'

Tactfully, Mathias changed the subject. 'Are you hungry? I bet you didn't eat lunch, did you?'

'Actually, no, I didn't, and, yes, I'm starving.'

'What would you like to eat, Serena?' His accent was strong, but not easily placeable. Mathias, the absolute fantasy of women, exuded raw masculinity. Mildly mannered, he spoke with an air of authority yet kindly. His impeccable presentation clearly pointed to a background of wealth. Very quickly, he began to appeal to Serena, much more than she cared to notice. Slowly she started to feel comfortable in his presence.

'I think I will have the sea bass.'

'Great choice. I will have the steak.' The maître d', waiting patiently to attend to them, acted as though they were his only customers.

'Would you like to stay with the Champagne or order some wine, Signor Leistra?'

'We will stick to the Champagne for now. Thank you, Antonio.'

'Oh, so you're on a first-name basis?'

Mathias smiled. 'Yes, I always stay here when I come to Milan.'

'What do you do?'

'I work in a bank. Nothing exciting, I'm afraid. You, what do you do?'

'I'm unemployed.'

'Really, how fascinating. That's amazing. Good for you. I really admire unemployed people. It's the best way to be; nobody should have to work in my opinion. Do you want a job? Do you want to work in a bank?' He laughed.

'No, thank you. I hate finance!'

'So do I. I hate finance too, but sadly somebody has to do it. So, you are just travelling, freely, deciding as you go? No commitment, just young and beautiful.'

'That sounds far more glamorous than it actually is. I'm probably going to spend a few days in Tuscany, lie on a beach for a few days, then head back to Chicago.'

'Are you meeting someone in Tuscany?'

'No. No, I'm not. I don't have anyone to meet. I'm just going to take it easy, do a bit of painting if I happen to find some paints and canvases on my travels, visit a few beaches. Relax a little. Things haven't worked out according to the way I planned.'

'Come to France. We have nice beaches there.'

She smiled. 'Maybe I will. Are you French?'

'No. I'm South African. My parents moved to France many years ago for my dad's job. Then, when they had the option to return, my sister had exams so we just stayed. I love Paris, but I'm nothing like the typical Parisian. Not at all.'

He seemed very Parisian to Serena. He poured her another glass of Champagne.

'How many drinks have you got lined up?'

'Just the one bottle. I'm not trying to get you drunk, I promise. You can stop whenever you want. If you want to.'

'No, it's fine. I'm not really much of a drinker. I've just recently discovered it, actually. It seems quite fun, but I don't want to drink too much.' She smiled. Her eyes sparkled. 'It just feels as if you have many bottles hidden away under the table or something.' They both laughed.

'That makes me sound like a predator,' Mathias said, bashfully.

Other diners continued to glance in their direction every so often, excited to see what would happen next.

'I'm serious. You can come to France any time you want.'

'Thank you.'

The food arrived.

'Please eat,' Mathias continued. 'You must be starving. There is nothing more satisfying than watching a young lady eat and enjoy her meal.'

'I love eating. In fact, I eat far too much.'

'I strongly doubt that.'

'So, tell me,' Serena put her cutlery down, 'where did you spot me?'

'When you were checking in. I was sitting at the bar on the phone. My back was turned so you couldn't see me.'

'How did you see me?'

'I have eyes at the back of my head.'

'How did you know I was going to accept your invitation?'

'I didn't.' Mathias shook his head, reassuring her, wiping his mouth with his napkin. 'I had nothing to lose.' He paused. 'I don't think you realise what effect you have on people. When you walked into the hotel, everyone stopped, almost breathless. All eyes were on you. The waiters, the staff; everyone saw and noticed you.'

Serena listened. *Was he over-exaggerating a tad?* She knew she was nice looking, but so were millions of other women. Luckily, she didn't take herself too seriously; her humility and positive approach to life rendered her calm and balanced, at least as far as her appearance was concerned.

'You were alone, so I thought I might ask you to dinner. The worst you could do was refuse; besides, you didn't know who I was. I had nothing to lose.

'Do you invite every pretty girl you see to dinner?'

'Now, yes.' He smiled facetiously.

'What does that mean?'

'Now that I'm free. I'm going through a very messy, not to mention costly, divorce, unfortunately.'

Another complicated man. Serena felt deflated and irritated.

'I've suddenly lost my appetite,' she mumbled, inaudibly.

'I know it's the most unfortunate boring subject, and terrible dinner conversation. I just want to be honest.'

'It's fine. You don't owe me an explanation.'

'It's the least I can do.'

'Really, you don't.'

'Are you annoyed? I'm sorry if this is not what you want to hear.'

'Honestly, I prefer you lie.'

'You don't mean that.'

Just when she'd started to feel comfortable, he had to come out with that! The last thing she needed was another man with baggage in a tricky situation. 'I'm a bit bored with complicated people.'

'I'm sorry. I understand.'

'No, you don't.'

'Serena, please.'

'Let's eat quickly, please. Sorry but I feel a bit tired, and I have a headache coming on. If you don't mind, I would like to go back to my room.'

Mathias wished he hadn't mentioned his pending divorce. Serena did not attempt to hide her disdain for this subject, openly allowing him to notice her fresh wounds.

'I'm sorry you are not feeling well; is there something I can do?'

'No, thank you.'

'If you want to or need to go, I will not insist you stay. I don't want you to be uncomfortable. I promise I will let you go, just...' he smiled broadly. 'The soufflé here is incredibly good. Won't you stay and just quickly try it?'

'I will order it to my room.'

'I can bring it to you.'

'No! Thank you.'

'Serena, please, listen to me. I know it's not ideal, but I am going through a divorce. I am not married. I am not betraying my wife or my mistress. I am going to be single very soon.'

Serena stared at him with sad and distant eyes.

He smiled at her. 'Joke. I don't have a mistress.' This was the first lie he'd told her. Mathias did have a mistress; he also had a casual girlfriend, as many men in Paris seemed to have. This, however, seemed not to be the reason for the divorce. 'My wife is divorcing me. She doesn't want to be married to me any longer.'

'Because you have been unfaithful!' Serena snapped at him accusingly.

'No. She was.' Serena shot him a sarcastic, pained look. 'She has been having an affair with her girlfriend for two years.'

Lost for words, Serena, dumbfounded, tried to understand what he had just said.

'Her *girlfriend?*'

'Yes. Our twelve-year-old son's music teacher.'

'Oh, why are you all so complicated? Why do you all have to lead such perplexing, problematic lives? I don't understand.'

'I'm trying not to be,' Mathias insisted defensively. 'I'm doing everything I can to save our marriage. I even told her she can continue seeing her girlfriend, but stay married to me so our kids can still live with both parents and continue their lives as normal, but she wants to marry her girlfriend and live with her.'

'I am sick of people with complicated, troublesome relationships. I don't want that in my life.'

'You've had enough, eh?'

'Yes. It was really nice to meet you. Thank you for dinner. It was lovely. I have to go. Goodbye.'

The maître d' ran to the table. 'Is everything okay, Madame?'

'Yes. I feel tired, I'm going to my room.' Not wanting to court further attention, Serena tried to whisper, but her frustrations were palpable for all to see. 'Thank you for the meal, it was delicious,' she repeated, wishing she could run away without fuss.

People in the restaurant were still mesmerised and continued to watch her with bated breath.

'What is she doing?' some of them could be heard whispering.

Mathias, defeated, could only watch helplessly as his date left the table, sauntering out of the restaurant till she disappeared from view. He paid the bill, but remained seated, motionless. 'Hmm... that wasn't meant to end this way,' he mumbled to himself, raising his eyebrows, oblivious to others around him who seemed to be watching him curiously.

The maître d' looked at him with the same powerless look in his eyes. 'I need to let her go.' Mathias lamented out loud.

'I understand, sir. I hope she is not sad. She is a beautiful lady.'

'Yes, Antonio, she is. She is very beautiful.' Mathias smiled weakly, hoping to drown his sorrows in a Cognac, which he knocked back as he got up to leave. From the corner of his eye, he noticed people watching both him and Serena as she disappeared through the big wooden doors.

'Go after her,' an old lady on the next table whispered to him.

'She is not mine!'

'Make her yours!' instructed the old lady's husband.

Mathias smiled, as though reflecting. 'Okay, I will go now.'

'Let us know what happens,' the old lady said as she winked at him, speaking in Italian.

Serena sank into her armchair and kicked off her heels. The steam from the kettle circled the spacious suite.

'Another complication,' she muttered. 'I just can't seem to escape them. I wish I had stuck to camomile tea and TV; it's so much easier.' She checked her phone; no messages. 'Nobody loves me. Nobody cares about me. All alone in this world, poor old me.' She held her mirror and slowly she began to remove her mascara, which seemed to weigh her down along with everything else. Her face appeared dull, as though it had taken a beating. She felt stupid and deflated, wishing she hadn't bothered going to supper.

'Right. What shall I watch?' she said out loud, trying to avoid thinking about her unsuccessful dinner date.

Just as she was about to remove her lipstick, she heard a loud knock on the door. She ignored it and continued. The knock got louder. She ignored it again. The knock now sounded like a heavy punch. She walked to the door and pulled it open forcefully.

'I brought you the soufflé...' Mathias offered her a small pretty box wrapped in red ribbon. His face pursed in an apologetic pout, he looked straight into her eyes.

'I don't want your soufflé.'

'Yes, you do. It's delicious.'

'No, I don't.'

'Can I please come in for a second?'

'No.'

'Please.'

'No.'

Mathias pushed open the door and barged in. 'I just need five minutes and I promise I will go after that, and then you won't have to see me ever again. I promise; just give me a few minutes. Can I sit down?'

'Do what you want. I'm getting ready for bed. I don't want to listen to anything you have to say.'

'What did I do wrong? What's my crime? Why are you so upset with me? I didn't lie to you, I didn't pretend. I told you everything straight away. Everything.'

Mathias blocked her from going to the bathroom, gently grabbing her hand. Compelled to listen to him, she felt his breath on her face, again noticing how pleasing to the eye he was. His voice was convincing and encouraging. 'I can't help that I am getting divorced. Isn't that a good thing? It means I am going to be free. I am already free. My ex and I don't even live in the same house. I am free. What is there to be so angry about?' he asked puzzled, as he gently pulled her close to him.

She didn't resist. 'What do you want?'

'I don't want you to be angry with me. I don't deserve it.'

'Why did the waiter know your name? Why did they tell you which room I was in? Why does everyone know you so well?'

Mathias shook his head, looking confused.

'Shall I tell you why? It's because you do this all the time. You see a girl and you prey on her. Then, when you get what you want, you probably dump her, leave and run back to your wife. I am not going to let you do that to me. I'm much better off alone.'

Serena's comments shocked Mathias. They were pretty harsh accusations, and might very well have been true, but in his case, they weren't. She knew nothing about him; she should perhaps hold off on her judgement. Poor girl; what on earth had she experienced to make her so bitter?

'You can't really think that. You can't think me so low. You don't know me; what have I done to give you that impression?'

They stared into each other's eyes. She with fury, he with passion.

'Okay, my dear, I apologise. I will not take up any more of your time.' He headed to the door, opened it and turned back. 'I told you I was getting a divorce because my wife was unfaithful. I haven't been in love with her for over ten years, yet I stayed with her, and it's only in the last year or so that I've been playing around since I found out she was doing the same. I work in a bank; I am surrounded by beautiful women all the time, but I still prioritised a loveless marriage for the sake of my kids. My kids, who, by the way, hate me, because their mother has poisoned their minds against me. Now you hate me too. There is no point. I tried. Take care of yourself.'

Serena slammed the door before he could turn his back. She leaned against the door, sad and wounded. Unsure what she was doing, in mad haste, she flung open the door - he was gone. With bare feet she crept out, but there was no sign of him; all she could hear was the sound of the lift.

Mechanically, without emotion, she dragged herself back to her room. Bitterly disappointed with her evening, she began to sob, feeling terribly sorry for herself. Such a promising start, how could such a lovely evening end so abruptly, so painfully? Why did she have to be so melodramatic? Why had she treated him with such contempt? He was so charming, so gallant; he'd tried so hard and she'd ruined it. A fun, charming, handsome man, the whole restaurant watching in awe, and it had ended like this, and it was all her fault.

'What have I done?' she sobbed louder. What a pity. What a mistake she had made. Why did she always overreact? She would probably never see him again. She lay on the sofa wondering if she would ever meet anyone else.

A few hours of turning and tossing in bed, unable to rest, her mind continued to speed in every direction. Had she blown it? Was she on her way to becoming a sad, lonely old spinster like those terribly unfortunate ladies her parents felt so sorry for all those years ago? The thought was frightening. She must do everything possible to avoid that. This must not be her fate, not ever. *Mathias must think me such a child*, she lamented. Buried under the blanket, she hoped to erase this unfortunate evening from her mind; perhaps if she hid deeper, it would all go away.

Suddenly she leapt out of bed, as if she'd had an electric shock, flicked the light on in a panic and frantically began to search.

'Where did I put it? Where did I put it? Damn, where is it?' she repeated to herself, searching wildly around the room. 'Where on earth is it...? Where...? Where? It's got to be here somewhere, come on, show up. Where are you?' By a stroke of magic, under a pile of hotel magazines, there it was: Mathias's card and his phone number.

I'm sorry. Serena. She deleted it. *I'm sorry. Please forgive me. Will you be at breakfast?* No. No, that sounds silly; it has to be something else.

I had a lovely evening. I'm sorry I overreacted. Can I make it up to you? She read it out loud, she read it again and again. She looked at the text. She read it again. She hit send, without thinking further.

Serena crept back into bed; it was still early and she couldn't sleep. She checked her phone; he hadn't read the message. She put her phone away, face down. She tried to sleep again, she checked her phone again; nothing had changed. She had no new messages. Even Max had stopped writing. She really was her own worst enemy. Why couldn't she relax and try to be a bit more grown-up? Why did she always have to overthink? Why couldn't she let things run their natural course? In fact, ever since she'd met Harry, she had witnessed gradual changes in herself, further reinforced by Max's revelation.

Mental note to self, don't ever overreact again.

She ordered the most expensive whisky on the menu, yet felt sick looking at it. She tried to read her book, but couldn't concentrate. She put the TV on; no, not appealing. She tried to listen to an audiobook, but again she couldn't concentrate. Covering her eyes with an eyeshade, she tried to close her eyes firmly shut.

11

After much deliberation, Harry gave in, fully succumbing to his mother's insistence on his taking a holiday; he lacked the energy to fight over this with her. As of late, he'd had enough of fighting the women in his life. Elizabeth took care of all the arrangements; little remained for him to contest. 'Mummy knows best,' he told himself, going along with whatever she had planned to do. Elizabeth and Gemma, in control of the planning, had mutually worked everything out, deliberately not involving Harry. His only job was to get to the airport on time. He hadn't even bothered asking his mother or his PA for the exact itinerary: what was the point? He would only forget it, and then stress himself out trying to remember all the details, again and again, a futile exercise. He felt his memory, perception and balance had begun to worsen. No longer in control, he hardly knew if he was decaying for real or if he was greatly exaggerating his condition to himself.

Lacking the ability to determine fact from fiction, the one thing he was certain about was that something was happening to his mind. Something evil was compromising his memory and his understanding. It was just a matter of time before he deteriorated and slowly wasted away. More often than not, he found himself involved in basic conflicts of communication within himself. The only way to understand things was to thoroughly break down the information, practically reteach himself the ropes, as though he were educating one of his children. Keeping on top of his work schedule and the boys seemed to be taking its toll on him mentally. He knew he was overthinking, and the stress of the situation only succeeded in making things worse.

With only mild symptoms, the immediate need to disclose to the family could still be delayed, but at some point, they would need to know. How he dreaded that conversation. How do you tell your family that you have early-onset Alzheimer's? The embarrassment and the stigma. People would look at him as if he were a freak. Who has early-onset dementia? Did anyone know of anyone with such a bizarre disease? At his young age? People might feel compelled to speak to him slowly, as though he were a ninety year old. He cringed thinking about it. So many terrible things awaited him. People would probably feel the need to repeat themselves constantly, assuming he had forgotten what he was saying. And what if he became one of those people that repeats themselves; an Alzheimer's sufferer who asks the same question over and over again?

His mind drifted to that time in Seville, all those years ago, when he was with an ex-girlfriend, and her eighty-eight-year-old grandmother. The poor woman had been suffering from terrible dementia; in the space of five minutes, she had asked them eight times how and when they met. What if he became like that? Is that what he had to look forward to? Was that to become his fate? The grandmother had repeated the same question time and time again, becoming very irritating. Were people going to be irritated by him when he repeated the same question? At least this woman had an excuse; she was old. What was his excuse? He was not old. And what about his work? Were his working days numbered? How could they not be; he was behaving so irrationally at the office. He could feel people sneering behind his back. Harry's head spun, thinking about his career failing; nothing was as difficult as giving up his career. Even divorce wasn't as hard as a dead career at such a young age.

Reflecting on his marriage, he wondered if it was realistic to expect a marriage to last in this day and age. Whose marriage had actually lasted? Who was happily married? Even his parents' generation hadn't managed very well. Harry sighed in disappointment. He thought about Laura: was it really realistic that such a high-achieving powerhouse like her would have stayed with him forever? Bye-bye all hopes of further romance. Bye-bye all hopes of future happiness. Indeed, any kind of life. Bye-bye the normal world as we know it. Laura was probably the last woman he was ever going to be with. His life would be over in a matter of years. He should make a bucket list. Drowned amid his morbid thoughts, head floating in the clouds, Harry hardly noticed when Gemma strolled casually into his office.

'Harry? Oh my goodness!' She'd startled him. 'I'm sorry. Didn't you see me walk in?'

'No, I didn't. Sorry, I was miles away.'

'No problem. By the way, your flight is Sunday to Sunday, so you won't be leaving from the office. I've booked a large people carrier to take you all to the airport together.'

Harry frowned. 'Really? My mother told me I just had to leave the office and meet them there. I thought we were leaving on Friday.'

'Well, you would have been if you had stuck to the original itinerary that you were considering with Laura.'

'Okay…'

'We changed your destination from Majorca to Tuscany.'

'Tuscany? I don't want to go to Tuscany; can't we stick to Majorca? I prefer the Spanish to the Italians. I don't really like Italians.'

'Why not?'

'No reason. Actually, that's not true, I don't care. They are all the same. I really don't care about much at the moment, to be honest.'

'You think your wife is romancing an Italian, don't you?' Gemma smiled. 'Actually. I don't think she is. But even if she is, you mustn't hate the country because you think that.'

'I promise you that isn't the reason, and to be perfectly honest I don't care who my soon-to-be ex-wife romances. I just think the Spanish are more chilled than Italians. I've always preferred Spanish islands to Italian and Greek ones.'

'I'm sorry, but it's been booked. Your mother is a big fan of Tuscany; she told me they had their second honeymoon there. They were very happy.'

'Well, you know how that ended.'

'Also, availability wise, it was much better. Anyway, you will all have a wonderful time and the kids will love it. You are staying in a magnificent villa between the town and the beach; you won't even need to hire a car unless you do long trips.'

What a relief, sighed Harry. Driving had recently become quite a challenge, requiring extra attention and actual thought. Even his eyesight seemed to be playing tricks with him. He could swear his vision appeared blurred every now and then. Perhaps he should visit an optician? But maybe his eyesight was fine and he was working himself up for no reason at all.

'Which town?'

'Pietrasanta. It's beautiful. A bit commercial now, but still quite stunning: lots to do, lots to see, delicious food. You will love it.'

Uninterested in anything she had to say, Harry cleared his desk, checked his diary and decided he was done for the day. A holiday was the last thing he cared about right now. In fact, what perfect misery spending a whole week with the kids, his know-it-all mother and depressed father. Perhaps he should play along and then cancel at the last minute; they would understand and might even have a better time without him.

What a day; he was glad it was over. All he had to do now was mentally prepare himself for the next task: the big one; the crap one, the shitty awful one…

The taxi dropped him at the exact spot he had requested. Not moving, Harry could do nothing but stare at the building. He stood still, stuck to the ground, unable to move. What was he doing here? This wasn't for him. He glanced at his phone, then at his watch: he was punctual and on time. Someone was probably inside waiting to see him, to speak to him, to offer him advice. To reassure him, tell him it was not as bad as it seemed; that there were ways to cope. It was still early. It might never get aggressive.

There were so many things they could say to him. Shouldn't he go inside? Shouldn't he listen to what they had to say? It might be helpful; perhaps they could even tell him if it was actually real, or if he were really exaggerating it all. He could ask questions; he could learn. He might even meet others in the same boat. No, he wouldn't meet anyone else in the same position; there was no one else in this tragic position; he was the only one. He was the only sad creature suffering this terrible fate.

Harry hailed a black cab and directed it straight home. He looked back through the rear window and waved a mental goodbye to the Alzheimer's Society. He couldn't face it today. He postponed his meeting in his diary until after his holiday. He would certainly be more relaxed after the holiday. He would definitely go then. Yes, that would be a much better time to go. It's okay, no harm. It's only a couple of days; no big deal.

To Harry's relief, the next few days remained largely uneventful and unexciting, thoroughly pleasing him. Having developed a new-found love for boring and mundane, nothing excited Harry more than 'nothing' itself. Fortunately, he had established a stable routine with the kids and work, not to mention dedicating ample time to his daily sports routine, something he was slowly becoming obsessed with.

Having his family close by proved a godsend for Harry, frequently relying on their help. Jane brought her kids over whenever she could; even Jane's dreadful husband had taken to visiting Harry regularly, helping him to drown his sorrows. With everybody's help and a regular nanny, Harry could breathe again; never had he imagined he would appreciate and need his family so much. The comfort of having his family around provided him with the strength he thought he'd lost forever; however, was it enough to fight Laura for custody? Was he really able to cope? Thinking about his children broke his heart; they were both so young; how were they ever going to learn to cope with their parents living in separate houses? And God forbid if Laura got a new boyfriend. The thought of her new boyfriend repulsed him; he had to stop thinking about that; it would make him sick. Too much thinking drained Harry's mind; he felt his muscles strained and his back stiff and painful. He was stressed. Perhaps it really was time for a holiday.

ooooo

The day of the holiday arrived. Charlie and Ollie were overjoyed at the thought, especially as it meant missing school. Harry – astonished at how well they had accepted the story 'their mother was staying with *her* mother for a while' – could hardly believe his luck. Complaining, nagging kids was really the last thing he needed right now. Laura FaceTimed the children every day, speaking to them for hours. Though they missed her immensely, somehow they found peace within themselves and with each other, and continued as normal. Laura's move had possibly benefited the children, particularly Ollie. Ollie's behaviour had improved dramatically; he was suddenly much kinder to his little brother and generally much calmer and easier to be around.

Thankfully the holiday got off to a flying start. Harry sat with the kids on the plane while Elizabeth and Eric, forced to spend a lot of time together recently, began to get used to one another again. Elizabeth forgave his foolish escapade with Maria, and Eric, deeply ashamed of his actions, welcomed the chance to be in Elizabeth's company once again. The constant talk of sun, sand and swimming had overwhelmed the boys so intensely that they passed out just before they reached their sumptuous villa. Ceremoniously, Eric swung open the spectacular doors to the grand villa and magically the boys instantly woke up, the grown-ups almost as excited as the children.

Unable to contain himself, Charlie ran to the huge blue pool, which glistened as the sun shone bright, high above it. Ollie ran over to join his brother, elated.

'This is the biggest pool I've ever seen,' shouted Ollie.

'I want to swim. Now!' demanded Charlie.

'Tomorrow, my darlings.' Elizabeth pulled them both into the house and allowed them to run around upstairs, exploring all the rooms and trying to settle everyone into the house before the pool became the only subject of importance.

ooooo

Dr Raza sat in front of his patient, typically calm, emotionless, yet permanently amiable and pleasant. His full attention was geared to Laura, who sat facing him, bold and upright, very different from her first few visits. Her face was pale but less gaunt, her posture more assured, with her legs firmly crossed. It was almost inconceivable to the doctor that this was the same desperate woman he'd met just a few weeks ago. Only a fool could ignore her confidence and self-assurance. It pleased the doctor to see his patient back to what he could only assume she used to be before she first came to see him.

'How are you, Mrs Hoffman?' Dr Raza always addressed his patients formally at the beginning of each session until they told him to do otherwise.

'Soon to be Ms Johnson.' She smiled.

'How do you feel about that?'

'I feel great about it, Doctor.'

'Fantastic. I'm very glad to hear you feel happy.'

'Yes, I feel free. I am very fond of my soon-to-be ex-husband, but I don't love him. I don't love him the way a wife should love a husband, or how a husband deserves to be loved. I... I actually stopped loving him quite a while ago. I am what you might call "setting him free".'

'I believe that sentence ends something like, "and if they really love you, they will come back...",' the doctor said, smiling discreetly.

'No, there is no coming back.' Laura pursed her lips together, shaking her head. The doctor felt compelled to believe her, her steely gaze impenetrable. 'I don't make decisions just to "un-make" them again after a few months. I am a woman of my word. I like to be consistent.'

'That's a very good quality indeed. It's admirable to be consistent. Not many of us have that quality.'

'Let's change the subject, How are you, Doctor?'

'Fine. I am very well, thank you.'

'Do you ever get asked how you are?'

'Sometimes. Usually when people are diverting from the question I am asking, and don't want to answer my question.' He smiled.

'I am not diverting. I would like to know something about you. Do psychiatrists ever have personal, emotional problems?'

'Yes. We are human too. We have many, many problems.'

'How do you deal with them?'

'The same way as everyone else. We discuss, analyse, ask for help.'

'Do you have a therapist?' she teased.

'Yes, I do.' He laughed; if he found the question uncomfortable, he didn't show it. 'Psychiatrists usually make it a rule not to discuss themselves. We like to focus wholly on our clients. When you come to see me, it is all about you.'

Laura nodded in agreement; she wasn't going to learn anything about him today.

'How are things? How is your husband?'

'Harry? Oh, he didn't take the news of the divorce well, but he is fine. He is coping perfectly well with the kids without me. He even wants custody.'

'How do you feel about that?'

She let out a sarcastic, patronising laugh. 'He is setting himself up for a big fall. He will never get it. I will crush him in court.'

'Do you think he is a good father?'

'Yes, he is okay. He loves the kids. Like most men, he is not that great at the day-to-day stuff, but he is okay. He probably wouldn't win the Dad of the Year title, but he is okay.'

'Why do you think you fell out of love with him? Was it a recent thing?'

Laura was silent. She looked Dr Raza straight in the eye and spoke firmly. 'I don't feel the need to discuss this.'

'Okay. What would you like to discuss?'

'I don't know. I think I am done. I don't think I need to see you anymore.'

'If that's how you feel, that's wonderful.'

'I'm asking myself if there is anything else I need to discuss with you, and I can't think of anything. My therapy was never meant to be long term.'

'When will you next see the children?'

'After their holiday. Harry and his parents have taken them to Italy.'

The doctor looked surprised. 'That's nice. Don't they have school?'

'My very charming mother-in-law organised the whole thing. She probably wanted to kidnap my kids and run away with them.'

The doctor gave her a puzzled, questioning look. 'Is that true?'

'No. I mean she does whatever she wants, she... she plans things with my kids without telling me, like this holiday. It was all planned behind my back.' Angrily, Laura began to summarise the details.

'I think it's a great idea. The break might do everyone some good. Have you considered taking time out yourself?'

'I will, but not yet. Once the divorce comes through and I have my children, I, too, will take them on holiday. I will destroy my husband in court if he tries to oppose any of my plans.'

'Why do you want to "destroy" and "crush" your husband? Do you feel hurt by him?'

'I want to punish him! He stole so much of my time.'

'The time when you were married?'

'Yes.'

'How much time?'

'Probably the last five years.'

Dr Raza looked surprised. 'Have you been having problems for that long?'

Laura looked pensive. 'No, not problems. How shall I explain it? I neglected my career. I had two kids; it became all about them: the kids, Harry, the house. I took time off work. I neglected everything: myself, my career, I lagged behind my juniors, I lost a lot of my network, my contacts. Meanwhile, Harry excelled in his career, he became a senior partner, got the respect he craved, the right salary, while I dwindled and fell monumentally behind. He didn't have any sympathy or understanding; it was perfect for him. He wanted me to stay at home and be a housewife and mother. I shouldn't have listened; I should have put my career first. I put him and the kids first, and now I'm divorcing him and my career is crap. Excuse my French.'

'Did he keep you at home against your wish?'

'It's hard to say.' She stared into the distance, in deep thought. 'He should have encouraged me not to neglect my career. He should have understood that my career was just as important as his. Why didn't he take time out of his career and stay at home and look after the house and the kids? Why did I have to sacrifice my life, my career?'

'Is that what was arranged?'

'Nothing was arranged. It was just assumed I would stay home and look after the kids, and that's what I did. No questions asked.'

'Why didn't you tell Harry you wanted to go back to work and prioritise your career?'

'I didn't think about it at the time.'

'Do you think he would have stopped you?'

Laura thought about this question. 'Probably not. That's not the point. My career is dead and it's his fault!'

ooooo

Finally, after a struggle, Serena managed to fall asleep. It was an unsatisfactory, broken sleep, full of strange, bizarre dreams, which surprised her as the next morning she felt as fresh as a daisy. *The beauty of youth*, she assumed humorously. Instinctively, her first thought was to reach out and grab her phone, unsure of what she was expecting to see, but nevertheless hopeful. There was one message at 3.48 in the morning.

Enjoy your trip to Tuscany. Matt.

Her heart sank. Was it really him? Were last night's actions today's reality? Was it a case of water under the bridge already? An uncontrollable glimmer, an indefinable yearning for him stirred her emotions. His handsome face flashed back and forth in front of her eyes, the seductive way he'd gazed at her throughout the dinner, as though he saw right through her. But what a cold, distant message this was! Surely, he could have written something a tad more personal and kind? She mustn't take it personally, she told herself. It may have sounded cold, but there was nothing more to it. At least he responded; she had practically given up hope.

How she had longed to 'accidentally' bump into him at breakfast, or spot him roaming around some corner of the hotel. However, from his message it appeared as though there stood little chance of that happening, forcing her to face the possibility of perhaps never seeing him again. What a loss! Unbeknown to herself, subconsciously, she had built up tremendous excitement at the prospect of seeing him again; getting to know him could have been wonderful, but he had gone.

Disappointed, she opted for breakfast to be served in her room while organising a car to drive her to Tuscany. Now that she had lost the chance of bumping into him, she felt a desperate urge to be with him, aching to see him, to speak with him. Even though she barely knew him, she thought he was different to other men she had known; superior, somehow. Mature, grown-up, responsible, and oh, so refined. A true gentleman, comfortable in his skin. Very different from Max and Harry, who both seemed to have an edge.

Mathias was a man with nothing to prove, a man rich in experience, unfazed by any challenge life had to offer. Above all, his integrity impressed Serena. Though not happy with his story, at least he was upfront and he had hidden nothing. From the very beginning, he was open and transparent. She was the one who had messed things up, she had hurt his feelings, and he had run away from her. It was over before it started, and it was all her fault.

Seeking to forgive herself, she threw her belongings in her suitcase and made her way to Reception, ready to check out. The sooner she was out of the hotel, the sooner she could forget, burying this awful memory in the archive of her mind.

Without even checking her bill, she handed her black American Express card to the receptionist and waited impatiently for her car to arrive.

'Your car is outside, Madame. Let me escort you.' The porter carried her luggage and led her to a fancy silver Mercedes S-Class, glistening regally in the golden sun. Heaving a huge sigh of relief at the tinted windows, she couldn't wait to get in. With total privacy all the way, she could disappear and wallow in self-pity without anyone knowing. The minute the porter opened the car door, she dived in, head first. Then her heart missed a beat.

'Good morning!'

Serena opened her mouth to respond, but no sound came out.

'I got you a coffee.'

'Thank you,' she whispered quietly. Was she in the midst of a dream, a beautiful fantasy? Was he really here, in front of her? The smile on her face widened, as though her heart wanted to cry out in joy. She could hardly believe it. She blushed, elated. Could this be real? Overjoyed and bursting with emotion, she could hardly take her eyes off him; she dared not blink in case he disappeared again.

'What are you doing here?' She could have cried tears of joy.

'You need to go to Tuscany, right?'

'Yes.' She nodded. What delight she felt sitting next to him, looking at him, smelling him. None of it seemed real. Where did he appear from? Had he just stopped her from an endless journey of self-loathing?

'I will drive you there. Well, Philippo will drive you there. I will just keep you company.' He winked. 'Did you have breakfast?'

'Yes. I did, thanks.'

'I have some croissants here for you if you get hungry.'

Serena imagined grabbing him in her arms and kissing him passionately, and hanging on to him forever. His kind gesture reaffirmed she had over-exaggerated her feelings the night before. She had been wrong to be so judgemental. He seemed genuine. Right now, she adored him. He'd even brought her croissants! She wished to devour him.

'Do you know exactly where you are going, or should we just head towards Tuscany and you can decide when we get closer?'

'Let's do that for now.'

'Are you okay?'

'Yes, thank you.' She paused. 'Thank you for last night, thank you for this, thank you for everything. I'm... I am really sorry about last night. I overreacted.'

'Tell me to mind my own business by all means, but did something happen?'

'I lost my father a few months ago, then I broke up with my boyfriend, then, to top it all off, a few other things caught me by surprise that... I simply... I... hadn't anticipated... and ... and I didn't deal with them very well.'

Staring at her face, Mathias listened intently.

'I am... I'm very vulnerable at the moment.' She fought back her tears and took a deep breath. 'Everything gets to me. I take things far too seriously. I am constantly overreacting; I'm petrified of getting hurt.' She smiled tearfully. 'I will be okay. It's just... it's just all a bit raw at the moment.'

Mathias slowly stroked her hand with the tips of his fingers, withdrawing his touch a few seconds later, mindful not to over-impose himself.

'You started telling me your story and... and I panicked. All I could see before me were complications. I couldn't deal with it... I just felt as though I couldn't knowingly expose myself to another... another complicated situation. Again, I am sorry if I overreacted.'

'It's okay, I understand. You don't need to explain. It's all okay.' He squeezed her hand. 'There's just one thing I want you to know. I wasn't expecting anything from you. I wasn't trying to spend the night with you; that wasn't my intention at all. You are an extraordinarily beautiful woman, I was just enjoying being with you, sharing a meal with you; it was a pleasure just to look at you. You are absolutely right, my life is very complicated at the moment; even if I wanted to, I couldn't offer you anything. I would love us to spend time together, to experience things together, but I have no idea what will happen one day to the next.' Serena listened to him, the dulcet tones of his voice like drops of honey. There were no words to describe her happiness.

'You are one hundred per cent right to avoid complications; you deserve far better. No one should knowingly walk into a complicated situation if they can avoid it. My wife has one of the best divorce lawyers in the country; she wants everything and she will probably get it. My children don't talk to me. Mentally I am not ready for a serious relationship, and I don't have the time either.'

'Why did you invite me to dinner then?' Serena pouted, unsure of what to think. She wanted him to want her as she wanted him.

'Because you looked hungry.' He smiled.

'That's not funny,' she frowned at him playfully, doe-eyed.

Delicately, he stroked her face. 'You have beautiful skin. I could just touch your face all day long.'

'Answer my question.' Serena pressed his hand against her cheek.

'I told you. I saw you checking in. It's impossible to miss you. I thought I would take a chance and invite you to supper. I was sure you wouldn't accept; besides, you could have been married or meeting someone; I didn't know. You are gorgeous; any man would try their chances with you. I just saw you first. Actually, I was shocked when you came to dinner.'

'You knew I would come.'

'No, I didn't.'

'Would you have called someone else if I hadn't come?'

'Of course not. I had some work I was planning on doing at dinner. I was meeting friends later.'

'Where did you go?'

'To a club.'

Serena raised her eyebrows. 'Is that why you didn't respond till four in the morning?'

'Yes. Unfortunately, it turned out to be a very late night...' He closed his eyes, shaking his head in regret.

'Did you go home alone?'

He smiled cheekily. 'No, I didn't.'

She pushed his hand off her face.

'Ouch!' He laughed. 'I have some colleagues staying here in Milan; I went home with them. I wanted to be with you, but you kicked me out of your room, remember?' She looked away timidly.

'Don't you have work now?'

'Yes. I arranged a meeting in a bank in Florence at seven this morning so I could spend some time with you before I head back to Paris.'

'Are you flying back today?' she asked, palpably disappointed. No matter how hard she tried, it was impossible to hide her feelings.

'Yes.' He pulled her close hugging her casually. 'Would you like to see me again?' he teased.

'No, not really.' She smirked at him.

'Really?'

'Okay. Yes. Yes, it might be nice to see you again.'

'What about my "complications"?'

'It's fine. I shouldn't care, and actually they are none of my business. Besides, I live in Chicago,' she shrugged. 'We are hardly going to be able to meet casually for dinner and a movie whenever we feel like it. Complications are fine, providing I know what's going on.'

'How long are you going to stay in Europe?'

'I don't know. I don't have a return flight.'

'So you can stay as long as you want?' Mathias's mood changed, suddenly more animated.

'Well, yes.'

'Come to Paris!'

'Stay in Tuscany!'

'I can't.'

'Stay.'

'I can't.'

'I won't come to Paris.'

'How long are you going to stay in Tuscany, and where will you go after?'

'I have no clue. I wasn't even meant to be in Italy, I was supposed to stay in Switzerland.' Serena proceeded to explain her recent unfortunate experience with Max and why she left.

'How old are you, if you don't mind me asking?'

'Why?' Serena asked.

'I'm curious.'

'You think I am super immature, don't you?'

He smiled. 'Better immature than old and cynical.'

'I told you, I haven't really been myself for a while.'

'So, you have no concrete plans and you can be flexible…?'

'Yes.'

'Then come to Paris.'

'If you stay with me for a few nights in Tuscany.'

'I really can't.'

'Then I can't come to Paris.'

'You really are a child, aren't you! Tell me your age. I don't want to be accused of grooming a minor!'

She laughed. 'Relax. You won't get arrested... well, at least not for that!' Her eyes lit up as she giggled. Mathias, blinded by desire, struggled in vain to control himself as he pictured himself doing wonderful things to her. Easily the most irresistible thing he had seen in a long time, she was simply perfect.

'Have you decided where you're going yet?'

'No. Your driver can drop me somewhere in Florence. I'll be fine. As you can see, I am travelling lightly. I can get a taxi to somewhere, or stay one night in Florence.' She paused. 'And have dinner with a handsome stranger.' She looked at him from the corner of her eye provocatively.

Mathias nodded. 'Yes, you certainly can. You could do that every night if you so wished,' he agreed. Then he stopped. 'Hang on a minute.' Mathias took out his phone, looking concerned. She watched as his expression dulled. Frown lines appeared on his face, indicating the possibility he might be much older than he looked, or that he wasn't ageing very well. His deep tan, clear skin, pearly white teeth showed a man who undoubtedly took pleasure in his appearance. Perfectly groomed, the advantage of his age rendered him even more attractive. His green-blue eyes dazzled like the perfect blue of the sea. Serena watched as he typed; he felt her gazing at him, turning around to face her. His face calm. Serious. Full of lust. She drew closer to him, her lips quivering. He felt her warm, fragrant breath on his cheek. Mathias, still as a rock, as Serena edged closer, gazed down at her soft pink lips, while her nose gently brushed against his. Closing her eyes, as though in torment, gently she pulled away from him. He let her move herself away; she leant back and looked out of the window. Squeezing her thigh reassuringly, he continued on his phone.

She sat in silence looking out of the window. She had almost forgotten where she was. From the minute she saw Mathias, nothing else mattered; she felt no interest or desire to find out where she was going, or what she was planning to do. All that was important to her was right there with her. She felt herself drowning in an ocean of desire; his appeal and her lust for him was nothing she could describe or quantify.

'Serena,' he said, placing his hand gently on her jeans-clad leg. She turned to face him. 'Do you want to meet after my meeting?'

She nodded excitedly.

'We could have lunch, then my driver will drive you to a hotel.'

'What will you do after lunch?' she interrupted him.

'I have another meeting.'

'After that meeting?'

He paused as if in thought. His phone rang. 'Hello.' Serena looked away again. She wasn't going to touch that subject again. She took out her phone and began to search the internet. *Five-star hotels in Florence.* Mathias spoke in Spanish, a language Serena did not understand. She avoided looking at him. Clearly, he was a busy man.

'After that meeting...' he gently turned her head to face him. '... after that meeting, I will come to the hotel and stay with you.'

Serena flung her arms around him, hugging him with all her might. She placed her head on his shoulder, hoping to lose herself in him. The sweet smell of his scent and the warmth of his skin made her want to attach herself to him.

'That will be perfect,' she purred, pushing against him further as though she wanted to be with him forever. He held her tightly, fully understanding and sympathising with her desperation to be loved. Deep in his bones, he felt her fragility. He tasted her wounds. Overcome by guilt, he remained still and pensive. What was he doing? He wasn't able to give her what she needed, what she deserved. He would only hurt her if he encouraged this; she could not handle another failure. She held him tighter; so fragile, so young, and so delicate. He was in no position to fulfil her dreams; he must pull away from her. He must not hurt her; he must not lead her on. He would never forgive himself if he caused her further pain. Conflicted between desire and guilt, Mathias slowly moved her away. He should never have encouraged this. He should have flown back to Paris first thing that morning. He was in deep trouble now.

'Why are you pushing me away?'

'I... I'm sorry. I don't mean to push you away. I don't want to hurt you. I can't give you what you want.'

Serena kissed him delicately on his lips. 'It's okay. I'm a big girl; I can take it.' Her porcelain features, the passion and vulnerability, her childlike innocence, a beautiful flower untouched by the twisted madness of the insane world he lived in. He must spare her; she deserved something far better than he could offer. He pulled her in and held her tight against his chest. She snuggled up to him. His actions contradicted his thoughts. The more she displayed her innocence, the more he hungered to be with her. Appalled with himself, he felt as though he was somehow taking advantage of her purity. Suspecting her of seeking a father figure, knowing she had fallen for him most ardently, against his own realisation, against his own advice to himself, he clung on to her, fully knowing he was no longer in charge of his emotions.

ooooo

Charlie and Oliver, wide awake from six-thirty in the morning, had been so impatient to jump in the pool, they had dreamt about it in their sleep. Harry found that despite his willingness to look after them, keeping them company on holiday was much harder than he'd imagined. Contrary to all his beliefs as a father, he quarantined them both for two hours with an iPad and went straight back to bed.

After breakfast he lazed in the sun by the pool, hoping to relax and clear his head. Laura swayed in and out of his mind like a pendulum; the more he thought about her, the more certain he became that there was someone else. Knowing it was unlikely that she would confess, he reckoned he would remain in the dark; all he could do was speculate. Why else would she want to walk away so easily? It could only be for another man. How could she give everything up? Shell-shocked by how little he knew his wife, the situation became more and more preposterous. It was inconceivable how she'd made life-changing or perhaps life-ending decisions without consulting him. Such decisions seemed to have been made almost overnight. She must be seeing someone; she must be so deeply in love with someone else that she was prepared to throw everything away.

Harry found it impossible to switch off his brain. Like an out of control rocket, he plunged into the pool, swimming aggressively for twenty minutes without a break. Elizabeth and Eric watched silently as Harry swam relentlessly from one side of the pool to the other, endless strokes back and forth, as though he were competing in the Olympic Games. Discreetly they exchanged glances, but remained silent. Relieved, Elizabeth thanked her lucky stars that at least he wasn't alone. She dreaded the forthcoming conversation about custody that she had promised Laura. Elizabeth believed that Laura was best suited to bring up the kids. An old-fashioned woman, set in traditional ways, Elizabeth was convinced children should be with their mother. She herself would not have survived a minute without her children. Even now her children were her top priority, though they were almost middle-aged themselves. However, she couldn't cope with taking on the boys on top of everything else. She was too old for such a responsibility.

To no one's amazement, the boys fell asleep immediately after an early supper, exhausted from their day. Harry's parents invited him to have a drink with them on the terrace, but Harry refused, fearful of being interrogated. Everybody had questions, which he simply had no way of answering. Preferring his own company, he chose to go for a walk alone, discover the local sights, maybe wander off to the nearby town where he had grocery shopped earlier with his father.

With so much to offer, the Tuscan town did not disappoint. Every corner was equipped with everything a tourist might want: cafés, bars, restaurants. Full of life, charm and happiness, it was certainly a stunning place. He caught himself reflecting and fantasising while he walked the cobbled streets, soaking in the views.

Fascinated, he watched a young couple dancing the tango with great precision; it felt as though he was back in Buenos Aires again. Usually he would be wondering these streets sharing a gelato with his wife; he couldn't remember the last time he'd had a holiday without Laura. Adapting to life without her seemed abnormal. Not one to be alone, he had never understood loneliness. Now he was forced to find a way of forgetting her; he just didn't know how.

He found a buzzing little square, with restaurants heaving both with tourists and locals alike. Assimilating the locals, Harry decided to order some freshly made ice cream and follow it with a strong espresso, which he vowed to enjoy while people-watching, undoubtedly the best pastime in such an elegant little town. Slowly he walked past the quaint restaurants, all of which looked similar, waiting for one to jump out at him. A discreet little table tucked away on the hilltop of La Sorella offered a panoramic view of the square as the faraway hills sparkled majestically in the evening light.

Dressed casually in shorts and a polo T-shirt, Harry walked towards the restaurant, eyeing up the table, when suddenly a woman caught his attention. Many stunning looking women sat dotted around the restaurant, but none of them caught his eye except for this particular one, who drew him in. Looking at her discreetly, he made his way to the table and sat down immediately. Beautiful beyond belief, he felt strongly attached to her; his heart was thundering. Her brown hair pulled loosely back, away from her face, her translucent skin so clear as though he could see his own reflection, he felt certain he knew her. Her toned, lithe body draped in a long floral dress as green as a four-leaved clover, she positively gleamed amongst the crowd, her long limbs faintly visible under her chiffon robe. He felt as though he was gravitating towards her.

Sitting closely next to an unusually handsome older man, she was clearly in her element; they appeared infatuated with each other. Harry envied their love, and he envied the lucky bastard who looked like the cat that got the cream as this gorgeous woman draped herself all over him. Who was she? Certain he had seen her somewhere, she dazzled. He could only but stare. He watched her doting over her partner, giggling with laughter. *This is what loves look like*, he moaned to himself.

Harry continued to stare at her, unaware of his surroundings. The same confusion he had recently become accustomed to again consumed him. He felt as though he were drowning in self-pity. Why did this woman look familiar? Who on earth was she? He took out his trusted companion, his mobile phone. He would find some answers there. He flicked through his photos, then suddenly, at the sight of the Chicago office, the penny dropped. Only Americans or Azerbaijanis living in America had teeth as perfect as those.

There was no doubt. It was Serena. Serena from Chicago. The same Serena he couldn't stop thinking about a few weeks ago. His heart in his mouth, he was captivated; it was impossible to look away. What a vision she was, almost beyond perfection. Owing to the recent stream of bad events in his life, he'd completely forgotten about her. But now he questioned himself: how does one forget this? This beauty, this face, her glow of youth. How could he have forgotten and, more to the point, why had he resisted this woman?

In light of what had transpired since, he wished he had fully exploited the chance to be with her. How ironic the whole story looked. But who was this man with her? How he wished the man would vanish, how he wished she were alone; he would have approached and spoken to her. But the man, who seemed to be whispering profuse sweet nothings in her ears, fondled her leg, making her giddy with laughter. This man was very much here; Harry's eyes were not playing tricks on him. Surely she could not have got married in that short space of time since he last saw her? Surely it couldn't be anything too serious? What if it was?

Hit by an avalanche of jealousy, despondent and morose, he loathed everything at that moment. Suffocating in profound sadness, he felt destroyed. Harry had never known such intense feelings. What sickening games fate could play, the very woman he'd nobly rejected for his loving wife now sat in front of him, openly manifesting her desire for a man old enough to be her father, yet his wife had left him for God knows who. He felt as though he had been kicked in the stomach; to him it was unfathomable. What was she doing with this sick pervert? He looked the same age as her dead father whom she'd apparently just buried! The very handsome man quickly became ugly and loathsome in his eyes.

Harry shuddered in anger, dripping in sweat around the collar. His vision gravitated towards its new, unpredictable journey of blurdom. His head begun to throb, his throat became parched. He downed a glass of water, almost choking, not having realised it was sparkling water.

Meanwhile, Serena, none the wiser, revelled in her euphoria. Oblivious to her surroundings, her attention remained fixated on her man; her heart fluttered, almost as though he'd become an obsession overnight. Mathias, having parked his concerns to the side and evidently living for the moment, couldn't have been happier. The envy of every man in the vicinity, she seemed more ravishing every time he looked at her. She smiled, she laughed, she ate and drank with a healthy appetite; her joie de vivre and zest for life appealed to Mathias as something that no longer existed in his life, which consisted solely of Botox-loving, salad-eating, yoga-obsessed divorcees who no longer smiled.

While these two lovebirds were united together, Harry burned with rage. He didn't know they had hardly touched as yet. They had hardly exchanged a kiss; they hadn't spoken about the next day; they didn't know if there would be a next day; this might be their last night together. Slowly sipping his coffee, Harry ignored his ice cream. Not even the sweetest gelato would ease his bitterness now. He continued to observe the love-struck teenage-like couple, slowly trying to control his anger. In his mind, he resisted the urge to curse them deeply.

'It must look to people as though we are deeply, madly in love. In a proper, serious relationship,' Serena said, as she giggled into Mathias's ear.

'It's great.' He grinned.

'I wish you could stay with me for a bit longer.'

'You might get sick of me if I stay too long.'

'I could never get sick of you. I don't like being alone. I didn't have much family growing up; I always craved a big family...' Serena smiled and stopped speaking, careful not to arouse sympathy. Petrified he would leave sooner rather than later, she was determined to enjoy every minute possible with him. Mathias knew exactly what she wanted to say, but didn't dwell on it.

'I have a nice big flat in Paris and a few other houses scattered around here and there; you can come and stay whenever you fancy.' Serena kissed him on the cheek.

Harry watched them, shocked at himself. Never did he anticipate he could feel such jealousy, such desire for someone. Someone he hardly knew. He'd loved Laura more than anything else, but failed to identify ever having felt this for her, or, indeed, for any other woman.

What he wouldn't do to trade places with this man; the way she looked at him would haunt Harry forever. He wanted her to look at him in that way; the passion she had in her eyes, he wished it was for him. There were so many things he wanted to tell her, so many things he wanted to share with her, to do with her; he'd missed his chance. Lost and depleted, he tried to look away as the man paid the bill, sweeping his lady into his arms and disappearing down the Tuscan hills. He fought the temptation to follow them. The warning signs of a migraine rang in his mind like an unstoppable alarm. It was time for a respite away from this madness; he needed to escape.

ooooo

Another day, another déjà vu. Charlie and Ollie scrambled into their father's room at six-thirty in the morning, desperate to jump into the pool. Harry politely escorted them to his parents and slept till late. By the time he surfaced, all was calm, the kids playing in the pool, his parents patiently watching them, and tanning themselves, quietly in discussion.

'They must be discussing me again,' he muttered, and then loudly said, 'Mum, Dad, I need to tell you both something. It's uh… it's quite serious. You might want to sit up and listen.'

He looked tense. Immediately they changed their posture, sitting upright and looking at him.

'I have early-onset Alzheimer's.'

ooooo

Holding hands tightly, Serena and Mathias made their way into the presidential suite like two turtle doves, reunited after a decade of separation. Mathias spoke on the phone, trying to clear his schedule in the hope of buying himself another day. This time Serena understood what he was saying. He sounded different in French, more authoritative, sexy. Delighted he was prolonging his stay, she squeezed his hand in appreciation. She laughed silently upon hearing his blatant lies to his colleagues.

'I don't want you to get into trouble because of me,' she whispered. 'You can fly back to Paris tomorrow.' She paused for a second, 'and… er… if… if it makes things easier, I can come. I can come with you.' She blushed.

'*Now* you tell me! I have just deceived my dear colleagues and bought two more days. Let's enjoy them now, and then, yes, I would love you to come to Paris. I have a lot of work, but there are plenty of things for you to do.'

She leant over to kiss him; how wonderful it felt to follow her heart, devoid of fear. She felt happy – maybe life wasn't all pain and misery. A glimmer of hope, reminiscent of a rainbow, appeared in the distance, visible only to her. She smiled secretly to herself.

He followed as she led, surrendering himself to her, fully at her disposal, though never daring to make the first move. She was the boss. It felt good. Using his body to maximise her fulfilment, discarding all apprehension, yet conflicted by her inbuilt, life-long, staunch Catholic faith, was she face-to-face with the devil, or was this her moment? His strapping, muscular body, hidden underneath his crisp, white shirt, left her breathless, as though she hadn't seen light for years. Through his calm temperament, his soft touch, he captured her soul, bewitching her almost instantly.

As she unfolded her body between his, she saw his raging heart yearning to embrace her affection and pain as his own. Lost in a labyrinth of ecstasy, fighting his own guilt as if he were indulging in sin, Mathias was beside himself with passion; nothing was going to deter him today. They were like two butterflies released from their cocoons, the intimate exchange between hungry hearts; he could no longer think rationally or intelligibly. In her own needy state, Serena instinctively realised how deeply Mathias was involved; she knew she'd got inside his head. He was drunk with desire, his face burning hot, his eyes wide. She relished the opportunity to act out all her fantasies this one night. Like a wild jungle cat, she ripped him apart, devouring every part of him.

At this precise moment, it was quite possible they both believed themselves to be in love.

ooooo

'What did you say?' asked Elizabeth, dazed. 'You have *what?*'

Both his parents raised their heads up, as if struck by a sudden pain. Wide-eyed and stunned, they both stared at him.

'Yes, it's true. I have Alzheimer's disease, early-onset. It's very rare and affects only a few people, but I have it.'

'But what do you mean? You are still so young.'

'I know, but it's been confirmed.'

'Since when?'

'I found out a few months ago.'

'Why didn't you tell us? Does Laura know?'

'No.' He shook his head despondently. 'No one knows. Just you two. You guys are the first to know. I... I haven't told anyone else.'

Eric began to fidget in his seat, unsettled and shocked. Elizabeth took a deep breath, her voice trembling. 'What does that mean for your future?'

'Nothing. It's the same as everyone else's. It could be a quick deterioration, which is very unlikely, or it could take years, decades even, though I'm already experiencing symptoms, but it's under control.'

'Why didn't you tell us before?' Elizabeth's voice cracked. Eric just stared at Harry, sad and shocked.

'It's not really the type of thing I want to discuss.'

'How bad is it?'

Harry wished he didn't have to answer these questions. All these questions did was to force him to say it out loud, and once again hear how it actually sounded.

Eric, silent, could do nothing but listen. Words failed him. How on earth was it possible that his dear son could be so unfortunate? What a horrific disease.

'It's okay. Please don't worry. I'm absolutely fine. I can still do everything without any problems. I can work, drive, take care of the kids, etc.; I am fine, but I don't know how long for.'

'What do the doctors say?'

Harry explained his history regarding the doctors and the treatment. The blood tests, the MRI scans, the CT scans, the further tests due, and his tendency to keep cancelling future appointments, or turning up then leaving, avoiding doctor's calls, pretending it wasn't happening, not reading the info; an endless, exhaustive list. As he spoke, he himself heard how ridiculous it all sounded; it was vital he took it all more seriously and at least turned up for his appointments.

His parents threw their arms around him, heartbroken. Elizabeth fought back her tears: what a devastating blow.

Calmly, she whispered in Harry's ear, 'Don't fight Laura for custody.'

'I won't,' he assured his mother, sadly.

12

By the time Serena woke up, Mathias, deep in work mode, had already been up for hours.

'How was your sleep, my dear?' He greeted her tired face with a long passionate kiss while serving her a fresh hot coffee.

'Amazing. I haven't slept so well in ages.' She giggled girlishly, lazily rolling to the side, covered in just a white sheet. 'You? What time did you get up?' She gazed into his expressionless eyes.

'Not long ago. I had some work to do, so thought I'd let you sleep while I got on with it.'

'Is everything all right?'

'Yes, thanks, all fine.'

'Can you still stay another night, or do you have to rush off?'

'I can manage another night, but will definitely have to go after that. And don't try to keep me!' He shook his forefinger at her playfully. She grinned, grabbing his finger and biting it.

'I will come to Paris at the weekend, I promise.' Mathias smiled at her adoringly, bending down for a kiss.

She continued to kiss him, pulling him back to bed. He didn't resist.

'It's nice here.'

'Yes, it is. Are you okay? Comfortable?'

'Yes. I could stay here forever. Shall we go for a run when you have a little break?'

'Yes. Give me an hour and I will be ready.' Mathias took his job very seriously; it was the only thing functioning in his life at that moment, and he voluntarily dedicated almost all his time and passion to it. Serena felt happy for him; she wished she, too, could possess a fraction of the qualities he had. Gradually, she began to understand that she would need to find a way to accept him for what he was. The fewer demands she made of him, the better their chance of sealing a long-term friendship. He was complicated, distracted, his head buried in his work, his heart confused; she needed to give him freedom, space. Undoubtedly, he remained in a position to offer her a lot, but what she sought was beyond what he was able to give, for now at least. Sincere and innocent, out of the corner of her eye, she watched him type on his laptop. Would she get a chance to know him? Would she find out what made him tick? Fascinating, yet shrouded in mystery, he was almost a mythical character, a paradox. His face seemed to give nothing away, the invisible lines masking a thousand adventures they had witnessed, yet a beacon of hope still gleamed in his eyes. She couldn't read him.

'Come on!' He leapt out of bed, dragging her away from her dreams. 'Let's run.'

The morning sun blazed high above, scorching away the darkness of the night, the resplendent rays filled the world with a golden glow and positive energy. Serena's heart sang and her feet danced as she floated with the breeze, amazed by the wondrous beauty of the earth and the miracles of nature in all its splendour.

'How fit you are for a man your age,' she teased.

'I aim to please.'

'Race you!' Serena shot down the promenade. He caught up with her in a flash.

'Impressive,' she purred.

'Thank you,' he fired back, grinning.

'I challenge you to a game of tennis. I will whip your arse.'

'I'm very good at tennis; you may not beat me.'

'We will see.' She tried to sprint past him again, but this time he stopped her, showering her with floods of kisses. What she wouldn't do to stop the clock, freeze this perfect moment in this idyllic place with this dream of a man. Already she dreaded the goodbyes looming over her head like a dark cloud, almost biting his lip in anguish as she kissed him back.

ooooo

At the Hoffman holiday home, the atmosphere remained sombre and mournful. Elizabeth and Eric, devastated at their son's confession, had barely moved from their seats. The boys, still playing in the pool, started to complain of being hungry, calling for their grandma. Coming out of his daze, Eric stood up. He placed a soft hand on his clearly distressed ex-partner's shoulder, who remained stock-still and white as a ghost.

'Stay where you are. I'll prepare something for the kids.'

Still in shock, Elizabeth's thoughts rushed back and forth: *how could such a disease affect someone as young as Harry?*

'I'm going for a jog,' said Harry as he ran past his mother before she could utter a word to him, like a young boy running away to avoid a telling off.

Heaving a sigh of relief, as soon as he turned the corner and was out of sight, he promptly lit a foul-tasting cigarette. Not usually a smoker, the cigarette made him feel sick. He hoped it would offer him some calm and sanity: it didn't. Despite wanting to shield his parents from his concerns, he now reckoned he had just added to their worries. Burdening them with such news at their age was probably as selfish as it was inconsiderate, but he could no longer carry the colossal weight alone; he had to share the news with someone else – his parents at least had each other to discuss it.

Coolly and calmly, Harry jogged to the same restaurant where he'd happened to spot Serena the day before. Not expecting to see her there again, his thoughts became disorientated. Had he actually really seen her or was it his fragile imagination playing tricks on him? Serena undoubtedly was nowhere to be seen. What did he expect? Why had he come here? Harry lived in the hope he could forget her. He wanted to cleanse his mind of the memory of her, wishing he'd never laid eyes on this young woman.

Reluctantly, once again he observed the happy folk unwinding in full holiday mode, with envy rushing through him like an electric shock. *Why is their life so easy and mine so complicated?* He quit the restaurant and sprinted away, hell-bent on rescuing himself from this irritatingly happy mass of the bourgeoisie, aiming to find a quiet spot for some solitude and peace.

As he ran, he visualised himself floating over a sunny field, capturing the sun setting off in the horizon, while the still, calm music of nature played around him. He ran faster, and a small, tidy colourful field of flowers, swaying and dancing in the vivid bright grass, came into sight. The air smelt sweet, he could hear the distant sound of waves lapping on the shore; paradise was almost in sight, tranquil and serene, away from the holiday commotion and toothy grins.

A few sun worshippers perched in the meadow, having turned their backs on the hustle and bustle of the noisy square in the town, and seemed just as happy to be lying on the grass. Harry's legs almost caved in as he collapsed and lay on his back, face up towards the pleasant, blue, cloudless sky, eyes firmly closed. His body still, dripping in sweat and panting for breath, his view was nothing but perfect. Once again, he imagined himself floating in the air, flying across the sky, free from life, free from turmoil, free from care. Paradise at last.

ooooo

The next morning, he went jogging to exactly the same spot. Once again, he let his mind do all the work as he lay on the grass, eyes shut. He imagined himself swaying with the clouds, circling the moon, over the mountains, flying with the birds as they flapped their wings. Faint sounds of faraway ships echoed back and forth as they set sail. Was he a bird or a heavenly star, floating in the air, away from the world, away from life?

But what was this noise disturbing his peace of mind, with the forces of gravity pushing him back down to earth, his dream ending with a thud? What was this banshee-like sound disturbing his state of harmony? He heard faint sounds of giggling.

Agitated, he sprung upright, and there once again he saw her. Reeling in pain, as though viciously stung by a venomous snake, he saw a clearly visible Serena lying on top of the same grey-haired man, nibbling at his face, relishing every moment. The richly tanned man, with his arms wrapped around her, seemed to be basking in the same pleasure. Harry curled his lips in contempt and hatred; he could hardly believe his eyes. What was she doing here, and who on earth was this man she couldn't keep her hands off? Defiantly, he found himself approaching them; eyes burning with rage, face ugly with anger, he could hardly control his actions. Deeply immersed in one another, Mathias and Serena were unaware of the outside world. Rejoicing in her victory of having kept him another day, she was elated.

Harry, however, realising his aggressive behaviour, turned back halfway, alarmed by the jealousy and outrage he felt. He continued to walk away from the desperately-in-love couple, but stopped again, like a madman. *What's got in to me?* he questioned himself. 'Calm down; take a deep breath,' he muttered inaudibly. Unsure whether to continue walking away or turn back to confront the lovers, he found himself at a loose end, silent and still. He paused. Determined and no longer worried about making a fool of himself, once again he turned towards the couple, this time calm and cool. He walked towards them with a contrived smile on his flustered face, as though nudged by an evil ghost, trying his hardest to be mellow and unruffled.

'Hello, Serena.'

Mathias and Serena both looked up in bewilderment from their compromising position.

Serena took a moment to collect her thoughts, Mathias, none the wiser.

'Oh my God! *Harry!*' Serena sat up in a frenzy, Mathias following her, as they both stared at him curiously.

'What are you doing here?' She didn't know what to do. What a crazy coincidence?

Harry relaxed his face into as pleasant a smile as he could manage. 'I'm here with my family.' He continued to smile, feeling awkward and embarrassed.

Mathias broke the awkward silence by clearing his throat, indicating that he expected an introduction.

'Oh, this is Mathias.'

Mathias held out his hand, Harry took it over-zealously. 'Harry, how do you do?' They both smiled at each other, almost genuinely. An uncomfortable silence ensued.

Mathias finally spoke. 'I'm hot. You two sit here while I go and buy some ice cream. Any particular flavour?'

'I'm fine, thank you.'

'Er... chocolate... for me, please,' mumbled Serena.

Mathias kissed Serena on the lips, quickly. 'Back in a minute; you two talk.' He stood up and looked at her. She looked at him blankly. He stroked her cheek and smiled at her reassuringly. 'I'll be back in a few minutes. Promise.'

Harry sat on the grass next to Serena.

'He's a handsome guy. New boyfriend?'

'How's your wife?' Serena replied frostily.

'She's divorcing me.'

Serena gawped at him in amazement. '*What?*'

Harry nodded, lowering his bottom lip. 'She doesn't want me anymore. She's leaving me and wants to take the kids with her.'

'I'm so sorry.'

'Thanks. Is it serious with this guy?'

'It's complicated.'

'Again? You seem to like complications. Why don't you find yourself someone easier?'

'Why don't you save your marriage?

'I can't. She doesn't want to save it. She's done. She wants out.'

'It must be hard.'

Harry looked at her. 'You have no idea.'

She raised her eyebrows. 'How long are you staying here?'

'Till Sunday. You?'

'I don't know.' She shook her head.

He looked at her inquisitively. 'Okay, how long is *he* staying?'

'He leaves tomorrow.' Serena felt sad uttering those words aloud. 'He's leaving me and going back to his life.'

'Is he married?'

Serena laughed sarcastically. 'He's getting divorced!' She looked at Harry as though to say, *There you go.* She paused. 'He is also getting divorced,' she repeated, and shook her head.

Harry held Serena's arm, turning her towards him. 'Can we talk?'

Mathias watched them carefully as he approached with the ice cream. It was crystal clear to him that the relationship he saw before him came with many challenges.

'Ice cream, everyone.'

Serena leapt up, throwing her arms around him, kissing him frantically. Harry looked away, trying to ignore what was happening. Mathias kissed her back, quickly but passionately.

'I know you said no, but I got you one anyway.'

They sat down together in silence, eating their ice creams awkwardly. Serena held Mathias tightly with her left arm, Harry sat on her right side, feeling terribly uncomfortable. Should he get up and leave? Neither Serena nor Mathias could anticipate what was going to happen next. She squeezed his arm tighter, he moved closer to her. Harry watched their body language out of the corner of his eye, unsure of what to do with himself, partly wanting to stay near Serena, but also wanting to disappear.

ooooo

Serena lay in bed gazing at Mathias as he spoke on the phone, fixing his tie, alive and animated. In one conversation, he delegated, made decisions, made deals, made jokes, agreed to meetings in far corners of the world. Was there anything this man couldn't do? He appeared perfectly composed, as though nothing could stop him. The sun of his smile, the grace of his style, the inner mystery yet the transparent joy, his slightest touch commanded respect and attention. Serena feared he was getting ready to saunter out of her life without the slightest regret. She felt great pain watching him taking charge of his life so strongly, almost certain she would never see him again.

Mathias felt her despair; he had touched her heart and kissed her delicate skin. He wished it could be easier; he wished he could sweep her in his arms and walk off into the sunset, but he had to leave. She would never understand how much he too dreaded this goodbye; he wasn't ready to let her go just yet.

Serena feared her affection for Mathias was merely one-sided: he was nothing but a player, an insatiable ladies' man; he couldn't possibly have any real feelings for her. But now with Harry possibly back in the picture, she was engulfed in complex thoughts and feelings she could hardly explain.

Mathias aimed for a swift, painless goodbye without too much hurt for either of them. In her eyes, he witnessed the residue of a tear as though reflecting her soul, her cheeks deep crimson like blood oranges. He needed to leave without causing her more pain. Being away from Serena would be a good test for him to understand if what he had experienced was simply a few nights of lust, or if there was something deeper. Either way, he was certain he would struggle to forget the intensity of the last extraordinary few days.

The very minute Mathias's car left for the airport, Serena began to panic. Pacing back and forth in her room, she couldn't help staring out of the window, desperately hanging on to his final wave. Should she call and speak to him on the phone? Should she write him a message, or was that too needy? Would it scare him? Maybe she could just write *Miss you already*. Without a minute's hesitation, she switched her phone on, desperate to write to him, but her heart missed a beat. To her immense pleasure, someone else had been thinking about her. Harry had wasted little time, bombarding her with messages, urging a proper meeting. Another complication. Should she see him? Meeting Harry would at least divert her attention away from Mathias, and save her from running to Paris on the next available flight. But she was painfully aware that Harry himself was hurting, and certainly not in the right frame of mind to help her; he would never be able to offer her anything, but perhaps they could use each other's shoulder to cry on.

Whilst reading Harry's messages, the complexity of their relationship unravelled before her like an open book. No misinterpretation, no misunderstanding; clear and evident in black and white, the obstacles screamed out to her. Just when she had managed to forget him, he'd come back full force in her life. She collapsed on the armchair and sat back, head heavy. This was too much. She had just said goodbye to Matthias; she needed to process what had recently happened before she could focus on Harry. She breathed, slowly inhaling, then exhaling with force as she often did during Bikram yoga. She remained silent, taking some time to catch up with her thoughts. She continued to breathe in and out loudly, allowing herself ample time to think.

Various scenarios ran through her mind, with several options available. She could continue to see Mathias until Harry was ready; she could forget about Mathias completely and concentrate solely on Harry; or she could forget about them both and continue her travels and see what great adventures awaited her. Too many thoughts and possibilities crowded into her mind.

Sure, she responded. *Come to my hotel, I'm alone* and sent him the address.

Harry confirmed back within seconds, and knocked on her door shortly after.

Serena couldn't help thinking of herself as a prostitute, saying goodbye to one man and welcoming another, but this would turn out to be a meeting she could not have predicted.

She opened a bottle of light, fruity Tuscan wine. Mathias had introduced her to some regional flavours, and helped her choose some of the more famous bottles in the area to try. With Mathias's encouragement, Serena had developed a taste for wine and was having fun exploring the local varieties. She made herself comfortable on the sofa and motioned for Harry to sit close to her. Harry, who was quickly losing all appreciation for most things, took little notice of his surroundings. The large, opulent room, the decadent, high ceilings, the rich, detailed frescos on the freshly painted walls, all went unnoticed. He sank onto the sofa and immediately downed the glass of wine he'd been offered.

The arresting joie de vivre, the brilliant humour, his curious analytical mind, so evidently visible in Chicago, was now replaced by tension and anxiety. Serena assumed his edgy behaviour was a result of his personal situation, but didn't question it. Leisurely sipping her wine, she observed Harry. Was this really the man she'd developed such intense feelings for? She'd remembered him as far more striking, far more dashing, supremely more masculine. But sitting in front of her was a nervous wreck: lost to the world, lost to himself, drowning in misfortune. What a stark difference to the handsome, debonair playboy she had just spent the last few days lusting over.

'I'm really sorry to hear about the divorce. If there is anything I can do to help, just… just let me know.'

'I didn't expect it; it came out of nowhere,' Harry sighed, gazing at the rich cream velvet curtains hanging off an elaborately designed brass pole. He took a deep breath and recounted the last few months, deliberately omitting the more delicate, intricate details of his health. That was far too painful to speak about, and did Serena really need to know?

'I am so grateful to have my parents. I don't know what I would have done without them; they have been my rock, my strength.' Harry went on. At last he could talk to someone; what a great feeling it was to be able to offload.

In return, Serena confessed her feelings for him, admitting how recklessly she'd fallen for him, knowing full well the consequences, and saying how angry she had been with him. She felt as though she were reading an excerpt from a teenage romance novel: how stupid it must have sounded! She cringed.

Harry listened, gobsmacked.

'I know, it's crazy, huh? What you've been through sounds absolutely terrible. I'm sorry, I had no clue. I thought you went back to London to continue leading your perfectly perfect life. You have my sympathy, you really do, but besides offering friendship and a shoulder to cry on, I wonder what else I can do.'

'Are you so desperately in love with this guy that you have no affection left for me?'

Serena looked puzzled.

'You've just explained your feelings for me, yet all you can offer me is sympathy and a friendship… nothing else?' Harry's voice grew louder as his eyes grew cold.

'Are you crazy? Do you realise what you are saying?'

'Yes, I do.'

'You cannot be serious; you are not even divorced yet. What do you expect me to say? What do you want me to do? I've just managed to forget about you, meet someone else, and now here you are again. You can't just waltz in and out of my life when and how you please. I don't know how to deal with any of this. I'm sorry your wife that you loved so much is divorcing you, but that is not my problem!' Serena sat up, animated. 'I don't even know what's going on between Mathias and me. Who he is, what he is, if he's real, even. I have absolutely no idea what I should do.' Harry edged closer to her as she spoke, but she moved away.

'I have to find out what I am going to do first, what's happening between Mathias and me, before I start to get involved with you.'

'Okay, I understand. I won't be a thorn in your side, or try to prevent you from finding true love with this chap. I want you to be happy. I know I cannot make you happy.' Harry poured himself another glass of wine.

Serena felt uncomfortable; it was early afternoon and she found his excessive drinking somewhat off-putting: the pace at which he knocked back this rather expensive wine could hardly translate to enjoyment or appreciation.

'How do you know that?' Serena glared at him. 'How do you know you can't make me happy? I thought you were wonderful when I met you in the US. You were genuine and honest, so different to Miles; I would have done anything for you. I mean, I didn't set out to fall in love with you, but you were so endearing and, yet oh so judgemental of me, my wealth, my life.' She laughed. 'You and Mathias are the only two men I have ever fallen for, very quickly, I must admit. I know it's crazy and nonsensical, but you have to appreciate that I don't usually meet interesting people and, given my background, I always had to be selective with whom I spent my time. If you only knew how inexperienced I am in these things, you would be shocked.'

She paused. 'I knew you were married, but something so strange happened, and I just felt so drawn to you. Of course it wasn't love, or maybe it was, I don't know. Whatever it was, it was unique and special. It was all rather confusing, so fleeting and so quick. Even if it had been just a friendship, I would have been so happy. It hurt like hell when you left without even a goodbye.'

Harry could do little else but stare at her, his head pounding in turmoil with both pity and desire.

'I doubt anything will come of Mathias and me, to be honest.' Serena tossed her hair to the side as she looked out of the window. A fierce sun streamed through the large windows, leaving the room scorching hot.

'It's over for me.'

'What do you mean?' She turned to face Harry.

Harry grabbed Serena's hand, pulling her face close to his. 'Serena...' With desperation in his eyes, he almost choked on his words, '... I need to tell you something.' He placed his hand on top of hers.

'Harry, what's going on?'

'I'm sick.'

She looked him in the eye, horrified, her face furrowed. 'What is it? Harry, what's wrong?'

'I have early-onset Alzheimer's.'

Serena froze. Harry's face darkened. Slowly trying to process the information and understand what she had just heard, she took a deep breath. Tears trickled down Harry's cheek. She held him in her arms, squeezing him with all her strength, overcome with sympathy, wanting to sob with him.

Embarrassed, he pulled himself away, frantically drying his tears on his sleeve. He couldn't believe he'd allowed himself to cry in front of this gorgeous woman. 'I'm sorry,' he laughed anxiously. 'I just... I just wanted you to know. I haven't told my wife... well, ex-wife, Laura. I haven't told her yet... and neither will I, I suppose.' The words 'ex-wife' still sounded absurd to Harry.

'Thanks for telling me. I appreciate it, I feel honoured you trust me enough to let me know this. I'm really so very sorry.'

Harry held her hand again. 'Do you now understand how complicated my life is? Why I didn't let you close to me? Plus, I was supposedly happily married at that time, and even now that I'm separated, would it be fair for me to start something with you?'

'That wouldn't stop me if I wanted to be with you.' Serena smiled.

Harry stared at her. 'Do you understand what this disease is? Do you have any idea how dangerous it is, especially for close family members? I couldn't, I wouldn't, ever put you through this.'

'You're not. You're not putting me through anything. I'm saying that if we were to be together. ... We are not together. If I wanted to be with you, nothing would stop me, not Alzheimer's, not anything.'

Harry kissed her hand, 'Thank you. That means so much to me. I am having an awful time at the moment… As you can… as you can no doubt imagine.'

'I can't begin to imagine what you are going through. I'm really very sorry. I don't know what to say. The divorce, the sickness, everything at once. It's a lot to deal with.' Serena smiled dryly. 'I can't seem to stop apologising. All I can say is I'm here for you, always.'

'Thank you. That means so much to me.'

Serena pointed out of the window. 'Look. It's a glorious day. We are in a beautiful place. Let's go out for a walk; it's very hot in this room, and I hate the air con.'

'Yes, let's; it *is* very hot in here.' Harry tried to cheer up, managing a half smile. 'Is this the room you shared with your lover boy?'

'Yes, but I don't want to discuss that with you.'

He offered her his arm, almost relieved.

'I could always be your nurse if all else fails,' she whispered in his ear humorously.

'Mmm… will you wear a sexy nurse's outfit for me?' he replied, sharing her humour.

Casually, they strolled out of the hotel arm in arm. Harry wanted time to stand still, to grasp each second and steal it away, to capture and forever preserve the moment. It felt wonderful to be with Serena again; she was so different to his everyday, normal world. So many things stirred through his mind, he felt like a hamster running in a wheel that he couldn't get off.

ooooo

Another day, another goodbye. If the first goodbye was challenging, the second felt almost impossible. Struggling to cope with constant uncertainty, it often appeared to Serena as if life was passing her by, forcing her to watch from the sidelines. How could it be that she had met two men, one after the other, and they were both as unsuitable as they were problematic? Certainly, this could not be her destiny.

With an aching heart, Harry hired a bike to cycle to Serena, wondering if this was the end. His calm, sedate life had turned into cyclones, swirling in every direction. At least he was able to console himself with the knowledge that he had laid his soul bare for Serena, opening his heart and revealing all. Serena waited eagerly for him in the hotel courtyard, clear water roaring down the lavish man-made waterfalls, and butterflies fluttering around the late summer magnolia blossoms, a little piece of paradise to drown all sorrows. This time, Harry noticed his surroundings and the goddess clad in a bright blue sheath dress, hair hanging loose, lightened by the sun and wavy from the salt of the sea. She waited for him beneath a pristine papaya tree, which, thanks to climate change, was able to grow and flourish in warm European regions.

'You look beautiful,' Harry said as he smiled at her. 'I don't want to leave you. I wish things could be different.'

'I know. Please sit down. How long have you got?'

'Thirty minutes.'

'Okay.'

'I told my parents about you.'

That was very sweet, she thought, *but was there anything to tell?* Had anything happened between them that deserved an explanation?

'Oh, really? What did you tell them?'

'How lovely you are.' He handed her a red rose. 'I stole this for you from the lobby.'

'You're very close to your parents. Lucky you.'

'Yes, I am, but sometimes it gets a bit too much. I recently told them my news; it was very hard for them, but they needed to know. From my knowledge and everything I have read on the internet, I will probably start behaving strangely and doing some odd things, which will probably only become worse. My parents will notice. And after the divorce, my parents will inevitably play a bigger part in my life: I will need them more than ever. Believe it or not, my mother objected to my "relationship" with you. She insisted it was far too soon.' Serena smiled. 'So I threatened to elope with the kids and cut them out of my life.'

'Oh, Harry, that's a bit harsh,' retorted Serena. 'They're only trying to help! Imagine being me; I have no one; you are so lucky you have your parents; they sound such lovely people.'

'They are lovely, and I'm very lucky to have them, but I am too old to seek their approval and explain myself all the time. I know that I will need them far more later on; they need to understand it will get very difficult for me. But at the moment I need them to just let me be and deal with things my own way.'

Serena squeezed Harry's hand. His palms were sweaty; it was evident the conversation was challenging.

'Now, let's talk about you. Will you go to Paris and see your friend?'

'Yes, I will. Does it make you sick?' She grinned at him cheekily.

'Yes, it really does. I really hate this guy; he is just so good-looking and just so perfect. I actually really hate him. What are you going to do with him?'

'*Do* with him?'

'Are you going to have sex with him? Yuk. How could you; he is so slick and slimy. Does he wake up every morning and grease himself everywhere?'

Serena laughed. 'Don't be rude! He is South African, not Latin. They don't do that.' She winked at him. 'I will go and see what happens. I'm sure by the time I get there he will already have two or three girlfriends.'

'South African? He doesn't look it. Is he racist? Does he have a strong accent?'

'Can you stop! No, he is not racist. And, no, he doesn't have a South African accent. In fact, he has a wonderful sweet accent.'

He shook his head. 'Let's talk about something else. When we met in Chicago, you were contemplating moving to London. Would you still consider it?'

'I don't know,' she sighed. 'So much has changed since then.'

'I'm really going to miss you. You did something to me; I wasn't expecting it.' Harry raised his eyes staring at her, yearning to hold her in his arms. Her dress thoroughly accentuated her toned figure, her breasts perky, her lips moist.

'Did you wear this dress on purpose? Oh, let's tease this sick guy one last time?'

'Don't be silly.' She looked down at herself. 'Is this dress so sexy?'

'Oh,' he swung his head, pupils dilated, 'you cannot imagine!'

'Really?' She genuinely hadn't meant to be so alluring. 'It's hot. I just threw something light and short on.'

'I cannot begin to tell you how I feel right now, I could tear that little dress off with my teeth and just simply… hmm…'

'Simply what?' Serena questioned him joyfully, though careful not to provoke him.

'Simply… simply… never mind. I need to control myself. I probably will never have sex ever again.'

'Oh, come on; stop being silly. You've got years before it gets bad; stop being so pessimistic.'

Harry continued to lament. 'I will have to control myself forever while you make a home with this South African French guy in a beautiful Parisian apartment adorned with diamonds and pearls overlooking the Eiffel Tower. Think of me in an old people's home with ninety-year-olds while you sip Champagne and change lovers, oh Marie Antoinette.'

They both laughed. *Marie Antoinette is probably the only woman who could sustain a life with Mathias*, thought

Serena. 'I will really miss you. I promise I will visit you when Mathias forces me to take part in orgies and insists I take on other lovers for his pleasure.'

'Don't let him take advantage of you. I'm sure he is a predator, and a pervert.'

'Stop it. I'll be fine. Kiss me once before you go.'

ooooo

Harry boarded the plane with his children and his parents, his thoughts weighing him down. Since leaving Serena, he'd failed to get her out of his mind. He knew he had to carefully consider and re-evaluate his life; would that be with or without Serena? Deep inside, he knew that few options were available to him. The best thing would be to forget her. Thinking about her constantly and obsessing over her Parisian affair would only be to his detriment. He must find a way to avoid her mentally, a task as impossible as it was painful. Perhaps he too should find himself a part-time lover to distract himself with, some young, hot student: a casual affair requiring no explanation. Someone he could see when he felt positive – or extremely negative.

The more he thought about this, the more he cracked up with laughter; the absurdity of finding a part-time lover shocked him. Would he be capable of finding a lover? Could he ever think with a rational mind, devoid of anxiety and concern? Perhaps he could remain relatively 'normal' for a long time; maybe it wasn't all doom and gloom. Harry leaned back in his seat, relieved he was still able to find something positive to think about. Thinking about romance, women, and falling in love, made him erratic, and he knew he must not see Serena again. The most beautiful woman he had ever met: he must forget her.

'What a shame,' he muttered to himself. He took out his little quiz book and continued with the Sudoku he hadn't quite managed to finish on his inbound flight.

Since his diagnosis, Harry had taken part in various online cognitive tests and brain-teasing games. He frequently carried around word and number games in his pocket, using them as a distraction the moment he started to feel negative or anxious. A genius with numbers, in the last few months simple Sudoku games had helped to keep his brain in check. His mind drifted off to all sorts of places as he tried to concentrate. *How difficult could it be to count to nine? Just kidding. This is easy.* Successfully, he completed the first puzzle then the second, then the third without any problem at all. Maybe he was okay and this was all a test. Wouldn't that be great?

ooooo

Serena booked herself a flight to Paris the minute Harry left her alone under the Caribbean papaya tree. Suddenly afraid, she hated being alone. Flying to Paris and chasing a ghost was not the ideal solution, but surely it was better than being alone in a foreign country, desperately seeking adventure. Since Harry's confession, Serena could think of nothing else but him. Divorce aside, she thought hard about what this might mean for her, what it meant for them, and if there really was a real possibility of a 'them'.

It had been a good few years since Serena had been to Charles de Gaulle Airport. She had little recollection of ever having been there. She consciously avoided rewinding her mind back. However, her heart skipped a beat at the sight of Mathias, hiding behind a dozen white roses. Unsure whether she had seen him, he watched happily as she approached, floating towards him like an exquisite gazelle. The airport was heaving with passengers, but all Mathias could see was Serena. She was a breath of fresh air.

'Lovely flowers. Who are they for?'

He stood up, calm and laid-back. Relaxed and rich in appearance, he oozed sophistication. Could it be possible she was even more beautiful than he remembered? A bright smile on her excited face, she stood head to head with him, and he stared into her eyes without effort. She had the same flawless skin and had caught a tan. Her eyes sparkled. The white of her blazer shone under the bright airport light, and she looked even better than he'd remembered.

'You can have them.' He offered her the flowers, grabbing her at the waist and kissing her lovingly.

'Have you missed me?'

'Guess.'

'I don't know. Are you happy to see me?'

'*Un petit peu.*' He winked.

He whisked her away in a silent, smooth, chauffeur driven, black Tesla.

'I'm so happy to see you. I'd already forgotten what you look like. Kiss me,' she pleaded as she sat on his lap, determined to make the most of every minute they spent together.

The mere sight of him gave her strength. She felt free, as if she could fly. He encouraged inner confidence she hardly knew existed. In his presence, she felt no boundaries or inhibitions. Even though he'd made it clear he had nothing solid to offer, she felt a deep sense of comfort next to him, almost as though he was releasing her from a self-imposed prison. He gave her the power to escape, to shed her fears and throw away her concerns. Her heart yearned for his; she could no longer wait. She was here. She was with him, wrapped in his arms. She felt him deep inside her. It was all here. Everything she wanted.

ooooo

Caught up in the usual Monday morning frenzy, Harry sat at his desk, blankly staring at his screen, coffee in hand, desk full of notes, reading material scattered around the table. Had he really been away last week? Had Serena really been there? With Laura out of the picture, he had all the time to indulge in his weird activities without fear of being sprung, at least at home. What a relief. He knew for certain that Italy was real. The photos on his iPhone proved it.

Flicking through his iPhone was no longer the same. Once upon a time, this very iPhone buzzed with endless photos of his perfect family, his doting wife and gorgeous kids, but now all he seemed to be faced with was facts. Day-to-day facts, directions, reminders, to-do lists, urgent 'don't forget' notes. It all felt torturous and a pain in the backside. He compared it to Groundhog Day, as though his thoughts were set on repeat mode, over and over again.

In a frenzy of overthinking, again he painfully tried to obliterate all memories of Serena. This would be the best moment to delete her existence and bury her deep in the ground. A woman like her deserved so much better. What was he realistically going to do with her? After one last yearning look at her photos, he hit the delete button and took out his reading glasses. Laura had sent him a long email detailing her demands, to which Harry simply responded *Okay*. The glasses still felt odd; did he really need them or was he being over-cautious?

Okay, what? Laura shot back instantly.

Okay to everything you want. You get custody as long as I get some time with the children. Okay to all your financial requirements. Let's keep it amicable.

Laura wasn't convinced. He must be up to something?

Are you sure? she challenged him.

Yes. It's hard enough already. I don't want to fight. Fine. My lawyers will draft all the papers. Please sign.

Okay.

Harry knew she would be confused; it amused him to think about it. Providing she was reasonable, he would gravely agree to all her demands; he now knew he was in no fit state to take her on as an opponent. What Laura wanted, Laura would get. It was, after all, in his own best interest to get all financial matters under control. God forbid his health should take a turn for the worst and all his affairs be left up in the air.

The divorce was as good a reason as any for him to write his will, to tie up all loose ends going forward. Harry shocked himself by so readily and willingly accepting a passive role in every aspect of his life going forward. Day and night, he thought about his illness, expecting disaster to strike any second. Unsure of what mistakes he would make, what he would forget, how he would embarrass himself, life started to become a curse. Reading through his to-do list, he could often hear the melancholic tune of his life slowly unravelling in front of him. The music so out of tune, the screechy sound of an instrument continuing to play ever more hopelessly, ringing in his ears like the screams of an animal in pain. Was he playing these wretched notes, or was it Laura? Was he watching nervously as she hijacked the entire orchestra the same way as she'd hijacked his life? Had he lost the melody altogether? Was he consenting to a disaster by agreeing to all her needs, or was his destiny simply to head towards the straight and easy path, the path that led to somewhere sensible – or was it a path to nowhere? Confused and empty, he didn't know what to think.

While in Italy, for a few minutes Serena had been a flicker of hope, but was she real, or was she just another figment of his imagination? He read Laura's messages again.

As full of sadness and contempt as he was, the wrath of a scorned woman, who also happened to be an excellent lawyer, was probably best avoided. Besides, did it need to get acrimonious? No, it didn't. Should he fight her? No, he couldn't afford to fight her. His fear smouldered on; sudden outbreaks of mild perspiration sent his dithering mind into trance-like semi-dreams, in which a forgotten image of happiness of how things used to be flashed in front of him: the kids playing, he and Laura laughing. How did all this misery happen?

Gemma had arranged the flowers on top of his filing cabinet, as she had done every Monday morning since she'd started to work for him. Harry shot a concerned look at the brightly assorted blooms: what resentment he felt for this disturbingly harmful, angry display. The bold, upright floral design enraged him, and tiny shots of sweat gathered on his nose. No matter how much he focused, all he could see was a blur. He loathed these flowers, wanting never to see them again. How relieved he was when the day was finally over and an email from Laura's legal team hit his inbox. All he had to do was print and sign. A hot green tea and the confines of his home would serve as the best place to close this deal. Close it once and for all, and strike Laura out of his heart and life.

Harry hardly heeded the negative comments about women from his friends. He adored the opposite sex, having had wonderful experiences and perfect memories. Women had not been at all complex in his eyes, well, not until now. He realised he had got it all wrong. Women were by far the superior and unpredictable sex, each and every one of them. He gave up trying to understand them, all of them, including the ever-lovely Serena. Was she really as innocent as she made out? He imagined her draped in the arms of the fabulously rich playboy in his Louis XIV-style apartment. She was probably having the time of her life. He pitied himself effusively, all the while forcing himself to finalise the divorce and deal with his disease.

Divorce papers signed. He ended his message with a 'relieved' emoji.

Serena replied instantly: *Amazing. Congratulations. Are you okay?*

Yes. Feel nothing. How's Paris?

Great.

How's the playboy?

No comment. Serena followed her message with a 'smiley' face, which infuriated Harry.

He stopped writing immediately. He should have deleted her phone number along with the memories. Why did he succumb and text her? Everything was perfect in her life. He didn't want to hear another word about how great everything was for her, or what she was doing, or how she was doing it.

Before he had the chance to put his phone down, he received a message from Laura.

I will take the boys this weekend and explain properly. Thanks for not being difficult, and I'm sorry for everything. One day I hope you will realise it was the right decision.

Okay, Harry responded, passively.

ooooo

Reasonably satisfied, he felt strangely confused yet relieved at the same time. He read the appointment in his calendar with the same dark fear and loathing he usually associated with these group meetings. Could he afford to miss it? Should he ignore it? He felt it was imperative to attend; in fact, now that he had the weekend free, wouldn't it be good to take advantage and explore his options?

The Early-Stage Social Engagement programme was the perfect thing for him to attend. He could discuss his diagnosis with like-minded people. He now knew for certain he wasn't the only one with early-onset Alzheimer's. Harry typed *early-onset Alzheimer's* into his internet browser to see if anything had changed. Maybe it had been updated with new advanced research promising a glimmer of hope? He noticed nothing new; it was the same as the last time he'd Googled.

Nervous and apprehensive, he began to key in the numbers on his phone, even though they had been saved in his contacts. Luckily it was anonymous; they couldn't see him; they didn't know it was him. Work wouldn't find out; no one would know. If anything, it was preparation for his face-to-face meeting next week.

'Hello, Alzheimer's Society,' said a friendly voice.

Harry stalled, then hung up. Stroking his chin, he cursed himself. Heaving a sigh, he took a deep breath and immediately redialled the number.

'Yes, hello… hi… yes, I was hoping you could help me.' Harry took another deep breath and spoke in a deep yet calm voice. 'I have been diagnosed with early-onset Alzheimer's, and I would like to speak to someone about it. Could you help me?'

Harry felt incredibly proud of himself. He'd done it. He'd asked for help. Like most proud men, he found it not only difficult, but almost impossible to ask for help. What a huge relief to know there were others who shared his grief, his pain, and had the same future to look forward to as himself! It was, however, still painfully evident that he was a little on the young side. The Dementia Connect support team did their best to instil a temporary calm in Harry. Knowing the call was confidential was the most important thing, giving him the confidence to talk openly about his diagnosis and his situation. He hoped he would have the courage to display the same strength during his face-to-face meeting.

13

Eight months later

Clearly visible from the window, a sudden late snow was falling outside, bright with just a touch of magic. Harry stood in front of the fireplace, admiring his early birthday gift from his parents. Staring down at him hung a huge painting Elizabeth had commissioned. His two boys flanked on both sides of a grinning Harry, sitting smugly on what appeared to humorously resemble a throne. It put the finishing touches to his new flat and finally gave it a homely feel, for up until now it had been nothing but an empty shell. With minimal furniture and very few personal effects, it was a spacious room, with towering ceilings. Harry had ignored his mother's suggestions and had banned her from buying or sneakily trying to decorate his new bachelor pad. The boys' rooms were the only places fully furnished and liveable.

Having lost direction over the last few months, Harry was now no stranger to battles and conflicts, mostly within himself. His vague search for a new path had led him only to further destruction. On a downward decline, his new circumstances were as alien to him as his uncontrollable state. Not only the victim of a broken marriage, but an uncontrollable illness also lurked in his mind, with no possibility of disappearing. When thinking rationally, he wondered if it was really that bad. It wasn't cancer or

HIV, or anything life-threatening. On the contrary, it was something that hadn't really even happened. Of course it was going to happen, and it would probably mean a slow decline, but no one knew how bad it would hit; he might be one of the lucky ones, and with the right medication, he might be able to deal with it. When feeling positive, Harry comforted himself with the constant words, 'It will be okay.' But within a few hours, he would habitually retort back to his low and depressed self.

Harry's colleagues at his office, many of them divorcees themselves, understood and sympathised with his new predicament, happily agreeing to him working less hours in the office, and more often from home. Preferring his own company whenever possible, gradually he begun to withdraw from the many activities with which he had previously been involved.

An inner struggle, a dark black spell, and a downward spiral sunk Harry to a very low point. The lack of sleep, the frequent nightmares, the erratic behaviour, were all too much for him. Being divorced and alone didn't suit him. Like a stone sinking in water, stirring up a murky cloud at the bottom, alarm bells began to ring when he found himself struggling to get out of bed in the mornings, especially when he had to get to work. His candid confession to Gemma forced her to take action. She pestered him endlessly to seek therapy, but Harry continued to resist.

Then one day she came across what sounded like a very skilled psychiatrist in a women's magazine. The magazine highly praised this doctor's abilities. Subsequently, after a few phone calls, Dr Raza finally took Gemma's calls but only to refuse her. He was treating Laura and therefore it was impossible he could treat Laura's ex-husband.

However, the doctor was kind enough to suggest another highly acclaimed psychiatrist, specifically renowned for young people with chronic problems.

After his initial refusal, Harry had no choice but to agree to talk to someone. Simultaneously, Harry's family doctor, worried about Harry's ignorance of his condition, sent a referral, prompting a local dementia adviser to contact him. Suddenly he found himself discussing his divorce with his therapist and his illness with an early-onset Alzheimer's support group.

Harry explained his reluctance to cooperate in an Alzheimer's social group was due largely to his fear of being stuck in a room with old-age pensioners, whom he'd assumed to be the only age group to suffer from this disease. The revelation of others not dissimilar in age and in the same shoes as himself was almost as welcome as a crisp winter morning. Conveniently for Harry, the local support group had reserved a small spot in a café, close to his own home, on a quiet side street.

Known as the Memory café, the group of five eagerly awaited Harry. A long, brisk walk later, disguised in sunglasses and a baseball cap, Harry, desperate to be in control, casually strolled into the café, unsure of what to expect but determined to experience whatever might occur. He told himself to try to be positive. He wasn't the only one. A fairly young-looking chap, whom he thought looked a similar age to him, immediately caught his attention.

'My wife couldn't cope with it; she turned to alcohol and now we sort of look after each other.' Harry listened carefully as the sprightly young man spoke. He sipped his cappuccino, impressed with the idea of the Memory café. Brushing his problems under the carpet was not the right thing to do, but did he really want to discuss his problems with these strangers?

'I'm already at that point where I can't drive or do my own banking. My husband does it all for me, and my kids take it in turn to visit me twice a week.' The woman had introduced herself to the group, but Harry had already forgotten her name and was more interested in trying to read the tattoo on her arm. She went on. 'I'm very grateful for the medication: the Donepezil is great.'

Yes, the medication, thought Harry, he needed to start taking the meds. Who knew, it might work wonders.

'I watched my mother die from it; I hoped to God I would be spared, but unfortunately for me I, too, have it. However, I have to say I have help, and these Memory cafés are great. The 'Singing for the Group' sessions I attend are also super helpful. I have made some friends and I have a care worker; she's very kind and helpful. We discuss my needs and she helps to make sure I am cared for and looked after. This disease is not going to beat me.' The man with the eighties' mullet hairstyle was quite endearing, though he spoke very fast. Harry struggled to keep up with him.

The organiser of the group, an older woman, probably in her sixties, turned her attention to Harry. She spoke slowly as if she were speaking to a child.

'Thanks for joining us, Harry. How are you today?'

Harry responded honestly, preferring just to listen for a while. Was it okay if he didn't speak?

'Of course it is. Would anyone else like to talk about their experiences so Harry can understand how others are coping?'

'I was so stressed from learning about my diagnosis, I got breast cancer.' A small blonde lady had Harry's full attention. 'Two months after my doctor gave me my early-onset diagnosis, I panicked. I cried every day, took sick leave off work and drove myself insane with worry. My boyfriend left me; my parents moved house to be closer to me; I felt as if I was going mad. I was a total mess.'

'I'm so sorry.' Harry didn't know what else to say.

'Thank you.' She gave him half a smile. 'The cancer was so aggressive, it grew very fast. I'm sure it was due to the crazy stress levels I was putting myself through.'

The others, already familiar with this story, nevertheless listened intently. No matter how many times they heard it, the seriousness of what was being said was still as poignant as the first time they heard it.

Harry waited for the session to end, politely said goodbye, and took the same long route home. *Never again*, he thought, wrapping his scarf around his neck and hiding his hands in leather gloves. This was far too depressing. As helpful as the support group was, he couldn't bear to listen to the problems of others. The immense sympathy he'd felt for the woman who had cancer forced him to realise that this was real; it wasn't going to go away. He needed help, but perhaps in the confines of his own home.

The therapist began visiting Harry at home once a week. Unsure and reluctant at first, he surprised himself at how rapidly he started to find the sessions increasingly helpful. He was encouraged to speak openly without barriers, without the threat of being sued, or fired. The ability to share personal thoughts, pains and fears was a skill Harry had not really learned. Undeniably, and rather quickly, he felt a great need for the therapist and held him in very high esteem. Given there was not much to elaborate on about the divorce at this point, Harry preferred to focus on his disease.

One of the few in his peer group never to have previously visited a therapist, the experience proved a great revelation to Harry, even though he had earlier often ridiculed and laughed at his friends on their weekly visits. Working together at a gradual but consistent pace, provided some immediate relief for Harry. Through hypnosis, he began to sleep better, and the nightmares, though not completely eradicated, lessened in frequency. He learned to appreciate living alone, yet still be good company. He kept a daily journal, recording not only his activities but also his thoughts and concerns. Most importantly, he was thankful for being able to discuss his innermost feelings and ugliest thoughts openly with another individual without concern. It was a colossal relief for a man who previously had not dared to question any aspect of his emotions or character.

Harry's therapist, a retired doctor who often wrote articles for a medical website, was fascinated by the diagnosis of early-onset Alzheimer's. He invested his own time, voluntarily dedicating numerous hours outside his scheduled paid hours, researching and trying to understand dementia, Alzheimer's and all its facets. Determined to help and increasingly curious about how the disease would continue to manifest itself, the doctor was keen to maintain long-term relations with Harry.

Working in the office two days a week and the rest of the time from home, with Fridays as a day off, was much easier with regular therapy. With Gemma close by, aware of his unconventional needs, office life was less daunting.

She was a godsend. She helped him with even the most menial tasks. Harry smirked at his smug expression staring down at him from the protruding portrait. *It couldn't be further from my current reality*, he thought as he shook his head ironically.

ooooo

Thank you, Mum, for the lovely birthday lunch and the amazing portrait, I love it. Thanks also for taking the kids; they'll have a great time with Luca and Mia. I guess I will be thanking you for the rest of my life. I'm now tired and will have an early night. Good night.

His guardian angel, one of the few women who hadn't let him down or destroyed his soul; he would buy her flowers to say thank you.

Just as he was browsing his phone, wondering how to order flowers online, the doorbell rang. He couldn't imagine who could possibly be ringing his doorbell at this time, for all those nearest and dearest to him had just shared his birthday lunch with him. Perplexed, he crept to the door, looking at his watch. He now hated surprises. Carefully, he opened the door. Shocked and lost for words, and not even trying to hide the obviously stunned expression on his face, his eyes dilated and his mouth wide open in amazement, the look of confusion rapidly switched to a look of joy and elation. Was this a dream?

'Er… what are you doing here?' He could hardly string a sentence together.

'Hello.' Serena smiled excitedly. Harry paused. 'How are you? Can I come in?'

'Yes, yes! Of course!' Harry showed her in.

'Lovely flat!' She looked around, smiling.

'How did you get my address?'

'You are a very hard man to track down.'

'Serena, I cannot believe you are here. I don't know what to say!'

'Are you happy to see me?' She sat down on the large grey sofa leaving her luggage in the corner.

'Yes. But before I get too happy and actually believe it, how come? How come you are here?'

'I wanted to see you, to make sure you were okay. I thought it might be nice to spend some time together.'

'How did you find me?'

'I begged Miles to give me your address.'

'Oh, I see. Miles... hmm... how is he?'

'He's well, I think. We don't speak that often, but when we do he is always very kind and helpful. Do you mind me being here?'

'I'm just a bit confused. I... I don't know if I am ready...' He smiled. 'I'm sorry. It's lovely to see you. You look beautiful. It's always lovely to see you.'

'I really wanted to see you. To wish you a happy birthday and maybe spend some time with you, if you're up for it.'

'Are you sure you want to spend time with me? You have the world at your feet; why would you want to spend time with someone like me?'

'I've done a lot of thinking recently. I've travelled, had some interesting experiences, learnt a few things, learnt about myself. Grown up a little.'

It felt wonderful to sit next to her, to hear her voice, smell her perfume.

'I've also thought about us. Believe it or not, I've missed you. I... I could stay if you want me to.'

'I would love you to stay.' They both grinned. He couldn't help it any more, she was irresistible. He leaned over and kissed her softly on her cheek. She stared in to his eyes and lovingly kissed him on his lips. Robbed for so long of happiness, Serena's presence seemed like a gift from heaven. They both continued to smile. She looked at him, recognising the pain in his eyes, holding him tight. She was really there. He kissed her again.

'I am so, so incredibly happy to see you. You can't imagine. I feel... I feel as though I'm in the midst of a beautiful dream, I can't express how I feel. You are so gorgeous. I have so missed you. I could just sit and stare at you all day.'

Serena smiled sweetly. 'You look really well. One could never guess what you have been through.'

'It's not been easy. I've struggled. But... but the thought of...'

'The thought of what?'

'The thought of trying to live a half-normal life has kept me going.'

'Is there space for me in your half-normal life?'

Harry stared at her again. 'What would you do here? You would be bored out of your mind. What could a man like me with all my problems, offer a young beautiful woman like you?'

'Are you happy to see me?'

'Yes.'

'Would you like me to stay?'

'Yes. But you know it's not that simple.'

'Why can't we just give things a go instead of planning years ahead?'

'You are far too special, far too important to me. You know how I feel about you. I'm not in a position to live recklessly.'

'Look, I did a lot of thinking, a lot of soul searching. I liked you the minute I met you back in Chicago, and now, after all this time, I still like you. That must surely mean something? I'm not scared of your sickness; I've done a lot of reading, educated myself about this disease, how to deal with being around someone who has it. I am not overwhelmed by it, I'll cope. I really think we have something special between us. Why don't we try to be together? Just give it a go, without any expectations?'

'Are you sure? I am not feeling very strong or very fortunate, not to mention attractive, at the moment.'

Serena held his face in her hands and kissed him. Slowly, she began to unbutton his shirt. 'I find you very attractive. Where do you sleep?'

He pointed to his bedroom, at the top of a small staircase. She stood up and reached for his hands. He held on to her and let himself be led.

'Serena... what are you doing...?'

'Shush. Don't speak.' She took him to his room and slowly continued to undress him.

'Serena, do you think this is a good idea?'

'Yes. Let's live a little.'

Harry stopped resisting.

They made love.

ooooo

'I never dreamt that I would have you in my bed. Making love to you was something I couldn't even imagine.'

They lay in bed staring into each other's eyes.

'I… I can easily say it: I think I love you. It's crazy I know.'

'Do you?' Serena smiled emphatically.

'Yes.' Harry kissed her on the lips. 'I love you. I do. I really do. I have had a… ' he rolled his eyes in disbelief, '…I have had a bad, bad year, it's been… it's been really hard.' He sighed.

Serena smiled at him. 'Are you sure you love me?'

'Yes. Yes. I really am. I don't know you very well, but what I do know, I like… I love… I've thought about you almost every day. I've missed you so much. I've wanted to see you so much. I've wanted to be with you; wanting you has forced me to tackle and try to beat my depression. I was in a bad way. I had to get better for you. I wanted to see you desperately, but knew I had to work on myself if there was ever to be a chance of seeing you again. It's true I had doubts, but not doubts about you. They were doubts as to whether it was fair on you, if I should drag you into my uncertain life. When I was feeling positive, I thought only about you, about us being together, and how to make it possible.'

Serena continued to listen; her mind focused, her heart open. She stroked his cheek, staring into his eyes, which glowed with the same telling passion she'd detected when she first met him. They were dramatically different from the last time she'd seen him in Tuscany. He seemed more relaxed, more at ease.

Harry continued. 'I went through a lot, both mentally and physically. I had very dark moments, I wasn't sure if I was ever going to make it back. I had a lot of time to think. A lot of time to think about what I want.'

'What do you want?'

He smiled wistfully. 'What I want and what I am able to have are two very different things.'

'Okay, what would you have if you could have it?

'You!' Holding her gaze, he smiled nervously. 'I... I want you. I... I... I tried everything possible to forget you. Everything. I tried to delete your number. I deleted your photos. I tried to obliterate you from my mind, I did everything possible not to love you, not to think about you. But I want you, and I love you.' He looked at her facial expression; was he laying it on too heavily? Was he frightening her off? She had literally just walked in through the door.

Harry smiled apprehensively. 'What about *him*?'

'You mean Mathias?'

'Yes, that pervert.'

Serena laughed. 'He is just fine, thank you, and he is not a pervert.'

'And…?'

'And what?'

'Are you still together?'

'No. Well actually, I don't really know. No, not really.'

Harry sat up. 'Care to explain?'

Serena shrugged, also sitting up and pulling the covers around her. 'There's nothing to explain, really. We are together if I want us to be. Whenever I go to Paris, or whenever I need or want him, he is there.'

'Is it an open relationship?' Harry felt a pang of jealousy. He had just made love to her, and now they were talking about her other lover.

'It's whatever we want it to be. I've been to Paris to visit him a couple of times, he's visited me in the States, we see each other quite a lot, but we are not in a relationship. I haven't seen anyone else, just him, on and off.'

'So why aren't you with him now?'

'Because I am here with you. I stayed away because it was the right thing to do. You clearly needed time, which I wanted to give you. You needed time and space.'

Harry took a deep breath. 'Thinking about you with that guy half-killed me. I had visions of wanting to hurt him whenever I thought you were with him.' He raised his eyebrows apologetically. She giggled.

He turned to face her. 'No, seriously, why did you come now? You haven't called or written, I haven't heard from you for months. I'm over the moon you are here, but why?'

Serena smiled. 'It felt like the right time. And I wanted to wish you a happy birthday and…' she skipped to the exercise bike where a clean T-shirt lay hanging. She yanked it over her head and then ran towards the small staircase.

'Where are you going?'

'Wait!' she shouted. She grabbed her bag, giggling as she ran up the stairs.

'I wanted to give you something. Happy birthday!' She handed him a little box, jumping up and down in glee, impatiently waiting for him to open it.

'What is it?' Harry smiled in excitement like an overgrown kid, desperate to unwrap the curious-looking object.

'Open it,' she commanded, more excited than he was.

He opened it. It was the size of a small jewellery box. Inside lay a key. He took it out, looking at her bewildered, awaiting an explanation.

'It's a key.' She grinned.

'Key to?'

'I bought a house.'

'Really?'

'I bought a house for... for... for us.' She looked at him, poker-faced.

He raised his eyebrows, looking at the key once again, dumbfounded. 'I'm confused.'

Serena held his face gently, drawing it close to hers. 'I bought a house in California. A house for us. For us to live in...' she hesitated, '...to live in together. If we ever decided we wanted to...'

Astounded, Harry remained very quiet. Serena waited for him to speak. He was obviously concerned. His blank expression endeared him even more to her.

'Aren't you happy?

'Yes.' He managed half a smile. 'Happy. Happy but I must say, very confused.'

'The kids?'

He nodded, relieved.

'They can come with us.'

A look of horror spread across his bright crimson face. 'Laura has custody.' He hoped not to put her off.

Serena flung her arms around him. 'They can visit every holiday.'

Harry fell silent again. His face was etched in a horrendous pale frown.

'Please, please don't feel any pressure. Mathias showed it to me; it's a great investment and a nice place to visit.'

Harry felt goose-pimply all over. Little drops of perspiration were formulating like small sparkly stones on the tip of his nose, before sprinting down his face. Was he about to lose her again? He couldn't bear that.

Serena continued in a desperate bid to calm him down. 'Since you and Miles were, may I say, both thoroughly incompetent and unable to manage my money,' she giggled, cheekily, 'I asked Mathias for his help. He has helped me to make some investments, introduced me to a few Swiss banks, and has given me some general direction. This house belonged to one of his ex-colleagues who needed to sell it quickly because of his divorce. It was a bargain, so I bought it!'

Harry tried to follow, but struggled; his mind went wandering off back to the darkness. His thoughts diverted to Laura; he was in no fit state to enter into a war with her over the kids, but neither did he want to lose Serena. *Why did this have to happen now? Why couldn't she just come back, say 'I love you,' and simply remain with me?*

'I bought the house… just somewhere to escape to, for holidays, retirement, whatever. It's beautiful, it's spacious… on top of a cliff in Monterey, with beautiful views of the ocean. You will love it when you see it.'

'What about the kids?' Harry repeated, like a broken record.

'You don't need to decide yet, or even think about it. It's just a house. It was a great way to park some money and it's easy to sell if I ever need to. It's there for us to enjoy. Please don't feel pressure. We can take the kids on holiday there; they will love it, I promise!'

Harry tried to take some reassurance from her words, but he was terrified. He couldn't move to California now; what about his kids? What would he tell Laura? Things were amicable with her now; he couldn't afford to rock the boat. Making an enemy of Laura was the worst thing he could possibly do, and what about his therapy? He was doing so well. What about his new flat? There was so much pressure. Careful not to stress in front of Serena, he took a deep breath and faked a contrived grin.

'We need not make any big decisions.' Serena held his hand tightly; she didn't want to frighten or corner him. She realised her gift was probably causing him more pain than pleasure right now. Wondering if she had made a mistake presenting him with this gift so soon, she discreetly tried to change the subject. 'The kids can come and go as they please, your parents can bring them; there's lots of space, everyone will fit in.' She smiled encouragingly, anything to calm him down.

Harry chewed the inside of his lip, a recent habit. *Calm down*, he told himself.

'Thank you. It's an amazing idea. I'm sure it's beautiful.' He kissed her on the cheek as one would kiss a friend and offered her another grateful, 'thank you'.

'Would you like to see it?'

He nodded. 'I would love to. We can take the kids for their next holiday.'

'It's absolutely stunning. I have a few more things to do to it, but other than that, it's fully furnished and ready to be lived in. I can't wait to go and sit by the ocean, sip cocktails and paint. That's all I want to do.'

'How do I fit into that plan?' Harry sat at the edge of the bed in his dressing gown staring at her, out of his mind, but daring not show it.

Serena sat next to him. 'I want you to live there with me. I want us to live together as a proper couple.'

'So I would have to leave London?'

'It's a twelve-hour flight; you could come back whenever you want.'

Harry was silent. Serena went on. 'It's calm, peaceful, with an amazing quality of life, clean air, no pollution, no stress, great hospitals and expert care. It's perfect for you. It's perfect for me too. I totally fell in love with the place the minute I laid eyes on it. It's where *Big Little Lies* was filmed.'

Harry, as pale as a sheet of paper, was still adjusting to Serena being in his new flat. A day ago he couldn't have anticipated her being here, yet here she was, larger than life, as was her outrageous proposal.

'You look like you've seen a ghost! Are you okay? Am I scaring you?'

'Do you want to live with someone like me? Do you know how sick I am?'

'You are not sick, Harry. You keep saying you are sick, I understand you are scared to death, but the Alzheimer's hasn't hit that bad yet, and when it does, it will most probably come slowly. You will be okay. Besides, I love you, Harry,' she said, in a matter-of-fact manner. 'I, too, as I said, have had time to think. It's you I want.'

'Do you realise what you are asking me to do? Can you not see how preposterous your proposal is? I'm coming out of a divorce. I've lost my kids. I'm sick. How can I just up sticks and leave with you?' Harry's voice trembled as he spoke.

Serena felt terrible. The last thing she had intended to do was to freak him out, but perhaps he was right and she hadn't thought it through. Bad timing.

'Not now, darling. Not now. We don't need to move there now or ever, it's just a house. It's an asset, an investment. I'm sorry, I didn't think; I was just excited.'

'Just lie here with me. I am so happy to see you. I don't want to think about anything else right now. I have waited so long to hold you in my arms; let me just enjoy this moment. I want to feel your skin against mine and feel your body close. I have dreamt about moments like these. We can discuss the complicated stuff later.'

Harry listened to his instincts. He felt he could trust her; she was probably telling the truth. Maybe she did love him. He truly hoped this to be the case. He had to hang on to her, no matter what. Overcome with desire, he tore off the T-shirt she was wearing and made love to her for what seemed like the whole night.

ooooo

Dr Stephan Raza looked through his weekly appointments and was more than surprised to see Laura Johnson had been pencilled in. She had stopped seeing him many months ago. He hoped she was okay and was very curious to have a session with her. He always felt suspicious when patients returned a few months later. The last time he'd seen her, she seemed much stronger and she had insisted she had recovered.

As usual, Laura waited for the doctor in Reception, but she was light years away from when she had last sat in this very seat. Gone was the weeping willow of a woman, now replaced by the fierce powerhouse of the lawyer that she was. Her mental state was perfectly reflected in her bold yet somewhat inviting choice of attire. Dr Raza was very happy to see her. He noticed the dress she wore, he realised her face was made up, and he saw and heard her heels tapping on the floorboards.

'It's very nice to see you, Ms Johnson. Please do come in.' As expected, they exchanged pleasantries, albeit formally. Laura confessed to the doctor that it had been hard after the divorce, and she had somewhat struggled, but she was now much better and had bounced back quicker than she had anticipated.

'Nothing makes me happier than to see my patients smile. It makes my job all the more worth it. Thank you for coming to see me. People's recovery is largely due to themselves; if we are able to help in any way to get them there, then that's all we can ask for. It never hurts to hear about it though.'

Laura looked the doctor straight in the eye without blinking. 'I didn't come to see you just to tell you I'm healed; there's another reason.'

Dr Raza smiled and nodded as he usually did.

'During our therapy sessions, I developed feelings for you. It wasn't intentional. But I fell for you.' She paused. 'I am in love with you.'

Dr Raza became motionless like a statue, his face deadly pale with his left eye twitching. Speechless, he felt ice cold. He took a large sip of water, carefully avoiding eye contact.

'I have feelings for you.' Laura repeated, feeling little sympathy about putting him on the spot. After all, confrontation was her daily routine.

'I came to see you specifically, not only because I needed to see a professional; I had already been told about you. You were very highly recommended, not just for your skills but for other qualities you possess.'

Dr Raza felt a little lump in his throat, as he was thrust beyond the usual limits of conventional thought or action. He could only respond with a stern firmness. 'You are putting me in an awkward position, Ms Johnson. I am both flattered and embarrassed. It's not unusual for a patient to develop feelings for their therapist, but the therapist must heed these sentiments. If this is the case, then your therapy with me must cease immediately.' He cleared his throat and paused. 'You can, of course, continue your therapy… if you so wish, with one of my colleagues.'

'No. That's not an option. Anyway, I am not here for therapy. My therapy is finished. I am here because I feel ready. I feel ready to be able to tell you. I have had a lot of time to think about things and think about what I want. In fact, part of my therapy is getting closure on this episode and to get closure I need to tell you how I feel. The rest is up to you.'

'It's not quite as simple as that. Also, I need to manage your expectations. Knowing what I now know can only be detrimental to any further treatment with me.'

'So you are professionally rejecting me too?' Laura smiled sarcastically.

'Please don't misunderstand me. You are a valued client of mine, but it would be very unprofessional for me to continue treating you; it would be an abuse of my power. I cannot offer you a personal relationship; you must know that already, and you are rejecting my professional help, so there isn't much left for us to discuss.'

Laura, unaccustomed to rejection, embraced the challenge like water off a duck's back, and continued relentlessly to voice her thoughts. Only when Dr Raza politely made it crystal clear he was very happily married and had been for twenty-five years, and had no intention of ever changing that, did she begin to back down.

'The more you reject me, the more I want you. I probably wouldn't have broken up with my husband if I hadn't developed feelings for you; it was so easy to fall for you.'

'I don't know that I can be held responsible for the breakdown of your marriage.'

Laura smiled cheekily.

'Why *did* you divorce your husband?'

'I had an affair with a colleague at work. We broke it off when he got seconded to another office. Then he returned earlier than expected and automatically we rekindled our romance. It was never meant to be anything serious, but I ended up falling for him quite badly. Harry was working like mad, he was busy, stressed, often behaved erratically, we were frequently sleeping in separate beds; things were a bit off between us. It was with this colleague that I went to Athens. I told Harry it was with my best friend, who was indeed also there, but she wasn't the only one.'

'Are you still together?'

'No. I thought I loved him but I was mistaken. Once I found out I was pregnant, he let me down tremendously.' Her lips quivered. The mighty lawyer now appeared to Dr Raza nothing more than a desperate woman let down in love, left to deal with the aftermath. 'The baby… ' she took a deep breath. '… the baby was his.'

'I'm sorry for all you've had to deal with Ms Johnson; so much you've had to bear. Please consider seeing one of my colleagues; they are all very good. I cannot recommend them highly enough.'

'No. I don't want to go there again. I cannot bring myself to talk again about the baby I aborted. It was easy with you, I felt a strong connection with you. I wanted to talk to you. I also wanted to fall in love with you.' She smiled. 'And I did.'

Dr Raza experienced an unknown tingling feeling rushing through his torso. Suddenly, he longed to gaze at her. He watched her lip curl into a gentle pout as she spoke. He couldn't help but notice the shape of her firm breasts beneath her tight dress. Her long, delicate fingers wiped away the stubborn tear on her pink cheek. A stunning looking woman, her vulnerability, her open declaration of love, unexpectedly piqued the good doctor's interest. He hadn't expected this.

That night, Dr Raza found himself lying in bed in the early hours of the morning, thinking about Laura and the very interesting exchange between them. Married to his work, Stephan had blocked even the slightest hint of romance and emotion from his life. Contrary to what he had Laura believe, he and his wife, though living under the same roof, led increasingly separate lives, and for the last five years, separate bedrooms, resulting in minimal communication. He glanced at Laura's work profile picture. He would need a cold shower and some strenuous butterfly strokes at the gym pool first thing tomorrow morning.

14

For the next few days, Serena and Harry remained locked away in his bachelor pad away from the world: no excuses and no explanations. They focused solely on each other, speaking candidly about their lives, their past, their childhood. They discussed their likes, dislikes, strengths, weaknesses, passions, everything that came to mind, each of them laying everything on the table, bare and available for the other's benefit. Determined to start the relationship off the right way, without any secrets, they both agreed that honesty, openness, and absolute transparency were the only way forward.

'It's all prepared for you, darling. The scented candles, the calm, ambient music, your own little sanctuary awaits you.' Serena was thrilled Harry was prepared to take her suggestions seriously. He was no longer a stranger to the world of healing and meditation, having recently learnt a lot from Gemma, who had exposed him to the very interesting world of psychedelics that had opened his mind, pulling him out of his darkest moments and generally reawakening him. With nothing to lose, Harry was now comfortable tapping into his new non-philistine side, and welcoming different experiences, however strange they might be.

An avid yogini herself, Serena was overjoyed she'd finally found someone to share her keen knowledge and experiences with. Harry was the perfect guinea pig; if anyone needed alternative therapy it was him; she would teach him everything she knew, from harmonious breathing to Buddhist, Hindu and Chinese meditation. Having a steady boyfriend meant she could do all the things she dreamt of with a partner, waking him up at the crack of dawn with yoga sessions, cleansing exercises. She had found her partner in crime and she was delighted.

'Thank you. It looks perfect.' He peered into his bedroom.

'What's the matter?'

'Nothing.'

'Are you sure?'

'Yes. It's just… it's just that I find it so hard to relax. I always feel as if I should be working, or writing something in my diary. I've never been into yoga, meditation-type things. I'm still getting used to it. Please don't come in; I'll be so embarrassed.'

'I know, I understand, but I promise you it really helps. I try to meditate as often as I can, but if I have a crisis I do it as a matter of urgency. It's really helpful. And I promise I won't come in.' She smiled, motioning with her head for him to go into the room.

'Okay. You, er… you will still be here when I come out? Or do you have any plans to leave or go somewhere?'

'No. I have nowhere to be. I will remain here and be right here when you finish. Besides, I have some calls to make.'

'*Who?*' Harry glared at her.

'Harry! Stop it. I know who you are referring to…
Please, go and meditate.'

Deeply infatuated with Serena, Harry felt his heart
dictating his moves. Was she his new zen? Was she the
one? Had he finally found the right person for him? Right
now, it seemed so. He tried to keep his mind free and not
think about anything. It was very difficult for him to relax;
his mind was swimming with information, desperate for
an outlet. He breathed hard and deep, trying to let go as
Serena had instructed. He closed his eyes tightly. As he
relaxed his muscles, he focused just on his breathing. His
mind still imprisoned, he thought about his kids, picturing
them running wild on a cold beach. Was this the beach
where Serena had bought her house? Was it Montecito, or
Monterey? It was all the same to him.

He tried to keep his posture straight. Part of him
thought to give up and sleep, the other part resisted, trying
to continue. 'Enjoy the peace, enjoy the peace,' he repeated
to himself. It was impossible; he felt fidgety; did he need to
go to the lavatory? Was he thirsty? Should he open his eyes?
Why was it so hard for him to relax? It was so much easier
to do these things with his shrink.

His mind drifted off to the weekend. Was it too soon
to introduce Serena to the kids? Should he wait a little?
Well, no; he had the kids this weekend anyway so he might
as well introduce them. So far, he'd managed to avoid them
meeting Serena, but she was living with him now. How long
could he continue to make excuses and look like a fool? He
missed them; they'd be bitterly disappointed if he cancelled.
He opened his eyes. It was too much; he couldn't relax.

'What happened?'

'I couldn't do it.'

'Why not?'

'I have too much on my mind. I couldn't stop thinking; I couldn't let go. I was drowning. I couldn't relax.'

'It's okay. Don't worry. Meditation is also an art; one has to learn how to do it. You can try again another day. Let me run a bath for you, with a more comfortable surrounding that you are used to.' She winked.

'I'm sorry. I promise I will try meditation again soon.'

'It's okay; it can be strange at first; next time we will do it together. It will really help you, I promise. So, orange and lavender or fig and lemon bath salts?' She kissed him and went to run the bath.

ooooo

Nervously excited and emotional, Serena began preparations for the children's stay at Harry's flat from seven o'clock in the morning.

'You must understand I know nothing about kids. I have never had any children around me, I have no siblings, no cousins, no friends with kids; I have precisely zero experience with children.'

'You'll be fine. Honestly. My kids are super easy.'

'I don't know what to do with them, how to be, how to talk to them. I'm useless with kids.'

Harry held Serena in his arms. 'Just be yourself. They already have a mother; you are not replacing their mother; you can just be a friend.'

'What if they hate me?'

'They won't.'

'How do you know?'

'Well, if they do, it's okay; you don't need to live with them.' Harry saw the panic spreading across her face, 'Relax. They will love you. Especially if they know you have a house in America, they will most certainly love you! Please don't worry.'

'I so desperately want to be a mum, now that I finally have a chance to play at being one, but I'm worried as hell.'

'You don't have to be their mum.'

'I know. But one day I will be, to my own kids. One day.'

Harry glared at her. 'What?' he asked. 'To your own kids? You want kids?'

Serena shot him a puzzled look.

'Yes. Yes, of course I want kids. Of course, I want kids for God's sake!' She almost shouted, frowning at him. 'What woman doesn't want kids?' She stared at him, waiting for an answer. He offered none.

'You don't?' Her face suddenly darkened, her eyes narrowed and she pursed her lips in worry. 'You don't want kids? Oh my God, you don't want kids. You don't want any more, do you?' Serena clasped her hands together with a loud clap, eyes shining fiercely in disappointment.

Oh dear. Not the kid conversation again, thought Harry. Their open, candid conversation had clearly omitted this one very small, unimportant topic. Harry wished he could hide somewhere and avoid this conversation. Was he about to lose her yet again over this? Surely not this subject… again.

'Serena, darling, please sit down. Sit next to me. We need to talk.'

'You don't want any more kids, do you?'

'No. No, I don't. I don't want any more kids.'

'I didn't know that.' Serena's face was worried and pasty as she shook her head ferociously, sinking next to him, shocked that they hadn't established this during their apparently open conversations.

'I didn't know you didn't want kids. I thought we wanted the same things. I thought you wanted what I want.'

'I do. I do want what you want, just... just not kids.'

Serena shook her head again in disbelief. 'Are you crazy? How could you have thought I didn't want kids? I'm a woman.' She continued to shake her head. 'I have no family. I have no one. How could you have thought I wouldn't want a family? I don't understand.'

Harry felt himself numbing up. He threw his head back, breathing heavily and not wanting to say any more.

'How could you think I didn't want to have kids? Just because you already have kids, you're satisfied. Well I deserve my own kids too. Say something.'

'I'm sorry. I should have known you wanted kids, and, yes, you are of course right and it's normal to want kids. I'm sorry, I didn't think. I didn't think that far.'

'Clearly.'

'I'm sick; I've just got divorced; I'm not in a fit state of mind to think that far. I understand you want kids. I... I get it.'

'Do you? Really? Do you get it now? I'm glad we finally understand each other. So what does this mean now?'

'I don't know. I really don't know. I didn't think about it. I'm sorry, please understand. It's not personal. I... I just haven't had the time or the need to think about it; that's the honest truth.'

'Well, we need to talk about it seriously. I can compromise and sacrifice on everything, but not this. I want to have children. End of.'

'I understand; you are absolutely right; it's not even a question; you don't need to explain. I understand. Can we please discuss it properly before you make any decisions?'

Serena shrugged her shoulders. 'I don't know, Harry, it's all so difficult.'

Harry grabbed her. 'Serena please, please listen to me. Please don't leave me. Please stay with me. We can discuss it. We can talk about it in peace. Please don't make any rash decisions over this.' Serena looked down at her feet, avoiding further eye contact with Harry.

'Let's get the house ready; the kids will be here soon.' She got up and walked out of the room without looking at Harry.

'I can live with anything, but not with losing you. Please don't leave me,' Harry muttered under his breath, wishing he wasn't so needy.

Promptly at ten in the morning, Harry's doorbell rang. The kids stood outside, eagerly shouting for their father to open the door. Laura waited in the car until the door opened. With an amicable wave goodbye, she sped off as the boys ran inside the house. Charlie looked forward to meeting Daddy's new friend, whereas Oliver, apprehensive as usual, pretended not to care.

Admirably Serena swept her sadness to one side and put on a splendid performance for the children. Within minutes they both found themselves under her spell. Charmed by her kindness and lavish gifts she had bought especially for them, they hardly left her side. She tried to play games with them, and ending up making a fool of herself, endearing herself more to them. She sang French folk songs, and told them stories about bears in the Russian forests. The best part was when she ordered Kentucky Fried Chicken for supper and allowed them to go to bed late, ignoring their usual routine.

'I like Serena, Daddy. She is really nice.' Charlie was in love.

'Yes, darling, she is lovely. I am very happy you like her; I think she likes you too.'

'She is your girlfriend, isn't she?' teased Oliver from the bed on the other side of the room.

Harry ignored the question. 'Do you like her, Ollie?'

'Are you going to marry her?'

'Marry her?' shouted Charlie. 'Is Daddy going to marry Serena?'

'No, darling, Daddy is not going to marry Serena; she is my friend.'

'She's his girlfriend.'

'Thank you, Oliver. Right, kids, sleepy time.'

'Daddy, if you are divorced from Mummy, does that mean you can marry Serena? I like Serena; she is cool. Can she play with us tomorrow? She promised to buy me more Lego. I really want it.'

'Yes, Charles. Being divorced means Daddy can marry again.' Oliver looked at the ceiling as he spoke in his most annoying voice.

'We'll make sure you get your Lego tomorrow, Charlie. Daddy is tired now, so please go to sleep and we'll have a nice day tomorrow.' He kissed them goodnight and swiftly left the room.

'That was a success. Thank you. You were wonderful.' Harry offered Serena a large glass of wine, but stuck to water himself.

'You are right; they are both lovely. Did they like me?'

'Yes. Especially Charlie. He told me twice that he really likes you.'

Serena was pleased. 'This is the first time I've ever spent the whole day with kids. I thought it'd be much harder.'

'Just you wait. But you're a natural. Nothing to worry about.'

Serena drank her wine in silence, staring at the ceiling. Disheartened, she felt broken inside. Perhaps she should have discussed things with him before jumping to wild conclusions. After all, it was a massive thing; well, for him anyway.

'Are you ignoring me?'

She turned to face him. 'No,' she replied. 'I'm not ignoring you,' she lied, wishing she could have left the room.

'You were great with the kids. Thank you. I really appreciate it. It hasn't been easy for them, and Oliver can be very difficult; you managed him well.'

'Thanks. It was no effort. Tiring, but not as hard as I thought.'

'Do you want to talk?'

'I'm tired. I would like to go to sleep.'

'It's nine o'clock.'

'What do you want to talk about?'

'You know what I want to talk about.'

'There's nothing to talk about. We want completely different things.'

'Serena, I don't want to lose you. Here, sit here on the sofa next to me. I've just found you, I don't want to lose you again.'

'So, what are you going to do about it?'

'Can we get a dog?'

'Oh, Harry, for God's sake. I'm going to bed.'

'No, wait. I'm just teasing. Please sit back down. Please. Serena, I'm just joking,' he begged. 'We need to talk; please don't get angry. We don't want different things; we want exactly the same things. We cannot break up over this. Please.'

'I don't want to break up with you. But I don't see what the solution is.'

'One of us will have to compromise.'

'Harry, I want children. I want my own children; there is no compromise for me.'

'I understand.'

'What does that mean? "I understand"?'

'It means I understand you want your own children, and you are, of course, entitled to have your own children. I just need a little bit of time to think.'

'What do you want to think about?'

'Don't put me on the spot, please. It's been a long day. I need to think about things. About us. About you, about your wants.'

'Will you? Will you think about it? Will you think about it seriously?'

'I promise; of course I will. If you promise not to get upset and go running back to France.'

'It's not funny. Do you really promise to think about it? To really, honestly, think about it?'

'Yes. But Serena we… we have just got together, and not even that. You literally just turned up to my house out of the blue, from nowhere, without any warning. We really hardly know each other. I didn't expect to see you ever again after Tuscany, truly. We didn't have a relationship; it was so weird between us. Nothing had been determined, and now you are in my house and we are fighting about kids. This is beyond absurd. Sure, I understand you are a woman; you have a biological clock, etc., but it's too soon in the relationship. I will think about things in due course, but this, this is insane. It's far, far too early to be having this discussion now; we don't even know what's going on between us.'

'No, Harry, you don't understand. This is the right time for us to be having this discussion. I need to know this is a serious relationship. I absolutely don't need a casual part-time lover.'

'Here we go again, you and your part-time lovers.'

'Exactly, I already have a part-time lover... or I had one. I certainly don't need another one. I want a proper relationship, not another casual waste of time. I need to know that you and I want the same things. Otherwise it makes no sense for us to be together.'

'What do you want me to say?'

'I want you to tell me the truth.'

'The truth about what? I have told you more than I have told anyone else. I have told you everything. What else is there left to tell?'

'Harry, one day I want to have children. Healthy, beautiful children like you have. I need to know now there is a possibility of that. I need to know there is a possibility of that between us. Otherwise what's the point of us being together?'

'I understand that, I really do. But I cannot say what you want to hear right now. I need time. Time to think. My head is all over the place; I am constantly thinking, overthinking, and I have to say, having kids was not at the forefront of my thoughts.'

'This is a real waste of time.'

Harry held Serena in his arms, gazing lovingly at her face.

'However, now you are here. Now you are here with me, living in my flat, playing with my kids, and you have made your wishes very clear... I now understand what you want. I promise to think carefully and not to waste your time.'

'That's all I ask.'

Heaving a big sigh of relief, she sipped her wine. Unwillingly he poured himself a glass, feeling defeated, as he was desperate to stop drinking alcohol.

'I'm living in constant fear that you will just get up and leave and go back to Paris. Before you came, in a way I was okay; I had nothing but myself, and my straightforward path. Now that you are here, I am somehow more vulnerable. I am almost dependent on you. I don't want to be alone any more. I am so all over the place, and I hate it.'

'I won't do that. I have nothing in Paris that I need so desperately to get back to.'

'Actually, you haven't told me what happened in France between you and your lover boy. Do you want to tell me?'

'Nothing happened. I had a great time.'

'Was it a proper relationship you had?'

'Absolutely it was.'

'So why did it end?'

'It didn't. We are what we want to be. He loves me; he will always be there for me.'

'Is he waiting for you?'

'No. Not exactly.'

'Not exactly?'

'The door is always open. I can come and go as I please, but there is nothing for me to gain from it.'

'I wish you would just spell it out. You are either together as a couple or you're not.'

'Obviously we are not together as a couple. He is divorced; has older kids; he doesn't need a wife or a serious girlfriend. I accept that. We have no expectations of each other. We've decided to keep things open.'

'Are you planning on closing things with him... ever?'

'That's why I came here. I gave you time to deal with your life, post-divorce, but not too much time in case you met someone else, and I had actually hoped things would be a bit easier. Especially with your... as you say so proudly, "uncomplicated divorce".'

'Things will get easier. I am a free man. I can do whatever I want. I can love whomever I want.'

'I've heard that before.'

'Serena!'

'But you don't want kids.'

'That's not fair.'

'It's the truth.'

'Serena, don't be like that. It's not so simple. I have to tell you something. Please don't be angry and listen to me.'

'What is it?' Serena asked, surprised there could be more to tell.

'Please listen to me; it's very difficult for me to talk about this. I try to avoid this subject as much as I can.'

Serena's sarcasm soon turned to concern.

Harry began to explain and reprised the actual reason for the divorce: the baby, everything. He opened his heart to her as genuinely as he could, telling her everything that came to his mind, unreservedly holding nothing back. Every fibre of his being told him that she was the one: she was so easy to love. He must not lose her.

Genuinely moved by his experiences, without a second thought, Serena cast her annoyance to one side, immediately sympathising with him. 'I'm so sorry. Your life hasn't been easy, has it?'

'No, it really hasn't. At the moment, it's a disaster. It's all a mess.' He kissed her hand. 'It will get better, now that you're here; I feel it in my bones. It's so good to have you here. Have I told you that I missed you?'

'You certainly have.'

'Did you miss me?'

'You know I did.'

'I'm surprised you had time.'

She looked at him again, raising her eyebrows. 'That again?'

'I can't help it.'

'Why are you so obsessed with him? Why does he bother you so much?'

'He doesn't. I'm just joking.'

'No, you're not. You keep going on about him. You don't know anything about him; he is not an arsehole. He is actually a nice guy.'

'I don't want to discuss him. I want you to stop seeing him.'

'Okay.'

'Really?'

'Yes.'

'You will stop seeing him?'

'I don't need him if I have you.'

'Do you promise?'

'Yes. He is just a fallback for when I am lonely, or don't find anyone else.'

'If things don't work out between us, will you go back to him?'

'Let's hope things do work out.'

'If they don't?'

'We will cross that bridge when we come to it.'

'Okay, but I would still like it if you didn't mention him again.'

'You're the one who brings him up!'

'Do I?'

'Yes. Seven, eight times a day, every day.'

'No, I don't.'

'Yes, you do!'

'Well, how do you think it makes me feel: my girlfriend having an open relationship with a known playboy?'

'I am single, and so is he.'

'But it was an open relationship.'

'We didn't see anyone else while we were together.'

'Yes, but you could have. You knew nothing serious was going to come of the relationship, yet you continued to be with him.'

'So?'

'It's quite indecent actually.'

'No, it's not. He's been nice to me.'

'It is.'

'Well, it's over now.'

'Are you sure you won't see him again?'

'No, not while I am with you.'

'Positive?'

'Yes.'

'Okay, let's stop talking about him now.'

'Okay.'

'I don't like him. I really, really don't like him. In fact, I hate him. I really hate him.'

'Okay. I don't need to talk about him.'

'Okay, great. End of conversation.'

Later that night, Harry lay in bed watching Serena go through her usual bedtime routine.

'It's really good to have you here. I thought I was done with relationships, but now I realise I wasn't. In so many ways it was good to be alone after Laura left; I really needed that time to focus on myself, and learn how to live with my illness and prepare for whatever I can, whatever is in my control.'

'I am so impressed. You have made such tremendous progress.' Serena paused as she got into bed. 'You are so different to when I saw you in Italy. I much prefer this version of you.'

'Yes, that was a really bad time. I am so glad that's over.' He leaned over and kissed her. 'Serena, can I ask you a question?'

She looked at him curiously. 'Yes. What is it? It sounds serious.'

'Why me?'

'What?'

'Why do you want to be with me? Please don't misunderstand what I'm saying, I'm obsessed with you, I love you. I wanted you from the minute you waltzed in to that office in Chicago. But why do you want me? Why do you like me? Every man in the world would do anything and everything to have you. How can I believe that you want me?'

Serena sighed. 'I've had an interesting life. My childhood was lonely and unstable; it took me years as a grown-up to deal with that. Then, after my father passed away, I went a bit crazy. I was on a mad mission to find a husband, settle down, get married, and have kids as soon as I could. The thought of being completely alone terrified me.

'For sure, I wasn't ready for any of that, and most of the men I was introduced to I found rather strange, resulting in disaster after disaster. Then I had a relationship that sadly ended horribly, so again I was single and lonely. After that disaster, I had different problems to deal with so I somewhat gave up on men. Before I arranged to meet you and Miles, I did a lot of research on investment banks, hedge funds and financial institutions. That's when it got interesting.

'"Harry Hoffman" was all over the internet. I think it was your year. You were winning awards, you were being interviewed by finance journals. "Harry Hoffman" was quoted in the news; you were quite the star.' She smiled sweetly. 'And then when I met you, you were just as handsome, just as charming as you were on your YouTube videos.'

'Were you stalking me?' Harry giggled.

'No. I wasn't. I was generally interested. Your industry is alien to me; I knew nothing about it. I tried to learn about it, but I didn't manage to do so. I was thinking of moving to London, and then your PA told me you were coming to Chicago so I took the opportunity. You were almost a celebrity in my eyes. I was very happy to meet you.'

'Was it love at first sight, a *coup de foudre*?'

She laughed.

'But you knew I was married.'

'Yes, I did. But I wasn't expecting anything. I came to see you because I needed an asset manager. But you and Miles were not very subtle, I must say.'

'Was it blatantly obvious that we were both lusting after you?'

'You can say that again.'

'But that still doesn't explain anything. Why did you come to my hotel that evening? What would you have done had I invited you to my room?'

'I would have accepted.'

'No way! So I could have had all of this back then?' He buried his head in her neck.

'Yes, but the point is, you didn't invite me to your room. There was something very grounded, very special in you, it was almost impossible not to fall for you. You were faithful to your wife, honest in your work, successful in your career, a stark contrast to your colleague, Miles. It was hard for me to accept. Miles, who was also married with kids, was prepared to do anything to have me and it seemed to me that you couldn't have cared less. You left without saying goodbye. I was so hurt. That made me want you even more. I couldn't believe you'd just disappeared.'

'I'm sorry about that.'

'I just hung on to it. I so wanted to see you again. Then, when I bumped into you in Italy, I felt it was more than just a coincidence.'

'I was a mess in Italy.'

'Then I compared you to all the other men I knew, and every time you came up trumps. I am far better suited to you than to any other man I know.'

'What if you get bored of me and my disease worsens, which it inevitably will, and you feel as if you can't cope?'

'I'm not afraid of sicknesses and illnesses. My mother was diagnosed with paranoia and schizophrenia when I was still quite young. I learned to deal with it, live with it.'

'But don't you want more from your life?'

'Trust me, there is nothing out there.'

'So you will settle for me then?'

'Why is it so hard for you to understand I like you, indeed, love you, and want to be with you?'

'I'm insecure. You know that.'

'Don't be. Just trust me and give it a go.'

ooooo

Once again, Harry found himself at another Alzheimer's support group.

'It would be so much easier if I were older. I just feel so awkward being here. I'm too young; people don't expect someone of my age to have Alzheimer's, and I really don't like the attention or the sympathy.'

'I understand, but at least you are young. It's actually an advantage; you are so much better equipped to deal with it.'

Kind words, thought Harry, *but not all that helpful.* The support group could have had far more potential. The average age of over sixty-five was just too gut-wrenching for Harry; he felt sick to the stomach. What did he have in common with these people? They were old, so much older than him. It was perfectly acceptable for them to be sick, but not him; he was far too young. A bathroom break acted as an excuse and Harry discreetly ducked out of the group meeting. The experience had left him daunted; he simply wasn't ready for it. Every month he forced himself to attend, but somehow, he could never bring himself to sit through an entire meeting. Besides, he was still in the very early stages of the disease. He thought he would certainly come again, once it became more aggressive, which it almost certainly would. But for now Serena was his medication.

He wanted her to be close by. He yearned to share his experiences with her, no matter how positive or negative. It was imperative she knew exactly where he was, and that he was taking responsibility and all conceivable measures to deal with his problems and helping himself. The mere thought of Serena automatically put a smile on his face, providing him with a deep sense of comfort. If any woman could deal with his Alzheimer's, it was Serena. Her kindness and laid-back ways, without passing judgement, put him at ease, sparing him the constant shame and disgrace he fought within himself.

Serena was dominant in his thoughts, but in his mind, he pictured Laura's face. How strange; they were nothing like each other, almost worlds and oceans apart. *Laura is Charlie's mum*, he reminded himself, *Laura is Ollie's mum. Who is Serena then? Serena is my girlfriend.* He stood on the stairs of the building, meaning to head home, but didn't dare do so until he'd figured out what was going on in his head. He was able to distinguish Laura and the kids perfectly, *but Serena, she is my girlfriend*, he insisted to himself. Serena's face flashed back and forth in front of him. Was she *really* here? Was she really with him? How quickly it all seemed to happen. It was as if it were only yesterday that he'd lived with Laura and his children in his beautiful house. Yet now he lived in a new flat without his kids and with a different woman. But it was the right thing to do? Laura had left him. Harry repeated in his mind all that had happened, challenging himself to put it all into words without chills running down his spine.

He took out his trusted phone, intending to do something specific. He looked at it blankly; what did he want to do with it? He'd definitely taken it out for a reason, but what was the reason? He looked at his phone, hoping an answer would present itself, but nothing sprung to mind. Why had he taken out his phone? Directly above him, the winter sun shone down, radiant and warm. Harry returned his phone back to his jacket pocket; he couldn't cope with feeling stupid right now. The best thing to do would be to head home and seek solace there. He would be safe in his own home and not need to answer any questions, or be accountable to anyone. Confidently Harry headed home, happy that he had made the effort to visit the Alzheimer's support group once again. *Next time, it would be so much easier*, he reassured himself.

Back at home, Serena had cleared a small space in a corner at the back of the kitchen which was not in use, reserving it for her artwork.

'What are you drawing?' he quizzed, nuzzling at the back of her neck.

'Mmm...' she kissed him, eyes closed. 'You'll see.'

'What is it? It looks like a foetus! Is it a baby?' Harry looked confused.

Serena smiled. 'Yes, it's a pregnant woman with her baby partially visible in her tummy.'

'Wow, that's freaky. Are you doing it for fun or are you "working"?'

'I always draw to sell; I don't like any of my work so much that I feel the need to keep any of it. Besides, I don't have any space to store any of my work.' She gave Harry a sarcastic look, which rather concerned him.

'What?'

She smiled again. 'I don't have anywhere to store my work.' She shrugged. 'In fact, I don't really have any space to work either.'

'Yes, it's quite a small flat, I guess.' Harry leant in for a kiss. All he got was a quick peck.

'I need space and I need to work. I will go crazy if I don't do something.'

'Okay, I'm... I'm not stopping you...' Harry said worriedly. '... am I?'

'No, you're not. It's just that there isn't really any space here. These flats in London are so small. One has no space to do anything. Everything is so crowded and so, and... and... so claustrophobic.' Her voice was more agitated after each word. 'It's impossible to work here. Look. Look around you. There is no space to do anything; no space to hardly move.'

'Are you uncomfortable here, darling?' Harry laid his hands on Serena's shoulders; she smelt of paint. A stain peeped out from under her baggy white painting shirt. Harry tried to clean it gently with his hands. 'This stubborn stain doesn't want to come off,' he said as he smiled nervously. She stared at him blankly. 'Serena... please tell me. Are you unhappy here?'

She fell to the floor, sitting down with a loud bang, yanking out the pencil that had been neatly holding up her hair. 'The damn pencil hurts my head.'

Harry repeated his question. 'Serena, are you unhappy here in this house with me?'

'No. I'm happy. It's not a question of being unhappy. I am fine. I just need space. Much more space than this.'

Harry sat next to her. 'I understand,' he mumbled reluctantly. 'I don't know what to say, what to say to make things easier for you... perhaps... perhaps we can create some space somewhere.' He smiled at her nervously, having no idea of how or where he was going to create space. The flat was already bursting at the seams.

'I'm sorry, my love.' Serena laid her head on his shoulder. 'I'm really sorry; I don't mean to keep stressing you out. I know things are so difficult for you. I just... I just feel a bit uneasy. I don't know what it is... I'm just used to space, a lot of space. It sounds so spoilt, I know, but I've always lived in big houses. It sounds very brattish, but that's not what I mean at all.' She pulled her head away from his shoulders and kissed him.

'C'mon, let's make dinner. I'm hungry.'

Later that night, Harry lay in bed, wide awake. Still as a corpse in the silence of the night, his body lay cold and motionless. Serena's beautiful face almost glowed in the dark, soft and flawless. *She must be the dream and envy of every poet*, thought Harry, admiring her perfect features. She was never going to get used to this mediocre life, his small flat, his kids, his trivial, monotonous, boring ways. Did he expect her to settle for this? A fabulously wealthy woman like her, and, to top it all, she had a beautiful house in a beautiful part of the world, ready to be lived in. Not to mention the fact that she desperately wanted kids and a family of her own. Where did he fit into all of this? What did he have to offer her? Why should she stay here with him?

A young, beautiful woman with crazy amounts of money and equally wealthy men falling at her feet, she has everything and more going for her – why shouldn't she go on to pursue her dreams? Why am I kidding myself? I'm nothing but a thorn in her side.

He gazed at her solemnly, his cheeks hollow from the weight he had lost since she'd put him on a low-carb alkaline diet. How was he going to keep her? She could have the choice of dozens of eligible men; what on earth was she doing here with him? The thoughts drove him insane, bringing with them deeper insecurities. Suddenly he envied every man who'd ever looked at Serena. Did they have more to offer than he did? Certainly, a steep road lay ahead, and realistically, how long was Serena going to last before she was bored out of her mind, or desperate to have the child conversation again? He begged for sleep, but the darkness of the night and the heavy raindrops outside robbed him of this comfort. Insomnia plagued him again. *Be prepared*, he warned himself, *there is going to be no sleep tonight.*

ooooo

Surprisingly, the next few months remained calm and rather uneventful. Serena and Harry found a way to live their day-to-day lives without drama. The kids seemed happy dividing their time equally between Laura and Harry, and much to Harry's delight, Serena grew closer to the kids and formed her own special relationship with them, away from Harry. He found himself more at peace with his health issues.

Gradually he managed to locate various ways of controlling his emotions and coming to terms with the future. Unsurprisingly, occasional bouts of depression hit him hard from time to time. However, with Serena's unconditional love and consistent support, they found a balanced, pragmatic yet comfortable way of giving 'normality' a shot. Ever grateful, no news was always good news for Harry. He craved a calm life, struggling to cope with his uncertain future. He felt blessed not to be burdened with stressful daily events requiring his effort and attention. If life would consistently remain this balanced and uneventful, what a happy man he would be.

Serena also found herself more relaxed, calm and balanced. She managed to sell a few pieces of her artwork while simultaneously establishing some seemingly solid and interesting friends along the way. Things were finally plodding along well for the new couple.

15

S till nervous about driving on the left-hand side of the road, Serena nevertheless decided to brave it and drive the boys to the park. She was keen to be outdoors and enjoy the chilly air. Constant paint fumes played havoc with her lungs.

Still not used to the unpredictable British weather, she decided to make the most of the winter sunshine before the rain started to chuck down. Driving along the relatively quiet roads was not as intimidating as she'd suspected. The boys sang songs, imitated their favourite movie characters, easing her fears and making her laugh.

Charlie and Oliver were great company; she adored her time with them. Learning different things, seeing life from their point of view, reminded her of her own childhood, which had long been buried in her mind. The more time she spent with the children, the more she longed for her own child. It would be a girl, she had decided. Her name would be Lila. She would have light brown hair, and eyes as blue as the ocean, or a charming green as her mother and her grandmother had. Harry would probably love being a father to a daughter, and the boys would be wonderful older brothers. How lucky Lila would be, and how much fun it would be to bring her up and watch her grow, surrounded by a ready-made, large, loving family.

ooooo

Delighted at his girlfriend's kindness and willingness to spend time with his kids, Harry assured Serena that all would be well; he was only but a phone call away should any problems arise. He waved them goodbye and ran into the house, feeling a sudden burst of energy. Determined to take advantage of his relaxed and positive mood, he was more than pleased and grateful to have a few hours alone on a Sunday afternoon. He would use the time effectively and be selfish.

Harry took out his laptop. Work had been the last thing on his mind for so long; it was high time to get back into the swing of things and realign himself with his work life. Logging on to his emails, he watched in amazement as his inbox filled up in a matter of seconds. A constant stream, and so many high priority emails, it was almost endless. How long would he need to go through all of these? He raised his eyebrows in amazement. The fun afternoon he'd so looked forward to was now a dream, but at least he would be back in the loop and soon on top of everything once again.

The email addresses, mostly unfamiliar, quickly brought him back down to earth; he felt his brain razor-sharp again. It felt good. He stared at the names, shocked at how quickly things had accumulated. A brief analysis would swiftly bring him back up to speed. The short working weeks had left him behind. A technical nerd, secretly he revelled at being in front of a screen. Fortunately this time it was a different kind of research, with nothing to fear, all black and white, scientifically proven, algorithms, calculations, equations, matrixes, analytics – his world, his language. How much he appreciated these systems, so easy, so reliable and, most importantly, requiring minimal effort. It would take a short time to obtain all the information on everyone, and luckily it was all available at his fingertips. *Such great stalking equipment*, he chuckled to himself.

The virtual private network was still open. Since working from home, and having taken a few weeks off, Harry used a VPN, a secure and highly encrypted point-to-point internet connection to access sensitive data from home. Everything one needed to know was simply a few clicks away.

The sound of his phone diverted his attention away for a few seconds. How his face beamed with happiness. Serena, in a sending frenzy, shot out photos from the park, which continued to arrive on his phone without a break. His kids looked excited, the happiness on their innocent faces an obvious manifestation of how much fun they were having. Thrilled to bits, he zoomed in on Serena's face; she looked just as happy as the children; even her eyes smiled. Harry couldn't help but admire how great she was with the boys. How much he loved her and what a profound sense of trust he felt for her. Never had he imagined falling in love again, or loving anyone as much as he loved Laura, yet here was this woman who had stolen his heart and was now living in his house, playing with his kids. *How strange life is*, he thought. He thought he knew Laura quite well, even though he actually didn't, and she'd ended up hurting him, while Serena he knew almost nothing about, yet she made him so happy. He looked back at his screen, his face frozen in a childish smile.

Actually, what did he know about Serena? Really not much at all. In fact, very little. He stared at his phone for a few seconds, then looked at his laptop. Staring back at him in black and white was a list of names, a list of people awaiting checks and investigation. He froze. He looked at his phone screen again, then again at the laptop. He shook his head; was he thinking what he thought he was thinking?

What was he thinking?

He shouldn't. Should he?

He couldn't. Could he?

Could he really do that? Surely not.

Harry closed his eyes firmly, shaking his head, trying to convince himself not to. *Surely not*, he thought again to himself. Should he really? Trembling, slowly he began to type *Serena Markhieva* on his keyboard. He deleted it immediately as though he had made a terrible mistake. What was he doing? This was an invasion of her privacy; this was morally wrong. This was not fair. She deserved better than this.

He looked at his phone again; the boys were enamoured by her. She had sent another selfie, this time with both boys, planting a big kiss on her cheeks, her eyes closed, her face bursting with laughter. Slowly sipping his Darjeeling tea, in deep thought, face in a full frown, he thought it was all here in front of him. In a matter of a few seconds, he could obtain an entire life story at his fingertips. He zoomed in on Serena's face again. A grown-up woman, yet such stunning, girlish innocence; this woman had nothing to hide. He could type away freely, but the search would turn up blank: there was nothing. Nothing to find. The VPN was still open. Here was his chance, his burning desire had been awakened; it could no longer be banished. It was safe. There was nothing, nothing at all to investigate. *Get on with your work and stop being silly*, he told himself.

Ah, wait a minute, he thought. The question of her recently inherited money suddenly dominated his mind. *Ah, yes, the money*. With one click, he could discover the true source of her wealth. He hadn't thought about her wealth even once – in fact, he had forgotten all about it. However, as her California mansion was at the forefront of his thoughts, and she often spoke about her financial investments, he now had the chance to realise that niggly question he was very eager to discover back in Chicago. It's not really an everyday occurrence to inherit so many millions. How many millions was it? He couldn't really ask her; she might get the wrong idea. But did he need to ask her? Did he really need to know? Why was he suddenly so suspicious? Giving in to his over-inquisitive mind, he recognised he could resist no longer. His hands shook as he keyed in her name on his keyboard.

Patience was not one of his virtues. He stood up, ready to walk away from the screen in guilt and disgust. There was nothing. Wait a minute, the computer seemed to disagree. It was doing something. Ah, well, it's a very common surname, there's bound to be thousands of data entries. The system will no doubt bring up hundreds of people with similar names. He expected to sift through a deluge of zero information, resulting in nothing, just further extending his workload. This is how these systems work: you drill down, a routine he learned during his training in the industry, whilst navigating through practically every department of the hedge fund.

World Check had completed the list, approximately ten pages long. Swiftly, Harry skimmed through the names. He felt his facial muscles tense up. Nevertheless, he reassured himself all would be well, nothing incriminating would be found.

Finally, *Serena Markhieva* flashed on his screen. It was too late now; he had to click; too late to give up now. He had to know. *It will be nothing*, he insisted to himself. He opened Serena's family tree with a tap of his mouse. A visualisation opened up with several names which seemed to be regional. One name in particular was highlighted in bold red letters. He ran to Serena's bedside drawer and pulled out her birth certificate. *Father – Aleksander Leonid Markhiev.*

Harry clicked on the name on the screen. Several aliases came up. One of them accompanied with a hefty alert:

General Leonid Ruslan Zavgayev – Missing In Action since 1998.

Harry's heart stopped beating.

Olginskaya Massacre. Leader of the central Asian FEDOSI troops.

The FEDOSI troops were one of central Asia's most notorious and feared special unit during the 1990s. Their mission was to ensure control and influence. To carry out special operations with ruthless precision and violence. To crackdown on civilian protests. Policy: Shoot to kill.

Hyperventilating by now, Harry logged off the VPN, typed *Olginskaya massacre* into Google at high speed, and read the Wikipedia page in horror and disgust.

The Olginskaya massacre, May 7–8 1998, in Olginskaya, a region between Russia and Azerbaijan. Over two hundred people died, mainly civilians, as a result of heavy fighting between the police and SWAT troops.

Harry glanced through it quickly, reading as fast as he could, heart pounding, head throbbing.

According to 25 eye-witnesses, soldiers deliberately and arbitrarily attacked civilians and civilian dwellings in Olginskaya by shooting residents and burning houses with flame-throwers. The witnesses reported that many FEDOSI troops were drunk or under the influence of opium. They opened fire, threw grenades into basements where residents, mostly women, the elderly and children, had been hiding.

Harry Googled *FEDOSI Leader: Leonid Ruslan Zavgayev,* and clicked on 'Images'. He fell to his knees; there was no doubt in his mind. The resemblance between this face and Serena's face was uncanny. It almost felt as though someone had cut out Serena's face, added a few wrinkles and accentuated the features to appear more masculine, resulting in Serena's father. He clicked on 'All', looking for further clues.

Presumed living under fake identity, wife dead, twin boys dead, one living relative, daughter – name, age, whereabouts unknown. Places of interest, Georgia, Turkey, Cyprus.

Harry clicked on 'Images' again and held his phone with Serena's face zoomed-in next to the screen; every single feature was as prominent, piercing and dominant as Serena's. There was no mistaking this man was Serena's father. His Serena, the woman he loved; how could this be possible? He stared blankly at the screen, daring not to move, confused and destroyed. He closed his laptop with a thud and threw himself on the sofa. His desk was scattered with Post-its and notes on just about everything, including how he got to working from home. It was a long trail of notes that lead to the dissolution of what was left of his life.

ooooo

'Daddy, Daddy wake up, look what we got for you. Wake up, Daddy! We got a present for you, Daddy.'

Harry opened his eyes in a flash.

'Hey, you guys are back.' He forced himself to sit up, surprised he had dozed off so quickly and so deeply. Serena kissed him sweetly, smiling at him proudly.

'Wake up, sleepy head, we are back and we are hungry. Have you cooked us dinner?'

In an almost sedate state, Harry managed half a smile. 'Sorry, guys, I was very tired. I had a quick nap...'

He sprung up for all to see how energetic he was, especially for Serena who was helping the kids out of their dirty clothes.

'I haven't cooked anything, sorry. How about I order us some delicious sushi, boys? Serena, is sushi okay for you?'

'Great. I'm happy with anything healthy.'

'Daddy, can Serena tuck us in today?'

Harry looked at Serena questioningly. She smiled with a wink. 'Let's quickly shower, eat, and then I would love to. Come on, let's go; race you both to the bathroom.' Oliver followed, half-walking, half-running, trying not to smile as he watched his little brother and Serena sprint to the bathroom.

After supper, as Serena led the boys up to bed, Harry shouted, 'I'll clean up here and come say goodnight.'

Harry sat staring at the empty plates feeling paralysed and useless, unsure how to proceed. Should he confront Serena? Should he not? What should he do? Who was she? Was she the daughter of a terrorist? Was it blood money she had, the money she'd wanted him to manage? Was it all obtained by massacres, the murder of women and children? Who was this woman alone with his children, tucking them into bed? What if she were like her father? *She does, after all, have his blood running through her veins. What if she is slitting their throats right now? Oh my God, what a thought.*

'Who is General Leonid Ruslan Zavgayev?' Harry's red bloodshot eyes frightened Serena as she walked into the kitchen, shattered after reading to the kids.

'What?'

'How much of his blood money did he leave you?'

'What? What are you talking about it?'

'I know. I know everything, Serena; no more lying to me. I want the truth, once and for all!'

'What the hell are you talking about, Harry?'

'Please sit down; we need to talk.'

'Harry, you are scaring me. What's this all about?'

Harry pulled out the chair. 'Sit down, please.'

'What the... Harry! What's got into you? What are you doing?'

'When were you going to tell me? Were you ever planning to tell me?'

'What on earth are you talking about? You are scaring the hell out of me. What should I tell you?'

'Why do you women always play games? Why are you always the innocent victims, so "beautiful", so "sweet"? Well, you're not actually that beautiful and sweet, are you? You are, in fact, the daughter of a terrorist.'

'*What?*'

'Yes, that's right, I know. I checked you out. I did a World Check on you; all your details and your piece of shit father's.'

'Control your mouth! Do not speak about my father in that way. You know nothing about him. How *dare* you!'

'Here you go. Deny this.'

Serena grabbed the papers from his hands, shaking with fear. She could never imagine her kind, vulnerable Harry could have so much aggression, so much rage in him. She could hardly recognise such fury and disgust in his face, in his actions. *What's got into him?*

He stared at her unforgivingly as she absorbed the writing on the paper. 'Well?'

Silence ensued.

'There's been a mistake.' Serena felt her insides bursting open as she tried her hardest to maintain some semblance of calm. 'There must be a mistake. This is not my father.'

'That girl is not you either?' Harry pointed at her name, boldly visible in black and white, which he'd managed to locate. 'This guy is not your father? *Really?* He is a carbon copy of you. Look at his face! It clearly says, "one living relative, daughter". I guess that's a mistake, too. I guess that's not you. Go on, deny it. Deny that's not you and your killer, murderer father!'

'How dare you! Stop it! Stop it right now; you are frightening me.'

'With those genes, I doubt anything would frighten you.'

Serena quickly grabbed some of her things and stormed out of the house.

Harry banged his head on the table, resting his arms on his forehead, in utter dismay and agony.

ooooo

Serena frantically tried to reach her accountant; he wasn't picking up. She called him again, repeatedly, leaving numerous messages.

Call me back. It's urgent. Call me as soon as possible. Urgent. She continued to call and call, desperate to somehow get hold of him. She had to reach him, no matter what.

'Is it true? Is it true, all those things that my father is accused of? Is it all true?'

'What things? What do you mean?' Roman, her accountant, had finally called her back

'Do not lie to me. I need to know the truth. You need to tell me the whole truth; no more lies. I need to know the full story, and I need to know it right now.'

'I don't know anything. I don't know any more than you do.'

'You are lying!' Serena screamed. 'Stop lying. Tell me the God damn truth! Please, I am begging you tell me the truth. I have no one else to ask, I have no one else in the world I can ask, I need to know the truth. Was my father a terrorist? Did he kill women and children? The money he left for me, is it blood money? Is it stolen money? Stolen from the people that he had killed? Please tell me, I beg you.'

'No. No. It's…it's far, far more complicated than that.'

'So it *is* true.' Serena sobbed into the phone. 'Oh my God, oh dear God, it is true! I am the daughter of a terrorist. He was right. Harry was right. Oh my God!'

'Serena, calm down. Let me explain. It's not true what you are reading. Please listen to me.'

Serena hung up and sat still on the park bench, short of breath as though she were suffocating. Her head whirling as though she were a spinning wheel, she felt sick. So many thoughts rotated in her head: all the money she had, she needed to give it back. It was all dirty. The house she'd bought, she needed to sell it. The investments she'd made, they were all criminal. She would be investigated. People would find out the actual source; she needed to get rid of the money. There was no way she could keep it. What kind of a family did she come from?

Her father was a mass murderer and her mother a paranoid schizophrenic who'd spent her last years in a straitjacket before she'd dropped dead, in the most notorious mental institute central Asia had ever known. What dirty, tainted genes did she have? She would be tarnished for the rest of her life. What part of the gutter had she emerged from? Was this her real identity? Was this who she really was?

Her phone continued to ring. Roman, now calling her as frantically as she had been calling him, was persistent. She ignored the calls, wishing she was dead. He sent her a text.

This is not true. It's very far from the truth. We need to talk. Where are you? I will get the first flight out tomorrow morning. You are right. You deserve an explanation. I am sorry. Roman.

She read the message over and over again, not believing a single word she read. She didn't want to see or hear any more lies from him or anyone else.

She looked around the empty park. She had just spent blissful hours here with Harry's boys a short while ago; she remained glued to the bench and burst into tears.

A few days ago, she'd spoken about having kids with the man she loved and today she was here, alone on a park bench. She was the daughter of a mass murderer, on the world's most wanted list. What a tragedy. How terribly unfair life was. She continued to sob.

She heard her phone beep, but ignored it, continuing to sob. Again her phone beeped and continued to beep relentlessly. But when she looked carefully, it wasn't Roman at all. It was Mathias!

I miss you!

I miss you!

I miss you!

I miss you!

For two weeks Mathias had been writing to her, fiercely pursuing her. By now deeply in love with Harry and keen to let the past be the past, Serena had purposely ignored his messages. Certain to never need Mathias again, she had hoped to delete his number and all the memories, but had not yet done so.

I miss you, he wrote again. *Fancy taking a little trip to Paris? I will run the bath. It will be ready by the time you get here. The Champagne is already chilling.*

She replied: *I'm coming.*

ooooo

Dr Raza's PA knocked on his door, walking in after a faint, 'Come in.'

'Here is your mail for the day, Doctor. This one I didn't open; it's confidential.'

'Thank you, Dina, that'll be all.'

Mechanically, the doctor opened the letter labelled confidential, not the faintest bit concerned about whom it might be from or what the contents might be.

'Oh?' he questioned under his breath. 'How interesting.' He began to read, now rather curious.

Dear Dr Raza, or can I call you Stephan now? I hope you are well.

I am writing first to apologise if I embarrassed or caused you discomfort the last time we met. I do not regret relaying my feelings to you, neither will I apologise for feeling what I feel, but making you uncomfortable was not my intention. I had rather hoped you felt the same and would be man enough to admit it, but clearly you don't feel the same, or, if you do, you didn't show it.

The second reason for my letter is to bid you farewell. I applied for a job in Vancouver when I was at my lowest, needing desperately to get away from the UK. I thought nothing of it. However, much to my surprise, the organisation got in touch a few weeks ago, and, to cut a long story short, I have been offered a job and I have accepted.

The next step in my journey is to inform Harry that I am moving to Canada and taking my children with me. It is a conversation which, as you can imagine, I am dreading.

If ever you happen to be in Canada or passing by, do give me a call. My feelings remain the same. I think about you often and I would love to see you again.

Warm regards, Laura

Dr Raza felt hot under the collar; he had somewhat hoped not to cross paths with Laura again so soon. He stared at the words and at her name, clearly remembering her visible curves in a tight red dress. *She must have worn that dress on purpose*, he thought. Not one to be shocked, Laura had had more of an impact on the doctor than he cared to admit. Quite the mystery she presented herself to be, and if he were being totally honest with himself, there was a certain attraction he undeniably felt for her. Since her candid confession that day, he was ever more guilty of thinking of her as more than just a patient. Instinctively he hid the letter in his white jacket pocket. Surely he could think of a reason to justify a business trip to Vancouver?

Perhaps the local university might benefit from a guest lecturer as soon as Laura got settled.

ooooo

'We have extensive databases with pretty much any and all information available at our fingertips, unless it's archived, I guess,' said Mathias as he grinned. 'I promise I will check as soon as I can, but what's up with this guy? Why did he freak out like this? He needs to chill out. First, we don't know the whole truth. These wanted lists are fucked up sometimes, and not even real. Someone decides they don't like your name and you're done; it happens all the time. Especially with an interesting name like that.'

'He has Alzheimer's.'

'*What?* How old is he?'

'Forty-eight.'

'You're kidding! No way. Isn't that way too young to have dementia?'

'You'd think.' She took a large sip of a watered-down Scotch whisky.

'Is that why he is so melodramatic and constantly looks like he has just seen a ghost?'

'He got diagnosed with this illness, got divorced, and I was pressurising him for a baby, all at the same time. Such a damn mess.'

'And now he thinks you are a liar and the daughter of a terrorist who has left you blood money?'

'Yes.'

'So what's the problem? At least you are rich and can afford the best care for him when he gets really sick.'

'Harry is not like that; he doesn't think about money. He loves me; he loves his kids; he's a family man. He doesn't come from your mad, insane world. He's a kind, sweet man and... I... I love him. But I think it's over.'

'No. It's not.'

'It is. He was so disgusted. You should have seen his face. I couldn't believe he could get so angry. He thought I knew and that I was hiding everything from him. He doesn't trust me. He never has, really. He was always so suspicious about my "source of funds" and he was massively let down by his ex-wife, and now, of course, he thinks I've done the same thing as her, even worse.'

Serena held her head in her hands about to sob again. Mathias gently put his arms around her. 'Stop that. Come, let's sit on the sofa. We can watch a film. You need to get your mind off things.'

Serena looked at him heartbroken.

'I am so destroyed. What if it is true? I feel sick.'

Mathias held her tightly, her head buried in his chest.

'It's not. Forget about everything for a while. Give your mind a rest. We will think of a plan tomorrow.'

ooooo

Taking strict instructions from his psychiatrist, Harry took every precaution to block Serena out of his mind, putting her things to the side of the room and hoping for them not to interfere with his daily life. He noticed her passport was not in her bedside drawer, clearly indicating she had run off to her sleazy French lover.

'Give it some time. In a calm state of mind, get in touch with her. Right now you are angry and worked up; this kind of stress is very bad for you. It is possible she didn't know any of this, and even if she did and if her father were a terrorist, she cannot be held responsible for her father's crimes or actions. Give her time and try not to hold anger and resentment against her. You need to discuss this with her, and let her explain. Assume her innocent till guilty – she deserves that.'

Trusting the doctor implicitly, Harry heeded his advice without question, and without further ado it was decided an online homoeopathic medicine course, learning Spanish, and now he had the space, piano lessons, were destined to be his new hobbies.

Jane laughed uncontrollably as both she and the piano arrived at Harry's flat at the same time. 'You've become like a seventy year old. Soon you are going to be heading off to an old folk's home. What's going on with you? You got divorced, for God's sake. Get over it. You're far better off without that aggressive woman. You are acting as if life is over. Look outside, there's a whole world out there.'

'Yes, yes, ha ha. Thanks, Jane, I appreciate it. See you on Sunday. Look after my kids, please. And remember Charlie's allergies. Bye. Have a lovely weekend, kids.' Harry felt guilty palming the kids off to Jane on his weekend with them, but she had offered and they were very happy to be with their cousins.

Not bad, thought Harry as he admired his new electric piano, excited to play and see if he could remember anything from his early years of piano lessons. Bored with the classics, he thought to try his hand at Jazz; the kids would like that. He smiled.

'What does she want?' He sighed when he spotted a message from Laura on his phone.

Oliver said they're at Jane's. Bored with your kids already?

Jane's kids invited the boys, and they wanted to join. Do you have a problem with that?

Can I pop over? I need to discuss something.

If you must.

I will be with you in an hour.

Can we meet out somewhere? The flat is in a mess.

At the coffee shop then.

Harry wished to be free of Laura; he could no longer bear her presence. He longed to be in an indifferent, carefree state, but the pain she had caused him lingered, the wounds fresh as ever, especially with Serena no longer in the picture.

ooooo

'I'll make this quick, and get straight to the point.'

'I wish you would.'

Laura ignored him, speaking calmly. 'I've been offered a job in Vancouver. I've accepted it.'

Did he hear right? 'Vancouver, Canada?'

'No. Vancouver, Africa! Yes, of course, Vancouver, Canada.'

'Are you serious?'

'Yes, I am. Yes. Vancouver. I applied for a job there a while ago, and they have offered it to me. I would like to take it. I need a new start. Of course, I need you to be on board. I can't take the kids without your consent.'

Lost for words again, Harry sat still, staring at his coffee, stirring it slowly, looking for something to do. *I'd like to smoke a cigarette now, maybe that should also be one of my new hobbies*, he thought.

'I understand this is big news; please understand it's not to hurt you. Take as much time as you need, I don't need an answer today. But I urge you, please let me go. I really need a clean break. I think it'll be best for everyone if I go.' Laura smiled lamely.

'I'm going to go home now. I will think about it.'

Laura nodded as Harry stood up. 'Thank you for your understanding. I appreciate it.'

'I'm happy to let you go, just so that I don't ever have to see you again. You broke my heart, you broke up my home, and now you are planning on taking my kids to the other side of the world. Before I leave, I just want you to know that I hate you. I hate you with every fibre of my being, and I will never forgive you.'

Harry left the coffee shop thoroughly pleased with himself. He had been waiting for the opportunity to say those words to Laura for a very long time. He hoped she was hurt. Even if it was only a little bit of the pain she had caused him, he hoped she felt it. Full of bitterness, he no longer had the constitution for unpleasant news.

16

Roman sat in a corner of a restaurant admiring Jeff Leatham's stunning flower display at the George V Hotel, anxiously waiting for Serena. His ten-minute wait already felt like ten hours. How naïve had he been, hoping he could have avoided this conversation forever; it was the height of stupidity. Terribly nervous, he felt hot under the collar, prompting him to order a whisky in the middle of the day. The busy restaurant resembled a small slice of a wealthy suburb of Beirut, or equally Moscow. Almost everyone spoke either Russian or Arabic, was middle-aged and stinking of money. Roman would have loved to have sat there the whole day long, watching how the other half live; however, right now his priorities were a bit more serious.

'Why are you here?' Serena aggressively accosted him, sitting opposite him like a bomb waiting to explode.

'It's nice to see you, Serena. I am sorry we have to meet in these circumstances.'

'Who is paying your travel expenses? Is it coming out of my dirty blood money? Does it make you happy to pay yourself out of this money?'

'I have some important documents for you; your father left me in charge of them, anticipating this day might one day come.'

'I don't want them. I don't care. I don't want to know. Keep them, and please return to the States. I don't want to discuss this anymore.'

'I will go straight after this meeting. Here are my flight details. But I will not leave until you have looked at these documents. Your father is innocent. It is essential you know the truth. Everything is there. It would be better if you let me explain before I go.'

'Go on then, explain. Let's hear it.'

'It is true; your father did work for an organisation, but he never killed anyone. He certainly didn't kill any women and children. The only person whose murder your father ordered happened to be the head of the very terrorist organisation it is said your father was involved in. Your father was wrongly framed by loyalists of the terror group. Everything written about your father was fabricated; it's all lies. Your father took back the money wrongfully stolen by the terror group. He had intended to distribute the money back to the families of the victims of the organisation, but unfortunately, he had to flee before he could do anything further. The rest of the money, or most of the money, rightfully belonged to your father, all earned legitimately. Every penny. I have the papers to prove it.'

Serena stared at Roman icily as he spoke, not sure what to believe.

'Upon failing to distribute the money to its rightful place, as it had become too dangerous, your father headed back to the village where he thought you were, only to discover you and your mother were gone, in fear of your lives. Word had got back to your mother that your father was being hunted, so she had to flee. Your father finally located your mother, years later in a mental institution, where she sadly died. Living in exile at that time, there was nothing much he could do. He made provisions for the money to be held in various secret trusts to be released in its entirety to you when he died.'

'None of this adds up.'

'It's the truth.'

'I haven't seen my father for many years. I thought he was dead the whole time. Then a year ago, I heard he had recently died and had left me this great wealth. If he was alive, why didn't he try to see me?'

'He couldn't travel. He had international arrest warrants and was wanted by the US and Russia. He wasn't even able to make contact with you in case he was intercepted and eventually put you in danger. I sent him regular photos and updates of you. He knew everything about you.'

'You knew where he was?'

'No. I sent them to various email addresses.'

'What did you send?'

'Photos of you, voice recordings of you, your whereabouts, what you were doing.'

'Why didn't you ever tell me?'

'I was sworn to secrecy. It was to protect both you and him.'

'Where was he?'

'Mostly in central Asia. Sometimes South America, but mostly hiding in central Asia.'

'How did he die?'

'Heart attack.'

'So at least that part was true.'

'A lot of things told to you were true. Whatever was kept from you was for your own safety, instructed directly by your father. There are messages for you, diaries, journals in these files.'

'Why didn't you give me these before now?'

'I was going to give them to you as soon as I had managed to get all your money to you.'

'I thought I had all the money.'

'There is more. It's held in complicated trusts. I am working on getting it all to you, but it's very complicated.'

'How much is it?'

'A lot. I don't know exactly.'

'Is it rightfully mine?'

'Yes. Your father worked extremely hard, and he had a very good business brain. He knew how to make money, and back in the eighties, it was much easier to make money: there was less bureaucracy, fewer checks, especially if you knew the right people.'

'I don't want it.'

'I understand. I can arrange for donations to any charities of your choice, but as I say, I don't have my hands on all of it yet.'

'And the money I already have in my possession? I haven't decided what I will do with it. If I will keep it.'

'That's your choice, but it's clean. It cannot be challenged. Your father made sure of that, and it's the result of your father's blood, sweat and hard work. Every penny is clean. He was wrongly framed. But it's your choice. I shall not interfere.'

'I don't understand. The last time I saw my father was in a beautiful mansion in Turkey. Was he in hiding already?'

'Yes.'

'But he seemed so relaxed.'

'The mansion was owned by an acquaintance; he borrowed it just for the meeting with you.'

'So he was lying to me?'

'No, he was protecting you. Everything was about protecting you. You were his only living relative: his everything. You were the one and only thing that could be used to hurt him. He had to protect you. Your father's wealth is honest and all above board, but unfortunately, he was in a powerful position and he was betrayed. No one could be trusted in those days; everyone was desperate for money.'

Serena fell silent. None of it made sense to her, but there was nothing left to ask. All the evidence lay in her hands if she cared to look at it.

ooooo

'I have to tell Harry,' she said to Mathias. 'He needs to know that I didn't lie to him. He is so broken he thinks all women are poisonous and evil. I don't want him to carry these feelings. They are probably destroying him.'

'You really love him, don't you?'

'Is it that obvious?'

'Yes. I wish you would love me like that.' Mathias ran his fingers through her hair. 'Such beautiful, shiny hair.' He kissed her on her head. 'It smells lovely.'

'I would have loved you like that, but you are far too complicated for me. Harry is simple. He is straightforward; he doesn't have skeletons in his cupboard. He has been badly hurt and dealt a bad hand by fate. I have to go back to him.'

'Yes, you do. Go. And remember I am always here for you. If he upsets you again, I am here. I can be anything you want me to be...' He winked at her.

Serena boarded the Eurostar in haste, feeling more nervous than ever before. What if Harry were truly done with her? What if he didn't want to know her anymore? What if he was finished with women altogether? *This is my last chance. I owe him and myself this one last attempt. If after this it still doesn't work, I will cut my losses and return back to the US.* The thought of her house and the unfinished work kept her sane, knowing there was something for her to do and somewhere for her to go. *Perhaps I should buy myself a ticket already. Harry is probably better off without me in his life.*

Once she had arrived at the Ritz Hotel, Serena threw her bag onto the beautiful bedspread and immediately wrote Harry an email.

Harry,

You're probably still upset with me. If I may, I would like to address the accusations you have made towards me. I have all the evidence to prove you wrong.

First, my father wasn't a terrorist. Secondly, I didn't know anything.

Lastly, all the money I have is mine, and I have decided to distribute most of it to charity.

After I left your house, I went to Paris and met with my accountant. If possible, I would like us to talk. I am in London staying at the Ritz. I would like you to come and see me so we can talk. If you don't want to, I will fly back to LA in the morning, as I have no reason to remain.

I love you. I hope we can resolve this.

Yours

Serena

Harry read the email as soon as he'd received it and immediately replied.

I am so embarrassed about my behaviour, I am so sorry. I don't know how to face you. Do you really still love me?

Relieved, Serena responded immediately.

Yes. I love you… still. Do you want to come here?

I can come and pick you up if you want to come home… Harry replied.

Serena paused. Was it too soon to go back to his house and pretend everything was fine and nothing had happened? Shouldn't she stay here for a while?

I will come for a few hours, that may be better.

Thank you, Harry promptly answered.

Before Serena had much time to think, the hotel phone rang.

'Mr Harry Hoffman is waiting for you in Reception, Madam.'

'I have booked a table for two at the restaurant. Please take Mr Hoffman to the table. I will be down in a moment, thank you.'

Serena headed down to the restaurant, her father's file carefully hidden in her handbag. Dressed down in a casual pair of black jeans and a black top, she felt very out of place. Harry jumped up at the sight of her, unsure of how to greet her, embarrassed as never before.

'I'm so ashamed. I can hardly look at you. I'm so sorry. I overreacted. Please forgive me.'

'Sit down. I have all the papers in my bag, I would like you to see them and read everything. I don't ever want to discuss this subject ever again. You must see it all for yourself and read every word thoroughly. When you are happy with what you have read, we can bury it. I have never been as hurt as I have been over this matter. I don't want to go through this again; my whole world fell apart. So much pain and hurt, and it isn't even true.'

'I am so sorry. What can I say?' Harry shook his head. What an uncomfortable conversation to have with the woman he loved. 'I am paranoid. I have been through so much recently. I am not even a fraction of my old self.' He reached for Serena's hand, desperation in his voice. 'I don't recognise myself any more. I cannot sleep. I have nightmares. I am damaged. I am broken. I overreacted. Please forgive me.'

'Please take what I'm giving you home and read it. If you want to see me afterwards, I will be here. If not, then let me know, so I can leave.'

'Please don't say that. Of course I want to see you.' He squeezed her hand. 'Please forgive me. I am so ashamed.'

'I want to tell you something. I have decided I don't want to live in London any more. I understand if this is unsuitable for you with your situation, and your kids, but a lot has happened recently, as you know. Reading my father's documents has changed almost everything in my life.' She felt her heart wince in pain. She hated ultimatums; she didn't want to lose him, but if ever there was a time to be honest and to put her cards on the table, this was it.

'I love you, but I cannot make any more compromises.' She looked up at him. 'I will accept your every decision; I didn't want to leave without explaining my father's... and my own innocence to you. The rest is up to you.'

'Laura is moving to Canada.'

Serena opened her eyes wide in shock.

'She was offered a new job which she has accepted; she needs my permission to take the kids with her to Vancouver.' Harry looked into her eyes.

'What did you say?'

'Nothing. Yet. It depends on you.'

'How?'

'If you still want me to come with you to LA.'

Serena's eyes widened even further.

'If you still want me to come to LA with you, it makes sense for Laura to take the kids. I will be closer to them there. However, if… if… if you decide you don't want me any more… I… I… will stay here. I will stay here and fight her, I suppose.'

Serena looked at him blankly. Did she hear what he'd said correctly?

'You'd move to LA with me?'

'Yes. If you want me to.' He smiled, staring at her intently. 'I have something for you too…'

He handed her a little bag, which contained a small box.

'What is it?' she asked, genuinely puzzled.

'Open it.'

'Oh my God!'

Harry squeezed her hand tighter.

'I don't understand?'

'I got it for you.'

'It's a ring.'

'Yes. It's an engagement ring!'

Serena looked at him confused. 'I don't understand,' she said naïvely, staring at the ring.

Just as Harry was about to drop to one knee, the penny dropped.

'Yes,' she cried. 'Yes, yes and yes again'.

Epilogue

Later that night, Harry lay next to Serena, stroking her arm. Calm and at peace, she was half asleep, tired from the recent stresses. It was wonderful to have her back. Euphoric, he hoped he wasn't in the middle of a dream. A few weeks ago, it would have been inconceivable that Serena would be back in his bed, yet here she was, and Harry was over the moon. Happiness and contentment were almost alien sentiments to him as of late; he wanted to make the most of this moment. He felt at ease, almost too excited to sleep. There were hardly any conflicts in his mind; what a novelty.

With no sign of fatigue, Harry sat up and opened his laptop. As had become the usual thing to do for the last few months, he Googled *Alzheimer Research Breakthrough*.

He gazed at Serena then looked at his bright screen. He felt hope; having her back gave him courage. He looked back at the screen. *San Francisco-based Biotech firm identifies highly specific mechanism of action deploying a nano-engineered peptide antigen*, he read silently. He read it again, this time out loud. A keen advisor for Biotech investments for many years, Harry understood precisely what was written. With a wealth of knowledge and hours of intense research carried out in the Biotech and Pharmaceutical industries, he read quickly, clicking on link after link, rapidly absorbing the recently released clinical data. His gaze locked on the screen and his face became tense and concentrated, while his eyes slowly started to register with a curious optimism. His facial expression began to relax.

'What are you doing?' Serena's voice was faint and dreamy.

Mesmerised by the literature, Harry smiled.

'Nothing,' he replied calmly. 'I think I may have found a glimmer of light in my darkness.'

<u>Acknowledgements</u>

I would like to thank my mother for always prioritising her five children, and my big sister, Shaheen, for always supporting and encouraging me to chase my dreams.

To my darling husband, Yasin, who gives me the best advice and insight into the more complex things in life.

To the biggest love of my life, Zack, my son, who drives me to be the best version of myself and forever makes me laugh.

And, to my wonderful publisher, Brenda and her team, without whom none of this would have happened.

Facts about Alzheimer's

Dementia is the name for a set of symptoms that includes memory loss and difficulties with thinking, problem-solving or language. Dementia develops when the brain is damaged by diseases, including Alzheimer's disease.

Alzheimer's disease is a physical disease that affects the brain and is also the most common cause of dementia.

Alzheimer's disease is the most common type of young-onset dementia and may affect around 1 in 3 younger people with dementia. However, up to 2 in 3 older people with dementia have Alzheimer's disease. Alzheimer's disease develops when proteins build up in the brain to form structures called 'plaques' and 'tangles'. This causes brain cells to die and so affects functions controlled by the brain.

For most older people with Alzheimer's disease, the first symptom they notice is likely to be memory loss. However, in younger people with Alzheimer's disease, memory loss is less likely to be the first symptom.

In some areas there are local support groups for younger people or those living with certain types of dementia. These can enable younger people with dementia and those close to them to meet or get in touch with other younger people affected by dementia.

If you need information, support or advice, please contact the Alzheimer's Society Dementia Connect support line on 0333 150 3456 or consider joining our online community, Talking Point. Your kind donations ensure that Alzheimer's Society can be there for every person affected by dementia. For more information, please go to alzheimers. org.uk/donate

Book 2
Coming soon!